The Freelands by John Galsworthy

"Liberty's a glorious feast."—**Burns**.

John Galsworthy was born at Kingston Upon Thames in Surrey, England, on August 14th 1867 to a wealthy and well established family. His schooling was at Harrow and New College, Oxford before training as a barrister and being called to the bar in 1890. However, Law was not attractive to him and he travelled abroad becoming great friends with the novelist Joseph Conrad, then a first mate on a sailing ship.

In 1895 Galsworthy began an affair with Ada Nemesis Pearson Cooper, the wife of his cousin Major Arthur Galsworthy. The affair was kept a secret for 10 years till she at last divorced and they married on 23rd September 1905.

Galsworthy first published in 1897 with a collection of short stories entitled "The Four Winds'. For the next 7 years he published these and all works under his pen name John Sinjohn. It was only upon the death of his father and the publication of "The Island Pharisees" in 1904 that he published as John Galsworthy.

His first play, The Silver Box in 1906 was a success and was followed by "The Man of Property" later that same year and was the first in the Forsyte trilogy.   Whilst today he is far more well know as a Nobel Prize winning novelist then he was considered a playwright dealing with social issues and the class system.   Here we publish Villa Rubein, a very fine story that captures Galsworthy's unique narrative and take on life of the time.

He is now far better known for his novels, particularly The Forsyte Saga, his trilogy about the eponymous family of the same name. These books, as with many of his other works, deal with social class, upper-middle class lives in particular. Although always sympathetic to his characters, he reveals their insular, snobbish, and somewhat greedy attitudes and suffocating moral codes. He is now viewed as one of the first from the Edwardian era to challenge some of the ideals of society depicted in the literature of Victorian England.

In his writings he campaigns for a variety of causes, including prison reform, women's rights, animal welfare, and the opposition of censorship as well as a recurring theme of an unhappy marriage from the women's side. During World War I he worked in a hospital in France as an orderly after being passed over for military service.

He was appointed to the Order of Merit in 1929, after earlier turning down a knighthood, and awarded the Nobel Prize in 1932 though he was too ill to attend.

John Galsworthy died from a brain tumour at his London home, Grove Lodge, Hampstead on January 31st 1933. In accordance with his will he was cremated at Woking with his ashes then being scattered over the South Downs from an aeroplane.

Index of Contents

PROLOGUE

One early April afternoon, in a Worcestershire field, the only field in that immediate landscape which was not down in grass, a man moved slowly athwart the furrows, sowing—a big man of heavy build, swinging his hairy brown arm with the grace of strength. He wore no coat or hat; a waistcoat, open over a blue-checked cotton shirt, flapped against belted corduroys that were somewhat the color of his square, pale-brown face and dusty hair. His eyes were sad, with the swimming yet fixed stare of epileptics; his mouth heavy-lipped, so that, but for the yearning eyes, the face would have been almost brutal. He looked as if he suffered from silence. The elm-trees bordering the field, though only just in leaf, showed dark against a white sky. A light wind blew, carrying already a scent from the earth and growth pushing up, for the year was early. The green Malvern hills rose in the west; and not far away, shrouded by trees, a long country house of weathered brick faced to the south. Save for the man sowing, and some rooks crossing from elm to elm, no life was visible in all the green land. And it was quiet—with a strange, a brooding tranquillity. The fields and hills seemed to mock the scars of road and ditch and furrow scraped on them, to mock at barriers of hedge and wall—between the green land and white sky was a conspiracy to disregard those small activities. So lonely was it, so plunged in a ground-bass of silence; so much too big and permanent for any figure of man.

Across and across the brown loam the laborer doggedly finished out his task; scattered the few last seeds into a corner, and stood still. Thrushes and blackbirds were just beginning that even-song whose blitheness, as nothing else on earth, seems to promise youth forever to the land. He picked up his coat, slung it on, and, heaving a straw bag over his shoulder, walked out on to the grass-bordered road between the elms.

"Tryst! Bob Tryst!"

At the gate of a creepered cottage amongst fruit-trees, high above the road, a youth with black hair and pale-brown face stood beside a girl with frizzy brown hair and cheeks like poppies.

"Have you had that notice?"

The laborer answered slowly:

"Yes, Mr. Derek. If she don't go, I've got to."

"What a d—d shame!"

The laborer moved his head, as though he would have spoken, but no words came.

"Don't do anything, Bob. We'll see about that."

"Evenin', Mr. Derek. Evenin', Miss Sheila," and the laborer moved on.

The two at the wicket gate also turned away. A black-haired woman dressed in blue came to the wicket gate in their place. There seemed no purpose in her standing there; it was perhaps an evening custom, some ceremony such as Moslems observe at the muezzin-call. And any one who saw her would have wondered what on earth she might be seeing, gazing out with her dark glowing eyes above the white, grass-bordered roads stretching empty this way and that between the elm-trees and green fields; while the blackbirds and thrushes shouted out their hearts, calling all to witness how hopeful and young was life in this English countryside....

CHAPTER I

Mayday afternoon in Oxford Street, and Felix Freeland, a little late, on his way from Hampstead to his brother John's house in Porchester Gardens. Felix Freeland, author, wearing the very first gray top hat of the season. A compromise, that—like many other things in his life and works—between individuality and the accepted view of things, aestheticism and fashion, the critical sense and authority. After the meeting at John's, to discuss the doings of the family of his brother Morton Freeland—better known as Tod—he would perhaps look in on the caricatures at the English Gallery, and visit one duchess in Mayfair, concerning the George Richard Memorial. And so, not the soft felt hat which really suited authorship, nor the black top hat which obliterated personality to the point of pain, but this gray thing with narrowish black band, very suitable, in truth, to a face of a pale buff color, to a moustache of a deep buff color streaked with a few gray hairs, to a black braided coat cut away from a buff-colored waistcoat, to his neat boots—not patent leather—faintly buffed with May-day dust. Even his eyes, Freeland gray, were a little buffed over by sedentary habit, and the number of things that he was conscious of. For instance, that the people passing him were distressingly plain, both men and women; plain with the particular plainness of those quite unaware of it. It struck him forcibly, while he went along, how very queer it was that with so many plain people in the country, the population managed to keep up even as well as it did. To his wonderfully keen sense of defect, it seemed little short of marvellous. A shambling, shoddy crew, this crowd of shoppers and labor demonstrators! A conglomeration of hopelessly mediocre visages! What was to be done about it? Ah! what indeed!— since they were evidently not aware of their own dismal mediocrity. Hardly a beautiful or a vivid face, hardly a wicked one, never anything transfigured, passionate, terrible, or grand. Nothing Greek, early Italian, Elizabethan, not even beefy, beery, broad old Georgian. Something clutched-in, and squashed-out about it all—on that collective face something of the look of a man almost comfortably and warmly wrapped round by a snake at the very beginning of its squeeze. It gave Felix Freeland a sort of faint excitement and pleasure to notice this. For it was his business to notice things, and embalm them afterward in ink. And he believed that not many people noticed it, so that it contributed in his mind to his own distinction, which was precious to him. Precious, and encouraged to be so by the press, which— as he well knew—must print his name several thousand times a year. And yet, as a man of culture and of principle, how he despised that kind of fame, and theoretically believed that a man's real distinction lay in his oblivion of the world's opinion, particularly as expressed by that flighty creature, the Fourth Estate. But here again, as in the matter of the gray top hat, he had instinctively compromised, taking in press cuttings which described himself and his works, while he never failed to describe those descriptions—good, bad, and indifferent—as 'that stuff,' and their writers as 'those fellows.'

Not that it was new to him to feel that the country was in a bad way. On the contrary, it was his established belief, and one for which he was prepared to furnish due and proper reasons. In the first place he traced it to the horrible hold Industrialism had in the last hundred years laid on the nation, draining the peasantry from 'the Land'; and in the second place to the influence of a narrow and insidious Officialism, sapping the independence of the People.

This was why, in going to a conclave with his brother John, high in Government employ, and his brother Stanley, a captain of industry, possessor of the Morton Plough Works, he was conscious of a certain superiority in that he, at all events, had no hand in this paralysis which was creeping on the country.

And getting more buff-colored every minute, he threaded his way on, till, past the Marble Arch, he secured the elbow-room of Hyde Park. Here groups of young men, with chivalrous idealism, were jeering at and chivying the broken remnants of a suffrage meeting. Felix debated whether he should oppose his body to their bodies, his tongue to theirs, or whether he should avert his consciousness and hurry on; but, that instinct which moved him to wear the gray top hat prevailing, he did neither, and stood instead, looking at them in silent anger, which quickly provoked endearments—such as: "Take it off," or "Keep it on," or "What cheer, Toppy!" but nothing more acute. And he meditated: Culture! Could culture ever make headway among the blind partisanships, the hand-to-mouth mentality, the cheap excitements of this town life? The faces of these youths, the tone of their voices, the very look of their bowler hats, said: No! You could not culturalize the impermeable texture of their vulgarity. And they were the coming manhood of the nation—this inexpressibly distasteful lot of youths! The country had indeed got too far away from 'the Land.' And this essential towny commonness was not confined to the classes from which these youths were drawn. He had even remarked it among his own son's school and college friends—an impatience of discipline, an insensibility to everything but excitement and having a good time, a permanent mental indigestion due to a permanent diet of tit-bits. What aspiration they possessed seemed devoted to securing for themselves the plums of official or industrial life. His boy Alan, even, was infected, in spite of home influences and the atmosphere of art in which he had been so sedulously soaked. He wished to enter his Uncle Stanley's plough works, seeing in it a 'soft thing.'

But the last of the woman-baiters had passed by now, and, conscious that he was really behind time, Felix hurried on....

In his study—a pleasant room, if rather tidy—John Freeland was standing before the fire smoking a pipe and looking thoughtfully at nothing. He was, in fact, thinking, with that continuity characteristic of a man who at fifty has won for himself a place of permanent importance in the Home Office. Starting life in the Royal Engineers, he still preserved something of a military look about his figure, and grave visage with steady eyes and drooping moustache (both a shade grayer than those of Felix), and a forehead bald from justness and knowing where to lay his hand on papers. His face was thinner, his head narrower, than his brother's, and he had acquired a way of making those he looked at doubt themselves and feel the sudden instability of all their facts. He was—as has been said—thinking. His brother Stanley had wired to him that morning: "Am motoring up to-day on business; can you get Felix to come at six o'clock and talk over the position at Tod's?" What position at Tod's? He had indeed heard something vague—of those youngsters of Tod's, and some fuss they were making about the laborers down there. He had not liked it. Too much of a piece with the general unrest, and these new democratic ideas that were playing old Harry with the country! For in his opinion the country was in a bad way, partly owing to Industrialism, with its rotting effect upon physique; partly to this modern analytic Intellectualism, with its destructive and anarchic influence on morals. It was difficult to overestimate the mischief of those two factors; and in the approaching conference with his brothers, one of whom was the head of an industrial undertaking, and the other a writer, whose books, extremely modern, he never read, he was perhaps vaguely conscious of his own cleaner hands. Hearing a car come to a halt outside. he went to the window and looked out. Yes, it was Stanley!...

Stanley Freeland, who had motored up from Becket—his country place, close to his plough works in Worcestershire—stood a moment on the pavement, stretching his long legs and giving directions to his chauffeur. He had been stopped twice on the road for not-exceeding the limit as he believed, and was still a little ruffled. Was it not his invariable principle to be moderate in speed as in all other things? And his feeling at the moment was stronger even than usual, that the country was in a bad way, eaten up by officialism, with its absurd limitations of speed and the liberty of the subject, and the advanced ideas of these new writers and intellectuals, always talking about the rights and sufferings of the poor. There was no progress along either of those roads. He had it in his heart, as he stood there on the pavement, to say something pretty definite to John about interference with the liberty of the subject, and he wouldn't mind giving old Felix a rap about his precious destructive doctrines, and continual girding at the upper classes, vested interests, and all the rest of it. If he had something to put in their place that would be another matter. Capital and those who controlled it were the backbone of the country—what there was left of the country, apart from these d—d officials and aesthetic fellows! And with a contraction of his straight eyebrows above his straight gray eyes, straight blunt nose, blunter moustaches, and blunt chin, he kept a tight rein on his blunt tongue, not choosing to give way even to his own anger.

Then, perceiving Felix coming—'in a white topper, by Jove!'—he crossed the pavement to the door; and, tall, square, personable, rang the bell.

CHAPTER II

"Well, what's the matter at Tod's?"

And Felix moved a little forward in his chair, his eyes fixed with interest on Stanley, who was about to speak.

"It's that wife of his, of course. It was all very well so long as she confined herself to writing, and talk, and that Land Society, or whatever it was she founded, the one that snuffed out the other day; but now she's getting herself and those two youngsters mixed up in our local broils, and really I think Tod's got to be spoken to."

"It's impossible for a husband to interfere with his wife's principles." So Felix.

"Principles!" The word came from John.

"Certainly! Kirsteen's a woman of great character; revolutionary by temperament. Why should you expect her to act as you would act yourselves?"

When Felix had said that, there was a silence.

Then Stanley muttered: "Poor old Tod!"

Felix sighed, lost for a moment in his last vision of his youngest brother. It was four years ago now, a summer evening—Tod standing between his youngsters Derek and Sheila, in a doorway of his white, black-timbered, creepered cottage, his sunburnt face and blue eyes the serenest things one could see in a day's march!

"Why 'poor'?" he said. "Tod's much happier than we are. You've only to look at him."

"Ah!" said Stanley suddenly. "D'you remember him at Father's funeral?—without his hat, and his head in the clouds. Fine-lookin' chap, old Tod—pity he's such a child of Nature."

Felix said quietly:

"If you'd offered him a partnership, Stanley—it would have been the making of him."

"Tod in the plough works? My hat!"

Felix smiled. At sight of that smile, Stanley grew red, and John refilled his pipe. It is always the devil to have a brother more sarcastic than oneself!

"How old are those two?" John said abruptly.

"Sheila's twenty, Derek nineteen."

"I thought the boy was at an agricultural college?"

"Finished."

"What's he like?"

"A black-haired, fiery fellow, not a bit like Tod."

John muttered: "That's her Celtic blood. Her father, old Colonel Moray, was just that sort; by George, he was a regular black Highlander. What's the trouble exactly?"

It was Stanley who answered: "That sort of agitation business is all very well until it begins to affect your neighbors; then it's time it stopped. You know the Mallorings who own all the land round Tod's. Well, they've fallen foul of the Mallorings over what they call injustice to some laborers. Questions of morality involved. I don't know all the details. A man's got notice to quit over his deceased wife's sister; and some girl or other in another cottage has kicked over—just ordinary country incidents. What I want is that Tod should be made to see that his family mustn't quarrel with his nearest neighbors in this way. We know the Mallorings well, they're only seven miles from us at Becket. It doesn't do; sooner or later it plays the devil all round. And the air's full of agitation about the laborers and 'the Land,' and all the rest of it—only wants a spark to make real trouble."

And having finished this oration, Stanley thrust his hands deep into his pockets, and jingled the money that was there.

John said abruptly:

"Felix, you'd better go down."

Felix was sitting back, his eyes for once withdrawn from his brothers' faces.

"Odd," he said, "really odd, that with a perfectly unique person like Tod for a brother, we only see him once in a blue moon."

"It's because he IS so d—d unique."

Felix got up and gravely extended his hand to Stanley.

"By Jove," he said, "you've spoken truth." And to John he added: "Well, I WILL go, and let you know the upshot."

When he had departed, the two elder brothers remained for some moments silent, then Stanley said:

"Old Felix is a bit tryin'! With the fuss they make of him in the papers, his head's swelled!"

John did not answer. One could not in so many words resent one's own brother being made a fuss of, and if it had been for something real, such as discovering the source of the Black River, conquering Bechuanaland, curing Blue-mange, or being made a Bishop, he would have been the first and most loyal in his appreciation; but for the sort of thing Felix made up—Fiction, and critical, acid, destructive sort of stuff, pretending to show John Freeland things that he hadn't seen before—as if Felix could!—not at all the jolly old romance which one could read well enough and enjoy till it sent you to sleep after a good day's work. No! that Felix should be made a fuss of for such work as that really almost hurt him. It was not quite decent, violating deep down one's sense of form, one's sense of health, one's traditions. Though he would not have admitted it, he secretly felt, too, that this fuss was dangerous to his own point of view, which was, of course, to him the only real one. And he merely said:

"Will you stay to dinner, Stan?"

CHAPTER III

If John had those sensations about Felix, so—when he was away from John—had Felix about himself. He had never quite grown out of the feeling that to make himself conspicuous in any way was bad form. In common with his three brothers he had been through the mills of gentility—those unique grinding machines of education only found in his native land. Tod, to be sure, had been publicly sacked at the end of his third term, for climbing on to the headmaster's roof and filling up two of his chimneys with football pants, from which he had omitted to remove his name. Felix still remembered the august scene—the horrid thrill of it, the ominous sound of that: "Freeland minimus!" the ominous sight of poor little Tod emerging from his obscurity near the roof of the Speech Room, and descending all those steps. How very small and rosy he had looked, his bright hair standing on end, and his little blue eyes staring up very hard from under a troubled frown. And the august hand holding up those sooty pants, and the august voice: "These appear to be yours, Freeland minimus. Were you so good as to put them down my chimneys?" And the little piping, "Yes, sir."

"May I ask why, Freeland minimus?"

"I don't know, sir."

"You must have had some reason, Freeland minimus?"

"It was the end of term, sir."

"Ah! You must not come back here, Freeland minimus. You are too dangerous, to yourself, and others. Go to your place."

And poor little Tod ascending again all those steps, cheeks more terribly rosy than ever, eyes bluer, from under a still more troubled frown; little mouth hard set; and breathing so that you could hear him six forms off. True, the new Head had been goaded by other outrages, the authors of which had not omitted to remove their names; but the want of humor, the amazing want of humor! As if it had not been a sign of first-rate stuff in Tod! And to this day Felix remembered with delight the little bubbling hiss that he himself had started, squelched at once, but rippling out again along the rows like tiny scattered lines of fire when a conflagration is suppressed. Expulsion had been the salvation of Tod! Or—his damnation? Which? God would know, but Felix was not certain. Having himself been fifteen years acquiring 'Mill' philosophy, and another fifteen years getting rid of it, he had now begun to think that after all there might be something in it. A philosophy that took everything, including itself, at face value, and questioned nothing, was sedative to nerves too highly strung by the continual examination of the insides of oneself and others, with a view to their alteration. Tod, of course, having been sent to Germany after his expulsion, as one naturally would be, and then put to farming, had never properly acquired 'Mill' manner, and never sloughed it off; and yet he was as sedative a man as you could meet.

Emerging from the Tube station at Hampstead, he moved toward home under a sky stranger than one might see in a whole year of evenings. Between the pine-trees on the ridge it was opaque and colored like pinkish stone, and all around violent purple with flames of the young green, and white spring blossom lit against it. Spring had been dull and unimaginative so far, but this evening it was all fire and gathered torrents; Felix wondered at the waiting passion of that sky.

He reached home just as those torrents began to fall.

The old house, beyond the Spaniard's Road, save for mice and a faint underlying savor of wood-rot in two rooms, well satisfied the aesthetic sense. Felix often stood in his hall, study, bedroom, and other apartments, admiring the rich and simple glow of them—admiring the rarity and look of studied negligence about the stuffs, the flowers, the books, the furniture, the china; and then quite suddenly the feeling would sweep over him: "By George, do I really own all this, when my ideal is 'bread and water, and on feast days a little bit of cheese'?" True, he was not to blame for the niceness of his things—Flora did it; but still—there they were, a little hard to swallow for an epicurean. It might, of course, have been worse, for if Flora had a passion for collecting, it was a very chaste one, and though what she collected cost no little money, it always looked as if it had been inherited, and—as everybody knows—what has been inherited must be put up with, whether it be a coronet or a cruet-stand.

To collect old things, and write poetry! It was a career; one would not have one's wife otherwise. She might, for instance, have been like Stanley's wife, Clara, whose career was wealth and station; or John's wife, Anne, whose career had been cut short; or even Tod's wife, Kirsteen, whose career was revolution. No—a wife who had two, and only two children, and treated them with affectionate surprise, who was never out of temper, never in a hurry, knew the points of a book or play, could cut your hair at a pinch; whose hand was dry, figure still good, verse tolerable, and—above all—who wished for no better fate than Fate had given her—was a wife not to be sneezed at. And Felix never had. He had depicted so many sneezing wives and husbands in his books, and knew the value of a happy marriage better perhaps than any one in England. He had laid marriage low a dozen times, wrecked it on all sorts of rocks, and had the greater veneration for his own, which had begun early, manifested every symptom of ending late, and in the meantime walked down the years holding hands fast, and by no means forgetting to touch lips.

Hanging up the gray top hat, he went in search of her. He found her in his dressing-room, surrounded by a number of little bottles, which she was examining vaguely, and putting one by one into an 'inherited' waste-paper basket. Having watched her for a little while with a certain pleasure, he said:

"Yes, my dear?"

Noticing his presence, and continuing to put bottles into the basket, she answered:

"I thought I must—they're what dear Mother's given us."

There they lay—little bottles filled with white and brown fluids, white and blue and brown powders; green and brown and yellow ointments; black lozenges; buff plasters; blue and pink and purple pills. All beautifully labelled and corked.

And he said in a rather faltering voice:

"Bless her! How she does give her things away! Haven't we used ANY?"

"Not one. And they have to be cleared away before they're stale, for fear we might take one by mistake."

"Poor Mother!"

"My dear, she's found something newer than them all by now."

Felix sighed.

"The nomadic spirit. I have it, too!"

And a sudden vision came to him of his mother's carved ivory face, kept free of wrinkles by sheer will-power, its firm chin, slightly aquiline nose, and measured brows; its eyes that saw everything so quickly, so fastidiously, its compressed mouth that smiled sweetly, with a resolute but pathetic acceptation. Of the piece of fine lace, sometimes black, sometimes white, over her gray hair. Of her hands, so thin now, always moving a little, as if all the composure and care not to offend any eye by allowing Time to ravage her face, were avenging themselves in that constant movement. Of her figure, that was short but did not seem so, still quick-moving, still alert, and always dressed in black or gray. A vision of that exact, fastidious, wandering spirit called Frances Fleeming Freeland—that spirit strangely compounded of domination and humility, of acceptation and cynicism; precise and actual to the point of desert dryness; generous to a point that caused her family to despair; and always, beyond all things, brave.

Flora dropped the last little bottle, and sitting on the edge of the bath let her eyebrows rise. How pleasant was that impersonal humor which made her superior to other wives!

"You—nomadic? How?"

"Mother travels unceasingly from place to place, person to person, thing to thing. I travel unceasingly from motive to motive, mind to mind; my native air is also desert air—hence the sterility of my work."

Flora rose, but her eyebrows descended.

"Your work," she said, "is not sterile."

"That, my dear," said Felix, "is prejudice." And perceiving that she was going to kiss him, he waited without annoyance. For a woman of forty-two, with two children and three books of poems—and not knowing which had taken least out of her—with hazel-gray eyes, wavy eyebrows darker than they should have been, a glint of red in her hair; wavy figure and lips; quaint, half-humorous indolence, quaint, half-humorous warmth—was she not as satisfactory a woman as a man could possibly have married!

"I have got to go down and see Tod," he said. "I like that wife of his; but she has no sense of humor. How much better principles are in theory than in practice!"

Flora repeated softly, as if to herself:

"I'm glad I have none." She was at the window leaning out, and Felix took his place beside her. The air was full of scent from wet leaves, alive with the song of birds thanking the sky. Suddenly he felt her arm round his ribs; either it or they—which, he could not at the moment tell—seemed extraordinarily soft....

Between Felix and his young daughter, Nedda, there existed the only kind of love, except a mother's, which has much permanence—love based on mutual admiration. Though why Nedda, with her starry innocence, should admire him, Felix could never understand, not realizing that she read his books, and even analyzed them for herself in the diary which she kept religiously, writing it when she ought to have been asleep. He had therefore no knowledge of the way his written thoughts stimulated the ceaseless questioning that was always going on within her; the thirst to know why this was and that was not. Why, for instance, her heart ached so some days and felt light and eager other days? Why, when people wrote and talked of God, they seemed to know what He was, and she never did? Why people had to suffer; and the world be black to so many millions? Why one could not love more than one man at a time? Why—a thousand things? Felix's books supplied no answers to these questions, but they were comforting; for her real need as yet was not for answers, but ever for more questions, as a young bird's need is for opening its beak without quite knowing what is coming out or going in. When she and her father walked, or sat, or went to concerts together, their talk was neither particularly intimate nor particularly voluble; they made to each other no great confidences. Yet each was certain that the other was not bored—a great thing; and they squeezed each other's little fingers a good deal—very warming. Now with his son Alan, Felix had a continual sensation of having to keep up to a mark and never succeeding—a feeling, as in his favorite nightmare, of trying to pass an examination for which he had neglected to prepare; of having to preserve, in fact, form proper to the father of Alan Freeland. With Nedda he had a sense of refreshment; the delight one has on a spring day, watching a clear stream, a bank of flowers, birds flying. And Nedda with her father—what feeling had she? To be with him was like a long stroking with a touch of tickle in it; to read his books, a long tickle with a nice touch of stroking now and then when one was not expecting it.

That night after dinner, when Alan had gone out and Flora into a dream, she snuggled up alongside her father, got hold of his little finger, and whispered:

"Come into the garden, Dad; I'll put on goloshes. It's an awfully nice moon."

The moon indeed was palest gold behind the pines, so that its radiance was a mere shower of pollen, just a brushing of white moth-down over the reeds of their little dark pond, and the black blur of the flowering currant bushes. And the young lime-trees, not yet in full leaf, quivered ecstatically in that moon-witchery, still letting fall raindrops of the past spring torrent, with soft hissing sounds. A real sense in the garden, of God holding his breath in the presence of his own youth swelling, growing, trembling toward perfection! Somewhere a bird—a thrush, they thought—mixed in its little mind as to night and day, was queerly chirruping. And Felix and his daughter went along the dark wet paths, holding each other's arms, not talking much. For, in him, very responsive to the moods of Nature, there was a flattered feeling, with that young arm in his, of Spring having chosen to confide in him this whispering, rustling hour. And in Nedda was so much of that night's unutterable youth—no wonder she was silent! Then, somehow—neither responsible—they stood motionless. How quiet it was, but for a distant dog or two, and the stilly shivering-down of the water drops, and the far vibration of the million-voiced city! How quiet and soft and fresh! Then Nedda spoke:

"Dad, I do so want to know everything."

Not rousing even a smile, with its sublime immodesty, that aspiration seemed to Felix infinitely touching. What less could youth want in the very heart of Spring? And, watching her face put up to the night, her parted lips, and the moon-gleam fingering her white throat, he answered:

"It'll all come soon enough, my pretty!"

To think that she must come to an end like the rest, having found out almost nothing, having discovered just herself, and the particle of God that was within her! But he could not, of course, say this.

"I want to FEEL. Can't I begin?"

How many millions of young creatures all the world over were sending up that white prayer to climb and twine toward the stars, and—fall to earth again! And nothing to be answered, but:

"Time enough, Nedda!"

"But, Dad, there are such heaps of things, such heaps of people, and reasons, and—and life; and I know nothing. Dreams are the only times, it seems to me, that one finds out anything."

"As for that, my child, I am exactly in your case. What's to be done for us?"

She slid her hand through his arm again.

"Don't laugh at me!"

"Heaven forbid! I meant it. You're finding out much quicker than I. It's all folk-music to you still; to me Strauss and the rest of the tired stuff. The variations my mind spins—wouldn't I just swap them for the tunes your mind is making?"

"I don't seem making tunes at all. I don't seem to have anything to make them of. Take me down to see 'the Tods,' Dad!"

Why not? And yet—! Just as in this spring night Felix felt so much, so very much, lying out there behind the still and moony dark, such marvellous holding of breath and waiting sentiency, so behind this innocent petition, he could not help the feeling of a lurking fatefulness. That was absurd. And he said: "If you wish it, by all means. You'll like your Uncle Tod; as to the others, I can't say, but your aunt is an experience, and experiences are what you want, it seems."

Fervently, without speech, Nedda squeezed his arm.

CHAPTER IV

Stanley Freeland's country house, Becket, was almost a show place. It stood in its park and pastures two miles from the little town of Transham and the Morton Plough Works; close to the ancestral home of the Moretons, his mother's family—that home burned down by Roundheads in the Civil War. The site— certain vagaries in the ground—Mrs. Stanley had caused to be walled round, and consecrated so to speak with a stone medallion on which were engraved the aged Moreton arms—arrows and crescent moons in proper juxtaposition. Peacocks, too—that bird 'parlant,' from the old Moreton crest—were encouraged to dwell there and utter their cries, as of passionate souls lost in too comfortable surroundings.

By one of those freaks of which Nature is so prodigal, Stanley—owner of this native Moreton soil—least of all four Freeland brothers, had the Moreton cast of mind and body. That was why he made so much more money than the other three put together, and had been able, with the aid of Clara's undoubted genius for rank and station, to restore a strain of Moreton blood to its rightful position among the county families of Worcestershire. Bluff and without sentiment, he himself set little store by that, smiling up his sleeve—for he was both kindly and prudent—at his wife who had been a Tomson. It was not in Stanley to appreciate the peculiar flavor of the Moretons, that something which in spite of their naivete and narrowness, had really been rather fine. To him, such Moretons as were left were 'dry enough sticks, clean out of it.' They were of a breed that was already gone, the simplest of all country gentlemen, dating back to the Conquest, without one solitary conspicuous ancestor, save the one who had been physician to a king and perished without issue—marrying from generation to generation exactly their own equals; living simple, pious, parochial lives; never in trade, never making money, having a tradition and a practice of gentility more punctilious than the so-called aristocracy; constitutionally paternal and maternal to their dependents, constitutionally so convinced that those dependents and all indeed who were not 'gentry,' were of different clay, that they were entirely simple and entirely without arrogance, carrying with them even now a sort of Early atmosphere of archery and home-made cordials, lavender and love of clergy, together with frequent use of the word 'nice,' a peculiar regularity of feature, and a complexion that was rather parchmenty. High Church people and Tories, naturally, to a man and woman, by sheer inbred absence of ideas, and sheer inbred conviction that nothing else was nice; but withal very considerate of others, really plucky in bearing their own ills; not greedy, and not wasteful.

Of Becket, as it now was, they would not have approved at all. By what chance Edmund Moreton (Stanley's mother's grandfather), in the middle of the eighteenth century, had suddenly diverged from family feeling and ideals, and taken that 'not quite nice' resolution to make ploughs and money, would never now be known. The fact remained, together with the plough works. A man apparently of curious energy and character, considering his origin, he had dropped the E from his name, and—though he continued the family tradition so far as to marry a Fleeming of Worcestershire, to be paternal to his workmen, to be known as Squire, and to bring his children up in the older Moreton 'niceness'—he had yet managed to make his ploughs quite celebrated, to found a little town, and die still handsome and clean-shaved at the age of sixty-six. Of his four sons, only two could be found sufficiently without the E to go on making ploughs. Stanley's grandfather, Stuart Morton, indeed, had tried hard, but in the end had reverted to the congenital instinct for being just a Moreton. An extremely amiable man, he took to wandering with his family, and died in France, leaving one daughter—Frances, Stanley's mother—and three sons, one of whom, absorbed in horses, wandered to Australia and was killed by falling from them; one of whom, a soldier, wandered to India, and the embraces of a snake; and one of whom wandered into the embraces of the Holy Roman Church.

The Morton Plough Works were dry and dwindling when Stanley's father, seeking an opening for his son, put him and money into them. From that moment they had never looked back, and now brought Stanley, the sole proprietor, an income of full fifteen thousand pounds a year. He wanted it. For Clara, his wife, had that energy of aspiration which before now has raised women to positions of importance in the counties which are not their own, and caused, incidentally, many acres to go out of cultivation. Not one plough was used on the whole of Becket, not even a Morton plough—these indeed were unsuitable to English soil and were all sent abroad. It was the corner-stone of his success that Stanley had completely seen through the talked-of revival of English agriculture, and sedulously cultivated the foreign market. This was why the Becket dining-room could contain without straining itself large quantities of local magnates and celebrities from London, all deploring the condition of 'the Land,' and discussing without end the regrettable position of the agricultural laborer. Except for literary men and painters, present in small quantities to leaven the lump, Becket was, in fact, a rallying point for the advanced spirits of Land Reform—one of those places where they were sure of being well done at week-ends, and of congenial and even stimulating talk about the undoubted need for doing something, and the designs which were being entertained upon 'the Land' by either party. This very heart of English country that the old Moretons in their paternal way had so religiously farmed, making out of its lush grass and waving corn a simple and by no means selfish or ungenerous subsistence, was now entirely lawns, park, coverts, and private golf course, together with enough grass to support the kine which yielded that continual stream of milk necessary to Clara's entertainments and children, all female, save little Francis, and still of tender years. Of gardeners, keepers, cow-men, chauffeurs, footmen, stablemen—full twenty were supported on those fifteen hundred acres that formed the little Becket demesne. Of agricultural laborers proper—that vexed individual so much in the air, so reluctant to stay on 'the Land,' and so difficult to house when he was there, there were fortunately none, so that it was possible for Stanley, whose wife meant him to 'put up' for the Division, and his guests, who were frequently in Parliament, to hold entirely unbiassed and impersonal views upon the whole question so long as they were at Becket.

It was beautiful there, too, with the bright open fields hedged with great elms, and that ever-rich serenity of its grass and trees. The white house, timbered with dark beams in true Worcestershire fashion, and added-to from time to time, had preserved, thanks to a fine architect, an old-fashioned air of spacious presidency above its gardens and lawns. On the long artificial lake, with innumerable rushy nooks and water-lilies and coverture of leaves floating flat and bright in the sun, the half-tame wild duck and shy water-hens had remote little worlds, and flew and splashed when all Becket was abed, quite as if the human spirit, with its monkey-tricks and its little divine flame, had not yet been born.

Under the shade of a copper-beech, just where the drive cut through into its circle before the house, an old lady was sitting that afternoon on a campstool. She was dressed in gray alpaca, light and cool, and had on her iron-gray hair a piece of black lace. A number of Hearth and Home and a little pair of scissors, suspended by an inexpensive chain from her waist, rested on her knee, for she had been meaning to cut out for dear Felix a certain recipe for keeping the head cool; but, as a fact, she sat without doing so, very still, save that, now and then, she compressed her pale fine lips, and continually moved her pale fine hands. She was evidently waiting for something that promised excitement, even pleasure, for a little rose-leaf flush had quavered up into a face that was colored like parchment; and her gray eyes under regular and still-dark brows, very far apart, between which there was no semblance of a wrinkle, seemed noting little definite things about her, almost unwillingly, as an Arab's or a Red Indian's eyes will continue to note things in the present, however their minds may be set on the future. So sat Frances Fleeming Freeland (nee Morton) waiting for the arrival of her son Felix and her grandchildren Alan and Nedda.

She marked presently an old man limping slowly on a stick toward where the drive debouched, and thought at once: "He oughtn't to be coming this way. I expect he doesn't know the way round to the back. Poor man, he's very lame. He looks respectable, too." She got up and went toward him, remarking that his face with nice gray moustaches was wonderfully regular, almost like a gentleman's, and that he touched his dusty hat with quite old-fashioned courtesy. And smiling—her smile was sweet but critical—she said: "You'll find the best way is to go back to that little path, and past the greenhouses. Have you hurt your leg?"

"My leg's been like that, m'm, fifteen year come Michaelmas."

"How did it happen?"

"Ploughin'. The bone was injured; an' now they say the muscle's dried up in a manner of speakin'."

"What do you do for it? The very best thing is this."

From the recesses of a deep pocket, placed where no one else wore such a thing, she brought out a little pot.

"You must let me give it you. Put it on when you go to bed, and rub it well in; you'll find it act splendidly."

The old man took the little pot with dubious reverence.

"Yes, m'm," he said; "thank you, m'm."

"What is your name?"

"Gaunt."

"And where do you live?"

"Over to Joyfields, m'm."

"Joyfields—another of my sons lives there—Mr. Morton Freeland. But it's seven miles."

"I got a lift half-way."

"And have you business at the house?" The old man was silent; the downcast, rather cynical look of his lined face deepened. And Frances Freeland thought: 'He's overtired. They must give him some tea and an egg. What can he want, coming all this way? He's evidently not a beggar.'

The old man who was not a beggar spoke suddenly:

"I know the Mr. Freeland at Joyfields. He's a good gentleman, too."

"Yes, he is. I wonder I don't know you."

"I'm not much about, owin' to my leg. It's my grand-daughter in service here, I come to see."

"Oh, yes! What is her name?"

"Gaunt her name is."

"I shouldn't know her by her surname."

"Alice."

"Ah! in the kitchen; a nice, pretty girl. I hope you're not in trouble."

Again the old man was silent, and again spoke suddenly:

"That's as you look at it, m'm," he said. "I've got a matter of a few words to have with her about the family. Her father he couldn't come, so I come instead."

"And how are you going to get back?"

"I'll have to walk, I expect, without I can pick up with a cart."

Frances Freeland compressed her lips. "With that leg you should have come by train."

The old man smiled.

"I hadn't the fare like," he said. "I only gets five shillin's a week, from the council, and two o' that I pays over to my son."

Frances Freeland thrust her hand once more into that deep pocket, and as she did so she noticed that the old man's left boot was flapping open, and that there were two buttons off his coat. Her mind was swiftly calculating: "It is more than seven weeks to quarter day. Of course I can't afford it, but I must just give him a sovereign."

She withdrew her hand from the recesses of her pocket and looked at the old man's nose. It was finely chiselled, and the same yellow as his face. "It looks nice, and quite sober," she thought. In her hand was her purse and a boot-lace. She took out a sovereign.

"Now, if I give you this," she said, "you must promise me not to spend any of it in the public-house. And this is for your boot. And you must go back by train. And get those buttons sewn on your coat. And tell cook, from me, please, to give you some tea and an egg." And noticing that he took the sovereign and the boot-lace very respectfully, and seemed altogether very respectable, and not at all coarse or beery-looking, she said:

"Good-by; don't forget to rub what I gave you into your leg every night and every morning," and went back to her camp-stool. Sitting down on it with the scissors in her hand, she still did not cut out that recipe, but remained as before, taking in small, definite things, and feeling with an inner trembling that dear Felix and Alan and Nedda would soon be here; and the little flush rose again in her cheeks, and again her lips and hands moved, expressing and compressing what was in her heart. And close behind her, a peacock, straying from the foundations of the old Moreton house, uttered a cry, and moved slowly, spreading its tail under the low-hanging boughs of the copper-beeches, as though it knew those dark burnished leaves were the proper setting for its 'parlant' magnificence.

CHAPTER V

The day after the little conference at John's, Felix had indeed received the following note:

"DEAR FELIX:

"When you go down to see old Tod, why not put up with us at Becket? Any time will suit, and the car can take you over to Joyfields when you like. Give the pen a rest. Clara joins in hoping you'll come, and Mother is still here. No use, I suppose, to ask Flora.

"Yours ever,

"STANLEY."

During the twenty years of his brother's sojourn there Felix had been down to Becket perhaps once a year, and latterly alone; for Flora, having accompanied him the first few times, had taken a firm stand.

"My dear," she said, "I feel all body there."

Felix had rejoined:

"No bad thing, once in a way."

But Flora had remained firm. Life was too short! She did not get on well with Clara. Neither did Felix feel too happy in his sister-in-law's presence; but the gray top-hat instinct had kept him going there, for one ought to keep in touch with one's brothers.

He replied to Stanley:

"DEAR STANLEY:

"Delighted; if I may bring my two youngsters. We'll arrive to-morrow at four-fifty.

"Yours affectionately,

"FELIX."

Travelling with Nedda was always jolly; one could watch her eyes noting, inquiring, and when occasion served, have one's little finger hooked in and squeezed. Travelling with Alan was convenient, the young man having a way with railways which Felix himself had long despaired of acquiring. Neither of the children had ever been at Becket, and though Alan was seldom curious, and Nedda too curious about everything to be specially so about this, yet Felix experienced in their company the sensations of a new adventure.

Arrived at Transham, that little town upon a hill which the Morton Plough Works had created, they were soon in Stanley's car, whirling into the sleepy peace of a Worcestershire afternoon. Would this young bird nestling up against him echo Flora's verdict: 'I feel all body there!' or would she take to its fatted luxury as a duck to water? And he said: "By the way, your aunt's 'Bigwigs' set in on a Saturday. Are you for staying and seeing the lions feed, or do we cut back?"

From Alan he got the answer he expected:

"If there's golf or something, I suppose we can make out all right." From Nedda: "What sort of Bigwigs are they, Dad?"

"A sort you've never seen, my dear."

"Then I should like to stay. Only, about dresses?"

"What war paint have you?"

"Only two white evenings. And Mums gave me her Mechlin."

"'Twill serve."

To Felix, Nedda in white 'evenings' was starry and all that man could desire.

"Only, Dad, do tell me about them, beforehand."

"My dear, I will. And God be with you. This is where Becket begins."

The car had swerved into a long drive between trees not yet full-grown, but decorously trying to look more than their twenty years. To the right, about a group of older elms, rooks were in commotion, for Stanley's three keepers' wives had just baked their annual rook pies, and the birds were not yet happy again. Those elms had stood there when the old Moretons walked past them through corn-fields to church of a Sunday. Away on the left above the lake, the little walled mound had come in view. Something in Felix always stirred at sight of it, and, squeezing Nedda's arm, he said:

"See that silly wall? Behind there Granny's ancients lived. Gone now—new house—new lake—new trees—new everything."

But he saw from his little daughter's calm eyes that the sentiment in him was not in her.

"I like the lake," she said. "There's Granny—oh, and a peacock!"

His mother's embrace, with its frail energy, and the pressure of her soft, dry lips, filled Felix always with remorse. Why could he not give the simple and direct expression to his feeling that she gave to hers? He watched those lips transferred to Nedda, heard her say: "Oh, my darling, how lovely to see you! Do you know this for midge-bites?" A hand, diving deep into a pocket, returned with a little silver-coated stick having a bluish end. Felix saw it rise and hover about Nedda's forehead, and descend with two little swift dabs. "It takes them away at once."

"Oh, but Granny, they're not midge-bites; they're only from my hat!"

"It doesn't matter, darling; it takes away anything like that."

And he thought: 'Mother is really wonderful!'

At the house the car had already disgorged their luggage. Only one man, but he absolutely the butler, awaited them, and they entered, at once conscious of Clara's special pot-pourri. Its fragrance steamed from blue china, in every nook and crevice, a sort of baptism into luxury. Clara herself, in the outer morning-room, smelled a little of it. Quick and dark of eye, capable, comely, perfectly buttoned, one of those women who know exactly how not to be superior to the general taste of the period. In addition to that great quality she was endowed with a fine nose, an instinct for co-ordination not to be excelled, and a genuine love of making people comfortable; so that it was no wonder that she had risen in the ranks of hostesses, till her house was celebrated for its ease, even among those who at their week-ends liked to feel 'all body.' In regard to that characteristic of Becket, not even Felix in his ironies had ever stood up to Clara; the matter was too delicate. Frances Freeland, indeed—not because she had any philosophic preconceptions on the matter, but because it was 'not nice, dear, to be wasteful' even if it were only of rose-leaves, or to 'have too much decoration,' such as Japanese prints in places where they hum—sometimes told her daughter-in-law frankly what was wrong, without, however, making the faintest impression upon Clara, for she was not sensitive, and, as she said to Stanley, it was 'only Mother.'

When they had drunk that special Chinese tea, all the rage, but which no one really liked, in the inner morning, or afternoon room—for the drawing-rooms were too large to be comfortable except at week-ends—they went to see the children, a special blend of Stanley and Clara, save the little Francis, who did not seem to be entirely body. Then Clara took them to their rooms. She lingered kindly in Nedda's, feeling that the girl could not yet feel quite at home, and looking in the soap-dish lest she might not have the right verbena, and about the dressing-table to see that she had pins and scent, and plenty of 'pot-pourri,' and thinking: 'The child is pretty—a nice girl, not like her mother.' Explaining carefully how, because of the approaching week-end, she had been obliged to put her in 'a very simple room' where she would be compelled to cross the corridor to her bath, she asked her if she had a quilted dressing-gown, and finding that she had not, left her saying she would send one—and could she do her frocks up, or should Sirrett come?

Abandoned, the girl stood in the middle of the room, so far more 'simple' than she had ever slept in, with its warm fragrance of rose-leaves and verbena, its Aubusson carpet, white silk-quilted bed, sofa, cushioned window-seat, dainty curtains, and little nickel box of biscuits on little spindly table. There she stood and sniffed, stretched herself, and thought: 'It's jolly—only, it smells too much!' and she went up to the pictures, one by one. They seemed to go splendidly with the room, and suddenly she felt homesick. Ridiculous, of course! Yet, if she had known where her father's room was, she would have run out to it; but her memory was too tangled up with stairs and corridors—to find her way down to the hall again was all she could have done.

A maid came in now with a blue silk gown very thick and soft. Could she do anything for Miss Freeland? No, thanks, she could not; only, did she know where Mr. Freeland's room was?

"Which Mr. Freeland, miss, the young or the old?"

"Oh, the old!" Having said which, Nedda felt unhappy; her Dad was not old! "No, miss; but I'll find out. It'll be in the walnut wing!" But with a little flutter at the thought of thus setting people to run about wings, Nedda murmured: "Oh! thanks, no; it doesn't matter."

She settled down now on the cushion of the window-seat, to look out and take it all in, right away to that line of hills gone blue in the haze of the warm evening. That would be Malvern; and there, farther to the south, the 'Tods' lived. 'Joyfields!' A pretty name! And it was lovely country all round; green and peaceful, with its white, timbered houses and cottages. People must be very happy, living here—happy and quiet like the stars and the birds; not like the crowds in London thronging streets and shops and Hampstead Heath; not like the people in all those disgruntled suburbs that led out for miles where London ought to have stopped but had not; not like the thousands and thousands of those poor creatures in Bethnal Green, where her slum work lay. The natives here must surely be happy. Only, were there any natives? She had not seen any. Away to the right below her window were the first trees of the fruit garden; for many of them Spring was over, but the apple-trees had just come into blossom, and the low sun shining through a gap in some far elms was slanting on their creamy pink, christening them—Nedda thought—with drops of light; and lovely the blackbirds' singing sounded in the perfect hush! How wonderful to be a bird, going where you would, and from high up in the air seeing everything; flying down a sunbeam, drinking a raindrop, sitting on the very top of a tall tree, running in grass so high that you were hidden, laying little perfect blue-green eggs, or pure-gray speckly ones; never changing your dress, yet always beautiful. Surely the spirit of the world was in the birds and the clouds, roaming, floating, and in the flowers and trees that never smelled anything but sweet, never looked anything but lovely, and were never restless. Why was one restless, wanting things that did not come—wanting to feel and know, wanting to love, and be loved? And at that thought which had come to her so unexpectedly—a thought never before shaped so definitely—Nedda planted her arms on the window-sill, with sleeves fallen down, and let her hands meet cup-shaped beneath her chin. Love! To have somebody with whom she could share everything—some one to whom and for whom she could give up—some one she could protect and comfort—some one who would bring her peace. Peace, rest—from what? Ah! that she could not make clear, even to herself. Love! What would love be like? Her father loved her, and she loved him. She loved her mother; and Alan on the whole was jolly to her—it was not that. What was it—where was it—when would it come and wake her, and kiss her to sleep, all in one? Come and fill her as with the warmth and color, the freshness, light, and shadow of this beautiful May evening, flood her as with the singing of those birds, and the warm light sunning the apple blossoms. And she sighed. Then—as with all young things whose attention after all is but as the hovering of a butterfly—her speculation was attracted to a thin, high-shouldered figure limping on a stick, away from the house, down one of the paths among the apple-trees. He wavered, not knowing, it seemed, his way. And Nedda thought: 'Poor old man, how lame he is!' She saw him stoop, screened, as he evidently thought, from sight, and take something very small from his pocket. He gazed, rubbed it, put it back; what it was she could not see. Then pressing his hand down, he smoothed and stretched his leg. His eyes seemed closed. So a stone man might have stood! Till very slowly he limped on, passing out of sight. And turning from the window, Nedda began hurrying into her evening things.

When she was ready she took a long time to decide whether to wear her mother's lace or keep it for the Bigwigs. But it was so nice and creamy that she simply could not take it off, and stood turning and turning before the glass. To stand before a glass was silly and old-fashioned; but Nedda could never help it, wanting so badly to be nicer to look at than she was, because of that something that some day was coming!

She was, in fact, pretty, but not merely pretty—there was in her face something alive and sweet, something clear and swift. She had still that way of a child raising its eyes very quickly and looking straight at you with an eager innocence that hides everything by its very wonder; and when those eyes looked down they seemed closed—their dark lashes were so long. Her eyebrows were wide apart, arching with a slight angle, and slanting a little down toward her nose. Her forehead under its burnt-brown hair was candid; her firm little chin just dimpled. Altogether, a face difficult to take one's eyes off. But Nedda was far from vain, and her face seemed to her too short and broad, her eyes too dark and indeterminate, neither gray nor brown. The straightness of her nose was certainly comforting, but it, too, was short. Being creamy in the throat and browning easily, she would have liked to be marble-white, with blue dreamy eyes and fair hair, or else like a Madonna. And was she tall enough? Only five foot five. And her arms were too thin. The only things that gave her perfect satisfaction were her legs, which, of course, she could not at the moment see; they really WERE rather jolly! Then, in a panic, fearing to be late, she turned and ran out, fluttering into the maze of stairs and corridors.

CHAPTER VI

Clara, Mrs. Stanley Freeland, was not a narrow woman either in mind or body; and years ago, soon indeed after she married Stanley, she had declared her intention of taking up her sister-in-law, Kirsteen, in spite of what she had heard were the woman's extraordinary notions. Those were the days of carriages, pairs, coachmen, grooms, and, with her usual promptitude, ordering out the lot, she had set forth. It is safe to say she had never forgotten that experience.

Imagine an old, white, timbered cottage with a thatched roof, and no single line about it quite straight. A cottage crazy with age, buried up to the thatch in sweetbrier, creepers, honeysuckle, and perched high above crossroads. A cottage almost unapproachable for beehives and their bees—an insect for which Clara had an aversion. Imagine on the rough, pebbled approach to the door of this cottage (and Clara had on thin shoes) a peculiar cradle with a dark-eyed baby that was staring placidly at two bees sleeping on a coverlet made of a rough linen such as Clara had never before seen. Imagine an absolutely naked little girl of three, sitting in a tub of sunlight in the very doorway. Clara had turned swiftly and closed the wicket gate between the pebbled pathway and the mossed steps that led down to where her coachman and her footman were sitting very still, as was the habit of those people. She had perceived at once that she was making no common call. Then, with real courage she had advanced, and, looking down at the little girl with a fearful smile, had tickled the door with the handle of her green parasol. A woman younger than herself, a girl, indeed, appeared in a low doorway. She had often told Stanley since that she would never forget her first sight (she had not yet had another) of Tod's wife. A brown face and black hair, fiery gray eyes, eyes all light, under black lashes, and "such a strange smile;" bare, brown, shapely arms and neck in a shirt of the same rough, creamy linen, and, from under a bright blue skirt, bare, brown, shapely ankles and feet! A voice so soft and deadly that, as Clara said: "What with her eyes, it really gave me the shivers. And, my dear," she had pursued, "white-washed walls, bare brick floors, not a picture, not a curtain, not even a fire-iron. Clean—oh, horribly! They must be the most awful cranks. The only thing I must say that was nice was the smell. Sweetbrier, and honey, coffee, and baked apples—really delicious. I must try what I can do with it. But that woman—girl, I suppose she is— stumped me. I'm sure she'd have cut my head off if I'd attempted to open my mouth on ordinary topics. The children were rather ducks; but imagine leaving them about like that amongst the bees. 'Kirsteen!' She looked it. Never again! And Tod I didn't see at all; I suppose he was mooning about amongst his creatures."

It was the memory of this visit, now seventeen years ago, that had made her smile so indulgently when Stanley came back from the conference. She had said at once that they must have Felix to stay, and for her part she would be only too glad to do anything she could for those poor children of Tod's, even to asking them to Becket, and trying to civilize them a little.... "But as for that woman, there'll be nothing to be done with her, I can assure you. And I expect Tod is completely under her thumb."

To Felix, who took her in to dinner, she spoke feelingly and in a low voice. She liked Felix, in spite of his wife, and respected him—he had a name. Lady Malloring—she told him—the Mallorings owned, of course, everything round Joyfields—had been telling her that of late Tod's wife had really become quite rabid over the land question. 'The Tods' were hand in glove with all the cottagers. She, Clara, had nothing to say against any one who sympathized with the condition of the agricultural laborer; quite the contrary. Becket was almost, as Felix knew—though perhaps it wasn't for her to say so—the centre of that movement; but there were ways of doing things, and one did so deprecate women like this Kirsteen—what an impossibly Celtic name!—putting her finger into any pie that really was of national importance. Nothing could come of anything done that sort of way. If Felix had any influence with Tod it would be a mercy to use it in getting those poor young creatures away from home, to mix a little with people who took a sane view of things. She would like very much to get them over to Becket, but with their notions it was doubtful whether they had evening clothes! She had, of course, never forgotten that naked mite in the tub of sunlight, nor the poor baby with its bees and its rough linen. Felix replied deferentially—he was invariably polite, and only just ironic enough, in the houses of others—that he had the very greatest respect for Tod, and that there could be nothing very wrong with the woman to whom Tod was so devoted. As for the children, his own young people would get at them and learn all about what was going on in a way that no fogey like himself could. In regard to the land question, there were, of course, many sides to that, and he, for one, would not be at all sorry to observe yet another. After all, the Tods were in real contact with the laborers, and that was the great thing. It would be very interesting.

Yes, Clara quite saw all that, but—and here she sank her voice so that there was hardly any left—as Felix was going over there, she really must put him au courant with the heart of this matter. Lady Malloring had told her the whole story. It appeared there were two cases: A family called Gaunt, an old man, and his son, who had two daughters—one of them, Alice, quite a nice girl, was kitchen-maid here at Becket, but the other sister—Wilmet—well! she was one of those girls that, as Felix must know, were always to be found in every village. She was leading the young men astray, and Lady Malloring had put her foot down, telling her bailiff to tell the farmer for whom Gaunt worked that he and his family must go, unless they sent the girl away somewhere. That was one case. And the other was of a laborer called Tryst, who wanted to marry his deceased wife's sister. Of course, whether Mildred Malloring was not rather too churchy and puritanical—now that a deceased wife's sister was legal—Clara did not want to say; but she was undoubtedly within her rights if she thought it for the good of the village. This man, Tryst, was a good workman, and his farmer had objected to losing him, but Lady Malloring had, of course, not given way, and if he persisted he would get put out. All the cottages about there were Sir Gerald Malloring's, so that in both cases it would mean leaving the neighborhood. In regard to village morality, as Felix knew, the line must be drawn somewhere.

Felix interrupted quietly:

"I draw it at Lady Malloring."

"Well, I won't argue that with you. But it really is a scandal that Tod's wife should incite her young people to stir up the villagers. Goodness knows where that mayn't lead! Tod's cottage and land, you see, are freehold, the only freehold thereabouts; and his being a brother of Stanley's makes it particularly awkward for the Mallorings."

"Quite so!" murmured Felix.

"Yes, but my dear Felix, when it comes to infecting those simple people with inflated ideas of their rights, it's serious, especially in the country. I'm told there's really quite a violent feeling. I hear from Alice Gaunt that the young Tods have been going about saying that dogs are better off than people treated in this fashion, which, of course, is all nonsense, and making far too much of a small matter. Don't you think so?"

But Felix only smiled his peculiar, sweetish smile, and answered:

"I'm glad to have come down just now."

Clara, who did not know that when Felix smiled like that he was angry, agreed.

"Yes," she said; "you're an observer. You will see the thing in right perspective."

"I shall endeavor to. What does Tod say?"

"Oh! Tod never seems to say anything. At least, I never hear of it."

Felix murmured:

"Tod is a well in the desert."

To which deep saying Clara made no reply, not indeed understanding in the least what it might signify.

That evening, when Alan, having had his fill of billiards, had left the smoking-room and gone to bed, Felix remarked to Stanley:

"I say, what sort of people are these Mallorings?"

Stanley, who was settling himself for the twenty minutes of whiskey, potash, and a Review, with which he commonly composed his mind before retiring, answered negligently:

"The Mallorings? Oh! about the best type of landowner we've got."

"What exactly do you mean by that?"

Stanley took his time to answer, for below his bluff good-nature he had the tenacious, if somewhat slow, precision of an English man of business, mingled with a certain mistrust of 'old Felix.'

"Well," he said at last, "they build good cottages, yellow brick, d—d ugly, I must say; look after the character of their tenants; give 'em rebate of rent if there's a bad harvest; encourage stock-breedin', and machinery—they've got some of my ploughs, but the people don't like 'em, and, as a matter of fact, they're right—they're not made for these small fields; set an example goin' to church; patronize the Rifle Range; buy up the pubs when they can, and run 'em themselves; send out jelly, and let people over their place on bank holidays. Dash it all, I don't know what they don't do. Why?"

"Are they liked?"

"Liked? No, I should hardly think they were liked; respected, and all that. Malloring's a steady fellow, keen man on housing, and a gentleman; she's a bit too much perhaps on the pious side. They've got one of the finest Georgian houses in the country. Altogether they're what you call 'model.'"

"But not human."

Stanley slightly lowered the Review and looked across it at his brother. It was evident to him that 'old Felix' was in one of his free-thinking moods.

"They're domestic," he said, "and fond of their children, and pleasant neighbors. I don't deny that they've got a tremendous sense of duty, but we want that in these days."

"Duty to what?"

Stanley raised his level eyebrows. It was a stumper. Without great care he felt that he would be getting over the border into the uncharted land of speculation and philosophy, wandering on paths that led him nowhere.

"If you lived in the country, old man," he said, "you wouldn't ask that sort of question."

"You don't imagine," said Felix, "that you or the Mallorings live in the country? Why, you landlords are every bit as much town dwellers as I am—thought, habit, dress, faith, souls, all town stuff. There IS no 'country' in England now for us of the 'upper classes.' It's gone. I repeat: Duty to what?"

And, rising, he went over to the window, looking out at the moonlit lawn, overcome by a sudden aversion from more talk. Of what use were words from a mind tuned in one key to a mind tuned in another? And yet, so ingrained was his habit of discussion, that he promptly went on:

"The Mallorings, I've not the slightest doubt, believe it their duty to look after the morals of those who live on their property. There are three things to be said about that: One—you can't make people moral by adopting the attitude of the schoolmaster. Two—it implies that they consider themselves more moral than their neighbors. Three—it's a theory so convenient to their security that they would be exceptionally good people if they did not adopt it; but, from your account, they are not so much exceptionally as just typically good people. What you call their sense of duty, Stanley, is really their sense of self-preservation coupled with their sense of superiority."

"H'm!" said Stanley; "I don't know that I quite follow you."

"I always hate an odor of sanctity. I'd prefer them to say frankly: 'This is my property, and you'll jolly well do what I tell you, on it.'"

"But, my dear chap, after all, they really ARE superior."

"That," said Felix, "I emphatically question. Put your Mallorings to earn their living on fifteen to eighteen shillings a week, and where would they be? The Mallorings have certain virtues, no doubt, natural to their fortunate environment, but of the primitive virtues of patience, hardihood, perpetual, almost unconscious self-sacrifice, and cheerfulness in the face of a hard fate, they are no more the equals of the people they pretend to be superior to than I am your equal as a man of business."

"Hang it!" was Stanley's answer, "what a d—d old heretic you are!"

Felix frowned. "Am I? Be honest! Take the life of a Malloring and take it at its best; see how it stands comparison in the ordinary virtues with those of an averagely good specimen of a farm-laborer. Your Malloring is called with a cup of tea, at, say, seven o'clock, out of a nice, clean, warm bed; he gets into a bath that has been got ready for him; into clothes and boots that have been brushed for him; and goes down to a room where there's a fire burning already if it's a cold day, writes a few letters, perhaps, before eating a breakfast of exactly what he likes, nicely prepared for him, and reading the newspaper that best comforts his soul; when he has eaten and read, he lights his cigar or his pipe and attends to his digestion in the most sanitary and comfortable fashion; then in his study he sits down to steady direction of other people, either by interview or by writing letters, or what not. In this way, between directing people and eating what he likes, he passes the whole day, except that for two or three hours, sometimes indeed seven or eight hours, he attends to his physique by riding, motoring, playing a game, or indulging in a sport that he has chosen for himself. And, at the end of all that, he probably has another bath that has been made ready for him, puts on clean clothes that have been put out for him, goes down to a good dinner that has been cooked for him, smokes, reads, learns, and inwardly digests, or else plays cards, billiards, and acts host till he is sleepy, and so to bed, in a clean, warm bed, in a clean, fresh room. Is that exaggerated?"

"No; but when you talk of his directing other people, you forget that he is doing what they couldn't."

"He may be doing what they couldn't; but ordinary directive ability is not born in a man; it's acquired by habit and training. Suppose fortune had reversed them at birth, the Gaunt or Tryst would by now have it and the Malloring would not. The accident that they were not reversed at birth has given the Malloring a thousandfold advantage."

"It's no joke directing things," muttered Stanley.

"No work is any joke; but I just put it to you: Simply as work, without taking in the question of reward, would you dream for a minute of swapping your work with the work of one of your workmen? No. Well, neither would a Malloring with one of his Gaunts. So that, my boy, for work which is intrinsically more interesting and pleasurable, the Malloring gets a hundred to a thousand times more money."

"All this is rank socialism, my dear fellow."

"No; rank truth. Now, to take the life of a Gaunt. He gets up summer and winter much earlier out of a bed that he cannot afford time or money to keep too clean or warm, in a small room that probably has not a large enough window; into clothes stiff with work and boots stiff with clay; makes something hot for himself, very likely brings some of it to his wife and children; goes out, attending to his digestion crudely and without comfort; works with his hands and feet from half past six or seven in the morning till past five at night, except that twice he stops for an hour or so and eats simple things that he would not altogether have chosen to eat if he could have had his will. He goes home to a tea that has been got ready for him, and has a clean-up without assistance, smokes a pipe of shag, reads a newspaper perhaps two days old, and goes out again to work for his own good, in his vegetable patch, or to sit on a wooden bench in an atmosphere of beer and 'baccy.' And so, dead tired, but not from directing other people, he drowses himself to early lying again in his doubtful bed. Is that exaggerated?"

"I suppose not, but he—"

"Has his compensations: Clean conscience—freedom from worry—fresh air, all the rest of it! I know. Clean conscience granted, but so has your Malloring, it would seem. Freedom from worry—yes, except when a pair of boots is wanted, or one of the children is ill; then he has to make up for lost time with a vengeance. Fresh air—and wet clothes, with a good chance of premature rheumatism. Candidly, which of those two lives demands more of the virtues on which human life is founded—courage and patience, hardihood and self-sacrifice? And which of two men who have lived those two lives well has most right to the word 'superior'?"

Stanley dropped the Review and for fully a minute paced the room without reply. Then he said:

"Felix, you're talking flat revolution."

Felix, who, faintly smiling, had watched him up and down, up and down the Turkey carpet, answered:

"Not so. I am by no means a revolutionary person, because with all the good-will in the world I have been unable to see how upheavals from the bottom, or violence of any sort, is going to equalize these lives or do any good. But I detest humbug, and I believe that so long as you and your Mallorings go on blindly dosing yourselves with humbug about duty and superiority, so long will you see things as they are not. And until you see things as they are, purged of all that sickening cant, you will none of you really move to make the conditions of life more and ever more just. For, mark you, Stanley, I, who do not believe in revolution from the bottom, the more believe that it is up to us in honour to revolutionize things from the top!"

"H'm!" said Stanley; "that's all very well; but the more you give the more they want, till there's no end to it."

Felix stared round that room, where indeed one was all body.

"By George," he said, "I've yet to see a beginning. But, anyway, if you give in a grudging spirit, or the spirit of a schoolmaster, what can you expect? If you offer out of real good-will, so it is taken." And suddenly conscious that he had uttered a constructive phrase, Felix cast down his eyes, and added:

"I am going to my clean, warm bed. Good night, old man!"

When his brother had taken up his candlestick and gone, Stanley, uttering a dubious sound, sat down on the lounge, drank deep out of his tumbler, and once more took up his Review.

CHAPTER VII

The next day Stanley's car, fraught with Felix and a note from Clara, moved swiftly along the grass-bordered roads toward Joyfields. Lying back on the cushioned seat, the warm air flying at his face, Felix contemplated with delight his favorite countryside. Certainly this garden of England was very lovely, its greenness, trees, and large, pied, lazy cattle; its very emptiness of human beings even was pleasing.

Nearing Joyfields he noted the Mallorings' park and their long Georgian house, carefully fronting south. There, too, was the pond of what village there was, with the usual ducks on it; and three well-remembered cottages in a row, neat and trim, of the old, thatched sort, but evidently restored. Out of the door of one of them two young people had just emerged, going in the same direction as the car. Felix passed them and turned to look. Yes, it was they! He stopped the car. They were walking, with eyes straight before them, frowning. And Felix thought: 'Nothing of Tod in either of them; regular Celts!'

The girl's vivid, open face, crisp, brown, untidy hair, cheeks brimful of color, thick lips, eyes that looked up and out as a Skye terrier's eyes look out of its shagginess—indeed, her whole figure struck Felix as almost frighteningly vital; and she walked as if she despised the ground she covered. The boy was even more arresting. What a strange, pale-dark face, with its black, uncovered hair, its straight black brows; what a proud, swan's-eyed, thin-lipped, straight-nosed young devil, marching like a very Highlander; though still rather run-up, from sheer youthfulness! They had come abreast of the car by now, and, leaning out, he said:

"You don't remember me, I'm afraid!" The boy shook his head. Wonderful eyes he had! But the girl put out her hand.

"Of course, Derek; it's Uncle Felix."

They both smiled now, the girl friendly, the boy rather drawn back into himself. And feeling strangely small and ill at ease, Felix murmured:

"I'm going to see your father. Can I give you a lift home?"

The answer came as he expected:

"No, thanks." Then, as if to tone it down, the girl added:

"We've got something to do first. You'll find him in the orchard."

She had a ringing voice, full of warmth. Lifting his hat, Felix passed on. They WERE a couple! Strange, attractive, almost frightening. Kirsteen had brought his brother a formidable little brood.

Arriving at the cottage, he went up its mossy stones and through the wicket gate. There was little change, indeed, since the days of Clara's visit, save that the beehives had been moved farther out. Nor did any one answer his knock; and mindful of the girl's words, "You'll find him in the orchard," he made his way out among the trees. The grass was long and starred with petals. Felix wandered over it among bees busy with the apple-blossom. At the very end he came on his brother, cutting down a pear-tree. Tod was in shirt-sleeves, his brown arms bare almost to the shoulders. How tremendous the fellow was! What resounding and terrific blows he was dealing! Down came the tree, and Tod drew his arm across his brow. This great, burnt, curly-headed fellow was more splendid to look upon than even Felix had remembered, and so well built that not a movement of his limbs was heavy. His cheek-bones were very broad and high; his brows thick and rather darker than his bright hair, so that his deep-set, very blue eyes seemed to look out of a thicket; his level white teeth gleamed from under his tawny moustache, and his brown, unshaven cheeks and jaw seemed covered with gold powder. Catching sight of Felix, he came forward.

"Fancy," he said, "old Gladstone spending his leisure cutting down trees—of all melancholy jobs!"

Felix did not quite know what to answer, so he put his arm within his brother's. Tod drew him toward the tree.

"Sit down!" he said. Then, looking sorrowfully at the pear-tree, he murmured:

"Seventy years—and down in seven minutes. Now we shall burn it. Well, it had to go. This is the third year it's had no blossom."

His speech was slow, like that of a man accustomed to think aloud. Felix admired him askance. "I might live next door," he thought, "for all the notice he's taken of my turning up!"

"I came over in Stanley's car," he said. "Met your two coming along—fine couple they are!"

"Ah!" said Tod. And there was something in the way he said it that was more than a mere declaration of pride or of affection. Then he looked at Felix.

"What have you come for, old man?"

Felix smiled. Quaint way to put it!

"For a talk."

"Ah!" said Tod, and he whistled.

A largish, well-made dog with a sleek black coat, white underneath, and a black tail white-tipped, came running up, and stood before Tod, with its head rather to one side and its yellow-brown eyes saying: 'I simply must get at what you're thinking, you know.'

"Go and tell your mistress to come—Mistress!"

The dog moved his tail, lowered it, and went off.

"A gypsy gave him to me," said Tod; "best dog that ever lived."

"Every one thinks that of his own dog, old man."

"Yes," said Tod; "but this IS."

"He looks intelligent."

"He's got a soul," said Tod. "The gypsy said he didn't steal him, but he did."

"Do you always know when people aren't speaking the truth, then?"

"Yes."

At such a monstrous remark from any other man, Felix would have smiled; but seeing it was Tod, he only asked: "How?"

"People who aren't speaking the truth look you in the face and never move their eyes."

"Some people do that when they are speaking the truth."

"Yes; but when they aren't, you can see them struggling to keep their eyes straight. A dog avoids your eye when he's something to conceal; a man stares at you. Listen!"

Felix listened and heard nothing.

"A wren;" and, screwing up his lips, Tod emitted a sound: "Look!"

Felix saw on the branch of an apple-tree a tiny brown bird with a little beak sticking out and a little tail sticking up. And he thought: 'Tod's hopeless!'

"That fellow," said Tod softly, "has got his nest there just behind us." Again he emitted the sound. Felix saw the little bird move its head with a sort of infinite curiosity, and hop twice on the branch.

"I can't get the hen to do that," Tod murmured.

Felix put his hand on his brother's arm—what an arm!

"Yes," he said; "but look here, old man—I really want to talk to you."

Tod shook his head. "Wait for her," he said.

Felix waited. Tod was getting awfully eccentric, living this queer, out-of-the-way life with a cranky woman year after year; never reading anything, never seeing any one but tramps and animals and villagers. And yet, sitting there beside his eccentric brother on that fallen tree, he had an extraordinary sense of rest. It was, perhaps, but the beauty and sweetness of the day with its dappling sunlight brightening the apple-blossoms, the wind-flowers, the wood-sorrel, and in the blue sky above the fields those clouds so unimaginably white. All the tiny noises of the orchard, too, struck on his ear with a peculiar meaning, a strange fulness, as if he had never heard such sounds before. Tod, who was looking at the sky, said suddenly:

"Are you hungry?"

And Felix remembered that they never had any proper meals, but, when hungry, went to the kitchen, where a wood-fire was always burning, and either heated up coffee, and porridge that was already made, with boiled eggs and baked potatoes and apples, or devoured bread, cheese, jam, honey, cream, tomatoes, butter, nuts, and fruit, that were always set out there on a wooden table, under a muslin awning; he remembered, too, that they washed up their own bowls and spoons and plates, and, having finished, went outside and drew themselves a draught of water. Queer life, and deuced uncomfortable—almost Chinese in its reversal of everything that every one else was doing.

"No," he said, "I'm not."

"I am. Here she is."

Felix felt his heart beating—Clara was not alone in being frightened of this woman. She was coming through the orchard with the dog; a remarkable-looking woman—oh, certainly remarkable! She greeted him without surprise and, sitting down close to Tod, said: "I'm glad to see you."

Why did this family somehow make him feel inferior? The way she sat there and looked at him so calmly! Still more the way she narrowed her eyes and wrinkled her lips, as if rather malicious thoughts were rising in her soul! Her hair, as is the way of fine, soft, almost indigo-colored hair, was already showing threads of silver; her whole face and figure thinner than he had remembered. But a striking woman still—with wonderful eyes! Her dress—Felix had scanned many a crank in his day—was not so alarming as it had once seemed to Clara; its coarse-woven, deep-blue linen and needle-worked yoke were pleasing to him, and he could hardly take his gaze from the kingfisher-blue band or fillet that she wore round that silver-threaded black hair.

He began by giving her Clara's note, the wording of which he had himself dictated:

"DEAR KIRSTEEN:

"Though we have not seen each other for so long, I am sure you will forgive my writing. It would give us so much pleasure if you and the two children would come over for a night or two while Felix and his young folk are staying with us. It is no use, I fear, to ask Tod; but of course if he would come, too, both Stanley and myself would be delighted.

"Yours cordially,

"CLARA FREELAND."

She read it, handed it to Tod, who also read it and handed it to Felix. Nobody said anything. It was so altogether simple and friendly a note that Felix felt pleased with it, thinking: 'I expressed that well!'

Then Tod said: "Go ahead, old man! You've got something to say about the youngsters, haven't you?"

How on earth did he know that? But then Tod HAD a sort of queer prescience.

"Well," he brought out with an effort, "don't you think it's a pity to embroil your young people in village troubles? We've been hearing from Stanley—"

Kirsteen interrupted in her calm, staccato voice with just the faintest lisp:

"Stanley would not understand."

She had put her arm through Tod's, but never removed her eyes from her brother-in-law's face.

"Possibly," said Felix, "but you must remember that Stanley, John, and myself represent ordinary—what shall we say—level-headed opinion."

"With which we have nothing in common, I'm afraid."

Felix glanced from her to Tod. The fellow had his head on one side and seemed listening to something in the distance. And Felix felt a certain irritation.

"It's all very well," he said, "but I think you really have got to look at your children's future from a larger point of view. You don't surely want them to fly out against things before they've had a chance to see life for themselves."

She answered:

"The children know more of life than most young people. They've seen it close to, they've seen its realities. They know what the tyranny of the countryside means."

"Yes, yes," said Felix, "but youth is youth."

"They are not too young to know and feel the truth."

Felix was impressed. How those narrowing eyes shone! What conviction in that faintly lisping voice!

'I am a fool for my pains,' he thought, and only said:

"Well, what about this invitation, anyway?"

"Yes; it will be just the thing for them at the moment."

The words had to Felix a somewhat sinister import. He knew well enough that she did not mean by them what others would have meant. But he said: "When shall we expect them? Tuesday, I suppose, would be best for Clara, after her weekend. Is there no chance of you and Tod?"

She quaintly wrinkled her lips into not quite a smile, and answered:

"Tod shall say. Do you hear, Tod?"

"In the meadow. It was there yesterday—first time this year."

Felix slipped his arm through his brother's.

"Quite so, old man."

"What?" said Tod. "Ah! let's go in. I'm awfully hungry...."

Sometimes out of a calm sky a few drops fall, the twigs rustle, and far away is heard the muttering of thunder; the traveller thinks: 'A storm somewhere about.' Then all once more is so quiet and peaceful that he forgets he ever had that thought, and goes on his way careless.

So with Felix returning to Becket in Stanley's car. That woman's face, those two young heathens—the unconscious Tod!

There was mischief in the air above that little household. But once more the smooth gliding of the cushioned car, the soft peace of the meadows so permanently at grass, the churches, mansions, cottages embowered among their elms, the slow-flapping flight of the rooks and crows lulled Felix to quietude, and the faint far muttering of that thunder died away.

Nedda was in the drive when he returned, gazing at a nymph set up there by Clara. It was a good thing, procured from Berlin, well known for sculpture, and beginning to green over already, as though it had been there a long time—a pretty creature with shoulders drooping, eyes modestly cast down, and a sparrow perching on her head.

"Well, Dad?"

"They're coming."

"When?"

"On Tuesday—the youngsters, only."

"You might tell me a little about them."

But Felix only smiled. His powers of description faltered before that task; and, proud of those powers, he did not choose to subject them to failure.

CHAPTER VIII

Not till three o'clock that Saturday did the Bigwigs begin to come. Lord and Lady Britto first from Erne by car; then Sir Gerald and Lady Malloring, also by car from Joyfields; an early afternoon train brought three members of the Lower House, who liked a round of golf—Colonel Martlett, Mr. Sleesor, and Sir John Fanfar—with their wives; also Miss Bawtrey, an American who went everywhere; and Moorsome, the landscape-painter, a short, very heavy man who went nowhere, and that in almost perfect silence, which he afterward avenged. By a train almost sure to bring no one else came Literature in Public Affairs, alone, Henry Wiltram, whom some believed to have been the very first to have ideas about the land. He was followed in the last possible train by Cuthcott, the advanced editor, in his habitual hurry, and Lady Maude Ughtred in her beauty. Clara was pleased, and said to Stanley, while dressing, that almost every shade of opinion about the land was represented this week-end. She was not, she said, afraid of anything, if she could keep Henry Wiltram and Cuthcott apart. The House of Commons men would, of course, be all right. Stanley assented: "They'll be 'fed up' with talk. But how about Britto—he can sometimes be very nasty, and Cuthcott's been pretty rough on him, in his rag."

Clara had remembered that, and she was putting Lady Maude on one side of Cuthcott, and Moorsome on the other, so that he would be quite safe at dinner, and afterward—Stanley must look out!

"What have you done with Nedda?" Stanley asked.

"Given her to Colonel Martlett, with Sir John Fanfar on the other side; they both like something fresh." She hoped, however, to foster a discussion, so that they might really get further this week-end; the opportunity was too good to throw away.

"H'm!" Stanley murmured. "Felix said some very queer things the other night. He, too, might make ructions."

Oh, no!—Clara persisted—Felix had too much good taste. She thought that something might be coming out of this occasion, something as it were national, that would bear fruit. And watching Stanley buttoning his braces, she grew enthusiastic. For, think how splendidly everything was represented! Britto, with his view that the thing had gone too far, and all the little efforts we might make now were no good, with Canada and those great spaces to outbid anything we could do; though she could not admit that he was right, there was a lot in what he said; he had great gifts—and some day might—who knew? Then there was Sir John—Clara pursued—who was almost the father of the new Tory policy: Assist the farmers to buy their own land. And Colonel Martlett, representing the older Tory policy of: What the devil would happen to the landowners if they did? Secretly (Clara felt sure) he would never go into a lobby to support that. He had said to her: 'Look at my brother James's property; if we bring this policy in, and the farmers take advantage, his house might stand there any day without an acre round it.' Quite true—it might. The same might even happen to Becket.

Stanley grunted.

Exactly!—Clara went on: And that was the beauty of having got the Mallorings; theirs was such a steady point of view, and she was not sure that they weren't right, and the whole thing really a question of model proprietorship.

"H'm!" Stanley muttered. "Felix will have his knife into that."

Clara did not think that mattered. The thing was to get everybody's opinion. Even Mr. Moorsome's would be valuable—if he weren't so terrifically silent, for he must think a lot, sitting all day, as he did, painting the land.

"He's a heavy ass," said Stanley.

Yes; but Clara did not wish to be narrow. That was why it was so splendid to have got Mr. Sleesor. If anybody knew the Radical mind he did, and he could give full force to what one always felt was at the bottom of it—that the Radicals' real supporters were the urban classes; so that their policy must not go too far with 'the Land,' for fear of seeming to neglect the towns. For, after all, in the end it was out of the pockets of the towns that 'the Land' would have to be financed, and nobody really could expect the towns to get anything out of it. Stanley paused in the adjustment of his tie; his wife was a shrewd woman.

"You've hit it there," he said. "Wiltram will give it him hot on that, though."

Of course, Clara assented. And it was magnificent that they had got Henry Wiltram, with his idealism and his really heavy corn tax; not caring what happened to the stunted products of the towns—and they truly were stunted, for all that the Radicals and the half-penny press said—till at all costs we could grow our own food. There was a lot in that.

"Yes," Stanley muttered, "and if he gets on to it, shan't I have a jolly time of it in the smoking-room? I know what Cuthcott's like with his shirt out."

Clara's eyes brightened; she was very curious herself to see Mr. Cuthcott with his—that is, to hear him expound the doctrine he was always writing up, namely, that 'the Land' was gone and, short of revolution, there was nothing for it but garden cities. She had heard he was so cutting and ferocious that he really did seem as if he hated his opponents. She hoped he would get a chance—perhaps Felix could encourage him.

"What about the women?" Stanley asked suddenly. "Will they stand a political powwow? One must think of them a bit."

Clara had. She was taking a farewell look at herself in the far-away mirror through the door into her bedroom. It was a mistake—she added—to suppose that women were not interested in 'the Land.' Lady Britto was most intelligent, and Mildred Malloring knew every cottage on her estate.

"Pokes her nose into 'em often enough," Stanley muttered.

Lady Fanfar again, and Mrs. Sleesor, and even Hilda Martlett, were interested in their husbands, and Miss Bawtrey, of course, interested in everything. As for Maude Ughtred, all talk would be the same to her; she was always week-ending. Stanley need not worry—it would be all right; some real work would get done, some real advance be made. So saying, she turned her fine shoulders twice, once this way and once that, and went out. She had never told even Stanley her ambition that at Becket, under her aegis, should be laid the foundation-stone of the real scheme, whatever it might be, that should regenerate 'the Land.' Stanley would only have laughed; even though it would be bound to make him Lord Freeland when it came to be known some day....

To the eyes and ears of Nedda that evening at dinner, all was new indeed, and all wonderful. It was not that she was unaccustomed to society or to conversation, for to their house at Hampstead many people came, uttering many words, but both the people and the words were so very different. After the first blush, the first reconnaissance of the two Bigwigs between whom she sat, her eyes WOULD stray and her ears would only half listen to them. Indeed, half her ears, she soon found out, were quite enough to deal with Colonel Martlett and Sir John Fanfar. Across the azaleas she let her glance come now and again to anchor on her father's face, and exchanged with him a most enjoyable blink. She tried once or twice to get through to Alan, but he was always eating; he looked very like a young Uncle Stanley this evening.

What was she feeling? Short, quick stabs of self-consciousness as to how she was looking; a sort of stunned excitement due to sheer noise and the number of things offered to her to eat and drink; keen pleasure in the consciousness that Colonel Martlett and Sir John Fanfar and other men, especially that nice one with the straggly moustache who looked as if he were going to bite, glanced at her when they saw she wasn't looking. If only she had been quite certain that it was not because they thought her too young to be there! She felt a sort of continual exhilaration, that this was the great world—the world where important things were said and done, together with an intense listening expectancy, and a sense most unexpected and almost frightening, that nothing important was being said or would be done. But this she knew to be impudent. On Sunday evenings at home people talked about a future existence, about Nietzsche, Tolstoy, Chinese pictures, post-impressionism, and would suddenly grow hot and furious about peace, and Strauss, justice, marriage, and De Maupassant, and whether people were losing their souls through materialism, and sometimes one of them would get up and walk about the room. But to-night the only words she could catch were the names of two politicians whom nobody seemed to approve of, except that nice one who was going to bite. Once very timidly she asked Colonel Martlett whether he liked Strauss, and was puzzled by his answer: "Rather; those 'Tales of Hoffmann' are rippin', don't you think? You go to the opera much?" She could not, of course, know that the thought which instantly rose within her was doing the governing classes a grave injustice—almost all of whom save Colonel Martlett knew that the 'Tales of Hoffmann' were by one Offenbach. But beyond all things she felt she would never, never learn to talk as they were all talking—so quickly, so continuously, so without caring whether everybody or only the person they were talking to heard what they said. She had always felt that what you said was only meant for the person you said it to, but here in the great world she must evidently not say anything that was not meant for everybody, and she felt terribly that she could not think of anything of that sort to say. And suddenly she began to want to be alone. That, however, was surely wicked and wasteful, when she ought to be learning such a tremendous lot; and yet, what was there to learn? And listening just sufficiently to Colonel Martlett, who was telling her how great a man he thought a certain general, she looked almost despairingly at the one who was going to bite. He was quite silent at that moment, gazing at his plate, which was strangely empty. And Nedda thought: 'He has jolly wrinkles about his eyes, only they might be heart disease; and I like the color of his face, so nice and yellow, only that might be liver. But I DO like him—I wish I'd been sitting next to him; he looks real.' From that thought, of the reality of a man whose name she did not know, she passed suddenly into the feeling that nothing else of this about her was real at all, neither the talk nor the faces, not even the things she was eating. It was all a queer, buzzing dream. Nor did that sensation of unreality cease when her aunt began collecting her gloves, and they trooped forth to the drawing-room. There, seated between Mrs. Sleesor and Lady Britto, with Lady Malloring opposite, and Miss Bawtrey leaning over the piano toward them, she pinched herself to get rid of the feeling that, when all these were out of sight of each other, they would become silent and have on their lips a little, bitter smile. Would it be like that up in their bedrooms, or would it only be on her (Nedda's) own lips that this little smile would come? It was a question she could not answer; nor could she very well ask it of any of these ladies. She looked them over as they sat there talking and felt very lonely. And suddenly her eyes fell on her grandmother. Frances Freeland was seated halfway down the long room in a sandalwood chair, somewhat insulated by a surrounding sea of polished floor. She sat with a smile on her lips, quite still, save for the continual movement of her white hands on her black lap. To her gray hair some lace of Chantilly was pinned with a little diamond brooch, and hung behind her delicate but rather long ears. And from her shoulders was depended a silvery garment, of stuff that looked like the mail shirt of a fairy, reaching the ground on either side. A tacit agreement had evidently been come to, that she was incapable of discussing 'the Land' or those other subjects such as the French murder, the Russian opera, the Chinese pictures, and the doings of one, L——, whose fate was just then in the air, so that she sat alone.

And Nedda thought: 'How much more of a lady she looks than anybody here! There's something deep in her to rest on that isn't in the Bigwigs; perhaps it's because she's of a different generation.' And, getting up, she went over and sat down beside her on a little chair.

Frances Freeland rose at once and said:

"Now, my darling, you can't be comfortable in that tiny chair. You must take mine."

"Oh, no, Granny; please!"

"Oh, yes; but you must! It's so comfortable, and I've simply been longing to sit in the chair you're in. Now, darling, to please me!"

Seeing that a prolonged struggle would follow if she did not get up, Nedda rose and changed chairs.

"Do you like these week-ends, Granny?"

Frances Freeland seemed to draw her smile more resolutely across her face. With her perfect articulation, in which there was, however, no trace of bigwiggery, she answered:

"I think they're most interesting, darling. It's so nice to see new people. Of course you don't get to know them, but it's very amusing to watch, especially the head-dresses!" And sinking her voice: "Just look at that one with the feather going straight up; did you ever see such a guy?" and she cackled with a very gentle archness. Gazing at that almost priceless feather, trying to reach God, Nedda felt suddenly how completely she was in her grandmother's little camp; how entirely she disliked bigwiggery.

Frances Freeland's voice brought her round.

"Do you know, darling, I've found the most splendid thing for eyebrows? You just put a little on every night and it keeps them in perfect order. I must give you my little pot."

"I don't like grease, Granny."

"Oh! but this isn't grease, darling. It's a special thing; and you only put on just the tiniest touch."

Diving suddenly into the recesses of something, she produced an exiguous round silver box. Prizing it open, she looked over her shoulder at the Bigwigs, then placed her little finger on the contents of the little box, and said very softly:

"You just take the merest touch, and you put it on like that, and it keeps them together beautifully. Let me! Nobody'll see!"

Quite well understanding that this was all part of her grandmother's passion for putting the best face upon things, and having no belief in her eyebrows, Nedda bent forward; but in a sudden flutter of fear lest the Bigwigs might observe the operation, she drew back, murmuring: "Oh, Granny, darling! Not just now!"

At that moment the men came in, and, under cover of the necessary confusion, she slipped away into the window.

It was pitch-black outside, with the moon not yet up. The bloomy, peaceful dark out there! Wistaria and early roses, clustering in, had but the ghost of color on their blossoms. Nedda took a rose in her fingers, feeling with delight its soft fragility, its coolness against her hot palm. Here in her hand was a living thing, here was a little soul! And out there in the darkness were millions upon millions of other little souls, of little flame-like or coiled-up shapes alive and true.

A voice behind her said:

"Nothing nicer than darkness, is there?"

She knew at once it was the one who was going to bite; the voice was proper for him, having a nice, smothery sound. And looking round gratefully, she said:

"Do you like dinner-parties?"

It was jolly to watch his eyes twinkle and his thin cheeks puff out. He shook his head and muttered through that straggly moustache:

"You're a niece, aren't you? I know your father. He's a big man."

Hearing those words spoken of her father, Nedda flushed.

"Yes, he is," she said fervently.

Her new acquaintance went on:

"He's got the gift of truth—can laugh at himself as well as others; that's what makes him precious. These humming-birds here to-night couldn't raise a smile at their own tomfoolery to save their silly souls."

He spoke still in that voice of smothery wrath, and Nedda thought: 'He IS nice!'

"They've been talking about 'the Land'"—he raised his hands and ran them through his palish hair—"'the Land!' Heavenly Father! 'The Land!' Why! Look at that fellow!"

Nedda looked and saw a man, like Richard Coeur de Lion in the history books, with a straw-colored moustache just going gray.

"Sir Gerald Malloring—hope he's not a friend of yours! Divine right of landowners to lead 'the Land' by the nose! And our friend Britto!"

Nedda, following his eyes, saw a robust, quick-eyed man with a suave insolence in his dark, clean-shaved face.

"Because at heart he's just a supercilious ruffian, too cold-blooded to feel, he'll demonstrate that it's no use to feel—waste of valuable time—ha! valuable!—to act in any direction. And that's a man they believe things of. And poor Henry Wiltram, with his pathetic: 'Grow our own food—maximum use of the land as food-producer, and let the rest take care of itself!' As if we weren't all long past that feeble individualism; as if in these days of world markets the land didn't stand or fall in this country as a breeding-ground of health and stamina and nothing else. Well, well!"

"Aren't they really in earnest, then?" asked Nedda timidly.

"Miss Freeland, this land question is a perfect tragedy. Bar one or two, they all want to make the omelette without breaking eggs; well, by the time they begin to think of breaking them, mark me—there'll be no eggs to break. We shall be all park and suburb. The real men on the land, what few are left, are dumb and helpless; and these fellows here for one reason or another don't mean business—they'll talk and tinker and top-dress—that's all. Does your father take any interest in this? He could write something very nice."

"He takes interest in everything," said Nedda. "Please go on, Mr.—Mr.—" She was terribly afraid he would suddenly remember that she was too young and stop his nice, angry talk.

"Cuthcott. I'm an editor, but I was brought up on a farm, and know something about it. You see, we English are grumblers, snobs to the backbone, want to be something better than we are; and education nowadays is all in the direction of despising what is quiet and humdrum. We never were a stay-at-home lot, like the French. That's at the back of this business—they may treat it as they like, Radicals or Tories, but if they can't get a fundamental change of opinion into the national mind as to what is a sane and profitable life; if they can't work a revolution in the spirit of our education, they'll do no good. There'll be lots of talk and tinkering, tariffs and tommy-rot, and, underneath, the land-bred men dying, dying all the time. No, madam, industrialism and vested interests have got us! Bar the most strenuous national heroism, there's nothing for it now but the garden city!"

"Then if we WERE all heroic, 'the Land' could still be saved?"

Mr. Cuthcott smiled.

"Of course we might have a European war or something that would shake everything up. But, short of that, when was a country ever consciously and homogeneously heroic—except China with its opium? When did it ever deliberately change the spirit of its education, the trend of its ideas; when did it ever, of its own free will, lay its vested interests on the altar; when did it ever say with a convinced and resolute heart: 'I will be healthy and simple before anything. I will not let the love of sanity and natural conditions die out of me!' When, Miss Freeland, when?"

And, looking so hard at Nedda that he almost winked, he added:

"You have the advantage of me by thirty years. You'll see what I shall not—the last of the English peasant. Did you ever read 'Erewhon,' where the people broke up their machines? It will take almost that sort of national heroism to save what's left of him, even."

For answer, Nedda wrinkled her brows horribly. Before her there had come a vision of the old, lame man, whose name she had found out was Gaunt, standing on the path under the apple-trees, looking at that little something he had taken from his pocket. Why she thought of him thus suddenly she had no idea, and she said quickly:

"It's awfully interesting. I do so want to hear about 'the Land.' I only know a little about sweated workers, because I see something of them."

"It's all of a piece," said Mr. Cuthcott; "not politics at all, but religion—touches the point of national self-knowledge and faith, the point of knowing what we want to become and of resolving to become it. Your father will tell you that we have no more idea of that at present than a cat of its own chemical composition. As for these good people here to-night—I don't want to be disrespectful, but if they think they're within a hundred miles of the land question, I'm a—I'm a Jingo—more I can't say."

And, as if to cool his head, he leaned out of the window.

"Nothing is nicer than darkness, as I said just now, because you can only see the way you MUST go instead of a hundred and fifty ways you MIGHT. In darkness your soul is something like your own; in daylight, lamplight, moonlight, never."

Nedda's spirit gave a jump; he seemed almost at last to be going to talk about the things she wanted, above all, to find out. Her cheeks went hot, she clenched her hands and said resolutely:

"Mr. Cuthcott, do you believe in God?"

Mr. Cuthcott made a queer, deep little noise; it was not a laugh, however, and it seemed as if he knew she could not bear him to look at her just then.

"H'm!" he said. "Every one does that—according to their natures. Some call God IT, some HIM, some HER, nowadays—that's all. You might as well ask—do I believe that I'm alive?"

"Yes," said Nedda, "but which do YOU call God?"

As she asked that, he gave a wriggle, and it flashed through her: 'He must think me an awful enfant terrible!' His face peered round at her, queer and pale and puffy, with nice, straight eyes; and she added hastily:

"It isn't a fair question, is it? Only you talked about darkness, and the only way—so I thought—"

"Quite a fair question. My answer is, of course: 'All three'; but the point is rather: Does one wish to make even an attempt to define God to oneself? Frankly, I don't! I'm content to feel that there is in one some kind of instinct toward perfection that one will still feel, I hope, when the lights are going out; some kind of honour forbidding one to let go and give up. That's all I've got; I really don't know that I want more."

Nedda clasped her hands.

"I like that," she said; "only—what is perfection, Mr. Cuthcott?"

Again he emitted that deep little sound.

"Ah!" he repeated, "what is perfection? Awkward, that—isn't it?"

"Is it"—Nedda rushed the words out—"is it always to be sacrificing yourself, or is it—is it always to be—to be expressing yourself?"

"To some—one; to some—the other; to some—half one, half the other."

"But which is it to me?"

"Ah! that you've got to find out for yourself. There's a sort of metronome inside us—wonderful, sell-adjusting little machine; most delicate bit of mechanism in the world—people call it conscience—that records the proper beat of our tempos. I guess that's all we have to go by."

Nedda said breathlessly:

"Yes; and it's frightfully hard, isn't it?"

"Exactly," Mr. Cuthcott answered. "That's why people devised religions and other ways of having the thing done second-hand. We all object to trouble and responsibility if we can possibly avoid it. Where do you live?"

"In Hampstead."

"Your father must be a stand-by, isn't he?"

"Oh, yes; Dad's splendid; only, you see, I AM a good deal younger than he. There was just one thing I was going to ask you. Are these very Bigwigs?"

Mr. Cuthcott turned to the room and let his screwed-up glance wander. He looked just then particularly as if he were going to bite.

"If you take 'em at their own valuation: Yes. If at the country's: So-so. If at mine: Ha! I know what you'd like to ask: Should I be a Bigwig in THEIR estimation? Not I! As you knock about, Miss Freeland, you'll find out one thing—all bigwiggery is founded on: Scratch my back, and I'll scratch yours. Seriously, these are only tenpenny ones; but the mischief is, that in the matter of 'the Land,' the men who really are in earnest are precious scarce. Nothing short of a rising such as there was in 1832 would make the land question real, even for the moment. Not that I want to see one—God forbid! Those poor doomed devils were treated worse than dogs, and would be again."

Before Nedda could pour out questions about the rising in 1832, Stanley's voice said:

"Cuthcott, I want to introduce you!"

Her new friend screwed his eyes up tighter and, muttering something, put out his hand to her.

"Thank you for our talk. I hope we shall meet again. Any time you want to know anything—I'll be only too glad. Good night!"

She felt the squeeze of his hand, warm and dry, but rather soft, as of a man who uses a pen too much; saw him following her uncle across the room, with his shoulders a little hunched, as if preparing to inflict, and ward off, blows. And with the thought: 'He must be jolly when he gives them one!' she turned once more to the darkness, than which he had said there was nothing nicer. It smelled of new-mown grass, was full of little shiverings of leaves, and all colored like the bloom of a black grape. And her heart felt soothed.

CHAPTER IX

"...When I first saw Derek I thought I should never feel anything but shy and hopeless. In four days, only in four days, the whole world is different.... And yet, if it hadn't been for that thunder-storm, I shouldn't have got over being shy in time. He has never loved anybody—nor have I. It can't often be like that—it makes it solemn. There's a picture somewhere—not a good one, I know—of a young Highlander being taken away by soldiers from his sweetheart. Derek is fiery and wild and shy and proud and dark—like the man in that picture. That last day along the hills—along and along—with the wind in our faces, I could have walked forever; and then Joyfields at the end! Their mother's wonderful; I'm afraid of her. But Uncle Tod is a perfect dear. I never saw any one before who noticed so many things that I didn't, and nothing that I did. I am sure he has in him what Mr. Cuthcott said we were all losing—the love of simple, natural conditions. And then, THE moment, when I stood with Derek at the end of the orchard, to say good-by. The field below covered with those moony-white flowers, and the cows all dark and sleepy; the holy feeling down there was wonderful, and in the branches over our heads, too, and the velvety, starry sky, and the dewiness against one's face, and the great, broad silence—it was all worshipping something, and I was worshipping—worshipping happiness. I WAS happy, and I think HE was. Perhaps I shall never be so happy again. When he kissed me I didn't think the whole world had so much happiness in it. I know now that I'm not cold a bit; I used to think I was. I believe I could go with him anywhere, and do anything he wanted. What would Dad think? Only the other day I was saying I wanted to know everything. One only knows through love. It's love that makes the world all beautiful—makes it like those pictures that seem to be wrapped in gold, makes it like a dream—no, not like a dream—like a wonderful tune. I suppose that's glamour—a goldeny, misty, lovely feeling, as if my soul were wandering about with his—not in my body at all. I want it to go on and on wandering—oh! I don't want it back in my body, all hard and inquisitive and aching! I shall never know anything so lovely as loving him and being loved. I don't want anything more—nothing! Stay with me, please—Happiness! Don't go away and leave me!... They frighten me, though; he frightens me—their idealism; wanting to do great things, and fight for justice. If only I'd been brought up more like that—but everything's been so different. It's their mother, I think, even more than themselves. I seem to have grown up just looking on at life as at a show; watching it, thinking about it, trying to understand—not living it at all. I must get over that; I will. I believe I can tell the very moment I began to love him. It was in the schoolroom the second evening. Sheila and I were sitting there just before dinner, and he came, in a rage, looking splendid. 'That footman put out everything just as if I were a baby—asked me for suspenders to fasten on my socks; hung the things on a chair in order, as if I couldn't find out for myself what to put on first; turned the tongues of my shoes out!—curled them over!' Then Derek looked at me and said: 'Do they do that for you?—And poor old Gaunt, who's sixty-six and lame, has three shillings a week to buy him everything. Just think of that! If we had the pluck of flies—' And he clenched his fists. But Sheila got up, looked hard at me, and said: 'That'll do, Derek.' Then he put his hand on my arm and said: 'It's only Cousin Nedda!' I began to love him then; and I believe he saw it, because I couldn't take my eyes away. But it was when Sheila sang 'The Red Sarafan,' after dinner, that I knew for certain. 'The Red Sarafan'— it's a wonderful song, all space and yearning, and yet such calm—it's the song of the soul; and he was looking at me while she sang. How can he love me? I am nothing—no good for anything! Alan calls him a 'run-up kid, all legs and wings.' Sometimes I hate Alan; he's conventional and stodgy—the funny thing is that he admires Sheila. She'll wake him up; she'll stick pins into him. No, I don't want Alan hurt—I want every one in the world to be happy, happy—as I am.... The next day was the thunder-storm. I never saw lightning so near—and didn't care a bit. If he were struck I knew I should be; that made it all right. When you love, you don't care, if only the something must happen to you both. When it was over, and we came out from behind the stack and walked home through the fields, all the beasts looked at us as if we were new and had never been seen before; and the air was ever so sweet, and that long, red line of cloud low down in the purple, and the elm-trees so heavy and almost black. He put his arm round me, and I let him.... It seems an age to wait till they come to stay with us next week. If only Mother likes them, and I can go and stay at Joyfields. Will she like them? It's all so different to what it would be if they were ordinary. But if he were ordinary I shouldn't love him; it's because there's nobody like him. That isn't a loverish fancy—you only have to look at him against Alan or Uncle Stanley or even Dad. Everything he does is so different; the way he walks, and the way he stands drawn back into himself, like a stag, and looks out as if he were burning and smouldering inside; even the way he smiles. Dad asked me what I thought of him! That was only the second day. I thought he was too proud, then. And Dad said: 'He ought to be in a Highland regiment; pity—great pity!' He is a fighter, of course. I don't like fighting, but if I'm not ready to, he'll stop loving me, perhaps. I've got to learn. O Darkness out there, help me! And Stars, help me! O God, make me brave, and I will believe in you forever! If you are the spirit that grows in things in spite of everything, until they're like the flowers, so perfect that we laugh and sing at their beauty, grow in me, too; make me beautiful and brave; then I shall be fit for him, alive or dead; and that's all I want. Every evening I shall stand in spirit with him at the end of that orchard in the darkness, under the trees above the white flowers and the sleepy cows, and perhaps I shall feel him kiss me again.... I'm glad I saw that old man Gaunt; it makes what they feel more real to me. He showed me that poor laborer Tryst, too, the one who mustn't marry his wife's sister, or have her staying in the house without marrying her. Why should people interfere with others like that? It does make your blood boil! Derek and Sheila have been brought up to be in sympathy with the poor and oppressed. If they had lived in London they would have been even more furious, I expect. And it's no use my saying to myself 'I don't know the laborer, I don't know his hardships,' because he is really just the country half of what I do know and see, here in London, when I don't hide my eyes. One talk showed me how desperately they feel; at night, in Sheila's room, when we had gone up, just we four. Alan began it; they didn't want to, I could see; but he was criticising what some of those Bigwigs had said—the 'Varsity makes boys awfully conceited. It was such a lovely night; we were all in the big, long window. A little bat kept flying past; and behind the copper-beech the moon was shining on the lake. Derek sat in the windowsill, and when he moved he touched me. To be touched by him gives me a warm shiver all through. I could hear him gritting his teeth at what Alan said—frightfully sententious, just like a newspaper: 'We can't go into land reform from feeling, we must go into it from reason.' Then Derek broke out: 'Walk through this country as we've walked; see the pigsties the people live in; see the water they drink; see the tiny patches of ground they have; see the way their roofs let in the rain; see their peeky children; see their patience and their hopelessness; see them working day in and day out, and coming on the parish at the end See all that, and then talk about reason! Reason! It's the coward's excuse, and the rich man's excuse, for doing nothing. It's the excuse of the man who takes jolly good care not to see for fear that he may come to feel! Reason never does anything, it's too reasonable. The thing is to act; then perhaps reason will be jolted into doing something.' But Sheila touched his arm, and he stopped very suddenly. She doesn't trust us. I shall always be being pushed away from him by her. He's just twenty, and I shall be eighteen in a week; couldn't we marry now at once? Then, whatever happened, I couldn't be cut off from him. If I could tell Dad, and ask him to help me! But I can't—it seems desecration to talk about it, even to Dad. All the way up in the train to-day, coming back home, I was struggling not to show anything; though it's hateful to keep things from Dad. Love alters everything; it melts up the whole world and makes it afresh. Love is the sun of our spirits, and it's the wind. Ah, and the rain, too! But I won't think of that!... I wonder if he's told Aunt Kirsteen!..."

CHAPTER X

While Nedda sat, long past midnight, writing her heart out in her little, white, lilac-curtained room of the old house above the Spaniard's Road, Derek, of whom she wrote, was walking along the Malvern hills, hurrying upward in the darkness. The stars were his companions; though he was no poet, having rather the fervid temper of the born swordsman, that expresses itself in physical ecstasies. He had come straight out from a stormy midnight talk with Sheila. What was he doing—had been the burden of her cry—falling in love just at this moment when they wanted all their wits and all their time and strength for this struggle with the Mallorings? It was foolish, it was weak; and with a sweet, soft sort of girl who could be no use. Hotly he had answered: What business was it of hers? As if one fell in love when one wished! She didn't know—her blood didn't run fast enough! Sheila had retorted, "I've more blood in my big toe than Nedda in all her body! A lot of use you'll be, with your heart mooning up in London!" And crouched together on the end of her bed, gazing fixedly up at him through her hair, she had chanted mockingly: "Here we go gathering wool and stars—wool and stars—wool and stars!"

He had not deigned to answer, but had gone out, furious with her, striding over the dark fields, scrambling his way through the hedges toward the high loom of the hills. Up on the short grass in the cooler air, with nothing between him and those swarming stars, he lost his rage. It never lasted long—hers was more enduring. With the innate lordliness of a brother he already put it down to jealousy. Sheila was hurt that he should want any one but her; as if his love for Nedda would make any difference to their resolution to get justice for Tryst and the Gaunts, and show those landed tyrants once for all that they could not ride roughshod.

Nedda! with her dark eyes, so quick and clear, so loving when they looked at him! Nedda, soft and innocent, the touch of whose lips had turned his heart to something strange within him, and wakened such feelings of chivalry! Nedda! To see whom for half a minute he felt he would walk a hundred miles.

This boy's education had been administered solely by his mother till he was fourteen, and she had brought him up on mathematics, French, and heroism. His extensive reading of history had been focussed on the personality of heroes, chiefly knights errant, and revolutionaries. He had carried the worship of them to the Agricultural College, where he had spent four years; and a rather rough time there had not succeeded in knocking romance out of him. He had found that you could not have such beliefs comfortably without fighting for them, and though he ended his career with the reputation of a rebel and a champion of the weak, he had to earn it. To this day he still fed himself on stories of rebellions and fine deeds. The figures of Spartacus, Montrose, Hofer, Garibaldi, Hampden, and John Nicholson, were more real to him than the people among whom he lived, though he had learned never to mention—especially not to the matter-of-fact Sheila—his encompassing cloud of heroes; but, when he was alone, he pranced a bit with them, and promised himself that he too would reach the stars. So you may sometimes see a little, grave boy walking through a field, unwatched as he believes, suddenly fling his feet and his head every which way. An active nature, romantic, without being dreamy and book-loving, is not too prone to the attacks of love; such a one is likely to survive unscathed to a maturer age. But Nedda had seduced him, partly by the appeal of her touchingly manifest love and admiration, and chiefly by her eyes, through which he seemed to see such a loyal, and loving little soul looking. She had that indefinable something which lovers know that they can never throw away. And he had at once made of her, secretly, the crown of his active romanticism—the lady waiting for the spoils of his lance. Queer is the heart of a boy—strange its blending of reality and idealism!

Climbing at a great pace, he reached Malvern Beacon just as it came dawn, and stood there on the top, watching. He had not much aesthetic sense; but he had enough to be impressed by the slow paling of the stars over space that seemed infinite, so little were its dreamy confines visible in the May morning haze, where the quivering crimson flags and spears of sunrise were forging up in a march upon the sky. That vision of the English land at dawn, wide and mysterious, hardly tallied with Mr. Cuthcott's view of a future dedicate to Park and Garden City. While Derek stood there gazing, the first lark soared up and began its ecstatic praise. Save for that song, silence possessed all the driven dark, right out to the Severn and the sea, and the fastnesses of the Welsh hills, and the Wrekin, away in the north, a black point in the gray. For a moment dark and light hovered and clung together. Would victory wing back into night or on into day? Then, as a town is taken, all was over in one overmastering rush, and light proclaimed. Derek tightened his belt and took a bee-line down over the slippery grass. He meant to reach the cottage of the laborer Tryst before that early bird was away to the fields. He meditated as he went. Bob Tryst was all right! If they only had a dozen or two like him! A dozen or two whom they could trust, and who would trust each other and stand firm to form the nucleus of a strike, which could be timed for hay harvest. What slaves these laborers still were! If only they could be relied on, if only they would stand together! Slavery! It WAS slavery; so long as they could be turned out of their homes at will in this fashion. His rebellion against the conditions of their lives, above all against the manifold petty tyrannies that he knew they underwent, came from use of his eyes and ears in daily contact with a class among whom he had been more or less brought up. In sympathy with, and yet not of them, he had the queer privilege of feeling their slights as if they were his own, together with feelings of protection, and even of contempt that they should let themselves be slighted. He was near enough to understand how they must feel; not near enough to understand why, feeling as they did, they did not act as he would have acted. In truth, he knew them no better than he should.

He found Tryst washing at his pump. In the early morning light the big laborer's square, stubborn face, with its strange, dog-like eyes, had a sodden, hungry, lost look. Cutting short ablutions that certainly were never protracted, he welcomed Derek, and motioned him to pass into the kitchen. The young man went in, and perched himself on the window-sill beside a pot of Bridal Wreath. The cottage was one of the Mallorings', and recently repaired. A little fire was burning, and a teapot of stewed tea sat there beside it. Four cups and spoons and some sugar were put out on a deal table, for Tryst was, in fact, brewing the morning draught of himself and children, who still lay abed up-stairs. The sight made Derek shiver and his eyes darken. He knew the full significance of what he saw.

"Did you ask him again, Bob?"

"Yes, I asked 'im."

"What did he say?"

"Said as orders was plain. 'So long as you lives there,' he says, 'along of yourself alone, you can't have her come back.'"

"Did you say the children wanted looking after badly? Did you make it clear? Did you say Mrs. Tryst wished it, before she—"

"I said that."

"What did he say then?"

"'Sorry for you, m'lad, but them's m'lady's orders, an' I can't go contrary. I don't wish to go into things,' he says; 'you know better'n I how far 'tis gone when she was 'ere before; but seein' as m'lady don't never give in to deceased wife's sister marryin', if she come back 'tis certain to be the other thing. So, as that won't do neither, you go elsewhere,' he says."

Having spoken thus at length, Tryst lifted the teapot and poured out the dark tea into the three cups.

"Will 'ee have some, sir?"

Derek shook his head.

Taking the cups, Tryst departed up the narrow stairway. And Derek remained motionless, staring at the Bridal Wreath, till the big man came down again and, retiring into a far corner, sat sipping at his own cup.

"Bob," said the boy suddenly, "do you LIKE being a dog; put to what company your master wishes?"

Tryst set his cup down, stood up, and crossed his thick arms—the swift movement from that stolid creature had in it something sinister; but he did not speak.

"Do you like it, Bob?"

"I'll not say what I feels, Mr. Derek; that's for me. What I does'll be for others, p'raps."

And he lifted his strange, lowering eyes to Derek's. For a full minute the two stared, then Derek said:

"Look out, then; be ready!" and, getting off the sill, he went out.

On the bright, slimy surface of the pond three ducks were quietly revelling in that hour before man and his damned soul, the dog, rose to put the fear of God into them. In the sunlight, against the green duckweed, their whiteness was truly marvellous; difficult to believe that they were not white all through. Passing the three cottages, in the last of which the Gaunts lived, he came next to his own home, but did not turn in, and made on toward the church. It was a very little one, very old, and had for him a curious fascination, never confessed to man or beast. To his mother, and Sheila, more intolerant, as became women, that little, lichened, gray stone building was the very emblem of hypocrisy, of a creed preached, not practised; to his father it was nothing, for it was not alive, and any tramp, dog, bird, or fruit-tree meant far more. But in Derek it roused a peculiar feeling, such as a man might have gazing at the shores of a native country, out of which he had been thrown for no fault of his own—a yearning deeply muffled up in pride and resentment. Not infrequently he would come and sit brooding on the grassy hillock just above the churchyard. Church-going, with its pageantry, its tradition, dogma, and demand for blind devotion, would have suited him very well, if only blind devotion to his mother had not stood across that threshold; he could not bring himself to bow to that which viewed his rebellious mother as lost. And yet the deep fibres of heredity from her papistic Highland ancestors, and from old pious Moretons, drew him constantly to this spot at times when no one would be about. It was his enemy, this little church, the fold of all the instincts and all the qualities against which he had been brought up to rebel; the very home of patronage and property and superiority; the school where his friends the laborers were taught their place! And yet it had that queer, ironical attraction for him. In some such sort had his pet hero Montrose rebelled, and then been drawn despite himself once more to the side of that against which he had taken arms.

While he leaned against the rail, gazing at that ancient edifice, he saw a girl walk into the churchyard at the far end, sit down on a gravestone, and begin digging a little hole in the grass with the toe of her boot. She did not seem to see him, and at his ease he studied her face, one of those broad, bright English country faces with deep-set rogue eyes and red, thick, soft lips, smiling on little provocation. In spite of her disgrace, in spite of the fact that she was sitting on her mother's grave, she did not look depressed. And Derek thought: 'Wilmet Gaunt is the jolliest of them all! She isn't a bit a bad girl, as they say; it's only that she must have fun. If they drive her out of here, she'll still want fun wherever she is; she'll go to a town and end up like those girls I saw in Bristol.' And the memory of those night girls, with their rouged faces and cringing boldness, came back to him with horror.

He went across the grass toward her.

She looked round as he came, and her face livened.

"Well, Wilmet?"

"You're an early bird, Mr. Derek."

"Haven't been to bed."

"Oh!"

"Been up Malvern Beacon to see the sun rise."

"You're tired, I expect!"

"No."

"Must be fine up there. You'd see a long ways from there; near to London I should think. Do you know London, Mr. Derek?"

"No."

"They say 'tis a funny place, too." Her rogue eyes gleamed from under a heavy frown. "It'd not be all 'Do this' an' 'Do that'; an' 'You bad girl' an' 'You little hussy!' in London. They say there's room for more'n one sort of girl there."

"All towns are beastly places, Wilmet."

Again her rogue's eyes gleamed. "I don' know so much about that, Mr. Derek. I'm going where I won't be chivied about and pointed at, like what I am here."

"Your dad's stuck to you; you ought to stick to him."

"Ah, Dad! He's losin' his place for me, but that don't stop his tongue at home. 'Tis no use to nag me—nag me. Suppose one of m'lady's daughters had a bit of fun—they say there's lots as do—I've heard tales—there'd be none comin' to chase her out of her home. 'No, my girl, you can't live here no more, endangerin' the young men. You go away. Best for you's where they'll teach you to be'ave. Go on! Out with you! I don't care where you go; but you just go!' 'Tis as if girls were all pats o' butter—same square, same pattern on it, same weight, an' all."

Derek had come closer; he put his hand down and gripped her arm. Her eloquence dried up before the intentness of his face, and she just stared up at him.

"Now, look here, Wilmet; you promise me not to scoot without letting us know. We'll get you a place to go to. Promise."

A little sheepishly the rogue-girl answered:

"I promise; only, I'm goin'."

Suddenly she dimpled and broke into her broad smile.

"Mr. Derek, d'you know what they say—they say you're in love. You was seen in th' orchard. Ah! 'tis all right for you and her! But if any one kiss and hug ME, I got to go!"

Derek drew back among the graves, as if he had been struck with a whip.

She looked up at him with coaxing sweetness.

"Don't you mind me, Mr. Derek, and don't you stay here neither. If they saw you here with me, they'd say: 'Aw—look! Endangerin' another young man—poor young man!' Good mornin', Mr. Derek!"

The rogue eyes followed him gravely, then once more began examining the grass, and the toe of her boot again began kicking a little hole. But Derek did not look back.

CHAPTER XI

It is in the nature of men and angels to pursue with death such birds as are uncommon, such animals as are rare; and Society had no use for one like Tod, so uncut to its pattern as to be practically unconscious of its existence. Not that he had deliberately turned his back on anything; he had merely begun as a very young man to keep bees. The better to do that he had gone on to the cultivation of flowers and fruit, together with just enough farming as kept his household in vegetables, milk, butter, and eggs. Living thus amongst insects, birds, cows, and the peace of trees, he had become queer. His was not a very reflective mind, it distilled but slowly certain large conclusions, and followed intently the minute happenings of his little world. To him a bee, a bird, a flower, a tree was well-nigh as interesting as a man; yet men, women, and especially children took to him, as one takes to a Newfoundland dog, because, though capable of anger, he seemed incapable of contempt, and to be endowed with a sort of permanent wonder at things. Then, too, he was good to look at, which counts for more than a little in the scales of our affections; indeed, the slight air of absence in his blue eyes was not chilling, as is that which portends a wandering of its owner on his own business. People recognized that it meant some bee or other in that bonnet, or elsewhere, some sound or scent or sight of life, suddenly perceived—always of life! He had often been observed gazing with peculiar gravity at a dead flower, bee, bird, or beetle, and, if spoken to at such a moment, would say, "Gone!" touching a wing or petal with his finger. To conceive of what happened after death did not apparently come within the few large conclusions of his reflective powers. That quaint grief of his in the presence of the death of things that were not human had, more than anything, fostered a habit among the gentry and clergy of the neighborhood of drawing up the mouth when they spoke of him, and slightly raising the shoulders. For the cottagers, to be sure, his eccentricity consisted rather in his being a 'gentleman,' yet neither eating flesh, drinking wine, nor telling them how they ought to behave themselves, together with the way he would sit down on anything and listen to what they had to tell him, without giving them the impression that he was proud of himself for doing so. In fact, it was the extraordinary impression he made of listening and answering without wanting anything either for himself or for them, that they could not understand. How on earth it came about that he did not give them advice about their politics, religion, morals, or monetary states, was to them a never-ending mystery; and though they were too well bred to shrug their shoulders, there did lurk in their dim minds the suspicion that 'the good gentleman,' as they called him, was 'a tiddy-bit off.' He had, of course, done many practical little things toward helping them and their beasts, but always, as it seemed, by accident, so that they could never make up their minds afterward whether he remembered having done them, which, in fact, he probably did not; and this seemed to them perhaps the most damning fact of all about his being—well, about his being—not quite all there. Another worrying habit he had, too, that of apparently not distinguishing between them and any tramps or strangers who might happen along and come across him. This was, in their eyes, undoubtedly a fault; for the village was, after all, their village, and he, as it were, their property. To crown all, there was a story, full ten years old now, which had lost nothing in the telling, of his treatment of a cattle-drover. To the village it had an eerie look, that windmill-like rage let loose upon a man who, after all, had only been twisting a bullock's tail and running a spiked stick into its softer parts, as any drover might. People said—the postman and a wagoner had seen the business, raconteurs born, so that the tale had perhaps lost nothing—that he had positively roared as he came leaping down into the lane upon the man, a stout and thick-set fellow, taken him up like a baby, popped him into a furzebush, and held him there. People said that his own bare arms had been pricked to the very shoulder from pressing the drover down into that uncompromising shrub, and the man's howls had pierced the very heavens. The postman, to this day, would tell how the mere recollection of seeing it still made him sore all over. Of the words assigned to Tod on this occasion, the mildest and probably most true were: "By the Lord God, if you treat a beast like that again, I'll cut your liver out, you hell-hearted sweep!"

The incident, which had produced a somewhat marked effect in regard to the treatment of animals all round that neighborhood, had never been forgotten, nor in a sense forgiven. In conjunction with the extraordinary peace and mildness of his general behavior, it had endowed Tod with mystery; and people, especially simple folk, cannot bring themselves to feel quite at home with mystery. Children only—to whom everything is so mysterious that nothing can be—treated him as he treated them, giving him their hands with confidence. But children, even his own, as they grew up, began to have a little of the village feeling toward Tod; his world was not theirs, and what exactly his world was they could not grasp. Possibly it was the sense that they partook of his interest and affection too much on a level with any other kind of living thing that might happen to be about, which discomfited their understanding. They held him, however, in a certain reverence.

That early morning he had already done a good two hours' work in connection with broad beans, of which he grew, perhaps, the best in the whole county, and had knocked off for a moment, to examine a spider's web. This marvellous creation, which the dew had visited and clustered over, as stars over the firmament, was hung on the gate of the vegetable garden, and the spider, a large and active one, was regarding Tod with the misgiving natural to its species. Intensely still Tod stood, absorbed in contemplation of that bright and dusty miracle. Then, taking up his hoe again, he went back to the weeds that threatened his broad beans. Now and again he stopped to listen, or to look at the sky, as is the way of husbandmen, thinking of nothing, enjoying the peace of his muscles.

"Please, sir, father's got into a fit again."

Two little girls were standing in the lane below. The elder, who had spoken in that small, anxious voice, had a pale little face with pointed chin; her hair, the color of over-ripe corn, hung fluffy on her thin shoulders, her flower-like eyes, with something motherly in them already, were the same hue as her pale-blue, almost clean, overall. She had her smaller, chubbier sister by the hand, and, having delivered her message, stood still, gazing up at Tod, as one might at God. Tod dropped his hoe.

"Biddy come with me; Susie go and tell Mrs. Freeland, or Miss Sheila."

He took the frail little hand of the elder Tryst and ran. They ran at the child's pace, the one so very massive, the other such a whiff of flesh and blood.

"Did you come at once, Biddy?"

"Yes, sir."

"Where was he taken?"

"In the kitchen—just as I was cookin' breakfast."

"Ah! Is it a bad one?"

"Yes, sir, awful bad—he's all foamy."

"What did you do for it?"

"Susie and me turned him over, and Billy's seein' he don't get his tongue down his throat—like what you told us, and we ran to you. Susie was frightened, he hollered so."

Past the three cottages, whence a woman at a window stared in amaze to see that queer couple running, past the pond where the ducks, whiter than ever in the brightening sunlight, dived and circled carelessly, into the Tryst kitchen. There on the brick floor lay the distressful man, already struggling back out of epilepsy, while his little frightened son sat manfully beside him.

"Towels, and hot water, Biddy!"

With extraordinary calm rapidity the small creature brought what might have been two towels, a basin, and the kettle; and in silence she and Tod steeped his forehead.

"Eyes look better, Biddy?"

"He don't look so funny now, sir."

Picking up that form, almost as big as his own, Tod carried it up impossibly narrow stairs and laid it on a dishevelled bed.

"Phew! Open the window, Biddy."

The small creature opened what there was of window.

"Now, go down and heat two bricks and wrap them in something, and bring them up."

Tryst's boots and socks removed, Tod rubbed the large, warped feet. While doing this he whistled, and the little boy crept up-stairs and squatted in the doorway, to watch and listen. The morning air overcame with its sweetness the natural odor of that small room, and a bird or two went flirting past. The small creature came back with the bricks, wrapped in petticoats of her own, and, placing them against the soles of her father's feet, she stood gazing at Tod, for all the world like a little mother dog with puppies.

"You can't go to school to-day, Biddy."

"Is Susie and Billy to go?"

"Yes; there's nothing to be frightened of now. He'll be nearly all right by evening. But some one shall stay with you."

At this moment Tryst lifted his hand, and the small creature went and stood beside him, listening to the whispering that emerged from his thick lips.

"Father says I'm to thank you, please."

"Yes. Have you had your breakfasts?"

The small creature and her smaller brother shook their heads.

"Go down and get them."

Whispering and twisting back, they went, and by the side of the bed Tod sat down. In Tryst's eyes was that same look of dog-like devotion he had bent on Derek earlier that morning. Tod stared out of the window and gave the man's big hand a squeeze. Of what did he think, watching a lime-tree outside, and the sunlight through its foliage painting bright the room's newly whitewashed wall, already gray-spotted with damp again; watching the shadows of the leaves playing in that sunlight? Almost cruel, that lovely shadow game of outside life so full and joyful, so careless of man and suffering; too gay almost, too alive! Of what did he think, watching the chase and dart of shadow on shadow, as of gray butterflies fluttering swift to the sack of flowers, while beside him on the bed the big laborer lay?...

When Kirsteen and Sheila came to relieve him of that vigil he went down-stairs. There in the kitchen Biddy was washing up, and Susie and Billy putting on their boots for school. They stopped to gaze at Tod feeling in his pockets, for they knew that things sometimes happened after that. To-day there came out two carrots, some lumps of sugar, some cord, a bill, a pruning knife, a bit of wax, a bit of chalk, three flints, a pouch of tobacco, two pipes, a match-box with a single match in it, a six-pence, a necktie, a stick of chocolate, a tomato, a handkerchief, a dead bee, an old razor, a bit of gauze, some tow, a stick of caustic, a reel of cotton, a needle, no thimble, two dock leaves, and some sheets of yellowish paper. He separated from the rest the sixpence, the dead bee, and what was edible. And in delighted silence the three little Trysts gazed, till Biddy with the tip of one wet finger touched the bee.

"Not good to eat, Biddy."

At those words, one after the other, cautiously, the three little Trysts smiled. Finding that Tod smiled too, they broadened, and Billy burst into chuckles. Then, clustering in the doorway, grasping the edibles and the sixpence, and consulting with each other, they looked long after his big figure passing down the road.

CHAPTER XII

Still later, that same morning, Derek and Sheila moved slowly up the Mallorings' well-swept drive. Their lips were set, as though they had spoken the last word before battle, and an old cock pheasant, running into the bushes close by, rose with a whir and skimmed out toward his covert, scared, perhaps, by something uncompromising in the footsteps of those two.

Only when actually under the shelter of the porch, which some folk thought enhanced the old Greek-temple effect of the Mallorings' house, Derek broke through that taciturnity:

"What if they won't?"

"Wait and see; and don't lose your head, Derek." The man who stood there when the door opened was tall, grave, wore his hair in powder, and waited without speech.

"Will you ask Sir Gerald and Lady Malloring if Miss Freeland and Mr. Derek Freeland could see them, please; and will you say the matter is urgent?"

The man bowed, left them, and soon came back.

"My lady will see you, miss; Sir Gerald is not in. This way."

Past the statuary, flowers, and antlers of the hall, they traversed a long, cool corridor, and through a white door entered a white room, not very large, and very pretty. Two children got up as they came in and flapped out past them like young partridges, and Lady Malloring rose from her writing-table and came forward, holding out her hand. The two young Freelands took it gravely. For all their hostility they could not withstand the feeling that she would think them terrible young prigs if they simply bowed. And they looked steadily at one with whom they had never before been at quite such close quarters. Lady Malloring, who had originally been the Honorable Mildred Killory, a daughter of Viscount Silport, was tall, slender, and not very striking, with very fair hair going rather gray; her expression in repose was pleasant, a little anxious; only by her eyes was the suspicion awakened that she was a woman of some character. They had that peculiar look of belonging to two worlds, so often to be met with in English eyes, a look of self-denying aspiration, tinctured with the suggestion that denial might not be confined to self.

In a quite friendly voice she said:

"Can I do anything for you?" And while she waited for an answer her glance travelled from face to face of the two young people, with a certain curiosity. After a silence of several seconds, Sheila answered:

"Not for us, thank you; for others, you can."

Lady Malloring's eyebrows rose a little, as if there seemed to her something rather unjust in those words—'for others.'

"Yes?" she said.

Sheila, whose hands were clenched, and whose face had been fiery red, grew suddenly almost white.

"Lady Malloring, will you please let the Gaunts stay in their cottage and Tryst's wife's sister come to live with the children and him?"

Lady Malloring raised one hand; the motion, quite involuntary, ended at the tiny cross on her breast. She said quietly:

"I'm afraid you don't understand."

"Yes," said Sheila, still very pale, "we understand quite well. We understand that you are acting in what you believe to be the interests of morality. All the same, won't you? Do!"

"I'm very sorry, but I can't."

"May we ask why?"

Lady Malloring started, and transferred her glance to Derek.

"I don't know," she said with a smile, "that I am obliged to account for my actions to you two young people. Besides, you must know why, quite well."

Sheila put out her hand.

"Wilmet Gaunt will go to the bad if you turn them out."

"I am afraid I think she has gone to the bad already, and I do not mean her to take others there with her. I am sorry for poor Tryst, and I wish he could find some nice woman to marry; but what he proposes is impossible."

The blood had flared up again in Sheila's cheeks; she was as red as the comb of a turkey-cock.

"Why shouldn't he marry his wife's sister? It's legal, now, and you've no right to stop it."

Lady Malloring bit her lips; she looked straight and hard at Sheila.

"I do not stop it; I have no means of stopping it. Only, he cannot do it and live in one of our cottages. I don't think we need discuss this further."

"I beg your pardon—"

The words had come from Derek. Lady Malloring paused in her walk toward the bell. With his peculiar thin-lipped smile the boy went on:

"We imagined you would say no; we really came because we thought it fair to warn you that there may be trouble."

Lady Malloring smiled.

"This is a private matter between us and our tenants, and we should be so glad if you could manage not to interfere."

Derek bowed, and put his hand within his sister's arm. But Sheila did not move; she was trembling with anger.

"Who are you," she suddenly burst out, "to dispose of the poor, body and soul? Who are you, to dictate their private lives? If they pay their rent, that should be enough for you."

Lady Malloring moved swiftly again toward the bell. She paused with her hand on it, and said:

"I am sorry for you two; you have been miserably brought up!"

There was a silence; then Derek said quietly:

"Thank you; we shall remember that insult to our people. Don't ring, please; we're going."

In a silence if anything more profound than that of their approach, the two young people retired down the drive. They had not yet learned—most difficult of lessons—how to believe that people could in their bones differ from them. It had always seemed to them that if only they had a chance of putting directly what they thought, the other side must at heart agree, and only go on saying they didn't out of mere self-interest. They came away, therefore, from this encounter with the enemy a little dazed by the discovery that Lady Malloring in her bones believed that she was right. It confused them, and heated the fires of their anger.

They had shaken off all private dust before Sheila spoke.

"They're all like that—can't see or feel—simply certain they're superior! It makes—it makes me hate them! It's terrible, ghastly." And while she stammered out those little stabs of speech, tears of rage rolled down her cheeks.

Derek put his arm round her waist.

"All right! No good groaning; let's think seriously what to do."

There was comfort to the girl in that curiously sudden reversal of their usual attitudes.

"Whatever's done," he went on, "has got to be startling. It's no good pottering and protesting, any more." And between his teeth he muttered: "'Men of England, wherefore plough?'..."

In the room where the encounter had taken place Mildred Malloring was taking her time to recover. From very childhood she had felt that the essence of her own goodness, the essence of her duty in life, was the doing of 'good' to others; from very childhood she had never doubted that she was in a position to do this, and that those to whom she did good, although they might kick against it as inconvenient, must admit that it WAS their 'good.' The thought: 'They don't admit that I am superior!' had never even occurred to her, so completely was she unselfconscious, in her convinced superiority. It was hard, indeed, to be flung against such outspoken rudeness. It shook her more than she gave sign of, for she was not by any means an insensitive woman—shook her almost to the point of feeling that there was something in the remonstrance of those dreadful young people. Yet, how could there be, when no one knew better than she that the laborers on the Malloring estate were better off than those on nine out of ten estates; better paid and better housed, and—better looked after in their morals. Was she to give up that?—when she knew that she WAS better able to tell what was good for them than they were themselves. After all, without stripping herself naked of every thought, experience, and action since her birth, how could she admit that she was not better able? And slowly, in the white room with the moss-green carpet, she recovered, till there was only just a touch of soreness left, at the injustice implicit in their words. Those two had been 'miserably brought up,' had never had a chance of finding their proper place, of understanding that they were just two callow young things, for whom Life had some fearful knocks in store. She could even feel now that she had meant that saying: 'I am sorry for you two!' She WAS sorry for them, sorry for their want of manners and their point of view, neither of which they could help, of course, with a mother like that. For all her gentleness and sensibility, there was much practical directness about Mildred Malloring; for her, a page turned was a page turned, an idea absorbed was never disgorged; she was of religious temperament, ever trimming her course down the exact channel marked out with buoys by the Port Authorities, and really incapable of imagining spiritual wants in others that could not be satisfied by what satisfied herself. And this pathetic strength she had in common with many of her fellow creatures in every class. Sitting down at the writing-table from which she had been disturbed, she leaned her thin, rather long, gentle, but stubborn face on her hand, thinking. These Gaunts were a source of irritation in the parish, a kind of open sore. It would be better if they could be got rid of before quarter day, up to which she had weakly said they might remain. Far better for them to go at once, if it could be arranged. As for the poor fellow Tryst, thinking that by plunging into sin he could improve his lot and his poor children's, it was really criminal of those Freelands to encourage him. She had refrained hitherto from seriously worrying Gerald on such points of village policy—his hands were so full; but he must now take his part. And she rang the bell.

"Tell Sir Gerald I'd like to see him, please, as soon as he gets back."

"Sir Gerald has just come in, my lady."

"Now, then!"

Gerald Malloring—an excellent fellow, as could be seen from his face of strictly Norman architecture, with blue stained-glass windows rather deep set in—had only one defect: he was not a poet. Not that this would have seemed to him anything but an advantage, had he been aware of it. His was one of those high-principled natures who hold that breadth is synonymous with weakness. It may be said without exaggeration that the few meetings of his life with those who had a touch of the poet in them had been exquisitely uncomfortable. Silent, almost taciturn by nature, he was a great reader of poetry, and seldom went to sleep without having digested a page or two of Wordsworth, Milton, Tennyson, or Scott. Byron, save such poems as 'Don Juan' or 'The Waltz,' he could but did not read, for fear of setting a bad example. Burns, Shelley, and Keats he did not care for. Browning pained him, except by such things as: 'How They Brought the Good News from Ghent to Aix' and the 'Cavalier Tunes'; while of 'Omar Khayyam' and 'The Hound of Heaven' he definitely disapproved. For Shakespeare he had no real liking, though he concealed this, from humility in the face of accepted opinion. His was a firm mind, sure of itself, but not self-assertive. His points were so good, and he had so many of them, that it was only when he met any one touched with poetry that his limitations became apparent; it was rare, however, and getting more so every year, for him to have this unpleasant experience.

When summoned by his wife, he came in with a wrinkle between his straight brows; he had just finished a morning's work on a drainage scheme, like the really good fellow that he was. She greeted him with a little special smile. Nothing could be friendlier than the relations between these two. Affection and trust, undeviating undemonstrativeness, identity of feeling as to religion, children, property; and, in regard to views on the question of sex, a really strange unanimity, considering that they were man and woman.

"It's about these Gaunts, Gerald. I feel they must go at once. They're only creating bad feeling by staying till quarter day. I have had the young Freelands here."

"Those young pups!"

"Can't it be managed?"

Malloring did not answer hastily. He had that best point of the good Englishman, a dislike to being moved out of a course of conduct by anything save the appeal of his own conscience.

"I don't know," he said, "why we should alter what we thought was just. Must give him time to look round and get a job elsewhere."

"I think the general state of feeling demands it. It's not fair to the villagers to let the Freelands have such a handle for agitating. Labor's badly wanted everywhere; he can't have any difficulty in getting a place, if he likes."

"No. Only, I rather admire the fellow for sticking by his girl, though he is such a 'land-lawyer.' I think it's a bit harsh to move him suddenly."

"So did I, till I saw from those young furies what harm it's doing. They really do infect the cottagers. You know how discontent spreads. And Tryst—they're egging him on, too."

Malloring very thoughtfully filled a pipe. He was not an alarmist; if anything, he erred on the side of not being alarmed until it was all over and there was no longer anything to be alarmed at! His imagination would then sometimes take fire, and he would say that such and such, or so and so, was dangerous.

"I'd rather go and have a talk with Freeland," he said. "He's queer, but he's not at all a bad chap."

Lady Malloring rose, and took one of his real-leather buttons in her hand.

"My dear Gerald, Mr. Freeland doesn't exist."

"Don't know about that; a man can always come to life, if he likes, in his own family."

Lady Malloring was silent. It was true. For all their unanimity of thought and feeling, for all the latitude she had in domestic and village affairs, Gerald had a habit of filling his pipe with her decisions. Quite honestly, she had no objection to their becoming smoke through HIS lips, though she might wriggle just a little. To her credit, she did entirely carry out in her life her professed belief that husbands should be the forefronts of their wives. For all that, there burst from her lips the words:

"That Freeland woman! When I think of the mischief she's always done here, by her example and her irreligion—I can't forgive her. I don't believe you'll make any impression on Mr. Freeland; he's entirely under her thumb."

Smoking slowly, and looking just over the top of his wife's head, Malloring answered:

"I'll have a try; and don't you worry!"

Lady Malloring turned away. Her soreness still wanted salve.

"Those two young people," she murmured, "said some very unpleasant things to me. The boy, I believe, might have some good in him, but the girl is simply terrible."

"H'm! I think just the reverse, you know."

"They'll come to awful grief if they're not brought up sharp. They ought to be sent to the colonies to learn reality."

Malloring nodded.

"Come out, Mildred, and see how they're getting on with the new vinery." And they went out together through the French window.

The vinery was of their own designing, and of extraordinary interest. In contemplation of its lofty glass and aluminium-cased pipes the feeling of soreness left her. It was very pleasant, standing with Gerald, looking at what they had planned together; there was a soothing sense of reality about that visit, after the morning's happening, with its disappointment, its reminder of immorality and discontent, and of folk ungrateful for what was done for their good. And, squeezing her husband's arm, she murmured:

"It's really exactly what we thought it would be, Gerald!"

CHAPTER XIII

About five o'clock of that same afternoon, Gerald Malloring went to see Tod. An open-air man himself, who often deplored the long hours he was compelled to spend in the special atmosphere of the House of Commons, he rather envied Tod his existence in this cottage, crazed from age, and clothed with wistaria, rambler roses, sweetbrier, honeysuckle, and Virginia creeper. Freeland had, in his opinion, quite a jolly life of it—the poor fellow not being able, of course, to help having a cranky wife and children like that. He pondered, as he went along, over a talk at Becket, when Stanley, still under the influence of Felix's outburst, had uttered some rather queer sayings. For instance, he had supposed that they (meaning, apparently, himself and Malloring) WERE rather unable to put themselves in the position of these Trysts and Gaunts. He seemed to speak of them as one might speak generically of Hodge, which had struck Malloring as singular, it not being his habit to see anything in common between an individual case, especially on his own estate, and the ethics of a general proposition. The place for general propositions was undoubtedly the House of Commons, where they could be supported one way or the other, out of blue books. He had little use for them in private life, where innumerable things such as human nature and all that came into play. He had stared rather hard at his host when Stanley had followed up that first remark with: "I'm bound to say, I shouldn't care to have to get up at half past five, and go out without a bath!" What that had to do with the land problem or the regulation of village morality Malloring had been unable to perceive. It all depended on what one was accustomed to; and in any case threw no light on the question, as to whether or not he was to tolerate on his estate conduct of which his wife and himself distinctly disapproved. At the back of national life there was always this problem of individual conduct, especially sexual conduct—without regularity in which, the family, as the unit of national life, was gravely threatened, to put it on the lowest ground. And he did not see how to bring it home to the villagers that they had got to be regular, without making examples now and then.

He had hoped very much to get through his call without coming across Freeland's wife and children, and was greatly relieved to find Tod, seated on a window-sill in front of his cottage, smoking, and gazing apparently at nothing. In taking the other corner of the window-sill, the thought passed through his mind that Freeland was really a very fine-looking fellow. Tod was, indeed, about Malloring's own height of six feet one, with the same fairness and straight build of figure and feature. But Tod's head was round and massive, his hair crisp and uncut; Malloring's head long and narrow, his hair smooth and close-cropped. Tod's eyes, blue and deep-set, seemed fixed on the horizon, Malloring's, blue and deep-set, on the nearest thing they could light on. Tod smiled, as it were, without knowing; Malloring seemed to know what he was smiling at almost too well. It was comforting, however, that Freeland was as shy and silent as himself, for this produced a feeling that there could not be any real difference between their points of view. Perceiving at last that if he did not speak they would continue sitting there dumb till it was time for him to go, Malloring said:

"Look here, Freeland; about my wife and yours and Tryst and the Gaunts, and all the rest of it! It's a pity, isn't it? This is a small place, you know. What's your own feeling?"

Tod answered:

"A man has only one life."

Malloring was a little puzzled.

"In this world. I don't follow."

"Live and let live."

A part of Malloring undoubtedly responded to that curt saying, a part of him as strongly rebelled against it; and which impulse he was going to follow was not at first patent.

"You see, YOU keep apart," he said at last. "You couldn't say that so easily if you had, like us, to take up the position in which we find ourselves."

"Why take it up?"

Malloring frowned. "How would things go on?"

"All right," said Tod.

Malloring got up from the sill. This was 'laisser-faire' with a vengeance! Such philosophy had always seemed to him to savor dangerously of anarchism. And yet twenty years' experience as a neighbor had shown him that Tod was in himself perhaps the most harmless person in Worcestershire, and held in a curious esteem by most of the people about. He was puzzled, and sat down again.

"I've never had a chance to talk things over with you," he said. "There are a good few people, Freeland, who can't behave themselves; we're not bees, you know!"

He stopped, having an uncomfortable suspicion that his hearer was not listening.

"First I've heard this year," said Tod.

For all the rudeness of that interruption, Malloring felt a stir of interest. He himself liked birds. Unfortunately, he could hear nothing but the general chorus of their songs.

"Thought they'd gone," murmured Tod.

Malloring again got up. "Look here, Freeland," he said, "I wish you'd give your mind to this. You really ought not to let your wife and children make trouble in the village."

Confound the fellow! He was smiling; there was a sort of twinkle in his smile, too, that Malloring found infectious!

"No, seriously," he said, "you don't know what harm you mayn't do."

"Have you ever watched a dog looking at a fire?" asked Tod.

"Yes, often; why?"

"He knows better than to touch it."

"You mean you're helpless? But you oughtn't to be."

The fellow was smiling again!

"Then you don't mean to do anything?"

Tod shook his head.

Malloring flushed. "Now, look here, Freeland," he said, "forgive my saying so, but this strikes me as a bit cynical. D'you think I enjoy trying to keep things straight?"

Tod looked up.

"Birds," he said, "animals, insects, vegetable life—they all eat each other more or less, but they don't fuss about it."

Malloring turned abruptly and went down the path. Fuss! He never fussed. Fuss! The word was an insult, addressed to him! If there was one thing he detested more than another, whether in public or private life, it was 'fussing.' Did he not belong to the League for Suppression of Interference with the Liberty of the Subject? Was he not a member of the party notoriously opposed to fussy legislation? Had any one ever used the word in connection with conduct of his, before? If so, he had never heard them. Was it fussy to try and help the Church to improve the standard of morals in the village? Was it fussy to make a simple decision and stick to it? The injustice of the word really hurt him. And the more it hurt him, the slower and more dignified and upright became his march toward his drive gate.

'Wild geese' in the morning sky had been forerunners; very heavy clouds were sweeping up from the west, and rain beginning to fall. He passed an old man leaning on the gate of a cottage garden and said: "Good evening!"

The old man touched his hat but did not speak.

"How's your leg, Gaunt?"

"'Tis much the same, Sir Gerald."

"Rain coming makes it shoot, I expect."

"It do."

Malloring stood still. The impulse was on him to see if, after all, the Gaunts' affair could not be disposed of without turning the old fellow and his son out.

"Look here!" he said; "about this unfortunate business. Why don't you and your son make up your minds without more ado to let your granddaughter go out to service? You've been here all your lives; I don't want to see you go."

The least touch of color invaded the old man's carved and grayish face.

"Askin' your pardon," he said, "my son sticks by his girl, and I sticks by my son!"

"Oh! very well; you know your own business, Gaunt. I spoke for your good."

A faint smile curled the corners of old Gaunt's mouth downward beneath his gray moustaches.

"Thank you kindly," he said.

Malloring raised a finger to his cap and passed on. Though he felt a longing to stride his feelings off, he did not increase his pace, knowing that the old man's eyes were following him. But how pig-headed they were, seeing nothing but their own point of view! Well, he could not alter his decision. They would go at the June quarter—not a day before, nor after.

Passing Tryst's cottage, he noticed a 'fly' drawn up outside, and its driver talking to a woman in hat and coat at the cottage doorway. She avoided his eye.

'The wife's sister again!' he thought. 'So that fellow's going to be an ass, too? Hopeless, stubborn lot!' And his mind passed on to his scheme for draining the bottom fields at Cantley Bromage. This village trouble was too small to occupy for long the mind of one who had so many duties....

Old Gaunt remained at the gate watching till the tall figure passed out of sight, then limped slowly down the path and entered his son's cottage. Tom Gaunt, not long in from work, was sitting in his shirtsleeves, reading the paper—a short, thick-set man with small eyes, round, ruddy cheeks, and humorous lips indifferently concealed by a ragged moustache. Even in repose there was about him something talkative and disputatious. He was clearly the kind of man whose eyes and wit would sparkle above a pewter pot. A good workman, he averaged out an income of perhaps eighteen shillings a week, counting the two shillings' worth of vegetables that he grew. His erring daughter washed for two old ladies in a bungalow, so that with old Gaunt's five shillings from the parish, the total resources of this family of five, including two small boys at school, was seven and twenty shillings a week. Quite a sum! His comparative wealth no doubt contributed to the reputation of Tom Gaunt, well known as local wag and disturber of political meetings. His method with these gatherings, whether Liberal or Tory, had a certain masterly simplicity. By interjecting questions that could not be understood, and commenting on the answers received, he insured perpetual laughter, with the most salutary effects on the over-consideration of any political question, together with a tendency to make his neighbors say: "Ah! Tom Gaunt, he's a proper caution, he is!" An encomium dear to his ears. What he seriously thought about anything in this world, no one knew; but some suspected him of voting Liberal, because he disturbed their meetings most. His loyalty to his daughter was not credited to affection. It was like Tom Gaunt to stick his toes in and kick—the Quality, for choice. To look at him and old Gaunt, one would not have thought they could be son and father, a relationship indeed ever dubious. As for his wife, she had been dead twelve years. Some said he had joked her out of life, others that she had gone into consumption. He was a reader—perhaps the only one in all the village, and could whistle like a blackbird. To work hard, but without too great method, to drink hard, but with perfect method, and to talk nineteen to the dozen anywhere except at home—was his mode of life. In a word, he was a 'character.'

Old Gaunt sat down in a wooden rocking-chair, and spoke.

"Sir Gerald 'e've a-just passed."

"Sir Gerald 'e can goo to hell. They'll know un there, by 'is little ears."

"'E've a-spoke about us stoppin'; so as Mettie goes out to sarvice."

"'E've a-spoke about what 'e don't know 'bout, then. Let un do what they like, they can't put Tom Gaunt about; he can get work anywhere—Tom Gaunt can, an' don't you forget that, old man."

The old man, placing his thin brown hands on his knees, was silent. And thoughts passed through and through him. 'If so be as Tom goes, there'll be no one as'll take me in for less than three bob a week. Two bob a week, that's what I'll 'ave to feed me—Two bob a week—two bob a week! But if so be's I go with Tom, I'll 'ave to reg'lar sit down under he for me bread and butter.' And he contemplated his son.

"Where are you goin', then?" he said.

Tom Gaunt rustled the greenish paper he was reading, and his little, hard gray eyes fixed his father.

"Who said I was going?"

Old Gaunt, smoothing and smoothing the lined, thin cheeks of the parchmenty, thin-nosed face that Frances Freeland had thought to be almost like a gentleman's, answered: "I thart you said you was goin'."

"You think too much, then—that's what 'tis. You think too much, old man."

With a slight deepening of the sardonic patience in his face, old Gaunt rose, took a bowl and spoon down from a shelf, and very slowly proceeded to make himself his evening meal. It consisted of crusts of bread soaked in hot water and tempered with salt, pepper, onion, and a touch of butter. And while he waited, crouched over the kettle, his son smoked his grayish clay and read his greenish journal; an old clock ticked and a little cat purred without provocation on the ledge of the tight-closed window. Then the door opened and the rogue-girl appeared. She shook her shoulders as though to dismiss the wetting she had got, took off her turn-down, speckly, straw hat, put on an apron, and rolled up her sleeves. Her arms were full and firm and red; the whole of her was full and firm. From her rosy cheeks to her stout ankles she was superabundant with vitality, the strangest contrast to her shadowy, thin old grandfather. About the preparation of her father's tea she moved with a sort of brooding stolidity, out of which would suddenly gleam a twinkle of rogue-sweetness, as when she stopped to stroke the little cat or to tickle the back of her grandfather's lean neck in passing. Having set the tea, she stood by the table and said slowly: "Tea's ready, father. I'm goin' to London."

Tom Gaunt put down his pipe and journal, took his seat at the table, filled his mouth with sausage, and said: "You're goin' where I tell you."

"I'm goin' to London."

Tom Gaunt stayed the morsel in one cheek and fixed her with his little, wild boar's eye.

"Ye're goin' to catch the stick," he said. "Look here, my girl, Tom Gaunt's been put about enough along of you already. Don't you make no mistake."

"I'm goin' to London," repeated the rogue-girl stolidly. "You can get Alice to come over."

"Oh! Can I? Ye're not goin' till I tell you. Don't you think it!"

"I'm goin'. I saw Mr. Derek this mornin'. They'll get me a place there."

Tom Gaunt remained with his fork as it were transfixed. The effort of devising contradiction to the chief supporters of his own rebellion was for the moment too much for him. He resumed mastication.

"You'll go where I want you to go; and don't you think you can tell me where that is."

In the silence that ensued the only sound was that of old Gaunt supping at his crusty-broth. Then the rogue-girl went to the window and, taking the little cat on her breast, sat looking out into the rain. Having finished his broth, old Gaunt got up, and, behind his son's back, he looked at his granddaughter and thought:

'Goin' to London! 'Twud be best for us all. WE shudn' need to be movin', then. Goin' to London!' But he felt desolate.

CHAPTER XIV

When Spring and first love meet in a girl's heart, then the birds sing.

The songs that blackbirds and dusty-coated thrushes flung through Nedda's window when she awoke in Hampstead those May mornings seemed to have been sung by herself all night. Whether the sun were flashing on the leaves, or rain-drops sieving through on a sou'west wind, the same warmth glowed up in her the moment her eyes opened. Whether the lawn below were a field of bright dew, or dry and darkish in a shiver of east wind, her eyes never grew dim all day; and her blood felt as light as ostrich feathers.

Stormed by an attack of his cacoethes scribendi, after those few blank days at Becket, Felix saw nothing amiss with his young daughter. The great observer was not observant of things that other people observed. Neither he nor Flora, occupied with matters of more spiritual importance, could tell, offhand, for example, on which hand a wedding-ring was worn. They had talked enough of Becket and the Tods to produce the impression on Flora's mind that one day or another two young people would arrive in her house on a visit; but she had begun a poem called 'Dionysus at the Well,' and Felix himself had plunged into a satiric allegory entitled 'The Last of the Laborers.' Nedda, therefore, walked alone; but at her side went always an invisible companion. In that long, imaginary walking-out she gave her thoughts and the whole of her heart, and to be doing this never surprised her, who, before, had not given them whole to anything. A bee knows the first summer day and clings intoxicated to its flowers; so did Nedda know and cling. She wrote him two letters and he wrote her one. It was not poetry; indeed, it was almost all concerned with Wilmet Gaunt, asking Nedda to find a place in London where the girl could go; but it ended with the words:

"Your lover,

"DEREK."

This letter troubled Nedda. She would have taken it at once to Felix or to Flora if it had not been for the first words, "Dearest Nedda," and those last three. Except her mother, she instinctively distrusted women in such a matter as that of Wilmet Gaunt, feeling they would want to know more than she could tell them, and not be too tolerant of what they heard. Casting about, at a loss, she thought suddenly of Mr. Cuthcott.

At dinner that day she fished round carefully. Felix spoke of him almost warmly. What Cuthcott could have been doing at Becket, of all places, he could not imagine—the last sort of man one expected to see there; a good fellow, rather desperate, perhaps, as men of his age were apt to get if they had too many women, or no woman, about them.

Which, said Nedda, had Mr. Cuthcott?

Oh! None. How had he struck Nedda? And Felix looked at his little daughter with a certain humble curiosity. He always felt that the young instinctively knew so much more than he did.

"I liked him awfully. He was like a dog."

"Ah!" said Felix, "he IS like a dog—very honest; he grins and runs about the city, and might be inclined to bay the moon."

'I don't mind that,' Nedda thought, 'so long as he's not "superior."'

"He's very human," Felix added.

And having found out that he lived in Gray's Inn, Nedda thought: 'I will; I'll ask him.'

To put her project into execution, she wrote this note:

"DEAR MR. CUTHCOTT:

"You were so kind as to tell me you wouldn't mind if I bothered you about things. I've got a very bothery thing to know what to do about, and I would be so glad of your advice. It so happens that I can't ask my father and mother. I hope you won't think me very horrible, wasting your time. And please say no, if you'd rather.

"Yours sincerely,

"NEDDA FREELAND."

The answer came:

"DEAR MISS FREELAND:

"Delighted. But if very bothery, better save time and ink, and have a snack of lunch with me to-morrow at the Elgin restaurant, close to the British Museum. Quiet and respectable. No flowers by request. One o'clock.

"Very truly yours,

"GILES CUTHCOTT."

Putting on 'no flowers' and with a fast-beating heart, Nedda, went on her first lonely adventure. To say truth she did not know in the least how ever she was going to ask this almost strange man about a girl of doubtful character. But she kept saying to herself: 'I don't care—he has nice eyes.' And her spirit would rise as she got nearer, because, after all, she was going to find things out, and to find things out was jolly. The new warmth and singing in her heart had not destroyed, but rather heightened, her sense of the extraordinary interest of all things that be. And very mysterious to her that morning was the kaleidoscope of Oxford Street and its innumerable girls, and women, each going about her business, with a life of her own that was not Nedda's. For men she had little use just now, they had acquired a certain insignificance, not having gray-black eyes that smoked and flared, nor Harris tweed suits that smelled delicious. Only once on her journey from Oxford Circus she felt the sense of curiosity rise in her, in relation to a man, and this was when she asked a policeman at Tottenham Court Road, and he put his head down fully a foot to listen to her. So huge, so broad, so red in the face, so stolid, it seemed wonderful to her that he paid her any attention! If he were a human being, could she really be one, too? But that, after all, was no more odd than everything. Why, for instance, the spring flowers in that woman's basket had been born; why that high white cloud floated over; why and what was Nedda Freeland?

At the entrance of the little restaurant she saw Mr. Cuthcott waiting. In a brown suit, with his pale but freckled face, and his gnawed-at, sandy moustache, and his eyes that looked out and beyond, he was certainly no beauty. But Nedda thought: 'He's even nicer than I remembered, and I'm sure he knows a lot.'

At first, to be sitting opposite to him, in front of little plates containing red substances and small fishes, was so exciting that she simply listened to his rapid, rather stammering voice mentioning that the English had no idea of life or cookery, that God had so made this country by mistake that everything, even the sun, knew it. What, however, would she drink? Chardonnet? It wasn't bad here.

She assented, not liking to confess that she did not know what Chardonnet might be, and hoping it was some kind of sherbet. She had never yet drunk wine, and after a glass felt suddenly extremely strong.

"Well," said Mr. Cuthcott, and his eyes twinkled, "what's your botheration? I suppose you want to strike out for yourself. MY daughters did that without consulting me."

"Oh! Have you got daughters?"

"Yes—funny ones; older than you."

"That's why you understand, then."

Mr. Cuthcott smiled. "They WERE a liberal education!"

And Nedda thought: 'Poor Dad, I wonder if I am!'

"Yes," Mr. Cuthcott murmured, "who would think a gosling would ever become a goose?"

"Ah!" said Nedda eagerly, "isn't it wonderful how things grow?"

She felt his eyes suddenly catch hold of hers.

"You're in love!" he said.

It seemed to her a great piece of luck that he had found that out. It made everything easy at once, and her words came out pell-mell.

"Yes, and I haven't told my people yet. I don't seem able. He's given me something to do, and I haven't much experience."

A funny little wriggle passed over Mr. Cuthcott's face. "Yes, yes; go on! Tell us about it."

She took a sip from her glass, and the feeling that he had been going to laugh passed away.

"It's about the daughter of a laborer, down there in Worcestershire, where he lives, not very far from Becket. He's my cousin, Derek, the son of my other uncle at Joyfields. He and his sister feel most awfully strongly about the laborers."

"Ah!" said Mr. Cuthcott, "the laborers! Queer how they're in the air, all of a sudden."

"This girl hasn't been very good, and she has to go from the village, or else her family have. He wants me to find a place for her in London."

"I see; and she hasn't been very good?"

"Not very." She knew that her cheeks were flushing, but her eyes felt steady, and seeing that his eyes never moved, she did not mind. She went on:

"It's Sir Gerald Malloring's estate. Lady Malloring—won't—"

She heard a snap. Mr. Cuthcott's mouth had closed.

"Oh!" he said, "say no more!"

'He CAN bite nicely!' she thought.

Mr. Cuthcott, who had begun lightly thumping the little table with his open hand, broke out suddenly:

"That petty bullying in the country! I know it! My God! Those prudes, those prisms! They're the ruination of half the girls on the—" He looked at Nedda and stopped short. "If she can do any kind of work, I'll find her a place. In fact, she'd better come, for a start, under my old housekeeper. Let your cousin know; she can turn up any day. Name? Wilmet Gaunt? Right you are!" He wrote it on his cuff.

Nedda rose to her feet, having an inclination to seize his hand, or stroke his head, or something. She subsided again with a fervid sigh, and sat exchanging with him a happy smile. At last she said:

"Mr. Cuthcott, is there any chance of things like that changing?"

"Changing?" He certainly had grown paler, and was again lightly thumping the table. "Changing? By gum! It's got to change! This d—d pluto-aristocratic ideal! The weed's so grown up that it's choking us. Yes, Miss Freeland, whether from inside or out I don't know yet, but there's a blazing row coming. Things are going to be made new before long."

Under his thumps the little plates had begun to rattle and leap. And Nedda thought: 'I DO like him.'

But she said anxiously:

"You believe there's something to be done, then? Derek is simply full of it; I want to feel like that, too, and I mean to."

His face grew twinkly; he put out his hand. And wondering a little whether he meant her to, Nedda timidly stretched forth her own and grasped it.

"I like you," he said. "Love your cousin and don't worry."

Nedda's eyes slipped into the distance.

"But I'm afraid for him. If you saw him, you'd know."

"One's always afraid for the fellows that are worth anything. There was another young Freeland at your uncle's the other night—"

"My brother Alan!"

"Oh! your brother? Well, I wasn't afraid for him, and it seemed a pity. Have some of this; it's about the only thing they do well here."

"Oh, thank you, no. I've had a lovely lunch. Mother and I generally have about nothing." And clasping her hands she added:

"This is a secret, isn't it, Mr. Cuthcott?"

"Dead."

He laughed and his face melted into a mass of wrinkles. Nedda laughed also and drank up the rest of her wine. She felt blissful.

"Yes," said Mr. Cuthcott, "there's nothing like loving. How long have you been at it?"

"Only five days, but it's everything."

Mr. Cuthcott sighed. "That's right. When you can't love, the only thing is to hate."

"Oh!" said Nedda.

Mr. Cuthcott again began banging on the little table. "Look at them, look at them!" His eyes wandered angrily about the room, wherein sat some few who had passed though the mills of gentility. "What do they know of life? Where are their souls and sympathies? They haven't any. I'd like to see their blood flow, the silly brutes."

Nedda looked at them with alarm and curiosity. They seemed to her somewhat like everybody she knew. She said timidly: "Do you think OUR blood ought to flow, too?"

Mr. Cuthcott relapsed into twinkles. "Rather! Mine first!"

'He IS human!' thought Nedda. And she got up: "I'm afraid I ought to go now. It's been awfully nice. Thank you so very much. Good-by!"

He shook her firm little hand with his frail thin one, and stood smiling till the restaurant door cut him off from her view.

The streets seemed so gorgeously full of life now that Nedda's head swam. She looked at it all with such absorption that she could not tell one thing from another. It seemed rather long to the Tottenham Court Road, though she noted carefully the names of all the streets she passed, and was sure she had not missed it. She came at last to one called POULTRY. 'Poultry!' she thought; 'I should have remembered that—Poultry?' And she laughed. It was so sweet and feathery a laugh that the driver of an old four-wheeler stopped his horse. He was old and anxious-looking, with a gray beard and deep folds in his red cheeks.

"Poultry!" she said. "Please, am I right for the Tottenham Court Road?"

The old man answered: "Glory, no, miss; you're goin' East!"

'East!' thought Nedda; 'I'd better take him.' And she got in. She sat in the four-wheeler, smiling. And how far this was due to Chardonnet she did not consider. She was to love and not worry. It was wonderful! In this mood she was put down, still smiling, at the Tottenham Court Road Tube, and getting out her purse she prepared to pay the cabman. The fare would be a shilling, but she felt like giving him two. He looked so anxious and worn, in spite of his red face. He took them, looked at her, and said: "Thank you, miss; I wanted that."

"Oh!" murmured Nedda, "then please take this, too. It's all I happen to have, except my Tube fare."

The old man took it, and water actually ran along his nose.

"God bless yer!" he said. And taking up his whip, he drove off quickly.

Rather choky, but still glowing, Nedda descended to her train. It was not till she was walking to the Spaniard's Road that a cloud seemed to come over her sky, and she reached home dejected.

In the garden of the Freelands' old house was a nook shut away by berberis and rhododendrons, where some bees were supposed to make honey, but, knowing its destination, and belonging to a union, made no more than they were obliged. In this retreat, which contained a rustic bench, Nedda was accustomed to sit and read; she went there now. And her eyes began filling with tears. Why must the poor old fellow who had driven her look so anxious and call on God to bless her for giving him that little present? Why must people grow old and helpless, like that Grandfather Gaunt she had seen at Becket? Why was there all the tyranny that made Derek and Sheila so wild? And all the grinding poverty that she herself could see when she went with her mother to their Girls' Club, in Bethnal Green? What was the use of being young and strong if nothing happened, nothing was really changed, so that one got old and died seeing still the same things as before? What was the use even of loving, if love itself had to yield to death? The trees! How they grew from tiny seeds to great and beautiful things, and then slowly, slowly dried and decayed away to dust. What was the good of it all? What comfort was there in a God so great and universal that he did not care to keep her and Derek alive and loving forever, and was not interested enough to see that the poor old cab-driver should not be haunted day and night with fear of the workhouse for himself and an old wife, perhaps? Nedda's tears fell fast, and how far THIS was Chardonnet no one could tell.

Felix, seeking inspiration from the sky in regard to 'The Last of the Laborers,' heard a noise like sobbing, and, searching, found his little daughter sitting there and crying as if her heart would break. The sight was so unusual and so utterly disturbing that he stood rooted, quite unable to bring her help. Should he sneak away? Should he go for Flora? What should he do? Like many men whose work keeps them centred within themselves, he instinctively avoided everything likely to pain or trouble him; for this reason, when anything did penetrate those mechanical defences he became almost strangely tender. Loath, for example, to believe that any one was ill, if once convinced of it, he made so good a nurse that Flora, at any rate, was in the habit of getting well with suspicious alacrity. Thoroughly moved now, he sat down on the bench beside Nedda, and said:

"My darling!"

She leaned her forehead against his arm and sobbed the more.

Felix waited, patting her far shoulder gently.

He had often dealt with such situations in his books, and now that one had come true was completely at a loss. He could not even begin to remember what was usually said or done, and he only made little soothing noises.

To Nedda this tenderness brought a sudden sharp sense of guilt and yearning. She began:

"It's not because of that I'm crying, Dad, but I want you to know that Derek and I are in love."

The words: 'You! What! In those few days!' rose, and got as far as Felix's teeth; he swallowed them and went on patting her shoulder. Nedda in love! He felt blank and ashy. That special feeling of owning her more than any one else, which was so warming and delightful, so really precious—it would be gone! What right had she to take it from him, thus, without warning! Then he remembered how odious he had always said the elderly were, to spoke the wheels of youth, and managed to murmur:

"Good luck to you, my pretty!"

He said it, conscious that a father ought to be saying:

'You're much too young, and he's your cousin!' But what a father ought to say appeared to him just then both sensible and ridiculous. Nedda rubbed her cheek against his hand.

"It won't make any difference, Dad, I promise you!"

And Felix thought: 'Not to you, only to me!' But he said:

"Not a scrap, my love! What WERE you crying about?"

"About the world; it seems so heartless."

And she told him about the water that had run along the nose of the old four-wheeler man.

But while he seemed to listen, Felix thought: 'I wish to God I were made of leather; then ı shouldn't feel as if I'd lost the warmth inside me. I mustn't let her see. Fathers ARE queer—I always suspected that. There goes my work for a good week!' Then he answered:

"No, my dear, the world is not heartless; it's only arranged according to certain necessary contraries: No pain, no pleasure; no dark, no light, and the rest of it. If you think, it couldn't be arranged differently."

As he spoke a blackbird came running with a chuckle from underneath the berberis, looked at them with alarm, and ran back. Nedda raised her face.

"Dad, I mean to do something with my life!"

Felix answered:

"Yes. That's right."

But long after Nedda had fallen into dreams that night, he lay awake, with his left foot enclosed between Floras', trying to regain that sense of warmth which he knew he must never confess to having lost.

CHAPTER XV

Flora took the news rather with the air of a mother-dog that says to her puppy: "Oh, very well, young thing! Go and stick your teeth in it and find out for yourself!" Sooner or later this always happened, and generally sooner nowadays. Besides, she could not help feeling that she would get more of Felix, to her a matter of greater importance than she gave sign of. But inwardly the news had given her a shock almost as sharp as that felt by him. Was she really the mother of one old enough to love? Was the child that used to cuddle up to her in the window-seat to be read to, gone from her; that used to rush in every morning at all inconvenient moments of her toilet; that used to be found sitting in the dark on the stairs, like a little sleepy owl, because, for-sooth, it was so 'cosey'?

Not having seen Derek, she did not as yet share her husband's anxiety on that score, though his description was dubious:

"Upstanding young cockerel, swinging his sporran and marching to pipes—a fine spurn about him! Born to trouble, if I know anything, trying to sweep the sky with his little broom!"

"Is he a prig?"

"No-o. There's simplicity about his scorn, and he seems to have been brought up on facts, not on literature, like most of these young monkeys. The cousinship I don't think matters; Kirsteen brings in too strong an out-strain. He's HER son, not Tod's. But perhaps," he added, sighing, "it won't last."

Flora shook her head. "It will last!" she said; "Nedda's deep."

And if Nedda held, so would Fate; no one would throw Nedda over! They naturally both felt that. 'Dionysus at the Well,' no less than 'The Last of the Laborers,' had a light week of it.

Though in a sense relieved at having parted with her secret, Nedda yet felt that she had committed desecration. Suppose Derek should mind her people knowing!

On the day that he and Sheila were to come, feeling she could not trust herself to seem even reasonably calm, she started out, meaning to go to the South Kensington Museum and wander the time away there; but once out-of-doors the sky seemed what she wanted, and, turning down the hill on the north side, she sat down under a gorse bush. Here tramps, coming in to London, passed the night under the stars; here was a vision, however dim, of nature. And nature alone could a little soothe her ecstatic nerves.

How would he greet her? Would he be exactly as he was when they stood at the edge of Tod's orchard, above the dreamy, darkening fields, joining hands and lips, moved as they had never been moved before?

May blossom was beginning to come out along the hedge of the private grounds that bordered that bit of Cockney Common, and from it, warmed by the sun, the scent stole up to her. Familiar, like so many children of the cultured classes, with the pagan and fairy-tales of nature, she forgot them all the moment she was really by herself with earth and sky. In their breadth, their soft and stirring continuity, they rejected bookish fancy, and woke in her rapture and yearning, a sort of long delight, a never-appeased hunger. Crouching, hands round knees, she turned her face to get the warmth of the sun, and see the white clouds go slowly by, and catch all the songs that the birds sang. And every now and then she drew a deep breath. It was true what Dad had said: There was no real heartlessness in nature. It was warm, beating, breathing. And if things ate each other, what did it matter? They had lived and died quickly, helping to make others live. The sacred swing and circle of it went on forever, full and harmonious under the lighted sky, under the friendly stars. It was wonderful to be alive! And all done by love. Love! More, more, more love! And then death, if it must come! For, after all, to Nedda death was so far away, so unimaginably dim and distant, that it did not really count.

While she sat, letting her fingers, that were growing slowly black, scrabble the grass and fern, a feeling came on her of a Presence, a creature with wings above and around, that seemed to have on its face a long, mysterious smile of which she, Nedda, was herself a tiny twinkle. She would bring Derek here. They two would sit together and let the clouds go over them, and she would learn all that he really thought, and tell him all her longings and fears; they would be silent, too, loving each other too much to talk. She made elaborate plans of what they were to do and see, beginning with the East End and the National Gallery, and ending with sunrise from Parliament Hill; but she somehow knew that nothing would happen as she had designed. If only the first moment were not different from what she hoped!

She sat there so long that she rose quite stiff, and so hungry that she could not help going home and stealing into the kitchen. It was three o'clock, and the old cook, as usual, asleep in an armchair, with her apron thrown up between her face and the fire. What would Cookie say if she knew? In that oven she had been allowed to bake in fancy perfect little doll loaves, while Cookie baked them in reality. Here she had watched the mysterious making of pink cream, had burned countless 'goes' of toffy, and cocoanut ice; and tasted all kinds of loveliness. Dear old Cookie! Stealing about on tiptoe, seeking what she might devour, she found four small jam tarts and ate them, while the cook snored softly. Then, by the table, that looked so like a great loaf-platter, she stood contemplating cook. Old darling, with her fat, pale, crumply face! Hung to the dresser, opposite, was a little mahogany looking-glass tilted forward. Nedda could see herself almost down to her toes. 'I mean to be prettier than I am!' she thought, putting her hands on her waist. 'I wonder if I can pull them in a bit!' Sliding her fingers under her blouse, she began to pull at certain strings. They would not budge. They were loose, yes, really too comfortable. She would have to get the next size smaller! And dropping her chin, she rubbed it on the lace edging of her chest, where it felt warm and smelled piny. Had Cookie ever been in love? Her gray hairs were coming, poor old duck! The windows, where a protection of wire gauze kept out the flies, were opened wide, and the sun shone in and dimmed the fire. The kitchen clock ticked like a conscience; a faint perfume of frying-pan and mint scented the air. And, for the first time since this new sensation of love had come to her, Nedda felt as if a favorite book, read through and done with, were dropping from her hands. The lovely times in that kitchen, in every nook of that old house and garden, would never come again! Gone! She felt suddenly cast down to sadness. They HAD been lovely times! To be deserting in spirit all that had been so good to her—it seemed like a crime! She slid down off the table and, passing behind the cook, put her arms round those substantial sides. Without meaning to, out of sheer emotion, she pressed them somewhat hard, and, as from a concertina emerges a jerked and drawn-out chord, so from the cook came a long, quaking sound; her apron fell, her body heaved, and her drowsy, flat, soft voice, greasy from pondering over dishes, murmured:

"Ah, Miss Nedda! it's you, my dear! Bless your pretty 'eart."

But down Nedda's cheeks, behind her, rolled two tears.

"Cookie, oh, Cookie!" And she ran out....

And the first moment? It was like nothing she had dreamed of. Strange, stiff! One darting look, and then eyes down; one convulsive squeeze, then such a formal shake of hot, dry hands, and off he had gone with Felix to his room, and she with Sheila to hers, bewildered, biting down consternation, trying desperately to behave 'like a little lady,' as her old nurse would have put it—before Sheila, especially, whose hostility she knew by instinct she had earned. All that evening, furtive watching, formal talk, and underneath a ferment of doubt and fear and longing. All a mistake! An awful mistake! Did he love her? Heaven! If he did not, she could never face any one again. He could not love her! His eyes were like those of a swan when its neck is drawn up and back in anger. Terrible—having to show nothing, having to smile at Sheila, at Dad, and Mother! And when at last she got to her room, she stood at the window and at first simply leaned her forehead against the glass and shivered. What had she done? Had she dreamed it all—dreamed that they had stood together under those boughs in the darkness, and through their lips exchanged their hearts? She must have dreamed it! Dreamed that most wonderful, false dream! And the walk home in the thunder-storm, and his arm round her, and her letters, and his letter—dreamed it all! And now she was awake! From her lips came a little moan, and she sank down huddled, and stayed there ever so long, numb and chilly. Undress—go to bed? Not for the world. By the time the morning came she had got to forget that she had dreamed. For very shame she had got to forget that; no one should see. Her cheeks and ears and lips were burning, but her body felt icy cold. Then—what time she did not know at all—she felt she must go out and sit on the stairs. They had always been her comforters, those wide, shallow, cosey stairs. Out and down the passage, past all their rooms—his the last—to the dark stairs, eerie at night, where the scent of age oozed out of the old house. All doors below, above, were closed; it was like looking down into a well, to sit with her head leaning against the banisters. And silent, so silent—just those faint creakings that come from nowhere, as it might be the breathing of the house. She put her arms round a cold banister and hugged it hard. It hurt her, and she embraced it the harder. The first tears of self-pity came welling up, and without warning a great sob burst out of her. Alarmed at the sound, she smothered her mouth with her arm. No good; they came breaking out! A door opened; all the blood rushed to her heart and away from it, and with a little dreadful gurgle she was silent. Some one was listening. How long that terrible listening lasted she had no idea; then footsteps, and she was conscious that it was standing in the dark behind her. A foot touched her back. She gave a little gasp. Derek's voice whispered hoarsely:

"What? Who are you?"

And, below her breath, she answered: "Nedda."

His arms wrenched her away from the banister, his voice in her ear said:

"Nedda, darling, Nedda!"

But despair had sunk too deep; she could only quiver and shake and try to drive sobbing out of her breath. Then, most queer, not his words, nor the feel of his arms, comforted her—any one could pity!— but the smell and the roughness of his Norfolk jacket. So he, too, had not been in bed; he, too, had been unhappy! And, burying her face in his sleeve, she murmured:

"Oh, Derek! Why?"

"I didn't want them all to see. I can't bear to give it away. Nedda, come down lower and let's love each other!"

Softly, stumbling, clinging together, they went down to the last turn of the wide stairs. How many times had she not sat there, in white frocks, her hair hanging down as now, twisting the tassels of little programmes covered with hieroglyphics only intelligible to herself, talking spasmodically to spasmodic boys with budding 'tails,' while Chinese lanterns let fall their rose and orange light on them and all the other little couples as exquisitely devoid of ease. Ah! it was worth those hours of torture to sit there together now, comforting each other with hands and lips and whisperings. It was more, as much more than that moment in the orchard, as sun shining after a Spring storm is more than sun in placid mid-July. To hear him say: "Nedda, I love you!" to feel it in his hand clasped on her heart was much more, now that she knew how difficult it was for him to say or show it, except in the dark with her alone. Many a long day they might have gone through together that would not have shown her so much of his real heart as that hour of whispering and kisses.

He had known she was unhappy, and yet he couldn't! It had only made him more dumb! It was awful to be like that! But now that she knew, she was glad to think that it was buried so deep in him and kept for her alone. And if he did it again she would just know that it was only shyness and pride. And he was not a brute and a beast, as he insisted. But suppose she had chanced not to come out! Would she ever have lived through the night? And she shivered.

"Are you cold, darling? Put on my coat."

It was put on her in spite of all effort to prevent him. Never was anything so warm, so delicious, wrapping her in something more than Harris tweed. And the hall clock struck—Two!

She could just see his face in the glimmer that filtered from the skylight at the top. And she felt that he was learning her, learning all that she had to give him, learning the trust that was shining through her eyes. There was just enough light for them to realize the old house watching from below and from above—a glint on the dark floor there, on the dark wall here; a blackness that seemed to be inhabited by some spirit, so that their hands clutched and twitched, when the tiny, tiny noises of Time, playing in wood and stone, clicked out.

That stare of the old house, with all its knowledge of lives past, of youth and kisses spent and gone, of hopes spun and faiths abashed, the old house cynical, stirred in them desire to clutch each other close and feel the thrill of peering out together into mystery that must hold for them so much of love and joy and trouble! And suddenly she put her fingers to his face, passed them softly, clingingly, over his hair, forehead, eyes, traced the sharp cheek-bones down to his jaw, round by the hard chin up to his lips, over the straight bone of his nose, lingering, back, to his eyes again.

"Now, if I go blind, I shall know you. Give me one kiss, Derek. You MUST be tired."

Buried in the old dark house that kiss lasted long; then, tiptoeing—she in front—pausing at every creak, holding breath, they stole up to their rooms. And the clock struck—Three!

CHAPTER XVI

Felix (nothing if not modern) had succumbed already to the feeling that youth ruled the roost. Whatever his misgivings, his and Flora's sense of loss, Nedda must be given a free hand! Derek gave no outward show of his condition, and but for his little daughter's happy serenity Felix would have thought as she had thought that first night. He had a feeling that his nephew rather despised one so soaked in mildness and reputation as Felix Freeland; and he got on better with Sheila, not because she was milder, but because she was devoid of that scornful tang which clung about her brother. No! Sheila was not mild. Rich-colored, downright of speech, with her mane of short hair, she was a no less startling companion. The smile of Felix had never been more whimsically employed than during that ten-day visit. The evening John Freeland came to dinner was the highwater mark of his alarmed amusement. Mr. Cuthcott, also bidden, at Nedda's instigation, seemed to take a mischievous delight in drawing out those two young people in face of their official uncle. The pleasure of the dinner to Felix—and it was not too great—was in watching Nedda's face. She hardly spoke, but how she listened! Nor did Derek say much, but what he did say had a queer, sarcastic twinge about it.

"An unpleasant young man," was John's comment afterward. "How the deuce did he ever come to be Tod's son? Sheila, of course, is one of these hot-headed young women that make themselves a nuisance nowadays, but she's intelligible. By the way, that fellow Cuthcott's a queer chap!"

One subject of conversation at dinner had been the morality of revolutionary violence. And the saying that had really upset John had been Derek's: "Conflagration first—morality afterward!" He had looked at his nephew from under brows which a constant need for rejecting petitions to the Home Office had drawn permanently down and in toward the nose, and made no answer.

To Felix these words had a more sinister significance. With his juster appreciation both of the fiery and the official points of view, his far greater insight into his nephew than ever John would have, he saw that they were more than a mere arrow of controversy. And he made up his mind that night that he would tackle his nephew and try to find out exactly what was smouldering within that crisp, black pate.

Following him into the garden next morning, he said to himself: 'No irony—that's fatal. Man to man—or boy to boy—whichever it is!' But, on the garden path, alongside that young spread-eagle, whose dark, glowering, self-contained face he secretly admired, he merely began:

"How do you like your Uncle John?"

"He doesn't like me, Uncle Felix."

Somewhat baffled, Felix proceeded:

"I say, Derek, fortunately or unfortunately, I've some claim now to a little knowledge of you. You've got to open out a bit to me. What are you going to do with yourself in life? You can't support Nedda on revolution."

Having drawn this bow at a venture, he paused, doubtful of his wisdom. A glance at Derek's face confirmed his doubt. It was closer than ever, more defiant.

"There's a lot of money in revolution, Uncle Felix—other people's."

Dash the young brute! There was something in him! He swerved off to a fresh line.

"How do you like London?"

"I don't like it. But, Uncle Felix, don't you wish YOU were seeing it for the first time? What books you'd write!"

Felix felt that unconscious thrust go 'home.' Revolt against staleness and clipped wings, against the terrible security of his too solid reputation, smote him.

"What strikes you most about it, then?" he asked.

"That it ought to be jolly well blown up. Everybody seems to know that, too—they look it, anyway, and yet they go on as if it oughtn't."

"Why ought it to be blown up?"

"Well, what's the good of anything while London and all these other big towns are sitting on the country's chest? England must have been a fine place once, though!"

"Some of us think it a fine place still."

"Of course it is, in a way. But anything new and keen gets sat on. England's like an old tom-cat by the fire: too jolly comfortable for anything!"

At this support to his own theory that the country was going to the dogs, owing to such as John and Stanley, Felix thought: 'Out of the mouths of babes!' But he merely said: "You're a cheerful young man!"

"It's got cramp," Derek muttered; "can't even give women votes. Fancy my mother without a vote! And going to wait till every laborer is off the land before it attends to them. It's like the port you gave us last night, Uncle Felix, wonderful crust!"

"And what is to be your contribution to its renovation?"

Derek's face instantly resumed its peculiar defiant smile, and Felix thought: 'Young beggar! He's as close as wax.' After their little talk, however, he had more understanding of his nephew. His defiant self-sufficiency seemed more genuine....

In spite of his sensations when dining with Felix, John Freeland (little if not punctilious) decided that it was incumbent on him to have the 'young Tods' to dinner, especially since Frances Freeland had come to stay with him the day after the arrival of those two young people at Hampstead. She had reached Porchester Gardens faintly flushed from the prospect of seeing darling John, with one large cane trunk, and a hand-bag of a pattern which the man in the shop had told her was the best thing out. It had a clasp which had worked beautifully in the shop, but which, for some reason, on the journey had caused her both pain and anxiety. Convinced, however, that she could cure it and open the bag the moment she could get to that splendid new pair of pincers in her trunk, which a man had only yesterday told her were the latest, she still felt that she had a soft thing, and dear John must have one like it if she could get him one at the Stores to-morrow.

John, who had come away early from the Home Office, met her in that dark hall, to which he had paid no attention since his young wife died, fifteen years ago. Embracing him, with a smile of love almost timorous from intensity, Frances Freeland looked him up and down, and, catching what light there was gleaming on his temples, determined that she had in her bag, as soon as she could get it open, the very thing for dear John's hair. He had such a nice moustache, and it was a pity he was getting bald. Brought to her room, she sat down rather suddenly, feeling, as a fact, very much like fainting—a condition of affairs to which she had never in the past and intended never in the future to come, making such a fuss! Owing to that nice new patent clasp, she had not been able to get at her smelling-salts, nor the little flask of brandy and the one hard-boiled egg without which she never travelled; and for want of a cup of tea her soul was nearly dying within her. Dear John would never think she had not had anything since breakfast (she travelled always by a slow train, disliking motion), and she would not for the world let him know—so near dinner-time, giving a lot of trouble! She therefore stayed quite quiet, smiling a little, for fear he might suspect her. Seeing John, however, put her bag down in the wrong place, she felt stronger.

"No, darling—not there—in the window."

And while he was changing the position of the bag, her heart swelled with joy because his back was so straight, and with the thought: 'What a pity the dear boy has never married again! It does so keep a man from getting moony!' With all that writing and thinking he had to do, such important work, too, it would have been so good for him, especially at night. She would not have expressed it thus in words—that would not have been quite nice—but in thought Frances Freeland was a realist.

When he was gone, and she could do as she liked, she sat stiller than ever, knowing by long experience that to indulge oneself in private only made it more difficult not to indulge oneself in public. It really was provoking that this nice new clasp should go wrong just this once, and that the first time it was used! And she took from her pocket a tiny prayer-book, and, holding it to the light, read the eighteenth psalm—it was a particularly good one, that never failed her when she felt low—she used no glasses, and up to the present had avoided any line between the brows, knowing it was her duty to remain as nice as she could to look at, so as not to spoil the pleasure of people round about her. Then saying to herself firmly, "I do not, I WILL not want any tea—but I shall be glad of dinner!" she rose and opened her cane trunk. Though she knew exactly where they were, she was some time finding the pincers, because there were so many interesting things above them, each raising a different train of thought. A pair of field-glasses, the very latest—the man had said—for darling Derek; they would be so useful to keep his mind from thinking about things that it was no good thinking about. And for dear Flora (how wonderful that she could write poetry—poetry!) a really splendid, and perfectly new, little pill. She herself had already taken two, and they had suited her to perfection. For darling Felix a new kind of eau de cologne, made in

Worcester, because that was the only scent he would use. For her pet Nedda, a piece of 'point de Venise' that she really could not be selfish enough to keep any longer, especially as she was particularly fond of it. For Alan, a new kind of tin-opener that the dear boy would like enormously; he was so nice and practical. For Sheila, such a nice new novel by Mr. and Mrs. Whirlingham—a bright, wholesome tale, with such a good description of quite a new country in it—the dear child was so clever, it would be a change for her. Then, actually resting on the pincers, she came on her pass-book, recently made up, containing little or no balance, just enough to get darling John that bag like hers with the new clasp, which would be so handy for his papers when he went travelling. And having reached the pincers, she took them in her hand, and sat down again to be quite quiet a moment, with her still-dark eyelashes resting on her ivory cheeks and her lips pressed to a colorless line; for her head swam from stooping over. In repose, with three flies circling above her fine gray hair, she might have served a sculptor for a study of the stoic spirit. Then, going to the bag, her compressed lips twitching, her gray eyes piercing into its clasp with a kind of distrustful optimism, she lifted the pincers and tweaked it hard.

If the atmosphere of that dinner, to which all six from Hampstead came, was less disturbed than John anticipated, it was due to his sense of hospitality, and to every one's feeling that controversy would puzzle and distress Granny. That there were things about which people differed, Frances Freeland well knew, but that they should so differ as to make them forget to smile and have good manners would not have seemed right to her at all. And of this, in her presence, they were all conscious; so that when they had reached the asparagus there was hardly anything left that could by any possibility be talked about. And this—for fear of seeming awkward—they at once proceeded to discuss, Flora remarking that London was very full. John agreed.

Frances Freeland, smiling, said:

"It's so nice for Derek and Sheila to be seeing it like this for the first time."

Sheila said:

"Why? Isn't it always as full as this?"

John answered:

"In August practically empty. They say a hundred thousand people, at least, go away."

"Double!" remarked Felix.

"The figures are variously given. My estimate—"

"One in sixty. That shows you!"

At this interruption of Derek's John frowned slightly. "What does it show you?" he said.

Derek glanced at his grandmother.

"Oh, nothing!"

"Of course it shows you," exclaimed Sheila, "what a heartless great place it is. All 'the world' goes out of town, and 'London's empty!' But if you weren't told so you'd never know the difference."

Derek muttered: "I think it shows more than that."

Under the table Flora was touching John's foot warningly; Nedda attempting to touch Derek's; Felix endeavoring to catch John's eye; Alan trying to catch Sheila's; John biting his lip and looking carefully at nothing. Only Frances Freeland was smiling and gazing lovingly at dear Derek, thinking he would be so handsome when he had grown a nice black moustache. And she said:

"Yes, dear. What were you going to say?"

Derek looked up.

"Do you really want it, Granny?"

Nedda murmured across the table: "No, Derek."

Frances Freeland raised her brows quizzically. She almost looked arch.

"But of course I do, darling. I want to hear immensely. It's so interesting."

"Derek was going to say, Mother"—every one at once looked at Felix, who had thus broken in—"that all we West-End people—John and I and Flora and Stanley, and even you—all we people born in purple and fine linen, are so accustomed to think we're all that matters, that when we're out of London there's nobody in it. He meant to say that this is appalling enough, but that what is still more appalling is the fact that we really ARE all that matters, and that if people try to disturb us, we can, and jolly well will, take care they don't disturb us long. Is that what you meant, Derek?"

Derek turned a rather startled look on Felix.

"What he meant to say," went on Felix, "was, that age and habit, vested interests, culture and security sit so heavy on this country's chest, that aspiration may wriggle and squirm but will never get from under. That, for all we pretend to admire enthusiasm and youth, and the rest of it, we push it out of us just a little faster than it grows up. Is that what you meant, Derek?"

"You'll try to, but you won't succeed!"

"I'm afraid we shall, and with a smile, too, so that you won't see us doing it."

"I call that devilish."

"I call it natural. Look at a man who's growing old; notice how very gracefully and gradually he does it. Take my hair—your aunt says she can't tell the difference from month to month. And there it is, or rather isn't—little by little."

Frances Freeland, who during Felix's long speech had almost closed her eyes, opened them, and looked piercingly at the top of his head.

"Darling," she said, "I've got the very thing for it. You must take some with you when you go tonight. John is going to try it."

Checked in the flow of his philosophy, Felix blinked like an owl surprised.

"Mother," he said, "YOU only have the gift of keeping young."

"Oh! my dear, I'm getting dreadfully old. I have the greatest difficulty in keeping awake sometimes when people are talking. But I mean to fight against it. It's so dreadfully rude, and ugly, too; I catch myself sometimes with my mouth open."

Flora said quietly: "Granny, I have the very best thing for that—quite new!"

A sweet but rather rueful smile passed over Frances Freeland's face. "Now," she said, "you're chaffing me," and her eyes looked loving.

It is doubtful if John understood the drift of Felix's exordium, it is doubtful if he had quite listened—he having so much to not listen to at the Home Office that the practice was growing on him. A vested interest to John was a vested interest, culture was culture, and security was certainly security—none of them were symbols of age. Further, the social question—at least so far as it had to do with outbreaks of youth and enthusiasm—was too familiar to him to have any general significance whatever. What with women, labor people, and the rest of it, he had no time for philosophy—a dubious process at the best. A man who had to get through so many daily hours of real work did not dissipate his energy in speculation. But, though he had not listened to Felix's remarks, they had ruffled him. There is no philosophy quite so irritating as that of a brother! True, no doubt, that the country was in a bad way, but as to vested interests and security, that was all nonsense! The guilty causes were free thought and industrialism.

Having seen them all off to Hampstead, he gave his mother her good-night kiss. He was proud of her, a wonderful woman, who always put a good face on everything! Even her funny way of always having some new thing or other to do you good—even that was all part of her wanting to make the best of things. She never lost her 'form'!

John worshipped that kind of stoicism which would die with its head up rather than live with its tail down. Perhaps the moment of which he was most proud in all his life was that, when, at the finish of his school mile, he overheard a vulgar bandsman say: "I like that young ——'s running; he breathes through his —— nose." At that moment, if he had stooped to breathe through his mouth, he must have won; as it was he had lost in great distress and perfect form.

When, then, he had kissed Frances Freeland, and watched her ascend the stairs, breathless because she WOULD breathe through her nose to the very last step, he turned into his study, lighted his pipe, and sat down to a couple of hours of a report upon the forces of constabulary available in the various counties, in the event of any further agricultural rioting, such as had recently taken place on a mild scale in one or two districts where there was still Danish blood. He worked at the numbers steadily, with just that engineer's touch of mechanical invention which had caused him to be so greatly valued in a department where the evolution of twelve policemen out of ten was constantly desired. His mastery of figures was highly prized, for, while it had not any of that flamboyance which has come from America and the game of poker, it possessed a kind of English optimism, only dangerous when, as rarely happened, it was put to the test. He worked two full pipes long, and looked at the clock. Twelve! No good knocking off just yet! He had no liking for bed this many a long year, having, from loyalty to memory and a drier sense of what became one in the Home Department, preserved his form against temptations of the flesh. Yet, somehow, to-night he felt no spring, no inspiration, in his handling of county constabulary. A kind of English stolidity about them baffled him—ten of them remained ten. And leaning that forehead, whose height so troubled Frances Freeland, on his neat hand, he fell to brooding. Those young people with everything before them! Did he envy them? Or was he glad of his own age? Fifty! Fifty already; a fogey! An official fogey! For all the world like an umbrella, that every day some one put into a stand and left there till it was time to take it out again. Neatly rolled, too, with an elastic and button! And this fancy, which had never come to him before, surprised him. One day he, too, would wear out, slit all up his seams, and they would leave him at home, or give him away to the butler.

He went to the window. A scent of—of May, or something! And nothing in sight save houses just like his own! He looked up at the strip of sky privileged to hang just there. He had got a bit rusty with his stars. There, however, certainly was Venus. And he thought of how he had stood by the ship's rail on that honeymoon trip of his twenty years ago, giving his young wife her first lesson in counting the stars. And something very deep down, very mossed and crusted over in John's heart, beat and stirred, and hurt him. Nedda—he had caught her looking at that young fellow just as Anne had once looked at him, John Freeland, now an official fogey, an umbrella in a stand. There was a policeman! How ridiculous the fellow looked, putting one foot before the other, flirting his lantern and trying the area gates! This confounded scent of hawthorn—could it be hawthorn?—got here into the heart of London! The look in that girl's eyes! What was he about, to let them make him feel as though he could give his soul for a face looking up into his own, for a breast touching his, and the scent of a woman's hair. Hang it! He would smoke a cigarette and go to bed! He turned out the light and began to mount the stairs; they creaked abominably—the felt must be wearing out. A woman about the place would have kept them quiet. Reaching the landing of the second floor, he paused a moment from habit, to look down into the dark hall. A voice, thin, sweet, almost young, said:

"Is that you, darling?" John's heart stood still. What—was that? Then he perceived that the door of the room that had been his wife's was open, and remembered that his mother was in there.

"What! Aren't you asleep, Mother?"

Frances Freeland's voice answered cheerfully: "Oh, no, dear; I'm never asleep before two. Come in."

John entered. Propped very high on her pillows, in perfect regularity, his mother lay. Her carved face was surmounted by a piece of fine lace, her thin, white fingers on the turnover of the sheet moved in continual interlocking, her lips smiled.

"There's something you must have," she said. "I left my door open on purpose. Give me that little bottle, darling."

John took from a small table by the bed a still smaller bottle. Frances Freeland opened it, and out came three tiny white globules.

"Now," she said, "pop them in! You've no idea how they'll send you to sleep! They're the most splendid things; perfectly harmless. Just let them rest on the tongue and swallow!"

John let them rest—they were sweetish—and swallowed.

"How is it, then," he said, "that you never go to sleep before two?"

Frances Freeland corked the little bottle, as if enclosing within it that awkward question.

"They don't happen to act with me, darling; but that's nothing. It's the very thing for any one who has to sit up so late," and her eyes searched his face. Yes—they seemed to say—I know you pretend to have work; but if you only had a dear little wife!

"I shall leave you this bottle when I go. Kiss me."

John bent down, and received one of those kisses of hers that had such sudden vitality in the middle of them, as if her lips were trying to get inside his cheek. From the door he looked back. She was smiling, composed again to her stoic wakefulness.

"Shall I shut the door, Mother?"

"Please, darling."

With a little lump in his throat John closed the door.

CHAPTER XVII

The London which Derek had said should be blown up was at its maximum of life those May days. Even on this outer rampart of Hampstead, people, engines, horses, all had a touch of the spring fever; indeed, especially on this rampart of Hampstead was there increase of the effort to believe that nature was not dead and embalmed in books. The poets, painters, talkers who lived up there were at each other all the time in their great game of make-believe. How could it be otherwise, when there was veritably blossom on the trees and the chimneys were ceasing to smoke? How otherwise, when the sun actually shone on the ponds? But the four young people (for Alan joined in—hypnotized by Sheila) did not stay in Hampstead. Chiefly on top of tram and 'bus they roamed the wilderness. Bethnal Green and Leytonstone, Kensington and Lambeth, St. James's and Soho, Whitechapel, Shoreditch, West Ham, and Piccadilly, they traversed the whole ant-heap at its most ebullient moment. They knew their Whitman and their Dostoievsky sufficiently to be aware that they ought to love and delight in everything—in the gentleman walking down Piccadilly with a flower in his buttonhole, and in the lady sewing that buttonhole in Bethnal Green; in the orator bawling himself hoarse close to the Marble Arch, the coster loading his barrow in Covent Garden; and in Uncle John Freeland rejecting petitions in Whitehall. All these things, of course, together with the long lines of little gray houses in Camden Town, long lines of carts with bobtail horses rattling over Blackfriars' Bridge, long smells drifting behind taxicabs—all these things were as delightful and as stimulating to the soul as the clouds that trailed the heavens, the fronds of the lilac, and Leonardo's Cartoon in the Diploma Gallery. All were equal manifestations of that energy in flower known as 'Life.' They knew that everything they saw and felt and smelled OUGHT equally to make them long to catch creatures to their hearts and cry: Hosanna! And Nedda and Alan, bred in Hampstead, even knew that to admit that these things did not all move them in the same way would be regarded as a sign of anaemia. Nevertheless—most queerly—these four young people confessed to each other all sorts of sensations besides that 'Hosanna' one. They even confessed to rage and pity and disgust one moment, and to joy and dreams the next, and they differed greatly as to what excited which. It was truly odd! The only thing on which they did seem to agree was that they were having 'a thundering good time.' A sort of sense of "Blow everything!" was in their wings, and this was due not to the fact that they were thinking of and loving and admiring the little gray streets and the gentleman in Piccadilly—as, no doubt, in accordance with modern culture, they should have been—but to the fact that they were loving and admiring themselves, and that entirely without the trouble of thinking about it at all. The practice, too, of dividing into couples was distinctly precious to them, for, though they never failed to start out together, they never failed to come home two by two. In this way did they put to confusion Whitman and Dostoievsky, and all the other thinkers in Hampstead. In the daytime they all, save Alan, felt that London ought to be blown up; but at night it undermined their philosophies so that they sat silent on the tops of their respective 'buses, with arms twined in each other's. For then a something seemed to have floated up from that mass of houses and machines, of men and trees, and to be hovering above them, violet-colored, caught between the stars and the lights, a spirit of such overpowering beauty that it drenched even Alan in a kind of awe. After all, the huge creature that sat with such a giant's weight on the country's chest, the monster that had spoiled so many fields and robbed so many lives of peace and health, could fly at night upon blue and gold and purple wings, murmur a passionate lullaby, and fall into deep sleep!

One such night they went to the gallery at the opera, to supper at an oyster-shop, under Alan's pilotage, and then set out to walk back to Hampstead, timing themselves to catch the dawn. They had not gone twenty steps up Southampton Row before Alan and Sheila were forty steps in front. A fellow-feeling had made Derek and Nedda stand to watch an old man who walked, tortuous, extremely happy, bidding them all come. And when they moved on, it was very slowly, just keeping sight of the others across the lumbered dimness of Covent Garden, where tarpaulin-covered carts and barrows seemed to slumber under the blink of lamps and watchmen's lanterns. Across Long Acre they came into a street where there was not a soul save the two others, a long way ahead. Walking with his arm tightly laced with hers, touching her all down one side, Derek felt that it would be glorious to be attacked by night-birds in this dark, lonely street, to have a splendid fight and drive them off, showing himself to Nedda for a man, and her protector. But nothing save one black cat came near, and that ran for its life. He bent round and looked under the blue veil-thing that wrapped Nedda's head. Her face seemed mysteriously lovely, and her eyes, lifted so quickly, mysteriously true. She said:

"Derek, I feel like a hill with the sun on it!"

"I feel like that yellow cloud with the wind in it."

"I feel like an apple-tree coming into blossom."

"I feel like a giant."

"I feel like a song."

"I feel I could sing you."

"On a river, floating along."

"A wide one, with great plains on each side, and beasts coming down to drink, and either the sun or a yellow moon shining, and some one singing, too, far off."

"The Red Sarafan."

"Let's run!"

From that yellow cloud sailing in moonlight a spurt of rain had driven into their faces, and they ran as fast as their blood was flowing, and the raindrops coming down, jumping half the width of the little dark streets, clutching each other's arms. And peering round into her face, so sweet and breathless, into her eyes, so dark and dancing, he felt he could run all night if he had her there to run beside him through the dark. Into another street they dashed, and again another, till she stopped, panting.

"Where are we now?"

Neither knew. A policeman put them right for Portland Place. Half past one! And it would be dawn soon after three! They walked soberly again now into the outer circle of Regent's Park; talked soberly, too, discussing sublunary matters, and every now and then, their arms, round each other, gave little convulsive squeezes. The rain had stopped and the moon shone clear; by its light the trees and flowers were clothed in colors whose blood had spilled away; the town's murmur was dying, the house lights dead already. They came out of the park into a road where the latest taxis were rattling past; a face, a bare neck, silk hat, or shirt-front gleamed in the window-squares, and now and then a laugh came floating through. They stopped to watch them from under the low-hanging branches of an acacia-tree, and Derek, gazing at her face, still wet with rain, so young and round and soft, thought: 'And she loves me!' Suddenly she clutched him round the neck, and their lips met.

They talked not at all for a long time after that kiss, walking slowly up the long, empty road, while the whitish clouds sailed across the dark river of the sky and the moon slowly sank. This was the most delicious part of all that long walk home, for the kiss had made them feel as though they had no bodies, but were just two spirits walking side by side. This is its curious effect sometimes in first love between the very young....

Having sent Flora to bed, Felix was sitting up among his books. There was no need to do this, for the young folk had latch-keys, but, having begun the vigil, he went on with it, a volume about Eastern philosophies on his knee, a bowl of narcissus blooms, giving forth unexpected whiffs of odor, beside him. And he sank into a long reverie.

Could it be said—as was said in this Eastern book—that man's life was really but a dream; could that be said with any more truth than it had once been said, that he rose again in his body, to perpetual life? Could anything be said with truth, save that we knew nothing? And was that not really what had always been said by man—that we knew nothing, but were just blown over and about the world like soughs of wind, in obedience to some immortal, unknowable coherence! But had that want of knowledge ever retarded what was known as the upward growth of man? Had it ever stopped man from working, fighting, loving, dying like a hero if need were? Had faith ever been anything but embroidery to an instinctive heroism, so strong that it needed no such trappings? Had faith ever been anything but anodyne, or gratification of the aesthetic sense? Or had it really body and substance of its own? Was it something absolute and solid, that he—Felix Freeland—had missed? Or again, was it, perhaps, but the natural concomitant of youth, a naive effervescence with which thought and brooding had to part? And, turning the page of his book, he noticed that he could no longer see to read, the lamp had grown too dim, and showed but a decorative glow in the bright moonlight flooding through the study window. He got up and put another log on the fire, for these last nights of May were chilly.

Nearly three! Where were these young people? Had he been asleep, and they come in? Sure enough, in the hall Alan's hat and Sheila's cloak—the dark-red one he had admired when she went forth—were lying on a chair. But of the other two—nothing! He crept up-stairs. Their doors were open. They certainly took their time—these young lovers. And the same sore feeling which had attacked Felix when Nedda first told him of her love came on him badly in that small of the night when his vitality was lowest. All the hours she had spent clambering about him, or quietly resting on his knee with her head tucked in just where his arm and shoulder met, listening while he read or told her stories, and now and again turning those clear eyes of hers wide open to his face, to see if he meant it; the wilful little tugs of her hand when they two went exploring the customs of birds, or bees, or flowers; all her 'Daddy, I love yous!' and her rushes to the front door, and long hugs when he came back from a travel; all those later crookings of her little finger in his, and the times he had sat when she did not know it, watching her, and thinking: 'That little creature, with all that's before her, is my very own daughter to take care of, and share joy and sorrow with....' Each one of all these seemed to come now and tweak at him, as the songs of blackbirds tweak the heart of one who lies, unable to get out into the Spring. His lamp had burned itself quite out; the moon was fallen below the clump of pines, and away to the north-east something stirred in the stain and texture of the sky. Felix opened the window. What peace out there! The chill, scentless peace of night, waiting for dawn's renewal of warmth and youth. Through that bay window facing north he could see on one side the town, still wan with the light of its lamps, on the other the country, whose dark bloom was graying fast. Suddenly a tiny bird twittered, and Felix saw his two truants coming slowly from the gate across the grass, his arm round her shoulders, hers round his waist. With their backs turned to him, they passed the corner of the house, across where the garden sloped away. There they stood above the wide country, their bodies outlined against a sky fast growing light, evidently waiting for the sun to rise. Silent they stood, while the birds, one by one, twittered out their first calls. And suddenly Felix saw the boy fling his hand up into the air. The Sun! Far away on the gray horizon was a flare of red!

CHAPTER XVIII

The anxieties of the Lady Mallorings of this life concerning the moral welfare of their humbler neighbors are inclined to march in front of events. The behavior in Tryst's cottage was more correct than it would have been in nine out of ten middle or upper class demesnes under similar conditions. Between the big laborer and 'that woman,' who, since the epileptic fit, had again come into residence, there had passed nothing whatever that might not have been witnessed by Biddy and her two nurslings. For love is an emotion singularly dumb and undemonstrative in those who live the life of the fields; passion a feeling severely beneath the thumb of a propriety born of the age-long absence of excitants, opportunities, and the aesthetic sense; and those two waited, almost as a matter of course, for the marriage which was forbidden them in this parish. The most they did was to sit and look at one another.

On the day of which Felix had seen the dawn at Hampstead, Sir Gerald's agent tapped on the door of Tryst's cottage, and was answered by Biddy, just in from school for the midday meal.

"Your father home, my dear?"

"No, sir; Auntie's in."

"Ask your auntie to come and speak to me."

The mother-child vanished up the narrow stairs, and the agent sighed. A strong-built, leathery-skinned man in a brown suit and leggings, with a bristly little moustache and yellow whites to his eyes, he did not, as he had said to his wife that morning, 'like the job a little bit.' And while he stood there waiting, Susie and Billy emerged from the kitchen and came to stare at him. The agent returned that stare till a voice behind him said: "Yes, sir?"

'That woman' was certainly no great shakes to look at: a fresh, decent, faithful sort of body! And he said gruffly: "Mornin', miss. Sorry to say my orders are to make a clearance here. I suppose Tryst didn't think we should act on it, but I'm afraid I've got to put his things out, you know. Now, where are you all going; that's the point?"

"I shall go home, I suppose; but Tryst and the children—we don't know."

The agent tapped his leggings with a riding-cane. "So you've been expecting it!" he said with relief. "That's right." And, staring down at the mother-child, he added: "Well, what d'you say, my dear; you look full of sense, you do!"

Biddy answered: "I'll go and tell Mr. Freeland, sir."

"Ah! You're a bright maid. He'll know where to put you for the time bein'. Have you had your dinner?"

"No, sir; it's just ready."

"Better have it—better have it first. No hurry. What've you got in the pot that smells so good?"

"Bubble and squeak, sir."

"Bubble and squeak! Ah!" And with those words the agent withdrew to where, in a farm wagon drawn up by the side of the road, three men were solemnly pulling at their pipes. He moved away from them a little, for, as he expressed it to his wife afterward: "Look bad, you know, look bad—anybody seeing me! Those three little children—that's where it is! If our friends at the Hall had to do these jobs for themselves, there wouldn't be any to do!"

Presently, from his discreet distance, he saw the mother-child going down the road toward Tod's, in her blue 'pinny' and corn-colored hair. Nice little thing! Pretty little thing, too! Pity, great pity! And he went back to the cottage. On his way a thought struck him so that he well-nigh shivered. Suppose the little thing brought back that Mrs. Freeland, the lady who always went about in blue, without a 'nat! Phew! Mr. Freeland—he was another sort; a bit off, certainly—harmless, quite harmless! But that lady! And he entered the cottage. The woman was washing up; seemed a sensible body. When the two kids cleared off to school he could go to work and get it over; the sooner the better, before people came hanging round. A job of this kind sometimes made nasty blood! His yellowish eyes took in the nature of the task before him. Funny jam-up they did get about them, to be sure! Every blessed little thing they'd ever bought, and more, too! Have to take precious good care nothing got smashed, or the law would be on the other leg! And he said to the woman:

"Now, miss, can I begin?"

"I can't stop you, sir."

'No,' he thought, 'you can't stop me, and I blamed well wish you could!' But he said: "Got an old wagon out here. Thought I'd save him damage by weather or anything; we'll put everything in that, and run it up into the empty barn at Marrow and leave it. And there they'll be for him when he wants 'em."

The woman answered: "You're very kind, I'm sure."

Perceiving that she meant no irony, the agent produced a sound from somewhere deep and went out to summon his men.

With the best intentions, however, it is not possible, even in villages so scattered that they cannot be said to exist, to do anything without every one's knowing; and the work of 'putting out' the household goods of the Tryst family, and placing them within the wagon, was not an hour in progress before the road in front of the cottage contained its knot of watchers. Old Gaunt first, alone—for the rogue-girl had gone to Mr. Cuthcott's and Tom Gaunt was at work. The old man had seen evictions in his time, and looked on silently, with a faint, sardonic grin. Four children, so small that not even school had any use for them as yet, soon gathered round his legs, followed by mothers coming to retrieve them, and there was no longer silence. Then came two laborers, on their way to a job, a stone-breaker, and two more women. It was through this little throng that the mother-child and Kirsteen passed into the fast-being-gutted cottage.

The agent was standing by Tryst's bed, keeping up a stream of comment to two of his men, who were taking that aged bed to pieces. It was his habit to feel less when he talked more; but no one could have fallen into a more perfect taciturnity than he when he saw Kirsteen coming up those narrow stairs. In so small a space as this room, where his head nearly touched the ceiling, was it fair to be confronted by that lady—he put it to his wife that same evening—"Was it fair?" He had seen a mother wild duck look like that when you took away its young—snaky fierce about the neck, and its dark eye! He had seen a mare, going to bite, look not half so vicious! "There she stood, and—let me have it?—not a bit! Too much the lady for that, you know!—Just looked at me, and said very quiet: 'Ah! Mr. Simmons, and are you really doing this?' and put her hand on that little girl of his. 'Orders are orders, ma'am!' What could I say? 'Ah!' she said, 'yes, orders are orders, but they needn't be obeyed.' 'As to that, ma'am,' I said—mind you, she's a lady; you can't help feeling that 'I'm a working man, the same as Tryst here; got to earn my living.' 'So have slave-drivers, Mr. Simmons.' 'Every profession,' I said, 'has got its dirty jobs, ma'am. And that's a fact.' 'And will have,' she said, 'so long as professional men consent to do the dirty work of their employers.' 'And where should I be, I should like to know,' I said, 'if I went on that lay? I've got to take the rough with the smooth.' 'Well,' she said, 'Mr. Freeland and I will take Tryst and the little ones in at present.' Good-hearted people, do a lot for the laborers, in their way. All the same, she's a bit of a vixen. Picture of a woman, too, standin' there; shows blood, mind you! Once said, all over—no nagging. She took the little girl off with her. And pretty small I felt, knowing I'd got to finish that job, and the folk outside gettin' nastier all the time—not sayin' much, of course, but lookin' a lot!" The agent paused in his recital and gazed fixedly at a bluebottle crawling up the windowpane. Stretching out his thumb and finger, he nipped it suddenly and threw it in the grate. "Blest if that fellow himself didn't turn up just as I was finishing. I was sorry for the man, you know. There was his home turned out-o'-doors. Big man, too! 'You blanky-blank!' he says; 'if I'd been here you shouldn't ha' done this!' Thought he was goin' to hit me. 'Come, Tryst!' I said, 'it's not my doing, you know!' 'Ah!' he said, 'I know that and it'll be blanky well the worse for THEM!' Rough tongue; no class of man at all, he is! 'Yes,' he said, 'let 'em look out; I'll be even with 'em yet!' 'None o' that!' I told him; 'you know which side the law's buttered. I'm making it easy for you, too, keeping your things in the wagon, ready to shift any time!' He gave me a look—he's got very queer eyes, swimmin', sad sort of eyes, like a man in liquor—and he said: 'I've been here twenty years,' he said. 'My wife died here.' And all of a sudden he went as dumb as a fish. Never let his eyes off us, though, while we finished up the last of it; made me feel funny, seein' him glowering like that all the time. He'll savage something over this, you mark my words!" Again the agent paused, and remained as though transfixed, holding that face of his, whose yellow had run into the whites of the eyes, as still as wood. "He's got some feeling for the place, I suppose," he said suddenly; "or maybe they've put it into him about his rights; there's plenty of 'em like that. Well, anyhow, nobody likes his private affairs turned inside out for every one to gape at. I wouldn't myself." And with that deeply felt remark the agent put out his leathery-yellow thumb and finger and nipped a second bluebottle....

While the agent was thus recounting to his wife the day's doings, the evicted Tryst sat on the end of his bed in a ground-floor room of Tod's cottage. He had taken off his heavy boots, and his feet, in their thick, soiled socks, were thrust into a pair of Tod's carpet slippers. He sat without moving, precisely as if some one had struck him a blow in the centre of the forehead, and over and over again he turned the heavy thought: 'They've turned me out o' there—I done nothing, and they turned me out o' there! Blast them—they turned me out o' there!'...

In the orchard Tod sat with a grave and puzzled face, surrounded by the three little Trysts. And at the wicket gate Kirsteen, awaiting the arrival of Derek and Sheila—summoned home by telegram—stood in the evening glow, her blue-clad figure still as that of any worshipper at the muezzin-call.

CHAPTER XIX

"A fire, causing the destruction of several ricks and an empty cowshed, occurred in the early morning of Thursday on the home farm of Sir Gerald Malloring's estate in Worcestershire. Grave suspicions of arson are entertained, but up to the present no arrest has been made. The authorities are in doubt whether the occurrence has any relation with recent similar outbreaks in the eastern counties."

So Stanley read at breakfast, in his favorite paper; and the little leader thereon:

"The outbreak of fire on Sir Gerald Malloring's Worcestershire property may or may not have any significance as a symptom of agrarian unrest. We shall watch the upshot with some anxiety. Certain it is that unless the authorities are prepared to deal sharply with arson, or other cases of deliberate damage to the property of landlords, we may bid good-by to any hope of ameliorating the lot of the laborer"

—and so on.

If Stanley had risen and paced the room there would have been a good deal to be said for him; for, though he did not know as much as Felix of the nature and sentiments of Tod's children, he knew enough to make any but an Englishman uneasy. The fact that he went on eating ham, and said to Clara,

"Half a cup!" was proof positive of that mysterious quality called phlegm which had long enabled his country to enjoy the peace of a weedy duck-pond.

Stanley, a man of some intelligence—witness his grasp of the secret of successful plough-making (none for the home market!)—had often considered this important proposition of phlegm. People said England was becoming degenerate and hysterical, growing soft, and nervous, and towny, and all the rest of it. In his view there was a good deal of bosh about that! "Look," he would say, "at the weight that chauffeurs put on! Look at the House of Commons, and the size of the upper classes!" If there were growing up little shrill types of working men and Socialists, and new women, and half-penny papers, and a rather larger crop of professors and long-haired chaps—all the better for the rest of the country! The flesh all these skimpy ones had lost, solid people had put on. The country might be suffering a bit from officialism, and the tendency of modern thought, but the breed was not changing. John Bull was there all right under his moustache. Take it off and clap on little side-whiskers, and you had as many Bulls as you liked, any day. There would be no social upheaval so long as the climate was what it was! And with this simple formula, and a kind of very deep-down throaty chuckle, he would pass to a subject of more immediate importance. There was something, indeed, rather masterly in his grasp of the fact that rain might be trusted to put out any fire—give it time. And he kept a special vessel in a special corner which recorded for him faithfully the number of inches that fell; and now and again he wrote to his paper to say that there were more inches in his vessel than there had been "for thirty years." His conviction that the country was in a bad way was nothing but a skin affection, causing him local irritation rather than affecting the deeper organs of his substantial body.

He did not readily confide in Clara concerning his own family, having in a marked degree the truly domestic quality of thinking it superior to his wife's. She had been a Tomson, not one of THE Tomsons, and it was quite a question whether he or she were trying to forget that fact the faster. But he did say to her as he was getting into the car:

"It's just possible I might go round by Tod's on my way home. I want a run."

She answered: "Be careful what you say to that woman. I don't want her here by any chance. The young ones were quite bad enough."

And when he had put in his day at the works he did turn the nose of his car toward Tod's. Travelling along grass-bordered roads, the beauty of this England struck his not too sensitive spirit and made him almost gasp. It was that moment of the year when the countryside seems to faint from its own loveliness, from the intoxication of its scents and sounds. Creamy-white may, splashed here and there with crimson, flooded the hedges in breaking waves of flower-foam; the fields were all buttercup glory; every tree had its cuckoo, calling; every bush its blackbird or thrush in full even-song. Swallows were flying rather low, and the sky, whose moods they watch, had the slumberous, surcharged beauty of a long, fine day, with showers not far away. Some orchards were still in blossom, and the great wild bees, hunting over flowers and grasses warm to their touch, kept the air deeply murmurous. Movement, light, color, song, scent, the warm air, and the fluttering leaves were confused, till one had almost become the other.

And Stanley thought, for he was not rhapsodic 'Wonderful pretty country! The way everything's looked after—you never see it abroad!'

But the car, a creature with little patience for natural beauty, had brought him to the crossroads and stood, panting slightly, under the cliff-bank whereon grew Tod's cottage, so loaded now with lilac, wistaria, and roses that from the road nothing but a peak or two of the thatched roof could be seen.

Stanley was distinctly nervous. It was not a weakness his face and figure were very capable of showing, but he felt that dryness of mouth and quivering of chest which precede adventures of the soul. Advancing up the steps and pebbled path, which Clara had trodden once, just nineteen years ago, and he himself but three times as yet in all, he cleared his throat and said to himself: 'Easy, old man! What is it, after all? She won't bite!' And in the very doorway he came upon her.

What there was about this woman to produce in a man of common sense such peculiar sensations, he no more knew after seeing her than before. Felix, on returning from his visit, had said, "She's like a Song of the Hebrides sung in the middle of a programme of English ballads." The remark, as any literary man's might, had conveyed nothing to Stanley, and that in a far-fetched way. Still, when she said: "Will you come in?" he felt heavier and thicker than he had ever remembered feeling; as a glass of stout might feel coming across a glass of claret. It was, perhaps, the gaze of her eyes, whose color he could not determine, under eyebrows that waved in the middle and twitched faintly, or a dress that was blue, with the queerest effect of another color at the back of it, or perhaps the feeling of a torrent flowing there under a coat of ice, that might give way in little holes, so that your leg went in but not the whole of you. Something, anyway, made him feel both small and heavy—that awkward combination for a man accustomed to associate himself with cheerful but solid dignity. In seating himself by request at a table, in what seemed to be a sort of kitchen, he experienced a singular sensation in the legs, and heard her say, as it might be to the air:

"Biddy, dear, take Susie and Billy out."

And thereupon a little girl with a sad and motherly face came crawling out from underneath the table, and dropped him a little courtesy. Then another still smaller girl came out, and a very small boy, staring with all his eyes.

All these things were against Stanley, and he felt that if he did not make it quite clear that he was there he would soon not know where he was.

"I came," he said, "to talk about this business up at Malloring's." And, encouraged by having begun, he added: "Whose kids were those?"

A level voice with a faint lisp answered him:

"They belong to a man called Tryst; he was turned out of his cottage on Wednesday because his dead wife's sister was staying with him, so we've taken them in. Did you notice the look on the face of the eldest?"

Stanley nodded. In truth, he had noticed something, though what he could not have said.

"At nine years old she has to do the housework and be a mother to the other two, besides going to school. This is all because Lady Malloring has conscientious scruples about marriage with a deceased wife's sister."

'Certainly'—thought Stanley—'that does sound a bit thick!' And he asked:

"Is the woman here, too?"

"No, she's gone home for the present."

He felt relief.

"I suppose Malloring's point is," he said, "whether or not you're to do what you like with your own property. For instance, if you had let this cottage to some one you thought was harming the neighborhood, wouldn't you terminate his tenancy?"

She answered, still in that level voice:

"Her action is cowardly, narrow, and tyrannical, and no amount of sophistry will make me think differently."

Stanley felt precisely as if one of his feet had gone through the ice into water so cold that it seemed burning hot! Sophistry! In a plain man like himself! He had always connected the word with Felix. He looked at her, realizing suddenly that the association of his brother's family with the outrage on Malloring's estate was probably even nearer than he had feared.

"Look here, Kirsteen!" he said, uttering the unlikely name with resolution, for, after all, she was his sister-in-law: "Did this fellow set fire to Malloring's ricks?"

He was aware of a queer flash, a quiver, a something all over her face, which passed at once back to its intent gravity.

"We have no reason to suppose so. But tyranny produces revenge, as you know."

Stanley shrugged his shoulders. "It's not my business to go into the rights and wrongs of what's been done. But, as a man of the world and a relative, I do ask you to look after your youngsters and see they don't get into a mess. They're an inflammable young couple—young blood, you know!"

Having made this speech, Stanley looked down, with a feeling that it would give her more chance.

"You are very kind," he heard her saying in that quiet, faintly lisping voice; "but there are certain principles involved."

And, suddenly, his curious fear of this woman took shape. Principles! He had unconsciously been waiting for that word, than which none was more like a red rag to him.

"What principles can possibly be involved in going against the law?"

"And where the law is unjust?"

Stanley was startled, but he said: "Remember that your principles, as you call them, may hurt other people besides yourself; Tod and your children most of all. How is the law unjust, may I ask?"

She had been sitting at the table opposite, but she got up now and went to the hearth. For a woman of forty-two—as he supposed she would be—she was extraordinarily lithe, and her eyes, fixed on him from under those twitching, wavy brows, had a curious glow in their darkness. The few silver threads in the mass of her over-fine black hair seemed to give it extra vitality. The whole of her had a sort of intensity that made him profoundly uncomfortable. And he thought suddenly: 'Poor old Tod! Fancy having to go to bed with that woman!'

Without raising her voice, she began answering his question.

"These poor people have no means of setting law in motion, no means of choosing where and how they will live, no means of doing anything except just what they are told; the Mallorings have the means to set the law in motion, to choose where and how to live, and to dictate to others. That is why the law is unjust. With every independent pound a year, this equal law of yours—varies!"

"Phew!" said Stanley. "That's a proposition!"

"I give you a simple case. If I had chosen not to marry Tod but to live with him in free love, we could have done it without inconvenience. We have some independent income; we could have afforded to disregard what people thought or did. We could have bought (as we did buy) our piece of land and our cottage, out of which we could not have been turned. Since we don't care for society, it would have made absolutely no difference to our present position. But Tryst, who does not even want to defy the law—what happens to him? What happens to hundreds of laborers all over the country who venture to differ in politics, religion, or morals from those who own them?"

'By George!' thought Stanley, 'it's true, in a way; I never looked at it quite like that.' But the feeling that he had come to persuade her to be reasonable, and the deeply rooted Englishry of him, conspired to make him say:

"That's all very well; but, you see, it's only a necessary incident of property-holding. You can't interfere with plain rights."

"You mean—an evil inherent in property-holding?"

"If you like; I don't split words. The lesser of two evils. What's your remedy? You don't want to abolish property; you've confessed that property gives YOU your independence!"

Again that curious quiver and flash!

"Yes; but if people haven't decency enough to see for themselves how the law favors their independence, they must be shown that it doesn't pay to do to others as they would hate to be done by."

"And you wouldn't try reasoning?"

"They are not amenable to reason."

Stanley took up his hat.

"Well, I think some of us are. I see your point; but, you know, violence never did any good; it isn't—isn't English."

She did not answer. And, nonplussed thereby, he added lamely: "I should have liked to have seen Tod and your youngsters. Remember me to them. Clara sent her regards;" and, looking round the room in a rather lost way, he held out his hand.

He had an impression of something warm and dry put into it, with even a little pressure.

Back in the car, he said to his chauffeur, "Go home the other way, Batter, past the church."

The vision of that kitchen, with its brick floor, its black oak beams, bright copper pans, the flowers on the window-sill, the great, open hearth, and the figure of that woman in her blue dress standing before it, with her foot poised on a log, clung to his mind's eye with curious fidelity. And those three kids, popping out like that—proof that the whole thing was not a rather bad dream! 'Queer business!' he thought; 'bad business! That woman's uncommonly all there, though. Lot in what she said, too. Where the deuce should we all be if there were many like her!' And suddenly he noticed, in a field to the right, a number of men coming along the hedge toward the road—evidently laborers. What were they doing? He stopped the car. There were fifteen or twenty of them, and back in the field he could see a girl's red blouse, where a little group of four still lingered. 'By George!' he thought, 'those must be the young Tods going it!' And, curious to see what it might mean, Stanley fixed his attention on the gate through which the men were bound to come. First emerged a fellow in corduroys tied below the knee, with long brown moustaches decorating a face that, for all its haggardness, had a jovial look. Next came a sturdy little red-faced, bow-legged man in shirt-sleeves rolled up, walking alongside a big, dark fellow with a cap pushed up on his head, who had evidently just made a joke. Then came two old men, one of whom was limping, and three striplings. Another big man came along next, in a little clearance, as it were, between main groups. He walked heavily, and looked up lowering at the car. The fellow's eyes were queer, and threatening, and sad—giving Stanley a feeling of discomfort. Then came a short, square man with an impudent, loquacious face and a bit of swagger in his walk. He, too, looked up at Stanley and made some remark which caused two thin-faced fellows with him to grin sheepishly. A spare old man, limping heavily, with a yellow face and drooping gray moustaches, walked next, alongside a warped, bent fellow, with yellowish hair all over his face, whose expression struck Stanley as half-idiotic. Then two more striplings of seventeen or so, whittling at bits of sticks; an active, clean-shorn chap with drawn-in cheeks; and, last of all, a small man by himself, without a cap on a round head covered with thin, light hair, moving at a 'dot-here, dot-there' walk, as though he had beasts to drive.

Stanley noted that all—save the big man with the threatening, sad eyes, the old, yellow-faced man with a limp, and the little man who came out last, lost in his imaginary beasts—looked at the car furtively as they went their ways. And Stanley thought: 'English peasant! Poor devil! Who is he? What is he? Who'd miss him if he did die out? What's the use of all this fuss about him? He's done for! Glad I've nothing to do with him at Becket, anyway! "Back to the land!" "Independent peasantry!" Not much! Shan't say that to Clara, though; knock the bottom out of her week-ends!' And to his chauffeur he muttered:

"Get on, Batter!"

So, through the peace of that country, all laid down in grass, through the dignity and loveliness of trees and meadows, this May evening, with the birds singing under a sky surcharged with warmth and color, he sped home to dinner.

CHAPTER XX

But next morning, turning on his back as it came dawn, Stanley thought, with the curious intensity which in those small hours so soon becomes fear: 'By Jove! I don't trust that woman a yard! I shall wire for Felix!' And the longer he lay on his back, the more the conviction bored a hole in him. There was a kind of fever in the air nowadays, that women seemed to catch, as children caught the measles. What did it all mean? England used to be a place to live in. One would have thought an old country like this would have got through its infantile diseases! Hysteria! No one gave in to that. Still, one must look out! Arson was about the limit! And Stanley had a vision, suddenly, of his plough-works in flames. Why not? The ploughs were not for the English market. Who knew whether these laboring fellows mightn't take that as a grievance, if trouble began to spread? This somewhat far-fetched notion, having started to burrow, threw up a really horrid mole-hill on Stanley. And it was only the habit, in the human mind, of saying suddenly to fears: Stop! I'm tired of you! that sent him to sleep about half past four.

He did not, however, neglect to wire to Felix:

"If at all possible, come down again at once; awkward business at Joyfields."

Nor, on the charitable pretext of employing two old fellows past ordinary work, did he om t to treble his night-watchman....

On Wednesday, the day of which he had seen the dawn rise, Felix had already been startled, on returning from his constitutional, to discover his niece and nephew in the act of departure. All the explanation vouchsafed had been: "Awfully sorry, Uncle Felix; Mother's wired for us." Save for the general uneasiness which attended on all actions of that woman, Felix would have felt rel eved at their going. They had disturbed his life, slipped between him and Nedda! So much so that he did not even expect her to come and tell him why they had gone, nor feel inclined to ask her. So little breaks the fine coherence of really tender ties! The deeper the quality of affection, the more it 'starts and puffs,' and from sheer sensitive feeling, each for the other, spares attempt to get back into touch!

His paper—though he did not apply to it the word 'favorite,' having that proper literary feeling toward all newspapers, that they took him in rather than he them—gave him on Friday morning precisely the same news, of the rick-burning, as it gave to Stanley at breakfast and to John on his way to the Home Office. To John, less in the know, it merely brought a knitting of the brow and a vague attempt to recollect the numbers of the Worcestershire constabulary. To Felix it brought a feeling of sickness. Men whose work in life demands that they shall daily whip their nerves, run, as a rule, a little in advance of everything. And goodness knows what he did not see at that moment. He said no word to Nedda, but debated with himself and Flora what, if anything, was to be done. Flora, whose sense of humor seldom deserted her, held the more comfortable theory that there was nothing to be done as yet. Soon enough to cry when milk was spilled! He did not agree, but, unable to suggest a better course, followed her advice. On Saturday, however, receiving Stanley's wire, he had much difficulty in not saying to her, "I told you so!" The question that agitated him now was whether or not to take Nedda with him. Flora said: "Yes. The child will be the best restraining influence, if there is really trouble brewing!" Some feeling fought against this in Felix, but, suspecting it to be mere jealousy, he decided to take her. And, to the girl's rather puzzled delight, they arrived at Becket that day in time for dinner. It was not too reassuring to find John there, too. Stanley had also wired to him. The matter must indeed be serious!

The usual week-end was in progress. Clara had made one of her greatest efforts. A Bulgarian had providentially written a book in which he showed, beyond doubt, that persons fed on brown bread, potatoes, and margarine, gave the most satisfactory results of all. It was a discovery of the first value as a topic for her dinner-table—seeming to solve the whole vexed problem of the laborers almost at one stroke. If they could only be got to feed themselves on this perfect programme, what a saving of the situation! On those three edibles, the Bulgarian said—and he had been well translated—a family of five could be maintained at full efficiency for a shilling per day. Why! that would leave nearly eight shillings a week, in many cases more, for rent, firing, insurance, the man's tobacco, and the children's boots. There would be no more of that terrible pinching by the mothers, to feed the husband and children properly, of which one heard so much; no more lamentable deterioration in our stock! Brown bread, potatoes, margarine—quite a great deal could be provided for seven shillings! And what was more delicious than a well-baked potato with margarine of good quality? The carbohydrates—or was it hybocardrates—ah, yes! the kybohardrates—would be present in really sufficient quantity! Little else was talked of all through dinner at her end of the table. Above the flowers which Frances Freeland always insisted on arranging—and very charmingly—when she was there—over bare shoulders and white shirt-fronts, those words bombed and rebombed. Brown bread, potatoes, margarine, carbohydrates, calorific! They mingled with the creaming sizzle of champagne, with the soft murmur of well-bred deglutition. White bosoms heaved and eyebrows rose at them. And now and again some Bigwig versed in science murmured the word 'Fats.' An agricultural population fed to the point of efficiency without disturbance of the existing state of things! Eureka! If only into the bargain they could be induced to bake their own brown bread and cook their potatoes well! Faces flushed, eyes brightened, and teeth shone. It was the best, the most stimulating, dinner ever swallowed in that room. Nor was it until each male guest had eaten, drunk, and talked himself into torpor suitable to the company of his wife, that the three brothers could sit in the smoking-room together, undisturbed.

When Stanley had described his interview with 'that woman,' his glimpse of the red blouse, and the laborers' meeting, there was a silence before John said:

"It might be as well if Tod would send his two youngsters abroad for a bit."

Felix shook his head.

"I don't think he would, and I don't think they'd go. But we might try to get those two to see that anything the poor devils of laborers do is bound to recoil on themselves, fourfold. I suppose," he added, with sudden malice, "a laborers' rising would have no chance?"

Neither John nor Stanley winced.

"Rising? Why should they rise?"

"They did in '32."

"In '32!" repeated John. "Agriculture had its importance then. Now it has none. Besides, they've no cohesion, no power, like the miners or railway men. Rising? No chance, no earthly! Weight of metal's dead against it."

Felix smiled.

"Money and guns! Guns and money! Confess with me, brethren, that we're glad of metal."

John stared and Stanley drank off his whiskey and potash. Felix really was a bit 'too thick' sometimes. Then Stanley said:

"Wonder what Tod thinks of it all. Will you go over, Felix, and advise that our young friends be more considerate to these poor beggars?"

Felix nodded. And with 'Good night, old man' all round, and no shaking of the hands, the three brothers dispersed.

But behind Felix, as he opened his bedroom door, a voice whispered:

"Dad!" And there, in the doorway of the adjoining room, was Nedda in her dressing-gown.

"Do come in for a minute. I've been waiting up. You ARE late."

Felix followed her into her room. The pleasure he would once have had in this midnight conspiracy was superseded now, and he stood blinking at her gravely. In that blue gown, with her dark hair falling on its lace collar and her face so round and childish, she seemed more than ever to have defrauded him. Hooking her arm in his, she drew him to the window; and Felix thought: 'She just wants to talk to me about Derek. Dog in the manger that I am! Here goes to be decent!' So he said:

"Well, my dear?"

Nedda pressed his hand with a little coaxing squeeze.

"Daddy, darling, I do love you!"

And, though Felix knew that she had grasped what he was feeling, a sort of warmth spread in him. She had begun counting his fingers with one of her own, sitting close beside him. The warmth in Felix deepened, but he thought: 'She must want a good deal out of me!' Then she began:

"Why did we come down again? I know there's something wrong! It's hard not to know, when you're anxious." And she sighed. That little sigh affected Felix.

"I'd always rather know the truth, Dad. Aunt Clara said something about a fire at the Mallorings'."

Felix stole a look at her. Yes! There was a lot in this child of his! Depth, warmth, and strength to hold to things. No use to treat her as a child! And he answered:

"My dear, there's really nothing beyond what you know—our young man and Sheila are hotheads, and things over there are working up a bit. We must try and smooth them down."

"Dad, ought I to back him whatever he does?"

What a question! The more so that one cannot answer superficially the questions of those whom one loves.

"Ah!" he said at last. "I don't know yet. Some things it's not your duty to do; that's certain. It can't be right to do things simply because he does them—THAT'S not real—however fond one is."

"No; I feel that. Only, it's so hard to know what I do really think—there's always such a lot trying to make one feel that only what's nice and cosey is right!"

And Felix thought: 'I've been brought up to believe that only Russian girls care for truth. It seems I was wrong. The saints forbid I should be a stumbling-block to my own daughter searching for it! And yet—where's it all leading? Is this the same child that told me only the other night she wanted to know everything? She's a woman now! So much for love!' And he said:

"Let's go forward quietly, without expecting too much of ourselves."

"Yes, Dad; only I distrust myself so."

"No one ever got near the truth who didn't."

"Can we go over to Joyfields to-morrow? I don't think I could bear a whole day of Bigwigs and eating, with this hanging—"

"Poor Bigwigs! All right! We'll go. And now, bed; and think of nothing!"

Her whisper tickled his ear:

"You are a darling to me, Dad!"

He went out comforted.

And for some time after she had forgotten everything he leaned out of his window, smoking cigarettes, and trying to see the body and soul of night. How quiet she was—night, with her mystery, bereft of moon, in whose darkness seemed to vibrate still the song of the cuckoos that had been calling so all day! And whisperings of leaves communed with Felix.

CHAPTER XXI

What Tod thought of all this was, perhaps, as much of an enigma to Tod as to his three brothers, and never more so than on that Sunday morning when two police constables appeared at his door with a warrant for the arrest of Tryst. After regarding them fixedly for full thirty seconds, he said, "Wait!" and left them in the doorway.

Kirsteen was washing breakfast things which had a leadless glaze, and Tryst's three children, extremely tidy, stood motionless at the edge of the little scullery, watching.

When she had joined him in the kitchen Tod shut the door.

"Two policemen," he said, "want Tryst. Are they to have him?"

In the life together of these two there had, from the very start, been a queer understanding as to who should decide what. It had become by now so much a matter of instinct that combative consultations, which bulk so large in married lives, had no place in theirs. A frowning tremor passed over her face.

"I suppose they must. Derek is out. Leave it to me, Tod, and take the tinies into the orchard."

Tod took the three little Trysts to the very spot where Derek and Nedda had gazed over the darkening fields in exchanging that first kiss, and, sitting on the stump of the apple-tree he had cut down, he presented each of them with an apple. While they ate, he stared. And his dog stared at him. How far there worked in Tod the feelings of an ordinary man watching three small children whose only parent the law was just taking into its charge it would be rash to say, but his eyes were extremely blue and there was a frown between them.

"Well, Biddy?" he said at last.

Biddy did not reply; the habit of being a mother had imposed on her, together with the gravity of her little, pale, oval face, a peculiar talent for silence. But the round-cheeked Susie said:

"Billy can eat cores."

After this statement, silence was broken only by munching, till Tod remarked:

"What makes things?"

The children, having the instinct that he had not asked them, but himself, came closer. He had in his hand a little beetle.

"This beetle lives in rotten wood; nice chap, isn't he?"

"We kill beetles; we're afraid of them." So Susie.

They were now round Tod so close that Billy was standing on one of his large feet, Susie leaning her elbows on one of his broad knees, and Biddy's slender little body pressed against his huge arm.

"No," said Tod; "beetles are nice chaps."

"The birds eats them," remarked Billy.

"This beetle," said Tod, "eats wood. It eats through trees and the trees get rotten."

Biddy spoke:

"Then they don't give no more apples." Tod put the beetle down and Billy got off his foot to tread on it. When he had done his best the beetle emerged and vanished in the grass. Tod, who had offered no remonstrance, stretched out his hand and replaced Billy on his foot.

"What about my treading on you, Billy?" he said.

"Why?"

"I'm big and you're little."

On Billy's square face came a puzzled defiance. If he had not been early taught his station he would evidently have found some poignant retort. An intoxicated humblebee broke the silence by buzzing into Biddy's fluffed-out, corn-gold hair. Tod took it off with his hand.

"Lovely chap, isn't he?"

The children, who had recoiled, drew close again, while the drunken bee crawled feebly in the cage of Tod's large hand.

"Bees sting," said Biddy; "I fell on a bee and it stang me!"

"You stang it first," said Tod. "This chap wouldn't sting—not for worlds. Stroke it!"

Biddy put out her little, pale finger but stayed it a couple of inches from the bee.

"Go on," said Tod.

Opening her mouth a little, Biddy went on and touched the bee.

"It's soft," she said. "Why don't it buzz?"

"I want to stroke it, too," said Susie. And Billy stamped a little on Tod's foot.

"No," said Tod; "only Biddy."

There was perfect silence till the dog, rising, approached its nose, black with a splash of pinky whiteness on the end of the bridge, as if to love the bee.

"No," said Tod. The dog looked at him, and his yellow-brown eyes were dark with anxiety.

"It'll sting the dog's nose," said Biddy, and Susie and Billy came yet closer.

It was at this moment, when the heads of the dog, the bee, Tod, Biddy, Susie, and Billy might have been contained within a noose three feet in diameter, that Felix dismounted from Stanley's car and, coming from the cottage, caught sight of that little idyll under the dappled sunlight, green, and blossom. It was something from the core of life, out of the heartbeat of things—like a rare picture or song, the revelation of the childlike wonder and delight, to which all other things are but the supernumerary casings—a little pool of simplicity into which fever and yearning sank and were for a moment drowned. And quite possibly he would have gone away without disturbing them if the dog had not growled and wagged his tail.

But when the children had been sent down into the field he experienced the usual difficulty in commencing a talk with Tod. How far was his big brother within reach of mere unphilosophic statements; how far was he going to attend to facts?

"We came back yesterday," he began; "Nedda and I. You know all about Derek and Nedda, I suppose?"

Tod nodded.

"What do you think of it?"

"He's a good chap."

"Yes," murmured Felix, "but a firebrand. This business at Malloring's—what's it going to lead to, Tod? We must look out, old man. Couldn't you send Derek and Sheila abroad for a bit?"

"Wouldn't go."

"But, after all, they're dependent on you."

"Don't say that to them; I should never see them again."

Felix, who felt the instinctive wisdom of that remark, answered helplessly:

"What's to be done, then?"

"Sit tight." And Tod's hand came down on Felix's shoulder.

"But suppose they get into real trouble? Stanley and John don't like it; and there's Mother." And Felix added, with sudden heat, "Besides, I can't stand Nedda being made anxious like this."

Tod removed his hand. Felix would have given a good deal to have been able to see into the brain behind the frowning stare of those blue eyes.

"Can't help by worrying. What must be, will. Look at the birds!"

The remark from any other man would have irritated Felix profoundly; coming from Tod, it seemed the unconscious expression of a really felt philosophy. And, after all, was he not right? What was this life they all lived but a ceaseless worrying over what was to come? Was not all man's unhappiness caused by nervous anticipations of the future? Was not that the disease, and the misfortune, of the age; perhaps of all the countless ages man had lived through?

With an effort he recalled his thoughts from that far flight. What if Tod had rediscovered the secret of the happiness that belonged to birds and lilies of the field—such overpowering interest in the moment that the future did not exist? Why not? Were not the only minutes when he himself was really happy those when he lost himself in work, or love? And why were they so few? For want of pressure to the square moment. Yes! All unhappiness was fear and lack of vitality to live the present fully. That was why love and fighting were such poignant ecstasies—they lived their present to the full. And so it would be almost comic to say to those young people: Go away; do nothing in this matter in which your interest and your feelings are concerned! Don't have a present, because you've got to have a future! And he said:

"I'd give a good deal for your power of losing yourself in the moment, old boy!"

"That's all right," said Tod. He was examining the bark of a tree, which had nothing the matter with it, so far as Felix could see; while his dog, who had followed them, carefully examined Tod. Both were obviously lost in the moment. And with a feeling of defeat Felix led the way back to the cottage.

In the brick-floored kitchen Derek was striding up and down; while around him, in an equilateral triangle, stood the three women, Sheila at the window, Kirsteen by the open hearth, Nedda against the wall opposite. Derek exclaimed at once:

"Why did you let them, Father? Why didn't you refuse to give him up?"

Felix looked at his brother. In the doorway, where his curly head nearly touched the wood, Tod's face was puzzled, rueful. He did not answer.

"Any one could have said he wasn't here. We could have smuggled him away. Now the brutes have got him! I don't know that, though—" And he made suddenly for the door.

Tod did not budge. "No," he said.

Derek turned; his mother was at the other door; at the window, the two girls.

The comedy of this scene, if there be comedy in the face of grief, was for the moment lost on Felix.

'It's come,' he thought. 'What now?'

Derek had flung himself down at the table and was burying his head in his hands. Sheila went up to him.

"Don't be a fool, Derek."

However right and natural that remark, it seemed inadequate.

And Felix looked at Nedda. The blue motor scarf she had worn had slipped off her dark head; her face was white; her eyes, fixed immovably on Derek, seemed waiting for him to recognize that she was there. The boy broke out again:

"It was treachery! We took him in; and now we've given him up. They wouldn't have touched US if we'd got him away. Not they!"

Felix literally heard the breathing of Tod on one side of him and of Kirsteen on the other. He crossed over and stood opposite his nephew.

"Look here, Derek," he said; "your mother was quite right. You might have put this off for a day or two; but it was bound to come. You don't know the reach of the law. Come, my dear fellow! It's no good making a fuss, that's childish—the thing is to see that the man gets every chance."

Derek looked up. Probably he had not yet realized that his uncle was in the room; and Felix was astonished at his really haggard face; as if the incident had bitten and twisted some vital in his body.

"He trusted us."

Felix saw Kirsteen quiver and flinch, and understood why they had none of them felt quite able to turn their backs on that display of passion. Something deep and unreasoning was on the boy's side; something that would not fit with common sense and the habits of civilized society; something from an Arab's tent or a Highland glen. Then Tod came up behind and put his hands on his son's shoulders.

"Come!" he said; "milk's spilt."

"All right!" said Derek gruffly, and he went to the door.

Felix made Nedda a sign and she slipped out after him.

CHAPTER XXII

Nedda, her blue head-gear trailing, followed along at the boy's side while he passed through the orchard and two fields; and when he threw himself down under an ash-tree she, too, subsided, waiting for him to notice her.

"I am here," she said at last.

At that ironic little speech Derek sat up.

"It'll kill him," he said.

"But—to burn things, Derek! To light horrible cruel flames, and burn things, even if they aren't alive!"

Derek said through his teeth:

"It's I who did it! If I'd never talked to him he'd have been like the others. They were taking him in a cart, like a calf."

Nedda got possession of his hand and held it tight.

That was a bitter and frightening hour under the faintly rustling ash-tree, while the wind sprinkled over her flakes of the may blossom, just past its prime. Love seemed now so little a thing, seemed to have lost warmth and power, seemed like a suppliant outside a door. Why did trouble come like this the moment one felt deeply?

The church bell was tolling; they could see the little congregation pass across the churchyard into that weekly dream they knew too well. And presently the drone emerged, mingling with the voices outside, of sighing trees and trickling water, of the rub of wings, birds' songs, and the callings of beasts everywhere beneath the sky.

In spite of suffering because love was not the first emotion in his heart, the girl could only feel he was right not to be loving her; that she ought to be glad of what was eating up all else within him. It was ungenerous, unworthy, to want to be loved at such a moment. Yet she could not help it! This was her first experience of the eternal tug between self and the loved one pulled in the hearts of lovers. Would she ever come to feel happy when he was just doing what he thought was right? And she drew a little away from him; then perceived that unwittingly she had done the right thing, for he at once tried to take her hand again. And this was her first lesson, too, in the nature of man. If she did not give her hand, he wanted it! But she was not one of those who calculate in love; so she gave him her hand at once. That went to his heart; and he put his arm round her, till he could feel the emotion under those stays that would not be drawn any closer. In this nest beneath the ash-tree they sat till they heard the organ wheeze and the furious sound of the last hymn, and saw the brisk coming-forth with its air of, 'Thank God! And now, to eat!' till at last there was no stir again about the little church—no stir at all save that of nature's ceaseless thanksgiving....

Tod, his brown face still rueful, had followed those two out into the air, and Sheila had gone quickly after him. Thus left alone with his sister-in-law, Felix said gravely:

"If you don't want the boy to get into real trouble, do all you can to show him that the last way in the world to help these poor fellows is to let them fall foul of the law. It's madness to light flames you can't put out. What happened this morning? Did the man resist?"

Her face still showed how bitter had been her mortification, and he was astonished that she kept her voice so level and emotionless.

"No. He went with them quite quietly. The back door was open; he could have walked out. I did not advise him to. I'm glad no one saw his face except myself. You see," she added, "he's devoted to Derek, and Derek knows it; that's why he feels it so, and will feel it more and more. The boy has a great sense of honour, Felix."

Under that tranquillity Felix caught the pain and yearning in her voice. Yes! This woman really felt and saw. She was not one of those who make disturbance with their brains and powers of criticism; rebellion leaped out from the heat in her heart. But he said:

"Is it right to fan this flame? Do you think any good end is being served?" Waiting for her answer, he found himself gazing at the ghost of dark down on her upper lip, wondering that he had never noticed it before.

Very low, as if to herself, she said:

"I would kill myself to-day if I didn't believe that tyranny and injustice must end."

"In our time?"

"Perhaps not."

"Are you content to go on working for an Utopia that you will never see?"

"While our laborers are treated and housed more like dogs than human beings, while the best life under the sun—because life on the soil might be the best life—is despised and starved, and made the plaything of people's tongues, neither I nor mine are going to rest."

The admiration she inspired in Felix at that moment was mingled with a kind of pity. He said impressively:

"Do you know the forces you are up against? Have you looked into the unfathomable heart of this trouble? Understood the tug of the towns, the call of money to money; grasped the destructive restlessness of modern life; the abysmal selfishness of people when you threaten their interests; the age-long apathy of those you want to help? Have you grasped all these?"

"And more!"

Felix held out his hand. "Then," he said, "you are truly brave!"

She shook her head.

"It got bitten into me very young. I was brought up in the Highlands among the crofters in their worst days. In some ways the people here are not so badly off, but they're still slaves."

"Except that they can go to Canada if they want, and save old England."

She flushed. "I hate irony."

Felix looked at her with ever-increasing interest; she certainly was of the kind that could be relied on to make trouble.

"Ah!" he murmured. "Don't forget that when we can no longer smile we can only swell and burst. It IS some consolation to reflect that by the time we've determined to do something really effectual for the ploughmen of England there'll be no ploughmen left!"

"I cannot smile at that."

And, studying her face, Felix thought, 'You're right there! You'll get no help from humor.'. .

Early that afternoon, with Nedda between them, Felix and his nephew were speeding toward Transham.

The little town—a hamlet when Edmund Moreton dropped the E from his name and put up the works which Stanley had so much enlarged—had monopolized by now the hill on which it stood. Living entirely on its ploughs, it yet had but little of the true look of a British factory town, having been for the most part built since ideas came into fashion. With its red roofs and chimneys, it was only moderately ugly, and here and there an old white, timbered house still testified to the fact that it had once been country. On this fine Sunday afternoon the population were in the streets, and presented all that long narrow-headedness, that twist and distortion of feature, that perfect absence of beauty in face, figure, and dress, which is the glory of the Briton who has been for three generations in a town. 'And my great-grandfather'—thought Felix—'did all this! God rest his soul!'

At a rather new church on the very top they halted, and went in to inspect the Morton memorials. There they were, in dedicated corners. 'Edmund and his wife Catherine'—'Charles Edmund and his wife Florence'—'Maurice Edmund and his wife Dorothy.' Clara had set her foot down against 'Stanley and his wife Clara' being in the fourth; her soul was above ploughs, and she, of course, intended to be buried at Becket, as Clara, dowager Lady Freeland, for her efforts in regard to the land. Felix, who had a tendency to note how things affected other people, watched Derek's inspection of these memorials and marked that they excited in him no tendency to ribaldry. The boy, indeed, could hardly be expected to see in them what Felix saw—an epitome of the great, perhaps fatal, change that had befallen his native country; a record of the beginning of that far-back fever, whose course ran ever faster, which had emptied country into town and slowly, surely, changed the whole spirit of life. When Edmund Moreton, about 1780, took the infection disseminated by the development of machinery, and left the farming of his acres to make money, that thing was done which they were all now talking about trying to undo, with their cries of: "Back to the land! Back to peace and sanity in the shade of the elms! Back to the simple and patriarchal state of feeling which old documents disclose. Back to a time before these little squashed heads and bodies and features jutted every which way; before there were long squashed streets of gray houses; long squashed chimneys emitting smoke-blight; long squashed rows of graves; and long squashed columns of the daily papers. Back to well-fed countrymen who could not read, with Common rights, and a kindly feeling for old 'Moretons,' who had a kindly feeling for them!" Back to all that? A dream! Sirs! A dream! There was nothing for it now, but—progress! Progress! On with the dance! Let engines rip, and the little, squash-headed fellows with them! Commerce, literature, religion, science, politics, all taking a hand; what a glorious chance had money, ugliness, and ill will! Such were the reflections of Felix before the brass tablet:

"IN LOVING MEMORY OF
EDMUND MORTON
AND
HIS DEVOTED WIFE
CATHERINE.

AT REST IN THE LORD. A.D., 1816."

From the church they went about their proper business, to interview a Mr. Pogram, of the firm of Pogram & Collet, solicitors, in whose hands the interests of many citizens of Transham and the country round were almost securely deposited. He occupied, curiously enough, the house where Edmund Morton himself had lived, conducting his works on the one hand and the squirearchy of the parish on the other. Incorporated now into the line of a long, loose street, it still stood rather apart from its neighbors, behind some large shrubs and trees of the holmoak variety.

Mr. Pogram, who was finishing his Sunday after-lunch cigar, was a short, clean-shaved man with strong cheeks and those rather lustful gray-blue eyes which accompany a sturdy figure. He rose when they were introduced, and, uncrossing his fat little thighs, asked what he could do for them.

Felix propounded the story of the arrest, so far as might be, in words of one syllable, avoiding the sentimental aspect of the question, and finding it hard to be on the side of disorder, as any modern writer might. There was something, however, about Mr. Pogram that reassured him. The small fellow looked a fighter—looked as if he would sympathize with Tryst's want of a woman about him. The tusky but soft-hearted little brute kept nodding his round, sparsely covered head while he listened, exuding a smell of lavender-water, cigars, and gutta-percha. When Felix ceased he said, rather dryly:

"Sir Gerald Malloring? Yes. Sir Gerald's country agents, I rather think, are Messrs. Porter of Worcester. Quite so."

And a conviction that Mr. Pogram thought they should have been Messrs. Pogram & Collet of Transham confirmed in Felix the feeling that they had come to the right man.

"I gather," Mr. Pogram said, and he looked at Nedda with a glance from which he obviously tried to remove all earthly desires, "that you, sir, and your nephew wish to go and see the man. Mrs. Pogram will be delighted to show Miss Freeland our garden. Your great-grandfather, sir, on the mother's side, lived in this house. Delighted to meet you; often heard of your books; Mrs. Pogram has read one—let me see—'The Bannister,' was it?"

"'The Balustrade,'" Felix answered gently.

Mr. Pogram rang the bell. "Quite so," he said. "Assizes are just over so that he can't come up for trial till August or September; pity—great pity! Bail in cases of arson—for a laborer, very doubtful! Ask your mistress to come, please."

There entered a faded rose of a woman on whom Mr. Pogram in his time had evidently made a great impression. A vista of two or three little Pograms behind her was hastily removed by the maid. And they all went into the garden.

"Through here," said Mr. Pogram, coming to a side door in the garden wall, "we can make a short cut to the police station. As we go along I shall ask you one or two blunt questions." And he thrust out his under lip:

"For instance, what's your interest in this matter?"

Before Felix could answer, Derek had broken in:

"My uncle has come out of kindness. It's my affair, sir. The man has been tyrannously treated."

Mr. Pogram cocked his eye. "Yes, yes; no doubt, no doubt! He's not confessed, I understand?"

"No; but—"

Mr. Pogram laid a finger on his lips.

"Never say die; that's what we're here for. So," he went on, "you're a rebel; Socialist, perhaps. Dear me! Well, we're all of us something, nowadays—I'm a humanitarian myself. Often say to Mrs. Pogram—humanity's the thing in this age—and so it is! Well, now, what line shall we take?" And he rubbed his hands. "Shall we have a try at once to upset what evidence they've got? We should want a strong alibi. Our friends here will commit if they can—nobody likes arson. I understand he was sleeping in your cottage. His room, now? Was it on the ground floor?"

"Yes; but—"

Mr. Pogram frowned, as who should say: Ah! Be careful! "He had better reserve his defence and give us time to turn round," he said rather shortly.

They had arrived at the police station and after a little parley were ushered into the presence of Tryst.

The big laborer was sitting on the stool in his cell, leaning back against the wall, his hands loose and open at his sides. His gaze passed at once from Felix and Mr. Pogram, who were in advance, to Derek; and the dumb soul seemed suddenly to look through, as one may see all there is of spirit in a dog reach out to its master. This was the first time Felix had seen him who had caused already so much anxiety, and that broad, almost brutal face, with the yearning fidelity in its tragic eyes, made a powerful impression on him. It was the sort of face one did not forget and might be glad of not remembering in dreams. What had put this yearning spirit into so gross a frame, destroying its solid coherence? Why could not Tryst have been left by nature just a beer-loving serf, devoid of grief for his dead wife, devoid of longing for the nearest he could get to her again, devoid of susceptibility to this young man's influence? And the thought of all that was before the mute creature, sitting there in heavy, hopeless patience, stung Felix's heart so that he could hardly bear to look him in the face.

Derek had taken the man's thick, brown hand; Felix could see with what effort the boy was biting back his feelings.

"This is Mr. Pogram, Bob. A solicitor who'll do all he can for you."

Felix looked at Mr. Pogram. The little man was standing with arms akimbo; his face the queerest mixture of shrewdness and compassion, and he was giving off an almost needlessly strong scent of gutta-percha.

"Yes, my man," he said, "you and I are going to have a talk when these gentlemen have done with you," and, turning on his heel, he began to touch up the points of his little pink nails with a penknife, in front of the constable who stood outside the cell door, with his professional air of giving a man a chance.

Invaded by a feeling, apt to come to him in Zoos, that he was watching a creature who had no chance to escape being watched, Felix also turned; but, though his eyes saw not, his ears could not help hearing.

"Forgive me, Bob! It's I who got you into this!"

"No, sir; naught to forgive. I'll soon be back, and then they'll see!"

By the reddening of Mr. Pogram's ears Felix formed the opinion that the little man, also, could hear.

"Tell her not to fret, Mr. Derek. I'd like a shirt, in case I've got to stop. The children needn' know where I be; though I an't ashamed."

"It may be a longer job than you think, Bob."

In the silence that followed Felix could not help turning. The laborer's eyes were moving quickly round his cell, as if for the first time he realized that he was shut up; suddenly he brought those big hands of his together and clasped them between his knees, and again his gaze ran round the cell. Felix heard the clearing of a throat close by, and, more than ever conscious of the scent of gutta-percha, grasped its connection with compassion in the heart of Mr. Pogram. He caught Derek's muttered, "Don't ever think we're forgetting you, Bob," and something that sounded like, "And don't ever say you did it." Then, passing Felix and the little lawyer, the boy went out. His head was held high, but tears were running down his cheeks. Felix followed.

A bank of clouds, gray-white, was rising just above the red-tiled roofs, but the sun still shone brightly. And the thought of the big laborer sitting there knocked and knocked at Felix's heart mournfully, miserably. He had a warmer feeling for his young nephew than he had ever had. Mr. Pogram rejoined them soon, and they walked on together,

"Well?" said Felix.

Mr. Pogram answered in a somewhat grumpy voice:

"Not guilty, and reserve defence. You have influence, young man! Dumb as a waiter. Poor devil!" And not another word did he say till they had re-entered his garden.

Here the ladies, surrounded by many little Pograms, were having tea. And seated next the little lawyer, whose eyes were fixed on Nedda, Felix was able to appreciate that in happier mood he exhaled almost exclusively the scent of lavender-water and cigars.

CHAPTER XXIII

On their way back to Becket, after the visit to Tryst, Felix and Nedda dropped Derek half-way on the road to Joyfields. They found that the Becket household already knew of the arrest. Woven into a dirge on the subject of 'the Land,' the last town doings, and adventures on golf courses, it formed the genial topic of the dinner-table; for the Bulgarian with his carbohydrates was already a wonder of the past. The Bigwigs of this week-end were quite a different lot from those of three weeks ago, and comparatively homogeneous, having only three different plans for settling the land question, none of which, fortunately, involved any more real disturbance of the existing state of things than the potato, brown-bread plan, for all were based on the belief held by the respectable press, and constructive portions of the community, that omelette can be made without breaking eggs. On one thing alone, the whole house party was agreed—the importance of the question. Indeed, a sincere conviction on this point was like the card one produces before one is admitted to certain functions. No one came to Becket without it; or, if he did, he begged, borrowed, or stole it the moment he smelled Clara's special pot-pourri in the hall; and, though he sometimes threw it out of the railway-carriage window in returning to town, there was nothing remarkable about that. The conversational debauch of the first night's dinner—and, alas! there were only two even at Becket during a week-end—had undoubtedly revealed the feeling, which had set in of late, that there was nothing really wrong with the condition of the agricultural laborer, the only trouble being that the unreasonable fellow did not stay on the land. It was believed that Henry Wiltram, in conjunction with Colonel Martlett, was on the point of promoting a policy for imposing penalties on those who attempted to leave it without good reason, such reason to be left to the discretion of impartial district boards, composed each of one laborer, one farmer, and one landowner, decision going by favor of majority. And though opinion was rather freely expressed that, since the voting would always be two to one against, this might trench on the liberty of the subject, many thought that the interests of the country were so much above this consideration that something of the sort would be found, after all, to be the best arrangement. The cruder early notions of resettling the land by fostering peasant proprietorship, with habitable houses and security of tenure, were already under a cloud, since it was more than suspected that they would interfere unduly with the game laws and other soundly vested interests. Mere penalization of those who (or whose fathers before them) had at great pains planted so much covert, enclosed so much common, and laid so much country down in grass was hardly a policy for statesmen. A section of the guests, and that perhaps strongest because most silent, distinctly favored this new departure of Henry Wiltram's. Coupled with his swinging corn tax, it was indubitably a stout platform.

A second section of the guests spoke openly in favor of Lord Settleham's policy of good-will. The whole thing, they thought, must be voluntary, and they did not see any reason why, if it were left to the kindness and good intentions of the landowner, there should be any land question at all. Boards would be formed in every county on which such model landowners as Sir Gerald Malloring, or Lord Settleham himself, would sit, to apply the principles of goodwill. Against this policy the only criticism was levelled by Felix. He could have agreed, he said, if he had not noticed that Lord Settleham, and nearly all landowners, were thoroughly satisfied with their existing good-will and averse to any changes in their education that might foster an increase of it. If—he asked—landowners were so full of good-will, and so satisfied that they could not be improved in that matter, why had they not already done what was now proposed, and settled the land question? He himself believed that the land question, like any other, was only capable of settlement through improvement in the spirit of all concerned, but he found it a little difficult to credit Lord Settleham and the rest of the landowners with sincerity in the matter so long as they were unconscious of any need for their own improvement. According to him, they wanted it both ways, and, so far as he could see, they meant to have it!

His use of the word sincere, in connection with Lord Settleham, was at once pounced on. He could not know Lord Settleham—one of the most sincere of men. Felix freely admitted that he did not, and hastened to explain that he did not question the—er—parliamentary sincerity of Lord Settleham and his followers. He only ventured to doubt whether they realized the hold that human nature had on them. His experience, he said, of the houses where they had been bred, and the seminaries where they had been trained, had convinced him that there was still a conspiracy on foot to blind Lord Settleham and those others concerning all this; and, since they were themselves part of the conspiracy, there was very little danger of their unmasking it. At this juncture Felix was felt to have exceeded the limit of fair criticism, and only that toleration toward literary men of a certain reputation, in country houses, as persons brought there to say clever and irresponsible things, prevented people from taking him seriously.

The third section of the guests, unquestionably more static than the others, confined themselves to pointing out that, though the land question was undoubtedly serious, nothing whatever would result from placing any further impositions upon landowners. For, after all, what was land? Simply capital invested in a certain way, and very poorly at that. And what was capital? Simply a means of causing wages to be paid. And whether they were paid to men who looked after birds and dogs, loaded your guns, beat your coverts, or drove you to the shoot, or paid to men who ploughed and fertilized the land, what did it matter? To dictate to a man to whom he was to pay wages was, in the last degree, un-English. Everybody knew the fate which had come, or was coming, upon capital. It was being driven out of the country by leaps and bounds—though, to be sure, it still perversely persisted in yielding every year a larger revenue by way of income tax. And it would be dastardly to take advantage of land just because it was the only sort of capital which could not fly the country in times of need. Stanley himself, though—as became a host—he spoke little and argued not at all, was distinctly of this faction; and Clara sometimes felt uneasy lest her efforts to focus at Becket all interest in the land question should not quite succeed in outweighing the passivity of her husband's attitude. But, knowing that it is bad policy to raise the whip too soon, she trusted to her genius to bring him 'with one run at the finish,' as they say, and was content to wait.

There was universal sympathy with the Mallorings. If a model landlord like Malloring had trouble with his people, who—who should be immune? Arson! It was the last word! Felix, who secretly shared Nedda's horror of the insensate cruelty of flames, listened, nevertheless, to the jubilation that they had caught the fellow, with profound disturbance. For the memory of the big laborer seated against the wall, his eyes haunting round his cell, quarrelled fiercely with his natural abhorrence of any kind of violence, and his equally natural dislike of what brought anxiety into his own life—and the life, almost as precious, of his little daughter. Scarcely a word of the evening's conversation but gave him in high degree the feeling: How glib all this is, how far from reality! How fatted up with shell after shell of comfort and security! What do these people know, what do they realize, of the pressure and beat of raw life that lies behind—what do even I, who have seen this prisoner, know? For us it's as simple as killing a rat that eats our corn, or a flea that sucks our blood. Arson! Destructive brute—lock him up! And something in Felix said: For order, for security, this may be necessary. But something also said: Our smug attitude is odious!

He watched his little daughter closely, and several times marked the color rush up in her face, and once could have sworn he saw tears in her eyes. If the temper of this talk were trying to him, hardened at a hundred dinner-tables, what must it be to a young and ardent creature! And he was relieved to find, on getting to the drawing-room, that she had slipped behind the piano and was chatting quietly with her Uncle John....

As to whether this or that man liked her, Nedda perhaps was not more ignorant than other women; and she had noted a certain warmth and twinkle in Uncle John's eyes the other evening, a certain rather jolly tendency to look at her when he should have been looking at the person to whom he was talking; so that she felt toward him a trustful kindliness not altogether unmingled with a sense that he was in that Office which controls the destinies of those who 'get into trouble.' The motives even of statesmen, they say, are mixed; how much more so, then, of girls in love! Tucked away behind a Steinway, which instinct told her was not for use, she looked up under her lashes at her uncle's still military figure and said softly:

"It was awfully good of you to come, too, Uncle John."

And John, gazing down at that round, dark head, and those slim, pretty, white shoulders, answered:

"Not at all—very glad to get a breath of fresh air."

And he stealthily tightened his white waistcoat—a rite neglected of late; the garment seemed to him at the moment unnecessarily loose.

"You have so much experience, Uncle. Do you think violent rebellion is ever justifiable?"

"I do not."

Nedda sighed. "I'm glad you think that," she murmured, "because I don't think it is, either. I do so want you to like Derek, Uncle John, because—it's a secret from nearly every one—he and I are engaged."

John jerked his head up a little, as though he had received a slight blow. The news was not palatable. He kept his form, however, and answered:

"Oh! Really! Ah!"

Nedda said still more softly: "Please don't judge him by the other night; he wasn't very nice then, I know."

John cleared his throat.

Instinct warned her that he agreed, and she said rather sadly:

"You see, we're both awfully young. It must be splendid to have experience."

Over John's face, with its double line between the brows, its double line in the thin cheeks, its single firm line of mouth beneath a gray moustache, there passed a little grimace.

"As to being young," he said, "that'll change for the—er—better only too fast."

What was it in this girl that reminded him of that one with whom he had lived but two years, and mourned fifteen? Was it her youth? Was it that quick way of lifting her eyes, and looking at him with such clear directness? Or the way her hair grew? Or what?

"Do you like the people here, Uncle John?"

The question caught John, as it were, between wind and water. Indeed, all her queries seemed to be trying to incite him to those wide efforts of mind which bring into use the philosophic nerve; and it was long since he had generalized afresh about either things or people, having fallen for many years past into the habit of reaching his opinions down out of some pigeonhole or other. To generalize was a youthful practice that one took off as one takes certain garments off babies when they come to years of discretion. But since he seemed to be in for it, he answered rather shortly: "Not at all."

Nedda sighed again.

"Nor do I. They make me ashamed of myself."

John, whose dislike of the Bigwigs was that of the dogged worker of this life for the dogged talkers, wrinkled his brows:

"How's that?"

"They make me feel as if I were part of something heavy sitting on something else, and all the time talking about how to make things lighter for the thing it's sitting on."

A vague recollection of somebody—some writer, a dangerous one—having said something of this sort flitted through John.

"Do YOU think England is done for, Uncle—I mean about 'the Land'?"

In spite of his conviction that 'the country was in a bad way,' John was deeply, intimately shocked by that simple little question. Done for! Never! Whatever might be happening underneath, there must be no confession of that. No! the country would keep its form. The country would breathe through its nose, even if it did lose the race. It must never know, or let others know, even if it were beaten. And he said:

"What on earth put that into your head?"

"Only that it seems funny, if we're getting richer and richer, and yet all the time farther and farther away from the life that every one agrees is the best for health and happiness. Father put it into my head, making me look at the little, towny people in Transham this afternoon. I know I mean to begin at once to learn about farm work."

"You?" This pretty young thing with the dark head and the pale, slim shoulders! Farm work! Women were certainly getting queer. In his department he had almost daily evidence of that!

"I should have thought art was more in your line!"

Nedda looked up at him; and he was touched by that look, so straight and young.

"It's this. I don't believe Derek will be able to stay in England. When you feel very strongly about things it must be awfully difficult to."

In bewilderment John answered:

"Why! I should have said this was the country of all others for movements, and social work, and—and—cranks—" he paused.

"Yes; but those are all for curing the skin, and I suppose we're really dying of heart disease, aren't we? Derek feels that, anyway, and, you see, he's not a bit wise, not even patient—so I expect he'll have to go. I mean to be ready, anyway."

And Nedda got up. "Only, if he does something rash, don't let them hurt him, Uncle John, if you can help it."

John felt her soft fingers squeezing his almost desperately, as if her emotions had for the moment got out of hand. And he was moved, though he knew that the squeeze expressed feeling for his nephew, not for himself. When she slid away out of the big room all friendliness seemed to go out with her, and very soon after he himself slipped away to the smoking-room. There he was alone, and, lighting a cigar, because he still had on his long-tailed coat which did not go with that pipe he would so much have preferred, he stepped out of the French window into the warm, dark night. He walked slowly in his evening pumps up a thin path between columbines and peonies, late tulips, forget-me-nots, and pansies peering up in the dark with queer, monkey faces. He had a love for flowers, rather starved for a long time past, and, strangely, liked to see them, not in the set and orderly masses that should seemingly have gone with his character, but in wilder beds, where one never knew what flower was coming next. Once or twice he stopped and bent down, ascertaining which kind it was, living its little life down there, then passed on in that mood of stammering thought which besets men of middle age who walk at night—a mood caught between memory of aspirations spun and over, and vision of aspirations that refuse to take shape. Why should they, any more—what was the use? And turning down another path he came on something rather taller than himself, that glowed in the darkness as though a great moon, or some white round body, had floated to within a few feet of the earth. Approaching, he saw it for what it was—a little magnolia-tree in the full of its white blossoms. Those clustering flower-stars, printed before him on the dark coat of the night, produced in John more feeling than should have been caused by a mere magnolia-tree; and he smoked somewhat furiously. Beauty, seeking whom it should upset, seemed, like a girl, to stretch out arms and say: "I am here!" And with a pang at heart, and a long ash on his cigar, between lips that quivered oddly, John turned on his heel and retraced his footsteps to the smoking-room. It was still deserted. Taking up a Review, he opened it at an article on 'the Land,' and, fixing his eyes on the first page, did not read it, but thought: 'That child! What folly! Engaged! H'm! To that young—! Why, they're babes! And what is it about her that reminds me—reminds me—What is it? Lucky devil, Felix—to have her for daughter! Engaged! The little thing's got her troubles before her. Wish I had! By George, yes—wish I had!' And with careful fingers he brushed off the ash that had fallen on his lapel....

The little thing who had her troubles before her, sitting in her bedroom window, had watched his white front and the glowing point of his cigar passing down there in the dark, and, though she did not know that they belonged to him, had thought: 'There's some one nice, anyway, who likes being out instead of in that stuffy drawing-room, playing bridge, and talking, talking.' Then she felt ashamed of her uncharitableness. After all, it was wrong to think of them like that. They did it for rest after all their hard work; and she—she did not work at all! If only Aunt Kirsteen would let her stay at Joyfields, and teach her all that Sheila knew! And lighting her candles, she opened her diary to write.

"Life," she wrote, "is like looking at the night. One never knows what's coming, only suspects, as in the darkness you suspect which trees are what, and try to see whether you are coming to the edge of anything.... A moth has just flown into my candle before I could stop it! Has it gone quite out of the world? If so, why should it be different for us? The same great Something makes all life and death, all light and dark, all love and hate—then why one fate for one living thing, and the opposite for another? But suppose there IS nothing after death—would it make me say: 'I'd rather not live'? It would only make me delight more in life of every kind. Only human beings brood and are discontented, and trouble about future life. While Derek and I were sitting in that field this morning, a bumblebee flew to the bank and tucked its head into the grass and went to sleep, just tired out with flying and working at its flowers; it simply snoozed its head down and went off. We ought to live every minute to the utmost, and when we're tired out, tuck in our heads and sleep.... If only Derek is not brooding over that poor man! Poor man—all alone in the dark, with months of misery before him! Poor soul! Oh! I am sorry for all the unhappiness of people! I can't bear to think of it. I simply can't." And dropping her pen, Nedda went again to her window and leaned out. So sweet the air smelled that it made her ache with delight to breathe it in. Each leaf that lived out there, each flower, each blade of grass, were sworn to conspiracy of perfume. And she thought: 'They MUST all love each other; it all goes together so beautifully!' Then, mingled with the incense of the night, she caught the savor of woodsmoke. It seemed to make the whole scent even more delicious, but she thought, bewildered: 'Smoke! Cruel fire—burning the wood that once grew leaves like those. Oh! it IS so mixed!' It was a thought others have had before her.

CHAPTER XXIV

To see for himself how it fared with the big laborer at the hands of Preliminary Justice, Felix went into Transham with Stanley the following morning. John having departed early for town, the brothers had not further exchanged sentiments on the subject of what Stanley called 'the kick-up at Joyfields.' And just as night will sometimes disperse the brooding moods of nature, so it had brought to all three the feeling: 'Haven't we made too much of this? Haven't we been a little extravagant, and aren't we rather bored with the whole subject?' Arson was arson; a man in prison more or less was a man in prison more or less! This was especially Stanley's view, and he took the opportunity to say to Felix: "Look here, old man, the thing is, of course, to see it in proportion."

It was with this intention, therefore, that Felix entered the building where the justice of that neighborhood was customarily dispensed. It was a species of small hall, somewhat resembling a chapel, with distempered walls, a platform, and benches for the public, rather well filled that morning—testimony to the stir the little affair had made. Felix, familiar with the appearance of London police courts, noted the efforts that had been made to create resemblance to those models of administration. The justices of the peace, hastily convoked and four in number, sat on the platform, with a semicircular backing of high gray screens and a green baize barrier in front of them, so that their legs and feet were quite invisible. In this way had been preserved the really essential feature of all human justice—at whose feet it is well known one must not look! Their faces, on the contrary, were entirely exposed to view, and presented that pleasing variety of type and unanimity of expression peculiar to men keeping an open mind. Below them, with his face toward the public, was placed a gray-bearded man at a table also covered with green baize, that emblem of authority. And to the side, at right angles, raised into the air, sat a little terrier of a man, with gingery, wired hair, obviously the more articulate soul of these proceedings. As Felix sat down to worship, he noticed Mr. Pogram at the green baize table, and received from the little man a nod and the faintest whiff of lavender and gutta-percha. The next moment he caught sight of Derek and Sheila, screwed sideways against one of the distempered walls, looking, with their frowning faces, for all the world like two young devils just turned out of hell. They did not greet him, and Felix set to work to study the visages of Justice. They impressed him, on the whole, more favorably than he had expected. The one to his extreme left, with a gray-whiskered face, was like a large and sleepy cat of mature age, who moved not, except to write a word now and then on the paper before him, or to hand back a document. Next to him, a man of middle age with bald forehead and dark, intelligent eyes seemed conscious now and again of the body of the court, and Felix thought: 'You have not been a magistrate long.' The chairman, who sat next, with the moustache of a heavy dragoon and gray hair parted in the middle, seemed, on the other hand, oblivious of the public, never once looking at them, and speaking so that they could not hear him, and Felix thought: 'You have been a magistrate too long.' Between him and the terrier man, the last of the four wrote diligently, below a clean, red face with clipped white moustache and little peaked beard. And Felix thought: 'Retired naval!' Then he saw that they were bringing in Tryst. The big laborer advanced between two constables, his broad, unshaven face held high, and his lowering eyes, through which his strange and tragical soul seemed looking, turned this way and that. Felix, who, no more than any one else, could keep his gaze off the trapped creature, felt again all the sensations of the previous afternoon.

"Guilty? or, Not guilty?" As if repeating something learned by heart, Tryst answered: "Not guilty, sir." And his big hands, at his sides, kept clenching and unclenching. The witnesses, four in number, began now to give their testimony. A sergeant of police recounted how he had been first summoned to the scene of burning, and afterward arrested Tryst; Sir Gerald's agent described the eviction and threats uttered by the evicted man; two persons, a stone-breaker and a tramp, narrated that they had seen him going in the direction of the rick and barn at five o'clock, and coming away therefrom at five-fifteen. Punctuated by the barking of the terrier clerk, all this took time, during which there passed through Felix many thoughts. Here was a man who had done a wicked, because an antisocial, act; the sort of act no sane person could defend; an act so barbarous, stupid, and unnatural that the very beasts of the field would turn noses away from it! How was it, then, that he himself could not feel incensed? Was it that in habitually delving into the motives of men's actions he had lost the power of dissociating what a man did from what he was; had come to see him, with his thoughts, deeds, and omissions, as a coherent growth? And he looked at Tryst. The big laborer was staring with all his soul at Derek. And, suddenly, he saw his nephew stand up—tilt his dark head back against the wall—and open his mouth to speak. In sheer alarm Felix touched Mr. Pogram on the arm. The little square man had already turned; he looked at that moment extremely like a frog.

"Gentlemen, I wish to say—"

"Who are you? Sit down!" It was the chairman, speaking for the first time in a voice that could be heard.

"I wish to say that he is not responsible. I—"

"Silence! Silence, sir! Sit down!"

Felix saw his nephew waver, and Sheila pulling at his sleeve; then, to his infinite relief, the boy sat down. His sallow face was red; his thin lips compressed to a white line. And slowly under the eyes of the whole court he grew deadly pale.

Distracted by fear that the boy might make another scene, Felix followed the proceedings vaguely. They were over soon enough: Tryst committed, defence reserved, bail refused—all as Mr. Pogram had predicted.

Derek and Sheila had vanished, and in the street outside, idle at this hour of a working-day, were only the cars of the four magistrates; two or three little knots of those who had been in court, talking of the case; and in the very centre of the street, an old, dark-whiskered man, lame, and leaning on a stick.

"Very nearly being awkward," said the voice of Mr. Pogram in his ear. "I say, do you think—no hand himself, surely no real hand himself?"

Felix shook his head violently. If the thought had once or twice occurred to him, he repudiated it with all his force when shaped by another's mouth—and such a mouth, so wide and rubbery!

"No, no! Strange boy! Extravagant sense of honour—too sensitive, that's all!"

"Quite so," murmured Mr. Pogram soothingly. "These young people! We live in a queer age, Mr. Freeland. All sorts of ideas about, nowadays. Young men like that—better in the army—safe in the army. No ideas there!"

"What happens now?" said Felix.

"Wait!" said Mr. Pogram. "Nothing else for it—wait. Three months—twiddle his thumbs. Bad system! Rotten!"

"And suppose in the end he's proved innocent?"

Mr. Pogram shook his little round head, whose ears were very red.

"Ah!" he said: "Often say to my wife: 'Wish I weren't a humanitarian!' Heart of india-rubber—excellent thing—the greatest blessing. Well, good-morning! Anything you want to say at any time, let me know!" And exhaling an overpowering whiff of gutta-percha, he grasped Felix's hand and passed into a house on the door of which was printed in brazen letters: "Edward Pogram, James Collet. Solicitors. Agents."

On leaving the little humanitarian, Felix drifted back toward the court. The cars were gone, the groups dispersed; alone, leaning on his stick, the old, dark-whiskered man stood like a jackdaw with a broken wing. Yearning, at that moment, for human intercourse, Felix went up to him.

"Fine day," he said.

"Yes, sir, 'tis fine enough." And they stood silent, side by side. The gulf fixed by class and habit between soul and human soul yawned before Felix as it had never before. Stirred and troubled, he longed to open his heart to this old, ragged, dark-eyed, whiskered creature with the game leg, who looked as if he had passed through all the thorns and thickets of hard and primitive existence; he longed that the old fellow should lay bare to him his heart. And for the life of him he could not think of any mortal words which might bridge the unreal gulf between them. At last he said:

"You a native here?"

"No, sir. From over Malvern way. Livin' here with my darter, owin' to my leg. Her 'usband works in this here factory."

"And I'm from London," Felix said.

"Thart you were. Fine place, London, they say!"

Felix shook his head. "Not so fine as this Worcestershire of yours."

The old man turned his quick, dark gaze. "Aye!" he said, "people'll be a bit nervy-like in towns, nowadays. The country be a good place for a healthy man, too; I don't want no better place than the country—never could abide bein' shut in."

"There aren't so very many like you, judging by the towns."

The old man smiled—that smile was the reverse of a bitter tonic coated with sweet stuff to make it palatable.

"'Tes the want of a life takes 'em," he said. "There's not a many like me. There's not so many as can't do without the smell of the earth. With these 'ere newspapers—'tesn't taught nowadays. The boys and gells they goes to school, and 'tes all in favor of the towns there. I can't work no more; I'm 's good as gone meself; but I feel sometimes I'll 'ave to go back. I don't like the streets, an' I guess 'tes worse in London."

"Ah! Perhaps," Felix said, "there are more of us like you than you think."

Again the old man turned his dark, quick glance.

"Well, an' I widden say no to that, neither. I've seen 'em terrible homesick. 'Tes certain sure there's lots would never go, ef 'twasn't so mortial hard on the land. 'Tisn't a bare livin', after that. An' they're put upon, right and left they're put upon. 'Tes only a man here and there that 'as something in 'im too strong. I widden never 'ave stayed in the country ef 'twasn't that I couldn't stand the town life. 'Tes like some breeds o' cattle—you take an' put 'em out o' their own country, an' you 'ave to take an' put 'em back again. Only some breeds, though. Others they don' mind where they go. Well, I've seen the country pass in my time, as you might say; where you used to see three men you only see one now."

"Are they ever going back onto the land?"

"They tark about it. I read my newspaper reg'lar. In some places I see they're makin' unions. That an't no good."

"Why?"

The old man smiled again.

"Why! Think of it! The land's different to anythin' else—that's why! Different work, different hours, four men's work to-day and one's to-morrow. Work land wi' unions, same as they've got in this 'ere factory, wi' their eight hours an' their do this an' don' do that? No! You've got no weather in factories, an' such-like. On the land 'tes a matter o' weather. On the land a man must be ready for anythin' at any time; you can't work it no other way. 'Tes along o' God's comin' into it; an' no use pullin' this way an' that. Union says to me: You mustn't work after hours. Hoh! I've 'ad to set up all night wi' ship an' cattle hundreds o' times, an' no extra for it. 'Tes not that way they'll do any good to keep people on the land. Oh, no!"

"How, then?"

"Well, you'll want new laws, o' course, to prevent farmers an' landowners takin' their advantage; you want laws to build new cottages; but mainly 'tes a case of hands together; can't be no other—the land's so ticklish. If 'tesn't hands together, 'tes nothing. I 'ad a master once that was never content so long's we wasn't content. That farm was better worked than any in the parish."

"Yes, but the difficulty is to get masters that can see the other side; a man doesn't care much to look at home."

The old man's dark eyes twinkled.

"No; an' when 'e does, 'tes generally to say: 'Lord, an' I right, an' an't they wrong, just?' That's powerful customary!"

"It is," said Felix; "God bless us all!"

"Ah! You may well say that, sir; an' we want it, too. A bit more wages wouldn't come amiss, neither. An' a bit more freedom; 'tes a man's liberty 'e prizes as well as money."

"Did you hear about this arson case?"

The old man cast a glance this way and that before he answered in a lower voice:

"They say 'e was put out of his cottage. I've seen men put out for votin' Liberal; I've seen 'em put out for free-thinkin'; all sorts o' things I seen em put out for. 'Tes that makes the bad blood. A man wants to call 'is soul 'is own, when all's said an' done. An' 'e can't, not in th' old country, unless 'e's got the dibs."

"And yet you never thought of emigrating?"

"Thart of it—ah! thart of it hundreds o' times; but some'ow cudden never bring mysel' to the scratch o' not seein' th' Beacon any more. I can just see it from 'ere, you know. But there's not so many like me, an' gettin' fewer every day."

"Yes," murmured Felix, "that I believe."

"'Tes a 'and-made piece o' goods—the land! You has to be fond of it, same as of your missis and yer chillen. These poor pitiful fellows that's workin' in this factory, makin' these here Colonial ploughs—union's all right for them—'tes all mechanical; but a man on the land, 'e's got to put the land first, whether 'tes his own or some one else's, or he'll never do no good; might as well go for a postman, any day. I'm keepin' of you, though, with my tattle!"

In truth, Felix had looked at the old man, for the accursed question had begun to worry him: Ought he or not to give the lame old fellow something? Would it hurt his feelings? Why could he not say simply: 'Friend, I'm better off than you; help me not to feel so unfairly favored'? Perhaps he might risk it. And, diving into his trousers pockets, he watched the old man's eyes. If they followed his hand, he would risk it. But they did not. Withdrawing his hand, he said:

"Have a cigar?"

The old fellow's dark face twinkled.

"I don' know," he said, "as I ever smoked one; but I can have a darned old try!"

"Take the lot," said Felix, and shuffled into the other's pocket the contents of his cigar-case. "If you get through one, you'll want the rest. They're pretty good."

"Ah!" said the old man. "Shuldn' wonder, neither."

"Good-by. I hope your leg will soon be better."

"Thank 'ee, sir. Good-by, thank 'ee!"

Looking back from the turning, Felix saw him still standing there in the middle of the empty street.

Having undertaken to meet his mother, who was returning this afternoon to Becket, he had still two hours to put away, and passing Mr. Pogram's house, he turned into a path across a clover-field and sat down on a stile. He had many thoughts, sitting at the foot of this little town—which his great-grandfather had brought about. And chiefly he thought of the old man he had been talking to, sent there, as it seemed to him, by Providence, to afford a prototype for his 'The Last of the Laborers.' Wonderful that the old fellow should talk of loving 'the Land,' whereon he must have toiled for sixty years or so, at a number of shillings per week, that would certainly not buy the cigars he had shovelled into that ragged pocket. Wonderful! And yet, a marvellous sweet thing, when all was said—this land! Changing its sheen and texture, the feel of its air, its very scent, from day to day. This land with myriad offspring of flowers and flying folk; the majestic and untiring march of seasons: Spring and its wistful ecstasy of saplings, and its yearning, wild, wind-loosened heart; gleam and song, blossom and cloud, and the swift white rain; each upturned leaf so little and so glad to flutter; each wood and field so full of peeping things! Summer! Ah! Summer, when on the solemn old trees the long days shone and lingered, and the glory of the meadows and the murmur of life and the scent of flowers bewildered tranquillity, till surcharge of warmth and beauty brooded into dark passion, and broke! And Autumn, in mellow haze down on the fields and woods; smears of gold already on the beeches, smears of crimson on the rowans, the apple-trees still burdened, and a flax-blue sky well-nigh merging with the misty air; the cattle browsing in the lingering golden stillness; not a breath to fan the blue smoke of the weed-fires—and in the fields no one moving—who would disturb such mellow peace? And Winter! The long spaces, the long dark; and yet—and yet, what delicate loveliness of twig tracery; what blur of rose and brown and purple caught in the bare boughs and in the early sunset sky! What sharp dark flights of birds in the gray-white firmament! Who cared what season held in its arms this land that had bred them all!

Not wonderful that into the veins of those who nursed it, tending, watching its perpetual fertility, should be distilled a love so deep and subtle that they could not bear to leave it, to abandon its hills, and greenness, and bird-songs, and all the impress of their forefathers throughout the ages.

Like so many of his fellows—cultured moderns, alien to the larger forms of patriotism, that rich liquor brewed of maps and figures, commercial profit, and high-cockalorum, which served so perfectly to swell smaller heads—Felix had a love of his native land resembling love for a woman, a kind of sensuous chivalry, a passion based on her charm, on her tranquillity, on the power she had to draw him into her embrace, to make him feel that he had come from her, from her alone, and into her alone was going back. And this green parcel of his native land, from which the half of his blood came, and that the dearest half, had a potency over his spirit that he might well be ashamed of in days when the true Briton was a town-bred creature with a foot of fancy in all four corners of the globe. There was ever to him a special flavor about the elm-girt fields, the flowery coppices, of this country of the old Moretons, a special fascination in its full, white-clouded skies, its grass-edged roads, its pied and creamy cattle, and the blue-green loom of the Malvern hills. If God walked anywhere for him, it was surely here. Sentiment! Without sentiment, without that love, each for his own corner, 'the Land' was lost indeed! Not if all Becket blew trumpets till kingdom came, would 'the Land' be reformed, if they lost sight of that! To fortify men in love for their motherland, to see that insecurity, grinding poverty, interference, petty tyranny, could no longer undermine that love—this was to be, surely must be, done! Monotony? Was that cry true? What work now performed by humble men was less monotonous than work on the land? What work was even a tenth part so varied? Never quite the same from day to day: Now weeding, now hay, now roots, now hedging; now corn, with sowing, reaping, threshing, stacking, thatching; the care of beasts, and their companionship; sheep-dipping, shearing, wood-gathering, apple-picking, cider-making; fashioning and tarring gates; whitewashing walls; carting; trenching—never, never two days quite the same! Monotony! The poor devils in factories, in shops, in mines; poor devils driving 'busses, punching tickets, cleaning roads; baking; cooking; sewing; typing! Stokers; machine-tenders; brick-layers; dockers; clerks! Ah! that great company from towns might well cry out: Monotony! True, they got their holidays; true, they had more social life—a point that might well be raised at Becket: Holidays and social life for men on the soil! But—and suddenly Felix thought of the long, long holiday that was before the laborer Tryst. 'Twiddle his thumbs'—in the words of the little humanitarian—twiddle his thumbs in a space twelve feet by seven! No sky to see, no grass to smell, no beast to bear him company; no anything—for, what resources in himself had this poor creature? No anything, but to sit with tragic eyes fixed on the wall before him for eighty days and eighty nights, before they tried him. And then— not till then—would his punishment for that moment's blind revenge for grievous wrong begin! What on this earth of God's was more disproportioned, and wickedly extravagant, more crassly stupid, than the arrangements of his most perfect creature, man? What a devil was man, who could yet rise to such sublime heights of love and heroism! What a ferocious brute, the most ferocious and cold-blooded brute that lived! Of all creatures most to be stampeded by fear into a callous torturer! 'Fear'—thought Felix—'fear! Not momentary panic, such as makes our brother animals do foolish things; conscious, calculating fear, paralyzing the reason of our minds and the generosity of our hearts. A detestable thing Tryst has done, a hateful act; but his punishment will be twentyfold as hateful!'

And, unable to sit and think of it, Felix rose and walked on through the fields....

CHAPTER XXV

He was duly at Transham station in time for the London train, and, after a minute consecrated to looking in the wrong direction, he saw his mother already on the platform with her bag, an air-cushion, and a beautifully neat roll.

'Travelling third!' he thought. 'Why will she do these things?'

Slightly flushed, she kissed Felix with an air of abstraction.

"How good of you to meet me, darling!"

Felix pointed in silence to the crowded carriage from which she had emerged. Frances Freeland looked a little rueful. "It would have been delightful," she said. "There was a dear baby there and, of course, I couldn't have the window down, so it WAS rather hot."

Felix, who could just see the dear baby, said dryly:

"So that's how you go about, is it? Have you had any lunch?"

Frances Freeland put her hand under his arm. "Now, don't fuss, darling! Here's sixpence for the porter. There's only one trunk—it's got a violet label. Do you know them? They're so useful. You see them at once. I must get you some."

"Let me take those things. You won't want this cushion. I'll let the air out."

"I'm afraid you won't be able, dear. It's quite the best screw I've ever come across—a splendid thing; I can't get it undone."

"Ah!" said Felix. "And now we may as well go out to the car!"

He was conscious of a slight stoppage in his mother's footsteps and rather a convulsive squeeze of her hand on his arm. Looking at her face, he discovered it occupied with a process whose secret he could not penetrate, a kind of disarray of her features, rapidly and severely checked, and capped with a resolute smile. They had already reached the station exit, where Stanley's car was snorting. Frances Freeland looked at it, then, mounting rather hastily, sat, compressing her lips.

When they were off, Felix said:

"Would you like to stop at the church and have a look at the brasses to your grandfather and the rest of them?"

His mother, who had slipped her hand under his arm again, answered:

"No, dear; I've seen them. The church is not at all beautiful. I like the old church at Becket so much better; it is such a pity your great-grandfather was not buried there."

She had never quite got over the lack of 'niceness' about those ploughs.

Going, as was the habit of Stanley's car, at considerable speed, Felix was not at first certain whether the peculiar little squeezes his arm was getting were due to the bounds of the creature under them or to some cause more closely connected with his mother, and it was not till they shaved a cart at the turning of the Becket drive that it suddenly dawned on him that she was in terror. He discovered it in looking round just as she drew her smile over a spasm of her face and throat. And, leaning out of the car, he said:

"Drive very slowly, Batter; I want to look at the trees."

A little sigh rewarded him. Since SHE had said nothing, He said nothing, and Clara's words in the hall seemed to him singularly tactless:

"Oh! I meant to have reminded you, Felix, to send the car back and take a fly. I thought you knew that Mother's terrified of motors." And at his mother's answer:

"Oh! no; I quite enjoyed it, dear," he thought: 'Bless her heart! She IS a stoic!'

Whether or no to tell her of the 'kick-up at Joyfields' exercised his mind. The question was intricate, for she had not yet been informed that Nedda and Derek were engaged, and Felix did not feel at liberty to forestall the young people. That was their business. On the other hand, she would certainly glean from Clara a garbled understanding of the recent events at Joyfields, if she were not first told of them by himself. And he decided to tell her, with the natural trepidation of one who, living among principles and theories, never quite knew what those, for whom each fact is unrelated to anything else under the moon, were going to think. Frances Freeland, he knew well, kept facts and theories especially unrelated, or, rather, modified her facts to suit her theories, instead of, like Felix, her theories to suit her facts. For example, her instinctive admiration for Church and State, her instinctive theory that they rested on gentility and people who were nice, was never for a moment shaken when she saw a half-starved baby of the slums. Her heart would impel her to pity and feed the poor little baby if she could, but to correlate the creature with millions of other such babies, and those millions with the Church and State, would not occur to her. And if Felix made an attempt to correlate them for her she would look at him and think: 'Dear boy! How good he is! I do wish he wouldn't let that line come in his forehead; it does so spoil it!' And she would say: "Yes, darling, I know, it's very sad; only I'm NOT clever." And, if a Liberal government chanced to be in power, would add: "Of course, I do think this Government is dreadful. I MUST show you a sermon of the dear Bishop of Walham. I cut it out of the 'Daily Mystery.' He puts things so well—he always has such nice ideas."

And Felix, getting up, would walk a little and sit down again too suddenly. Then, as if entreating him to look over her want of 'cleverness,' she would put out a hand that, for all its whiteness, had never been idle and smooth his forehead. It had sometimes touched him horribly to see with what despair she made attempts to follow him in his correlating efforts, and with what relief she heard him cease enough to let her say: "Yes, dear; only, I must show you this new kind of expanding cork. It's simply splendid. It bottles up everything!" And after staring at her just a moment he would acquit her of irony. Very often after these occasions he had thought, and sometimes said: "Mother, you're the best Conservative I ever met." She would glance at him then, with a special loving doubtfulness, at a loss as to whether or no he had designed to compliment her.

When he had given her half an hour to rest he made his way to the blue corridor, where a certain room was always kept for her, who never occupied it long enough at a time to get tired of it. She was lying on a sofa in a loose gray cashmere gown. The windows were open, and the light breeze just moved in the folds of the chintz curtains and stirred perfume from a bowl of pinks—her favorite flowers. There was no bed in this bedroom, which in all respects differed from any other in Clara's house, as though the spirit of another age and temper had marched in and dispossessed the owner. Felix had a sensation that one was by no means all body here. On the contrary. There was not a trace of the body anywhere; as if some one had decided that the body was not quite nice. No bed, no wash-stand, no chest of drawers, no wardrobe, no mirror, not even a jar of Clara's special pot-pourri. And Felix said:

"This can't be your bedroom, Mother?"

Frances Freeland answered, with a touch of deprecating quizzicality:

"Oh yes, darling. I must show you my arrangements." And she rose. "This," she said, "you see, goes under there, and that under here; and that again goes under this. Then they all go under that, and then I pull this. It's lovely."

"But why?" said Felix.

"Oh! but don't you see? It's so nice; nobody can tell. And it doesn't give any trouble."

"And when you go to bed?"

"Oh! I just pop my clothes into this and open that. And there I am. It's simply splendid."

"I see," said Felix. "Do you think I might sit down, or shall I go through?"

Frances Freeland loved him with her eyes, and said:

"Naughty boy!"

And Felix sat down on what appeared to be a window-seat.

"Well," he said, with slight uneasiness, for she was hovering, "I think you're wonderful."

Frances Freeland put away an impeachment that she evidently felt to be too soft.

"Oh! but it's all so simple, darling." And Felix saw that she had something in her hand, and mind.

"This is my little electric brush. It'll do wonders with your hair. While you sit there, I'll just try it."

A clicking and a whirring had begun to occur close to his ear, and something darted like a gadfly at his scalp.

"I came to tell you something serious, Mother."

"Yes, darling; it'll be simply lovely to hear it; and you mustn't mind this, because it really is a first-rate thing—quite new."

Now, how is it, thought Felix, that any one who loves the new as she does, when it's made of matter, will not even look at it when it's made of mind? And, while the little machine buzzed about his head, he proceeded to detail to her the facts of the state of things that existed at Joyfields.

When he had finished, she said:

"Now, darling, bend down a little."

Felix bent down. And the little machine began severely tweaking the hairs on the nape of his neck. He sat up again rather suddenly.

Frances Freeland was contemplating the little machine.

"How very provoking! It's never done that before!"

"Quite so!" Felix murmured. "But about Joyfields?"

"Oh, my dear, it IS such a pity they don't get on with those Mallorings! I do think it sad they weren't brought up to go to church."

Felix stared, not knowing whether to be glad or sorry that his recital had not roused within her the faintest suspicion of disaster. How he envied her that single-minded power of not seeing further than was absolutely needful! And suddenly he thought: 'She really is wonderful! With her love of church, how it must hurt her that we none of us go, not even John! And yet she never says a word. There really is width about her; a power of accepting the inevitable. Never was woman more determined to make the best of a bad job. It's a great quality!' And he heard her say:

"Now, darling, if I give you this, you must promise me to use it every morning. You'll find you'll soon have a splendid crop of little young hairs."

"I know," he said gloomily; "but they won't come to anything. Age has got my head, Mother, just as it's got 'the Land's.'"

"Oh, nonsense! You must go on with it, that's all!"

Felix turned so that he could look at her. She was moving round the room now, meticulously adjusting the framed photographs of her family that were the only decoration of the walls. How formal, chiselled, and delicate her face, yet how almost fanatically decisive! How frail and light her figure, yet how indomitably active! And the memory assailed him of how, four years ago, she had defeated double pneumonia without having a doctor, simply by lying on her back. 'She leaves trouble,' he thought, 'until it's under her nose, then simply tells it that it isn't there. There's something very English about that.'

She was chasing a bluebottle now with a little fan made of wire, and, coming close to Felix, said:

"Have you seen these, darling? You've only to hit the fly and it kills him at once."

"But do you ever hit the fly?"

"Oh, yes!" And she waved the fan at the bluebottle, which avoided it without seeming difficulty.

"I can't bear hurting them, but I DON'T like flies. There!"

The bluebottle flew out of the window behind Felix and in at the one that was not behind him. He rose.

"You ought to rest before tea, Mother."

He felt her searching him with her eyes, as if trying desperately to find something she might bestow upon or do for him.

"Would you like this wire—"

With a feeling that he was defrauding love, he turned and fled. She would never rest while he was there! And yet there was that in her face which made him feel a brute to go.

Passing out of the house, sunk in its Monday hush, no vestige of a Bigwig left, Felix came to that new-walled mound where the old house of the Moretons had been burned 'by soldiers from Tewkesbury and Gloucester,' as said the old chronicles dear to the heart of Clara. And on the wall he sat him down.

Above, in the uncut grass, he could see the burning blue of a peacock's breast, where the heraldic bird stood digesting grain in the repose of perfect breeding, and below him gardeners were busy with the gooseberries. 'Gardeners and the gooseberries of the great!' he thought. 'Such is the future of our Land.' And he watched them. How methodically they went to work! How patient and well-done-for they looked! After all, was it not the ideal future? Gardeners, gooseberries, and the great! Each of the three content in that station of life into which—! What more could a country want? Gardeners, gooseberries, and the great! The phrase had a certain hypnotic value. Why trouble? Why fuss? Gardeners, gooseberries, and the great! A perfect land! A land dedicate to the week-end! Gardeners, goose—! And suddenly he saw that he was not alone. Half hidden by the angle of the wall, on a stone of the foundations, carefully preserved and nearly embedded in the nettles which Clara had allowed to grow because they added age to the appearance, was sitting a Bigwig. One of the Settleham faction, he had impressed Felix alike by his reticence, the steady sincerity of his gray eyes, a countenance that, beneath a simple and delicate urbanity, had still in it something of the best type of schoolboy. 'How comes he to have stayed?' he mused. 'I thought they always fed and scattered!' And having received an answer to his salutation, he moved across and said:

"I imagined you'd gone."

"I've been having a look round. It's very jolly here. My affections are in the North, but I suppose this is pretty well the heart of England."

"Near 'the big song,'" Felix answered. "There'll never be anything more English than Shakespeare, when all's said and done." And he took a steady, sidelong squint at his companion. 'This is another of the types I've been looking for,' he reflected. The peculiar 'don't-quite-touch-me' accent of the aristocrat—and of those who would be—had almost left this particular one, as though he secretly aspired to rise superior and only employed it in the nervousness of his first greetings. 'Yes,' thought Felix, 'he's just about the very best we can do among those who sit upon 'the Land.' I would wager there's not a better landlord nor a better fellow in all his class, than this one. He's chalks away superior to Malloring, if I know anything of faces—would never have turned poor Tryst out. If this exception were the rule! And yet—! Does he, can he, go quite far enough to meet the case? If not—what hope of regeneration from above? Would he give up his shooting? Could he give up feeling he's a leader? Would he give up his town house and collecting whatever it is he collects? Could he let himself sink down and merge till he was just unseen leaven of good-fellowship and good-will, working in the common bread?' And squinting at that sincere, clean, charming, almost fine face, he answered himself unwillingly: 'He could not!' And suddenly he knew that he was face to face with the tremendous question which soon or late confronts all thinkers. Sitting beside him—was the highest product of the present system! With its charm, humanity, courage, chivalry up to a point, its culture, and its cleanliness, this decidedly rare flower at the end of a tall stalk, with dark and tortuous roots and rank foliage, was in a sense the sole justification of power wielded from above. And was it good enough? Was it quite good enough? Like so many other thinkers, Felix hesitated to reply. If only merit and the goods of this world could be finally divorced! If the reward of virtue were just men's love and an unconscious self-respect! If only 'to have nothing' were the highest honour! And yet, to do away with this beside him and put in its place—What? No kiss-me-quick change had a chance of producing anything better. To scrap the long growth of man and start afresh was but to say: 'Since in the past the best that man has done has not been good enough, I have a perfect faith in him for the future!' No! That was a creed for archangels and other extremists. Safer to work on what we had! And he began:

"Next door to this estate I'm told there's ten thousand acres almost entirely grass and covert, owned by Lord Baltimore, who lives in Norfolk, London, Cannes, and anywhere else that the whim takes him. He comes down here twice a year to shoot. The case is extremely common. Surely it spells paralysis. If land is to be owned at all in such great lumps, owners ought at least to live on the lumps, and to pass very high examinations as practical farmers. They ought to be the life and soul, the radiating sun, of their little universes; or else they ought to be cleared out. How expect keen farming to start from such an example? It really looks to me as if the game laws would have to go." And he redoubled his scrutiny of the Bigwig's face. A little furrow in its brow had deepened visibly, but nodding, he said:

"The absentee landlord is a curse, of course. I'm afraid I'm a bit of a one myself. And I'm bound to say—though I'm keen on shooting—if the game laws were abolished, it might do a lot."

"YOU wouldn't move in that direction, I suppose?"

The Bigwig smiled—charming, rather whimsical, that smile.

"Honestly, I'm not up to it. The spirit, you know, but the flesh—! My line is housing and wages, of course."

'There it is,' thought Felix. 'Up to a point, they'll move—not up to THE point. It's all fiddling. One won't give up his shooting; another won't give up his power; a third won't give up her week-ends: a fourth won't give up his freedom. Our interest in the thing is all lackadaisical, a kind of bun-fight of pet notions. There's no real steam.' And abruptly changing the subject, he talked of pictures to the pleasant Bigwig in the sleepy afternoon. Of how this man could paint, and that man couldn't. And in the uncut grass the peacock slowly moved, displaying his breast of burning blue; and below, the gardeners worked among the gooseberries.

CHAPTER XXVI

Nedda, borrowing the bicycle of Clara's maid, Sirrett, had been over to Joyfields, and only learned on her return of her grandmother's arrival. In her bath before dinner there came to her one of those strategic thoughts that even such as are no longer quite children will sometimes conceive. She hurried desperately into her clothes, and, ready full twenty minutes before the gong was due to sound, made her way to her grandmother's room. Frances Freeland had just pulled THIS, and, to her astonishment, THAT had not gone in properly. She was looking at it somewhat severely, when she heard Nedda's knock. Drawing a screen temporarily over the imperfection, she said: "Come in!"

The dear child looked charming in her white evening dress with one red flower in her hair; and while she kissed her, she noted that the neck of her dress was just a little too open to be quite nice, and at once thought: 'I've got the very thing for that.'

Going to a drawer that no one could have suspected of being there, she took from it a little diamond star. Getting delicate but firm hold of the Mechlin at the top of the frock, she popped it in, so that the neck was covered at least an inch higher, and said:

"Now, ducky, you're to keep that as a little present. You've no idea how perfectly it suits you just like this." And having satisfied for the moment her sense of niceness and that continual itch to part with everything she had, she surveyed her granddaughter, lighted up by that red flower, and said:

"How sweet you look!"

Nedda, looking down past cheeks colored by pleasure at the new little star on a neck rather browned by her day in the sun, murmured:

"Oh, Granny! it's much too lovely! You mustn't give it to me!"

These were moments that Frances Freeland loved best in life; and, with the untruthfulness in which she only indulged when she gave things away, or otherwise benefited her neighbors with or without their will, she added: "It's quite wasted; I never wear it myself." And, seeing Nedda's smile, for the girl recollected perfectly having admired it during dinner at Uncle John's, and at Becket itself, she said decisively, "So that's that!" and settled her down on the sofa. But just as she was thinking, 'I have the very thing for the dear child's sunburn,' Nedda said: "Granny, dear, I've been meaning to tell you— Derek and I are engaged."

For the moment Frances Freeland could do nothing but tremulously interlace her fingers.

"Oh, but, darling," she said very gravely, "have you thought?"

"I think of nothing else, Granny."

"But has he thought?"

Nedda nodded.

Frances Freeland sat staring straight before her. Nedda and Derek, Derek and Nedda! The news was almost unintelligible; those two were still for her barely more than little creatures to be tucked up at night. Engaged! Marriage! Between those who were both as near to her, almost, as her own children had been! The effort was for the moment quite too much for her, and a sort of pain disturbed her heart. Then the crowning principle of her existence came a little to her aid. No use in making a fuss; must put the best face on it, whether it were going to come to anything or not! And she said:

"Well, darling, I don't know, I'm sure. I dare say it's very lovely for you. But do you think you've seen enough of him?"

Nedda gave her a swift look, then dropped her lashes, so that her eyes seemed closed. Snuggling up, she said:

"No, Granny, I do wish I could see more; if only I could go and stay with them a little!"

And as she planted that dart of suggestion, the gong sounded.

In Frances Freeland, lying awake till two, as was her habit, the suggestion grew. To this growth not only her custom of putting the best face on things, but her incurable desire to make others happy, and an instinctive sympathy with love-affairs, all contributed; moreover, Felix had said something about Derek's having been concerned in something rash. If darling Nedda were there it would occupy his mind and help to make him careful. Never dilatory in forming resolutions, she decided to take the girl over with her on the morrow. Kirsteen had a dear little spare room, and Nedda should take her bag. It would be a nice surprise for them all. Accordingly, next morning, not wanting to give any trouble, she sent Thomas down to the Red Lion, where they had a comfortable fly, with a very steady, respectable driver, and ordered it to come at half past two. Then, without saying anything to Clara, she told Nedda to be ready to pop in her bag, trusting to her powers of explaining everything to everybody without letting anybody know anything. Little difficulties of this sort never bunkered her; she was essentially a woman of action. And on the drive to Joyfields she stilled the girl's quavering with:

"It's all right, darling; it'll be very nice for them."

She was perhaps the only person in the world who was not just a little bit afraid of Kirsteen. Indeed, she was constitutionally unable to be afraid of anything, except motor-cars, and, of course, earwigs, and even them one must put up with. Her critical sense told her that this woman in blue was just like anybody else, besides her father had been the colonel of a Highland regiment, which was quite nice, and one must put the best face on her.

In this way, pointing out the beauty of each feature of the scenery, and not permitting herself or Nedda to think about the bag, they drove until they came to Joyfields.

Kirsteen alone was in, and, having sent Nedda into the orchard to look for her uncle, Frances Freeland came at once to the point. It was so important, she thought, that darling Nedda should see more of dear Derek. They were very young, and if she could stay for a few weeks, they would both know their minds so much better. She had made her bring her bag, because she knew dear Kirsteen would agree with her; and it would be so nice for them all. Felix had told her about that poor man who had done this dreadful thing, and she thought that if Nedda were here it would be a distraction. She was a very good child, and quite useful in the house. And while she was speaking she watched Kirsteen, and thought: 'She is very handsome, and altogether ladylike; only it is such a pity she wears that blue thing in her hair—it makes her so conspicuous.' And rather unexpectedly she said:

"Do you know, dear, I believe I know the very thing to keep your hair from getting loose. It's such lovely hair. And this is quite a new thing, and doesn't show at all; invented by a very nice hairdresser in Worcester. It's simplicity itself. Do let me show you!" Quickly going over, she removed the kingfisher-blue fillet, and making certain passes with her fingers through the hair, murmured:

"It's so beautifully fine; it seems such a pity not to show it all, dear. Now look at yourself!" And from the recesses of her pocket she produced a little mirror. "I'm sure Tod will simply love it like that. It'll be such a nice change for him."

Kirsteen, with just a faint wrinkling of her lips and eyebrows, waited till she had finished. Then she said:

"Yes, Mother, dear, I'm sure he will," and replaced the fillet. A patient, half-sad, half-quizzical smile visited Frances Freeland's lips, as who should say: 'Yes, I know you think that I'm a fuss-box, but it really is a pity that you wear it so, darling!'

At sight of that smile, Kirsteen got up and kissed her gravely on the forehead.

When Nedda came back from a fruitless search for Tod, her bag was already in the little spare bedroom and Frances Freeland gone. The girl had never yet been alone with her aunt, for whom she had a fervent admiration not unmixed with awe. She idealized her, of course, thinking of her as one might think of a picture or statue, a symbolic figure, standing for liberty and justice and the redress of wrong. Her never-varying garb of blue assisted the girl's fancy, for blue was always the color of ideals and aspiration—was not blue sky the nearest one could get to heaven—were not blue violets the flowers of spring? Then, too, Kirsteen was a woman with whom it would be quite impossible to gossip or small-talk; with her one could but simply and directly say what one felt, and only that over things which really mattered. And this seemed to Nedda so splendid that it sufficed in itself to prevent the girl from saying anything whatever. She longed to, all the same, feeling that to be closer to her aunt meant to be closer to Derek. Yet, with all, she knew that her own nature was very different; this, perhaps, egged her on, and made her aunt seem all the more exciting. She waited breathless till Kirsteen said:

"Yes, you and Derek must know each other better. The worst kind of prison in the world is a mistaken marriage."

Nedda nodded fervently. "It must be. But I think one knows, Aunt Kirsteen!"

She felt as if she were being searched right down to the soul before the answer came:

"Perhaps. I knew myself. I have seen others who did—a few. I think you might."

Nedda flushed from sheer joy. "I could never go on if I didn't love. I feel I couldn't, even if I'd started."

With another long look through narrowing eyes, Kirsteen answered:

"Yes. You would want truth. But after marriage truth is an unhappy thing, Nedda, if you have made a mistake."

"It must be dreadful. Awful."

"So don't make a mistake, my dear—and don't let him."

Nedda answered solemnly:

"I won't—oh, I won't!"

Kirsteen had turned away to the window, and Nedda heard her say quietly to herself:

"'Liberty's a glorious feast!'"

Trembling all over with the desire to express what was in her, Nedda stammered:

"I would never keep anything that wanted to be free—never, never! I would never try to make any one do what they didn't want to!"

She saw her aunt smile, and wondered whether she had said anything exceptionally foolish. But it was not foolish—surely not—to say what one really felt.

"Some day, Nedda, all the world will say that with you. Until then we'll fight those who won't say it. Have you got everything in your room you want? Let's come and see."

To pass from Becket to Joyfields was really a singular experience. At Becket you were certainly supposed to do exactly what you liked, but the tyranny of meals, baths, scents, and other accompaniments of the 'all-body' regime soon annihilated every impulse to do anything but just obey it. At Joyfields, bodily existence was a kind of perpetual skirmish, a sort of grudged accompaniment to a state of soul. You might be alone in the house at any meal-time. You might or might not have water in your jug. And as to baths, you had to go out to a little white-washed shed at the back, with a brick floor, where you pumped on yourself, prepared to shout out, "Halloo! I'm here!" in case any one else came wanting to do the same. The conditions were in fact almost perfect for seeing more of one another. Nobody asked where you were going, with whom going, or how going. You might be away by day or night without exciting curiosity or comment. And yet you were conscious of a certain something always there, holding the house together; some principle of life, or perhaps—just a woman in blue. There, too, was that strangest of all phenomena in an English home—no game ever played, outdoors or in.

The next fortnight, while the grass was ripening, was a wonderful time for Nedda, given up to her single passion—of seeing more of him who so completely occupied her heart. She was at peace now with Sheila, whose virility forbade that she should dispute pride of place with this soft and truthful guest, so evidently immersed in rapture. Besides, Nedda had that quality of getting on well with her own sex, found in those women who, though tenacious, are not possessive; who, though humble, are secretly very self-respecting; who, though they do not say much about it, put all their eggs in one basket; above all, who disengage, no matter what their age, a candid but subtle charm.

But that fortnight was even more wonderful for Derek, caught between two passions—both so fervid. For though the passion of his revolt against the Mallorings did not pull against his passion for Nedda, they both tugged at him. And this had one curious psychological effect. It made his love for Nedda more actual, less of an idealization. Now that she was close to him, under the same roof, he felt the full allurement of her innocent warmth; he would have been cold-blooded indeed if he had not taken fire, and, his pride always checking the expression of his feelings, they glowed ever hotter underneath.

Yet, over those sunshiny days there hung a shadow, as of something kept back, not shared between them; a kind of waiting menace. Nedda learned of Kirsteen and Sheila all the useful things she could; the evenings she passed with Derek, those long evenings of late May and early June, this year so warm and golden. They walked generally in the direction of the hills. A favorite spot was a wood of larches whose green shoots had not yet quite ceased to smell of lemons. Tall, slender things those trees, whose stems and dried lower branch-growth were gray, almost sooty, up to the feathery green of the tops, that swayed and creaked faintly in a wind, with a soughing of their branches like the sound of the sea. From the shelter of those Highland trees, rather strange in such a countryside, they two could peer forth at the last sunlight gold-powdering the fringed branches, at the sunset flush dyeing the sky above the Beacon; watch light slowly folding gray wings above the hay-fields and the elms; mark the squirrels scurry along, and the pigeons' evening flight. A stream ran there at the edge, and beech-trees grew beside it. In the tawny-dappled sand bed of that clear water, and the gray-green dappled trunks of those beeches with their great, sinuous, long-muscled roots, was that something which man can never tame or garden out of the land: the strength of unconquerable fertility—the remote deep life in Nature's heart. Men and women had their spans of existence; those trees seemed as if there forever! From generation to generation lovers might come and, looking on this strength and beauty, feel in their veins the sap of the world. Here the laborer and his master, hearing the wind in the branches and the water murmuring down, might for a brief minute grasp the land's unchangeable wild majesty. And on the far side of that little stream was a field of moon-colored flowers that had for Nedda a strange fascination. Once the boy jumped across and brought her back a handkerchief full. They were of two kinds: close to the water's edge the marsh orchis, and farther back, a small marguerite. Out of this they made a crown of the alternate flowers, and a girdle for her waist. That was an evening of rare beauty, and warm enough already for an early chafer to go blooming in the dusk. An evening when they wandered with their arms round each other a long time, silent, stopping to listen to an owl; stopping to point out each star coming so shyly up in the gray-violet of the sky. And that was the evening when they had a strange little quarrel, sudden as a white squall on a blue sea, or the tiff of two birds shooting up in a swift spiral of attack and then—all over. Would he come to-morrow to see her milking? He could not. Why? He could not; he would be out. Ah! he never told her where he went; he never let her come with him among the laborers like Sheila.

"I can't; I'm pledged not."

"Then you don't trust me!"

"Of course I trust you; but a promise is a promise. You oughtn't to ask me, Nedda."

"No; but I would never have promised to keep anything from you."

"You don't understand."

"Oh! yes, I do. Love doesn't mean the same to you that it does to me."

"How do you know what it means to me?"

"I couldn't have a secret from you."

"Then you don't count honour."

"Honour only binds oneself!"

"What d'you mean by that?"

"I include you—you don't include me in yourself, that's all."

"I think you're very unjust. I was obliged to promise; it doesn't only concern myself."

Then silent, motionless, a yard apart, they looked fiercely at each other, their hearts stiff and sore, and in their brains no glimmer of perception of anything but tragedy. What more tragic than to have come out of an elysium of warm arms round each other, to this sudden hostility! And the owl went on hooting, and the larches smelled sweet! And all around was the same soft dusk wherein the flowers in her hair and round her waist gleamed white! But for Nedda the world had suddenly collapsed. Tears rushed into her eyes; she shook her head and turned away, hiding them passionately.... A full minute passed, each straining to make no sound and catch the faintest sound from the other, till in her breathing there was a little clutch. His fingers came stealing round, touched her cheeks, and were wetted. His arms suddenly squeezed all breath out of her; his lips fastened on hers. She answered those lips with her own desperately, bending her head back, shutting her wet eyes. And the owl hooted, and the white flowers fell into the dusk off her hair and waist.

After that, they walked once more enlaced, avoiding with what perfect care any allusion to the sudden tragedy, giving themselves up to the bewildering ecstasy that had started throbbing in their blood with that kiss, longing only not to spoil it. And through the sheltering larch wood their figures moved from edge to edge, like two little souls in paradise, unwilling to come forth.

After that evening love had a poignancy it had not quite had before; at once deeper, sweeter, tinged for both of them with the rich darkness of passion, and with discovery that love does not mean a perfect merger of one within another. For both felt themselves in the right over that little quarrel. The boy that he could not, must not, resign what was not his to resign; feeling dimly, without being quite able to shape the thought even to himself, that a man has a life of action into which a woman cannot always enter, with which she cannot always be identified. The girl feeling that she did not want any life into which he did not enter, so that it was hard that he should want to exclude her from anything. For all that, she did not try again to move him to let her into the secret of his plans of revolt and revenge, and disdained completely to find them out from Sheila or her aunt.

And the grass went on ripening. Many and various as the breeds of men, or the trees of a forest, were the stalks that made up that greenish jungle with the waving, fawn-colored surface; of rye-grass and brome-grass, of timothy, plantain, and yarrow; of bent-grass and quake-grass, foxtail, and the green-hearted trefoil; of dandelion, dock, musk-thistle, and sweet-scented vernal.

On the 10th of June Tod began cutting his three fields; the whole family, with Nedda and the three Tryst children, working like slaves. Old Gaunt, who looked to the harvests to clothe him for the year, came to do his share of raking, and any other who could find some evening hours to spare. The whole was cut and carried in three days of glorious weather.

The lovers were too tired the last evening of hay harvest to go rambling, and sat in the orchard watching the moon slide up through the coppice behind the church. They sat on Tod's log, deliciously weary, in the scent of the new-mown hay, while moths flitted gray among the blue darkness of the leaves, and the whitened trunks of the apple-trees gleamed ghostly. It was very warm; a night of whispering air, opening all hearts. And Derek said:

"You'll know to-morrow, Nedda."

A flutter of fear overtook her. What would she know?

CHAPTER XXVII

On the 13th of June Sir Gerald Malloring, returning home to dinner from the House of Commons, found on his hall table, enclosed in a letter from his agent, the following paper:

"We, the undersigned laborers on Sir Gerald Malloring's estate, beg respectfully to inform him that we consider it unjust that any laborer should be evicted from his cottage for any reason connected with private life, or social or political convictions. And we respectfully demand that, before a laborer receives notice to quit for any such reason, the case shall be submitted to all his fellow laborers on the estate; and that in the future he shall only receive such notice if a majority of his fellow laborers record their votes in favor of the notice being given. In the event of this demand being refused, we regretfully decline to take any hand in getting in the hay on Sir Gerald Malloring's estate."

Then followed ninety-three signatures, or signs of the cross with names printed after them.

The agent's letter which enclosed this document mentioned that the hay was already ripe for cutting; that everything had been done to induce the men to withdraw the demand, without success, and that the farmers were very much upset. The thing had been sprung on them, the agent having no notion that anything of the sort was on foot. It had been very secretly, very cleverly, managed; and, in the agent's opinion, was due to Mr. Freeland's family. He awaited Sir Gerald's instructions. Working double tides, with luck and good weather, the farmers and their families might perhaps save half of the hay.

Malloring read this letter twice, and the enclosure three times, and crammed them deep down into his pocket.

It was pre-eminently one of those moments which bring out the qualities of Norman blood. And the first thing he did was to look at the barometer. It was going slowly down. After a month of first-class weather it would not do that without some sinister intention. An old glass, he believed in it implicitly. He tapped, and it sank further. He stood there frowning. Should he consult his wife? General friendliness said: Yes! A Norman instinct of chivalry, and perhaps the deeper Norman instinct, that, when it came to the point, women were too violent, said, No! He went up-stairs three at a time, and came down two. And all through dinner he sat thinking it over, and talking as if nothing had happened; so that he hardly spoke. Three-quarters of the hay at stake, if it rained soon! A big loss to the farmers, a further reduction in rents already far too low. Should he grin and bear it, and by doing nothing show these fellows that he could afford to despise their cowardly device? For it WAS cowardly to let his grass get ripe and play it this low trick! But if he left things unfought this time, they would try it on again with the corn—not that there was much of that on the estate of a man who only believed in corn as a policy.

Should he make the farmers sack the lot and get in other labor? But where? Agricultural laborers were made, not born. And it took a deuce of a lot of making, at that! Should he suspend wages till they withdrew their demand? That might do—but he would still lose the hay. The hay! After all, anybody, pretty well, could make hay; it was the least skilled of all farm work, so long as the farmers were there to drive the machines and direct. Why not act vigorously? And his jaws set so suddenly on a piece of salmon that he bit his tongue. The action served to harden a growing purpose. So do small events influence great! Suspend those fellows' wages, get down strike-breakers, save the hay! And if there were a row—well, let there be a row! The constabulary would have to act. It was characteristic of his really Norman spirit that the notion of agreeing to the demand, or even considering whether it were just, never once came into his mind. He was one of those, comprising nowadays nearly all his class, together with their press, who habitually referred to his country as a democratic power, a champion of democracy—but did not at present suspect the meaning of the word; nor, to say truth, was it likely they ever would. Nothing, however, made him more miserable than indecision. And so, now that he was on the point of deciding, and the decision promised vigorous consequences, he felt almost elated. Closing his jaws once more too firmly, this time on lamb, he bit his tongue again. It was impossible to confess what he had done, for two of his children were there, expected to eat with that well-bred detachment which precludes such happenings; and he rose from dinner with his mind made up. Instead of going back to the House of Commons, he went straight to a strike-breaking agency. No grass should grow under the feet of his decision! Thence he sought the one post-office still open, despatched a long telegram to his agent, another to the chief constable of Worcestershire; and, feeling he had done all he could for the moment, returned to the 'House,' where they were debating the rural housing question. He sat there, paying only moderate attention to a subject on which he was acknowledged an authority. To-morrow, in all probability, the papers would have got hold of the affair! How he loathed people poking their noses into his concerns! And suddenly he was assailed, very deep down, by a feeling with which in his firmness he had not reckoned—a sort of remorse that he was going to let a lot of loafing blackguards down onto his land, to toss about his grass, and swill their beastly beer above it. And all the real love he had for his fields and coverts, all the fastidiousness of an English gentleman, and, to do him justice, the qualms of a conscience telling him that he owed better things than this to those born on his estate, assaulted him in force. He sat back in his seat, driving his long legs hard against the pew in front. His thick, wavy, still brown hair was beautifully parted above the square brow that frowned over deep-set eyes and a perfectly straight nose. Now and again he bit into a side of his straw-colored moustache, or raised a hand and twisted the other side. Without doubt one of the handsomest and perhaps the most Norman-looking man in the whole 'House.' There was a feeling among those round him that he was thinking deeply. And so he was. But he had decided, and he was not a man who went back on his decisions.

Morning brought even worse sensations. Those ruffians that he had ordered down—the farmers would never consent to put them up! They would have to camp. Camp on his land! It was then that for two seconds the thought flashed through him: Ought I to have considered whether I could agree to that demand? Gone in another flash. If there was one thing a man could not tolerate, it was dictation! Out of the question! But perhaps he had been a little hasty about strike-breakers. Was there not still time to save the situation from that, if he caught the first train? The personal touch was everything. If he put it to the men on the spot, with these strike-breakers up his sleeve, surely they must listen! After all, they were his own people. And suddenly he was overcome with amazement that they should have taken such a step. What had got into them? Spiritless enough, as a rule, in all conscience; the sort of fellows who hadn't steam even to join the miniature rifle-range that he had given them! And visions of them, as he was accustomed to pass them in the lanes, slouching along with their straw bags, their hoes, and their shamefaced greetings, passed before him. Yes! It was all that fellow Freeland's family! The men had been put up to it—put up to it! The very wording of their demand showed that! Very bitterly he thought of the unneighborly conduct of that woman and her cubs. It was impossible to keep it from his wife! And so he told her. Rather to his surprise, she had no scruples about the strike-breakers. Of course, the hay must be saved! And the laborers be taught a lesson! All the unpleasantness he and she had gone through over Tryst and that Gaunt girl must not go for nothing! It must never be said or thought that the Freeland woman and her children had scored over them! If the lesson were once driven home, they would have no further trouble.

He admired her firmness, though with a certain impatience. Women never quite looked ahead; never quite realized all the consequences of anything. And he thought: 'By George! I'd no idea she was so hard! But, then, she always felt more strongly about Tryst and that Gaunt girl than I did.'

In the hall the glass was still going down. He caught the 9.15, wiring to his agent to meet him at the station, and to the impresario of the strike-breakers to hold up their departure until he telegraphed. The three-mile drive up from the station, fully half of which was through his own land, put him in possession of all the agent had to tell: Nasty spirit abroad—men dumb as fishes—the farmers, puzzled and angry, had begun cutting as best they could. Not a man had budged. He had seen young Mr. and Miss Freeland going about. The thing had been worked very cleverly. He had suspected nothing—utterly unlike the laborers as he knew them. They had no real grievance, either! Yes, they were going on with all their other work—milking, horses, and that; it was only the hay they wouldn't touch. Their demand was certainly a very funny one—very funny—had never heard of anything like it. Amounted almost to security of tenure. The Tryst affair no doubt had done it! Malloring cut him short:

"Till they've withdrawn this demand, Simmons, I can't discuss that or anything."

The agent coughed behind his hand.

Naturally! Only perhaps there might be a way of wording it that would satisfy them. Never do to really let them have such decisions in their hands, of course!

They were just passing Tod's. The cottage wore its usual air of embowered peace. And for the life of him Malloring could not restrain a gesture of annoyance.

On reaching home he sent gardeners and grooms in all directions with word that he would be glad to meet the men at four o'clock at the home farm. Much thought, and interviews with several of the farmers, who all but one—a shaky fellow at best—were for giving the laborers a sharp lesson, occupied the interval. Though he had refused to admit the notion that the men could be chicaned, as his agent had implied, he certainly did wonder a little whether a certain measure of security might not in some way be guaranteed, which would still leave him and the farmers a free hand. But the more he meditated on the whole episode, the more he perceived how intimately it interfered with the fundamental policy of all good landowners—of knowing what was good for their people better than those people knew themselves.

As four o'clock approached, he walked down to the home farm. The sky was lightly overcast, and a rather chill, draughty, rustling wind had risen. Resolved to handle the men with the personal touch, he had discouraged his agent and the farmers from coming to the conference, and passed the gate with the braced-up feeling of one who goes to an encounter. In that very spick-and-span farmyard ducks were swimming leisurely on the greenish pond, white pigeons strutting and preening on the eaves of the barn, and his keen eye noted that some tiles were out of order up there. Four o'clock! Ah, here was a fellow coming! And instinctively he crisped his hands that were buried in his pockets, and ran over to himself his opening words. Then, with a sensation of disgust, he saw that the advancing laborer was that incorrigible 'land lawyer' Gaunt. The short, square man with the ruffled head and the little bright-gray eyes saluted, uttered an "Afternoon, Sir Gerald!" in his teasing voice, and stood still. His face wore the jeering twinkle that had disconcerted so many political meetings. Two lean fellows, rather alike, with lined faces and bitten, drooped moustaches, were the next to come through the yard gate. They halted behind Gaunt, touching their forelocks, shuffling a little, and looking sidelong at each other. And Malloring waited. Five past four! Ten past! Then he said:

"D'you mind telling the others that I'm here?"

Gaunt answered:

"If so be as you was waitin' for the meetin', I fancy as 'ow you've got it, Sir Gerald!"

A wave of anger surged up in Malloring, dyeing his face brick-red. So! He had come all that way with the best intentions—to be treated like this; to meet this 'land lawyer,' who, he could see, was only here to sharpen his tongue, and those two scarecrow-looking chaps, who had come to testify, no doubt, to his discomfiture. And he said sharply:

"So that's the best you can do to meet me, is it?"

Gaunt answered imperturbably:

"I think it is, Sir Gerald."

"Then you've mistaken your man."

"I don't think so, Sir Gerald."

Without another look Malloring passed the three by, and walked back to the house. In the hall was the agent, whose face clearly showed that he had foreseen this defeat. Malloring did not wait for him to speak.

"Make arrangements. The strike-breakers will be down by noon to-morrow. I shall go through with it now, Simmons, if I have to clear the whole lot out. You'd better go in and see that they're ready to send police if there's any nonsense. I'll be down again in a day or two." And, without waiting for reply, he passed into his study. There, while the car was being got ready, he stood in the window, very sore; thinking of what he had meant to do; thinking of his good intentions; thinking of what was coming to the country, when a man could not even get his laborers to come and hear what he had to say. And a sense of injustice, of anger, of bewilderment, harrowed his very soul.

CHAPTER XXVIII

For the first two days of this new 'kick-up,' that 'fellow Freeland's' family undoubtedly tasted the sweets of successful mutiny. The fellow himself alone shook his head. He, like Nedda, had known nothing, and there was to him something unnatural and rather awful in this conduct toward dumb crops.

From the moment he heard of it he hardly spoke, and a perpetual little frown creased a brow usually so serene. In the early morning of the day after Malloring went back to town, he crossed the road to a field where the farmer, aided by his family and one of Malloring's gardeners, was already carrying the hay; and, taking up a pitchfork, without a word to anybody, he joined in the work. The action was deeper revelation of his feeling than any expostulation, and the young people watched it rather aghast.

"It's nothing," Derek said at last; "Father never has understood, and never will, that you can't get things without fighting. He cares more for trees and bees and birds than he does for human beings."

"That doesn't explain why he goes over to the enemy, when it's only a lot of grass."

Kirsteen answered:

"He hasn't gone over to the enemy, Sheila. You don't understand your father; to neglect the land is sacrilege to him. It feeds us—he would say—we live on it; we've no business to forget that but for the land we should all be dead."

"That's beautiful," said Nedda quickly; "and true."

Sheila answered angrily:

"It may be true in France with their bread and wine. People don't live off the land here; they hardly eat anything they grow themselves. How can we feel like that when we're all brought up on mongrel food? Besides, it's simply sentimental, when there are real wrongs to fight about."

"Your father is not sentimental, Sheila. It's too deep with him for that, and too unconscious. He simply feels so unhappy about the waste of that hay that he can't keep his hands off it."

Derek broke in: "Mother's right. And it doesn't matter, except that we've got to see that the men don't follow his example. They've a funny feeling about him."

Kirsteen shook her head.

"You needn't be afraid. He's always been too strange to them!"

"Well, I'm going to stiffen their backs. Coming Sheila?" And they went.

Left, as she seemed always to be in these days of open mutiny, Nedda said sadly:

"What is coming, Aunt Kirsteen?"

Her aunt was standing in the porch, looking straight before her; a trail of clematis had drooped over her fine black hair down on to the blue of her linen dress. She answered, without turning:

"Have you ever seen, on jubilee nights, bonfire to bonfire, from hill to hill, to the end of the land? This is the first lighted."

Nedda felt something clutch her heart. What was that figure in blue? Priestess? Prophetess? And for a moment the girl felt herself swept into the vision those dark glowing eyes were seeing; some violent, exalted, inexorable, flaming vision. Then something within her revolted, as though one had tried to hypnotize her into seeing what was not true; as though she had been forced for the moment to look, not at what was really there, but at what those eyes saw projected from the soul behind them. And she said quietly:

"I don't believe, Aunt Kirsteen. I don't really believe. I think it must go out."

Kirsteen turned.

"You are like your father," she said—"a doubter."

Nedda shook her head.

"I can't persuade myself to see what isn't there. I never can, Aunt Kirsteen."

Without reply, save a quiver of her brows, Kirsteen went back into the house. And Nedda stayed on the pebbled path before the cottage, unhappy, searching her own soul. Did she fail to see because she was afraid to see, because she was too dull to see; or because, as she had said, there was really nothing there—no flames to leap from hill to hill, no lift, no tearing in the sky that hung over the land? And she thought: 'London—all those big towns, their smoke, the things they make, the things we want them to make, that we shall always want them to make. Aren't they there? For every laborer who's a slave Dad says there are five town workers who are just as much slaves! And all those Bigwigs with their great houses, and their talk, and their interest in keeping things where they are! Aren't they there? I don't—I can't believe anything much can happen, or be changed. Oh! I shall never see visions, and dream dreams!' And from her heart she sighed.

In the meantime Derek and Sheila were going their round on bicycles, to stiffen the backs of the laborers. They had hunted lately, always in a couple, desiring no complications, having decided that it was less likely to provoke definite assault and opposition from the farmers. To their mother was assigned all correspondence; to themselves the verbal exhortations, the personal touch. It was past noon, and they were already returning, when they came on the char-a-bancs containing the head of the strike-breaking column. The two vehicles were drawn up opposite the gate leading to Marrow Farm, and the agent was detaching the four men destined to that locality, with their camping-gear. By the open gate the farmer stood eying his new material askance. Dejected enough creatures they looked—poor devils picked up at ten pound the dozen, who, by the mingled apathy and sheepish amusement on their faces, might never have seen a pitchfork, or smelled a field of clover, in their lives.

The two young Freelands rode slowly past; the boy's face scornfully drawn back into itself; the girl's flaming scarlet.

"Don't take notice," Derek said; "we'll soon stop that."

And they had gone another mile before he added:

"We've got to make our round again; that's all."

The words of Mr. Pogram, 'You have influence, young man,' were just. There was about Derek the sort of quality that belongs to the good regimental officer; men followed and asked themselves why the devil they had, afterward. And if it be said that no worse leader than a fiery young fool can be desired for any movement, it may also be said that without youth and fire and folly there is usually no movement at all.

Late in the afternoon they returned home, dead beat. That evening the farmers and their wives milked the cows, tended the horses, did everything that must be done, not without curses. And next morning the men, with Gaunt and a big, dark fellow, called Tulley, for spokesmen, again proffered their demand. The agent took counsel with Malloring by wire. His answer, "Concede nothing," was communicated to the men in the afternoon, and received by Gaunt with the remark: "I thart we should be hearin' that. Please to thank Sir Gerald. The men concedes their gratitood...."

That night it began to rain. Nedda, waking, could hear the heavy drops pattering on the sweetbrier and clematis thatching her open window. The scent of rain-cooled leaves came in drifts, and it seemed a shame to sleep. She got up; put on her dressing-gown, and went to thrust her nose into that bath of dripping sweetness. Dark as the clouds had made the night, there was still the faint light of a moon somewhere behind. The leaves of the fruit-trees joined in the long, gentle hissing, and now and again rustled and sighed sharply; a cock somewhere, as by accident, let off a single crow. There were no stars. All was dark and soft as velvet. And Nedda thought: 'The world is dressed in living creatures! Trees, flowers, grass, insects, ourselves—woven together—the world is dressed in life! I understand Uncle Tod's feeling! If only it would rain till they have to send these strike-breakers back because there's no hay worth fighting about!' Suddenly her heart beat fast. The wicket gate had clicked. There was something darker than the darkness coming along the path! Scared, but with all protective instinct roused, she leaned out, straining to see. A faint grating sound from underneath came up to her. A window being opened! And she flew to her door. She neither barred it, however, nor cried out, for in that second it had flashed across her: 'Suppose it's he! Gone out to do something desperate, as Tryst did!' If it were, he would come up-stairs and pass her door, going to his room. She opened it an inch, holding her breath. At first, nothing! Was it fancy? Or was some one noiselessly rifling the room down-stairs? But surely no one would steal of Uncle Tod, who, everybody knew, had nothing valuable. Then came a sound as of bootless feet pressing the stairs stealthily! And the thought darted through her, 'If it isn't he, what shall I do?' And then—'What shall I do—if it IS!'

Desperately she opened the door, clasping her hands on the place whence her heart had slipped down to her bare feet. But she knew it was he before she heard him whisper: "Nedda!" and, clutching him by the sleeve, she drew him in and closed the door. He was wet through, dripping; so wet that the mere brushing against him made her skin feel moist through its thin coverings.

"Where have you been? What have you been doing? Oh, Derek!"

There was just light enough to see his face, his teeth, the whites of his eyes.

"Cutting their tent-ropes in the rain. Hooroosh!"

It was such a relief that she just let out a little gasping "Oh!" and leaned her forehead against his coat. Then she felt his wet arms round her, his wet body pressed to hers, and in a second he was dancing with her a sort of silent, ecstatic war dance. Suddenly he stopped, went down on his knees, pressing his face to her waist, and whispering: "What a brute, what a brute! Making her wet! Poor little Nedda!"

Nedda bent over him; her hair covered his wet head, her hands trembled on his shoulders. Her heart felt as if it would melt right out of her; she longed so to warm and dry him with herself. And, in turn, his wet arms clutched her close, his wet hands could not keep still on her. Then he drew back, and whispering: "Oh, Nedda! Nedda!" fled out like a dark ghost. Oblivious that she was damp from head to foot, Nedda stood swaying, her eyes closed and her lips just open; then, putting out her arms, she drew them suddenly in and clasped herself....

When she came down to breakfast the next morning, he had gone out already, and Uncle Tod, too; her aunt was writing at the bureau. Sheila greeted her gruffly, and almost at once went out. Nedda swallowed coffee, ate her egg, and bread and honey, with a heavy heart. A newspaper lay open on the table; she read it idly till these words caught her eye:

"The revolt which has paralyzed the hay harvest on Sir Gerald Malloring's Worcestershire estate and led to the introduction of strike-breakers, shows no sign of abatement. A very wanton spirit of mischief seems to be abroad in this neighborhood. No reason can be ascertained for the arson committed a short time back, nor for this further outbreak of discontent. The economic condition of the laborers on this estate is admittedly rather above than below the average."

And at once she thought: "'Mischief!' What a shame!' Were people, then, to know nothing of the real cause of the revolt—nothing of the Tryst eviction, the threatened eviction of the Gaunts? Were they not to know that it was on principle, and to protest against that sort of petty tyranny to the laborers all over the country, that this rebellion had been started? For liberty! only simple liberty not to be treated as though they had no minds or souls of their own—weren't the public to know that? If they were allowed to think that it was all wanton mischief—that Derek was just a mischief-maker—it would be dreadful! Some one must write and make this known? Her father? But Dad might think it too personal—his own relations! Mr. Cuthcott! Into whose household Wilmet Gaunt had gone. Ah! Mr. Cuthcott who had told her that he was always at her service! Why not? And the thought that she might really do something at last to help made her tingle all over. If she borrowed Sheila's bicycle she could catch the nine-o'clock train to London, see him herself, make him do something, perhaps even bring him back with her! She examined her purse. Yes, she had money. She would say nothing, here, because, of course, he might refuse! At the back of her mind was the idea that, if a real newspaper took the part of the laborers, Derek's position would no longer be so dangerous; he would be, as it were, legally recognized, and that, in itself, would make him more careful and responsible. Whence she got this belief in the legalizing power of the press it is difficult to say, unless that, reading newspapers but seldom, she still took them at their own valuation, and thought that when they said: "We shall do this," or "We must do that," they really were speaking for the country, and that forty-five millions of people were deliberately going to do something, whereas, in truth, as was known to those older than Nedda, they were speaking, and not too conclusively at that, for single anonymous gentlemen in a hurry who were not going to do anything. She knew that the press had power, great power—for she was always hearing that—and it had not occurred to her as yet to examine the composition of that power so as to discover that, while the press certainly had a certain monopoly of expression, and that same 'spirit of body' which makes police constables swear by one another, it yet contained within its ring fence the sane and advisable futility of a perfectly balanced contradiction; so that its only functions, practically speaking, were the dissemination of news, seven-tenths of which would have been happier in obscurity; and—'irritation of the Dutch!' Not, of course, that the press realized this; nor was it probable that any one would tell it, for it had power— great power.

She caught her train—glowing outwardly from the speed of her ride, and inwardly from the heat of adventure and the thought that at last she was being of some use.

The only other occupants of her third-class compartment were a friendly looking man, who might have been a sailor or other wanderer on leave, and his thin, dried-up, black-clothed cottage woman of an old mother. They sat opposite each other. The son looked at his mother with beaming eyes, and she remarked: "An' I says to him, says I, I says, 'What?' I says; so 'e says to me, he says, 'Yes,' he says; 'that's what I say,' he says." And Nedda thought: 'What an old dear! And the son looks nice too; I do like simple people.'

They got out at the first stop and she journeyed on alone. Taking a taxicab from Paddington, she drove toward Gray's Inn. But now that she was getting close she felt very nervous. How expect a busy man like Mr. Cuthcott to spare time to come down all that way? It would be something, though, if she could get him even to understand what was really happening, and why; so that he could contradict that man in the other paper. It must be wonderful to be writing, daily, what thousands and thousands of people read! Yes! It must be a very sacred-feeling life! To be able to say things in that particularly authoritative way which must take such a lot of people in—that is, make such a lot of people think in the same way! It must give a man a terrible sense of responsibility, make him feel that he simply must be noble, even if he naturally wasn't. Yes! it must be a wonderful profession, and only fit for the highest! In addition to Mr. Cuthcott, she knew as yet but three young journalists, and those all weekly.

At her timid ring the door was opened by a broad-cheeked girl, enticingly compact in apron and black frock, whose bright color, thick lips, and rogue eyes came of anything but London. It flashed across Nedda that this must be the girl for whose sake she had faced Mr. Cuthcott at the luncheon-table! And she said: "Are you Wilmet Gaunt?"

The girl smiled till her eyes almost disappeared, and answered: "Yes, miss."

"I'm Nedda Freeland, Miss Sheila's cousin. I've just come from Joyfields. How are you getting on?"

"Fine, thank you, miss. Plenty of life here."

Nedda thought: 'That's what Derek said of her. Bursting with life! And so she is.' And she gazed doubtfully at the girl, whose prim black dress and apron seemed scarcely able to contain her.

"Is Mr. Cuthcott in?"

"No, miss; he'll be down at the paper. Two hundred and five Floodgate Street."

'Oh!' thought Nedda with dismay; 'I shall never venture there!' And glancing once more at the girl, whose rogue slits of eyes, deep sunk between check-bones and brow, seemed to be quizzing her and saying: 'You and Mr. Derek—oh! I know!' she went sadly away. And first she thought she would go home to Hampstead, then that she would go back to the station, then: 'After all, why shouldn't I go and try? They can't eat me. I will!'

She reached her destination at the luncheon-hour, so that the offices of the great evening journal were somewhat deserted. Producing her card, she was passed from hand to hand till she rested in a small bleak apartment where a young woman was typing fast. She longed to ask her how she liked it, but did not dare. The whole atmosphere seemed to her charged with a strenuous solemnity, as though everything said, 'We have power—great power.' And she waited, sitting by the window which faced the street. On the buildings opposite she could read the name of another great evening journal. Why, it was the one which had contained the paragraph she had read at breakfast! She had bought a copy of it at the station. Its temperament, she knew, was precisely opposed to that of Mr. Cuthcott's paper. Over in that building, no doubt there would be the same strenuously loaded atmosphere, so that if they opened the windows on both sides little puffs of power would meet in mid-air, above the heads of the passers-by, as might the broadsides of old three-deckers, above the green, green sea.

And for the first time an inkling of the great comic equipoise in Floodgate Street and human affairs stole on Nedda's consciousness. They puffed and puffed, and only made smoke in the middle! That must be why Dad always called them: 'Those fellows!' She had scarcely, however, finished beginning to think these thoughts when a handbell sounded sharply in some adjoining room, and the young woman nearly fell into her typewriter. Readjusting her balance, she rose, and, going to the door, passed out in haste. Through the open doorway Nedda could see a large and pleasant room, whose walls seemed covered with prints of men standing in attitudes such that she was almost sure they were statesmen; and, at a table in the centre, the back of Mr. Cuthcott in a twiddly chair, surrounded by sheets of paper reposing on the floor, shining like autumn leaves on a pool of water. She heard his voice, smothery, hurried, but still pleasant, say: "Take these, Miss Mayne, take these! Begin on them, begin! Confound it! What's the time?" And the young woman's voice: "Half past one, Mr. Cuthcott!" And a noise from Mr. Cuthcott's throat that sounded like an adjuration to the Deity not to pass over something. Then the young woman dipped and began gathering those leaves of paper, and over her comely back Nedda had a clear view of Mr. Cuthcott hunching one brown shoulder as though warding something off, and of one of his thin hands ploughing up and throwing back his brown hair on one side, and heard the sound of his furiously scratching pen. And her heart pattered; it was so clear that he was 'giving them one' and had no time for her. And involuntarily she looked at the windows beyond him to see if there were any puffs of power issuing therefrom. But they were closed. She saw the young woman rise and come back toward her, putting the sheets of paper in order; and, as the door was closing, from the twiddly chair a noise that seemed to couple God with the condemnation of silly souls. When the young woman was once more at the typewriter she rose and said: "Have you given him my card yet?"

The young woman looked at her surprised, as if she had broken some rule of etiquette, and answered: "No."

"Then don't, please. I can see that he's too busy. I won't wait."

The young woman abstractedly placed a sheet of paper in her typewriter.

"Very well," she said. "Good morning!"

And before Nedda reached the door she heard the click-click of the machine, reducing Mr. Cuthcott to legibility.

'I was stupid to come,' she thought. 'He must be terribly overworked. Poor man! He does say lovely things!' And, crestfallen, she went along the passages, and once more out into Floodgate Street. She walked along it frowning, till a man who was selling newspapers said as she passed: "Mind ye don't smile, lydy!"

Seeing that he was selling Mr. Cuthcott's paper, she felt for a coin to buy one, and, while searching, scrutinized the news-vender's figure, almost entirely hidden by the words:

GREAT HOUSING SCHEME

HOPE FOR THE MILLION!

on a buff-colored board; while above it, his face, that had not quite blood enough to be scorbutic, was wrapped in the expression of those philosophers to whom a hope would be fatal. He was, in fact, just what he looked—a street stoic. And a dim perception of the great social truth: "The smell of half a loaf is not better than no bread!" flickered in Nedda's brain as she passed on. Was that what Derek was doing with the laborers—giving them half the smell of a liberty that was not there? And a sudden craving for her father came over her. He—he only, was any good, because he, only, loved her enough to feel how distracted and unhappy she was feeling, how afraid of what was coming. So, making for a Tube station, she took train to Hampstead....

It was past two, and Felix, on the point of his constitutional. He had left Becket the day after Nedda's rather startling removal to Joyfields, and since then had done his level best to put the whole Tryst affair, with all its somewhat sinister relevance to her life and his own, out of his mind as something beyond control. He had but imperfectly succeeded.

Flora, herself not too present-minded, had in these days occasion to speak to him about the absent-minded way in which he fulfilled even the most domestic duties, and Alan was always saying to him, "Buck up, Dad!" With Nedda's absorption into the little Joyfields whirlpool, the sun shone but dimly for Felix. And a somewhat febrile attention to 'The Last of the Laborers' had not brought it up to his expectations. He fluttered under his buff waistcoat when he saw her coming in at the gate. She must want something of him! For to this pitch of resignation, as to his little daughter's love for him, had he come! And if she wanted something of him, things would be going wrong again down there! Nor did the warmth of her embrace, and her: "Oh! Dad, it IS nice to see you!" remove that instinctive conviction; though delicacy, born of love, forbade him to ask her what she wanted. Talking of the sky and other matters, thinking how pretty she was looking, he waited for the new, inevitable proof that youth was first, and a mere father only second fiddle now. A note from Stanley had already informed him of the strike. The news had been something of a relief. Strikes, at all events, were respectable and legitimate means of protest, and to hear that one was in progress had not forced him out of his laborious attempt to believe the whole affair only a mole-hill. He had not, however, heard of the strike-breakers, nor had he seen any newspaper mention of the matter; and when she had shown him the paragraph; recounted her visit to Mr. Cuthcott, and how she had wanted to take him back with her to see for himself—he waited a moment, then said almost timidly: "Should I be of any use, my dear?" She flushed and squeezed his hand in silence; and he knew he would.

When he had packed a handbag and left a note for Flora, he rejoined her in the hall.

It was past seven when they reached their destination, and, taking the station 'fly,' drove slowly up to Joyfields, under a showery sky.

CHAPTER XXIX

When Felix and Nedda reached Tod's cottage, the three little Trysts, whose activity could never be quite called play, were all the living creatures about the house.

"Where is Mrs. Freeland, Biddy?"

"We don't know; a man came, and she went."

"And Miss Sheila?"

"She went out in the mornin'. And Mr. Freeland's gone."

Susie added: "The dog's gone, too."

"Then help me to get some tea."

"Yes."

With the assistance of the mother-child, and the hindrance of Susie and Billy, Nedda made and laid tea, with an anxious heart. The absence of her aunt, who so seldom went outside the cottage, fields, and orchard, disturbed her; and, while Felix refreshed himself, she fluttered several times on varying pretexts to the wicket gate.

At her third visit, from the direction of the church, she saw figures coming on the road—dark figures carrying something, followed by others walking alongside. What sun there had been had quite given in to heavy clouds; the light was dull, the elm-trees dark; and not till they were within two hundred yards could Nedda make out that these were figures of policemen. Then, alongside that which they were carrying, she saw her aunt's blue dress. WHAT were they carrying like that? She dashed down the steps, and stopped. No! If it were HE they would bring him in! She rushed back again, distracted. She could see now a form stretched on a hurdle. It WAS he!

"Dad! Quick!"

Felix came, startled at that cry, to find his little daughter on the path wringing her hands and flying back to the wicket gate. They were close now. She saw them begin to mount the steps, those behind raising their arms so that the hurdle should be level. Derek lay on his back, with head and forehead swathed in wet blue linen, torn from his mother's skirt; and the rest of his face very white. He lay quite still, his clothes covered with mud. Terrified, Nedda plucked at Kirsteen's sleeve.

"What is it?"

"Concussion!" The stillness of that blue-clothed figure, so calm beside her, gave her strength to say quietly:

"Put him in my room, Aunt Kirsteen; there's more air there!" And she flew up-stairs, flinging wide her door, making the bed ready, snatching her night things from the pillow; pouring out cold water, sprinkling the air with eau de cologne. Then she stood still. Perhaps, they would not bring him there? Yes, they were coming up. They brought him in, and laid him on the bed. She heard one say: "Doctor'll be here directly, ma'am. Let him lie quiet." Then she and his mother were alone beside him.

"Undo his boots," said Kirsteen.

Nedda's fingers trembled, and she hated them for fumbling so, while she drew off those muddy boots. Then her aunt said softly: "Hold him up, dear, while I get his things off."

And, with a strange rapture that she was allowed to hold him thus, she supported him against her breast till he was freed and lying back inert. Then, and only then, she whispered:

"How long before he—?"

Kirsteen shook her head; and, slipping her arm round the girl, murmured: "Courage, Nedda!"

The girl felt fear and love rush up desperately to overwhelm her. She choked them back, and said quite quietly: "I will. I promise. Only let me help nurse him!"

Kirsteen nodded. And they sat down to wait.

That quarter of an hour was the longest of her life. To see him thus, living, yet not living, with the spirit driven from him by a cruel blow, perhaps never to come back! Curious, how things still got themselves noticed when all her faculties were centred in gazing at his face. She knew that it was raining again; heard the swish and drip, and smelled the cool wet perfume through the scent of the eau de cologne that she had spilled. She noted her aunt's arm, as it hovered, wetting the bandage; the veins and rounded whiteness from under the loose blue sleeve slipped up to the elbow. One of his feet lay close to her at the bed's edge; she stole her hand beneath the sheet. That foot felt very cold, and she grasped it tight. If only she could pass life into him through her hot hand. She heard the ticking of her little travelling-clock, and was conscious of flies wheeling close up beneath the white ceiling, of how one by one they darted at each other, making swift zigzags in the air. And something in her she had not yet known came welling up, softening her eyes, her face, even the very pose of her young body—the hidden passion of a motherliness, that yearned so to 'kiss the place,' to make him well, to nurse and tend, restore and comfort him. And with all her might she watched the movements of those rounded arms under the blue sleeves—how firm and exact they were, how soft and quiet and swift, bathing the dark head! Then from beneath the bandage she caught sight suddenly of his eyes. And her heart turned sick. Oh, they were not quite closed! As if he hadn't life enough to close them! She bit into her lip to stop a cry. It was so terrible to see them without light. Why did not that doctor come? Over and over and over again within her the prayer turned: Let him live! Oh, let him live!

The blackbirds out in the orchard were tuning up for evening. It seemed almost dreadful they should be able to sing like that. All the world was going on just the same! If he died, the world would have no more light for her than there was now in his poor eyes—and yet it would go on the same! How was that possible? It was not possible, because she would die too! She saw her aunt turn her head like a startled animal; some one was coming up the stairs! It was the doctor, wiping his wet face—a young man in gaiters. How young—dreadfully young! No; there was a little gray at the sides of his hair! What would he say? And Nedda sat with hands tight clenched in her lap, motionless as a young crouching sphinx. An interminable testing, and questioning, and answer! Never smoked—never drank—never been ill! The blow—ah, here! Just here! Concussion—yes! Then long staring into the eyes, the eyelids lifted between thumb and finger. And at last (how could he talk so loud! Yet it was a comfort too—he would not talk like that if Derek were going to die!)—Hair cut shorter—ice—watch him like a lynx! This and that, if he came to. Nothing else to be done. And then those blessed words:

"But don't worry too much. I think it'll be all right." She could not help a little sigh escaping her clenched teeth.

The doctor was looking at her. His eyes were nice.

"Sister?"

"Cousin."

"Ah! Well, I'll get back now, and send you out some ice, at once."

More talk outside the door. Nedda, alone with her lover, crouched forward on her knees, and put her lips to his. They were not so cold as his foot, and the first real hope and comfort came to her. Watch him like a lynx—wouldn't she? But how had it all happened? And where was Sheila? and Uncle Tod?

Her aunt had come back and was stroking her shoulder. There had been fighting in the barn at Marrow Farm. They had arrested Sheila. Derek had jumped down to rescue her and struck his head against a grindstone. Her uncle had gone with Sheila. They would watch, turn and turn about. Nedda must go now and eat something, and get ready to take the watch from eight to midnight.

Following her resolve to make no fuss, the girl went out. The police had gone. The mother-child was putting her little folk to bed; and in the kitchen Felix was arranging the wherewithal to eat. He made her sit down and kept handing things; watching like a cat to see that she put them in her mouth, in the way from which only Flora had suffered hitherto; he seemed so anxious and unhappy, and so awfully sweet, that Nedda forced herself to swallow what she thought would never go down a dry and choky throat. He kept coming up and touching her shoulder or forehead. Once he said:

"It's all right, you know, my pet; concussion often takes two days."

Two days with his eyes like that! The consolation was not so vivid as Felix might have wished; but she quite understood that he was doing his best to give it. She suddenly remembered that he had no room to sleep in. He must use Derek's. No! That, it appeared, was to be for her when she came off duty. Felix was going to have an all-night sitting in the kitchen. He had been looking forward to an all-night sitting for many years, and now he had got his chance. It was a magnificent opportunity—"without your mother, my dear, to insist on my sleeping." And staring at his smile, Nedda thought: 'He's like Granny— he comes out under difficulties. If only I did!'

The ice arrived by motor-cycle just before her watch began. It was some comfort to have that definite thing to see to. How timorous and humble are thoughts in a sick-room, above all when the sick are stretched behind the muffle of unconsciousness, withdrawn from the watcher by half-death! And yet, for him or her who loves, there is at least the sense of being alone with the loved one, of doing all that can be done; and in some strange way of twining hearts with the exiled spirit. To Nedda, sitting at his feet, and hardly ever turning eyes away from his still face, it sometimes seemed that the flown spirit was there beside her. And she saw into his soul in those three hours of watching, as one looking into a stream sees the leopard-like dapple of its sand and dark-strewn floor, just reached by sunlight. She saw all his pride, courage, and impatience, his reserve, and strange unwilling tenderness, as she had never seen them. And a queer dreadful feeling moved her that in some previous existence she had looked at that face dead on a field of battle, frowning up at the stars. That was absurd—there were no previous existences! Or was it prevision of what would come some day?

When, at half past nine, the light began to fail, she lighted two candles in tall, thin, iron candlesticks beside her. They burned without flicker, those spires of yellow flame, slowly conquering the dying twilight, till in their soft radiance the room was full of warm dusky shadows, the night outside ever a deeper black. Two or three times his mother came, looked at him, asked her if she should stay, and, receiving a little silent shake of the head, went away again. At eleven o'clock, when once more she changed the ice-cap, his eyes had still no lustre, and for a moment her courage failed her utterly. It seemed to her that he could never win back, that death possessed the room already, possessed those candle-flames, the ticking of the clock, the dark, dripping night, possessed her heart. Could he be gone before she had been his! Gone! Where? She sank down on her knees, covering her eyes. What good to watch, if he were never coming back! A long time—it seemed hours—passed thus, with the feeling growing deeper in her that no good would come while she was watching. And behind the barrier of her hands she tried desperately to rally courage. If things were—they were! One must look them in the face! She took her hands away. His eyes! Was it light in them? Was it? They were seeing—surely they saw. And his lips made the tiniest movement. In that turmoil of exultation she never knew how she managed to continue kneeling there, with her hands on his. But all her soul shone down to him out of her eyes, and drew and drew at his spirit struggling back from the depths of him. For many minutes that struggle lasted; then he smiled. It was the feeblest smile that ever was on lips, but it made the tears pour down Nedda's cheeks and trickle off on to his hands. Then, with a stoicism that she could not believe in, so hopelessly unreal it seemed, so utterly the negation of the tumult within her, she settled back again at his feet to watch and not excite him. And still his lips smiled that faint smile, and his opened eyes grew dark and darker with meaning.

So at midnight Kirsteen found them.

CHAPTER XXX

In the early hours of his all-night sitting Felix had first only memories, and then Kirsteen for companion.

"I worry most about Tod," she said. "He had that look in his face when he went off from Marrow Farm. He might do something terrible if they ill-treat Sheila. If only she has sense enough to see and not provoke them."

"Surely she will," Felix murmured.

"Yes, if she realizes. But she won't, I'm afraid. Even I have only known him look like that three times. Tod is so gentle—passion stores itself in him; and when it comes, it's awful. If he sees cruelty, he goes almost mad. Once he would have killed a man if I hadn't got between them. He doesn't know what he's doing at such moments. I wish—I wish he were back. It's hard one can't pierce through, and see him."

Gazing at her eyes so dark and intent, Felix thought: 'If YOU can't pierce through—none can.'

He learned the story of the disaster.

Early that morning Derek had assembled twenty of the strongest laborers, and taken them a round of the farms to force the strike-breakers to desist. There had been several fights, in all of which the strike-breakers had been beaten. Derek himself had fought three times. In the afternoon the police had come, and the laborers had rushed with Derek and Sheila, who had joined them, into a barn at Marrow Farm, barred it, and thrown mangolds at the police, when they tried to force an entrance. One by one the laborers had slipped away by a rope out of a ventilation-hole high up at the back, and they had just got Sheila down when the police appeared on that side, too. Derek, who had stayed to the last, covering their escape with mangolds, had jumped down twenty feet when he saw them taking Sheila, and, pitching forward, hit his head against a grindstone. Then, just as they were marching Sheila and two of the laborers away, Tod had arrived and had fallen in alongside the policemen—he and the dog. It was then she had seen that look on his face.

Felix, who had never beheld his big brother in Berserk mood, could offer no consolation; nor had he the heart to adorn the tale, and inflict on this poor woman his reflection: 'This, you see, is what comes of the ferment you have fostered. This is the reward of violence!' He longed, rather, to comfort her; she seemed so lonely and, in spite of all her stoicism, so distraught and sad. His heart went out, too, to Tod. How would he himself have felt, walking by the side of policemen whose arms were twisted n Nedda's! But so mixed are the minds of men that at this very moment there was born within him the germ of a real revolt against the entry of his little daughter into this family of hotheads. It was more new than mere soreness and jealousy; it was fear of a danger hitherto but sniffed at, but now only too sharply savored.

When she left him to go up-stairs, Felix stayed consulting the dark night. As ever, in hours of ebbed vitality, the shapes of fear and doubt grew clearer and more positive; they loomed huge out there among the apple-trees, where the drip-drip of the rain made music. But his thoughts were still nebulous, not amounting to resolve. It was no moment for resolves—with the boy lying up there between the tides of chance; and goodness knew what happening to Tod and Sheila. The air grew sharper; he withdrew to the hearth, where a wood fire still burned, gray ash, red glow, scent oozing from it. And while he crouched there, blowing it with bellows, he heard soft footsteps, and saw Nedda standing behind him transformed.

But in the midst of all his glad sympathy Felix could not help thinking: 'Better for you, perhaps, if he had never returned from darkness!'

She came and crouched down by him.

"Let me sit with you, Dad. It smells so good."

"Very well; but you must sleep."

"I don't believe I'll ever want to sleep again."

And at the glow in her Felix glowed too. What is so infectious as delight? They sat a long time talking, as they had not talked since the first fatal visit to Becket. Of how love, and mountains, works of art, and doing things for others were the only sources of happiness; except scents, and lying on one's back looking through tree-tops at the sky; and tea, and sunlight, flowers, and hard exercise; oh, and the sea! Of how, when things went hard, one prayed—but what did one pray to? Was it not to something in oneself? It was of no use to pray to the great mysterious Force that made one thing a cabbage, and the other a king; for That could obviously not be weak-minded enough to attend. And gradually little pauses began to creep into their talk; then a big pause, and Nedda, who would never want to sleep again, was fast asleep.

Felix watched those long, dark lashes resting on her cheeks; the slow, soft rise of her breast; the touching look of trust and goodness in that young face abandoned to oblivion after these hours of stress; watched the little tired shadows under the eyes, the tremors of the just-parted lips. And, getting up, stealthy as a cat, he found a light rug, and ever more stealthily laid it over her. She stirred at that, smiled up at him, and instantly went off again. And he thought: 'Poor little sweetheart, she WAS tired!' And a passionate desire to guard her from trials and troubles came on him.

At four o'clock Kirsteen slipped in again, and whispered: "She made me promise to come for her. How pretty she looks, sleeping!"

"Yes," Felix answered; "pretty and good!"

Nedda raised her head, stared up at her aunt, and a delighted smile spread over her face. "Is it time again? How lovely!" Then, before either could speak or stop her, she was gone.

"She is more in love," Kirsteen murmured, "than I ever saw a girl of her age."

"She is more in love," Felix answered, "than is good to see."

"She is not truer than Derek is."

"That may be, but she will suffer from him."

"Women who love must always suffer."

Her cheeks were sunken, shadowy; she looked very tired. When she had gone to get some sleep, Felix restored the fire and put on a kettle, meaning to make himself some coffee. Morning had broken, clear and sparkling after the long rain, and full of scent and song. What glory equalled this early morning radiance, the dewy wonder of everything! What hour of the day was such a web of youth and beauty as this, when all the stars from all the skies had fallen into the grass! A cold nose was thrust into his hand, and he saw beside him Tod's dog. The animal was wet, and lightly moved his white-tipped tail; while his dark-yellow eyes inquired of Felix what he was going to give a dog to eat. Then Felix saw his brother coming in. Tod's face was wild and absent as a man with all his thoughts turned on something painful in the distance. His ruffled hair had lost its brightness; his eyes looked as if driven back into his head; he was splashed with mud, and wet from head to foot. He walked up to the hearth without a word.

"Well, old man?" said Felix anxiously.

Tod looked at him, but did not answer.

"Come," said Felix; "tell us!"

"Locked up," said Tod in a voice unlike his own. "I didn't knock them down."

"Heavens! I should hope not."

"I ought to have."

Felix put his hand within his brother's arm.

"They twisted her arms; one of them pushed her from behind. I can't understand it. How was it I didn't? I can't understand."

"I can," said Felix. "They were the Law. If they had been mere men you'd have done it, fast enough."

"I can't understand," Tod repeated. "I've been walking ever since."

Felix stroked his shoulder.

"Go up-stairs, old man. Kirsteen's anxious."

Tod sat down and took his boots off.

"I can't understand," he said once more. Then, without another word, or even a look at Felix, he went out and up the stairs.

And Felix thought: 'Poor Kirsteen! Ah, well—they're all about as queer, one as the other! How to get Nedda out of it?'

And, with that question gnawing at him, he went out into the orchard. The grass was drenching wet, so he descended to the road. Two wood-pigeons were crooning to each other, truest of all sounds of summer; there was no wind, and the flies had begun humming. In the air, cleared of dust, the scent of hay was everywhere. What about those poor devils of laborers, now? They would get the sack for this! and he was suddenly beset with a feeling of disgust. This world where men, and women too, held what they had, took what they could; this world of seeing only one thing at a time; this world of force, and cunning, of struggle, and primitive appetites; of such good things, too, such patience, endurance, heroism—and yet at heart so unutterably savage!

He was very tired; but it was too wet to sit down, so he walked on. Now and again he passed a laborer going to work; but very few in all those miles, and they quite silent. 'Did they ever really whistle?' Felix thought. 'Were they ever jolly ploughmen? Or was that always a fiction? Surely, if they can't give tongue this morning, they never can!' He crossed a stile and took a slanting path through a little wood. The scent of leaves and sap, the dapple of sunlight—all the bright early glow and beauty struck him with such force that he could have cried out in the sharpness of sensation. At that hour when man was still abed and the land lived its own life, how full and sweet and wild that life seemed, how in love with itself! Truly all the trouble in the world came from the manifold disharmonies of the self-conscious animal called Man!

Then, coming out on the road again, he saw that he must be within a mile or two of Becket; and finding himself suddenly very hungry, determined to go there and get some breakfast.

CHAPTER XXXI

Duly shaved with one of Stanley's razors, bathed, and breakfasted, Felix was on the point of getting into the car to return to Joyfields when he received a message from his mother: Would he please go up and see her before he went?

He found her looking anxious and endeavoring to conceal it.

Having kissed him, she drew him to her sofa and said: "Now, darling, come and sit down here, and tell me all about this DREADFUL business." And taking up an odorator she blew over him a little cloud of scent. "It's quite a new perfume; isn't it delicious?"

Felix, who dreaded scent, concealed his feelings, sat down, and told her. And while he told her he was conscious of how pathetically her fastidiousness was quivering under those gruesome details—fighting with policemen, fighting with common men, prison—FOR A LADY; conscious too of her still more pathetic effort to put a good face on it. When he had finished she remained so perfectly still, with lips so hard compressed, that he said:

"It's no good worrying, Mother."

Frances Freeland rose, pulled something hard, and a cupboard appeared. She opened it, and took out a travelling-bag.

"I must go back with you at once," she said.

"I don't think it's in the least necessary, and you'll only knock yourself up."

"Oh, nonsense, darling! I must."

Knowing that further dissuasion would harden her determination, Felix said: "I'm going in the car."

"That doesn't matter. I shall be ready in ten minutes. Oh! and do you know this? It's splendid for taking lines out under the eyes!" She was holding out a little round box with the lid off. "Just wet your finger with it, and dab it gently on."

Touched by this evidence of her deep desire that he should put as good a face on it as herself, Felix dabbed himself under the eyes.

"That's right. Now, wait for me, dear; I shan't be a minute. I've only to get my things. They'll all go splendidly in this little bag."

In a quarter of an hour they had started. During that journey Frances Freeland betrayed no sign of tremor. She was going into action, and, therefore, had no patience with her nerves.

"Are you proposing to stay, Mother?" Felix hazarded; "because I don't think there's a room for you."

"Oh! that's nothing, darling. I sleep beautifully in a chair. It suits me better than lying down." Felix cast up his eyes, and made no answer.

On arriving, they found that the doctor had been there, expressed his satisfaction, and enjoined perfect quiet. Tod was on the point of starting back to Transham, where Sheila and the two laborers would be brought up before the magistrates. Felix and Kirsteen took hurried counsel. Now that Mother, whose nursing was beyond reproach, had come, it would be better if they went with Tod. All three started forthwith in the car.

Left alone, Frances Freeland took her bag—a noticeably old one, without any patent clasp whatever, so that she could open it—went noiselessly upstairs, tapped on Derek's door, and went in. A faint but cheerful voice remarked: "Halloo, Granny!"

Frances Freeland went up to the bed, smiled down on him ineffably, laid a finger on his lips, and said, in the stillest voice: "You mustn't talk, darling!" Then she sat down in the window with her bag beside her. Half a tear had run down her nose, and she had no intention that it should be seen. She therefore opened her bag, and, having taken out a little bottle, beckoned Nedda.

"Now, darling," she whispered, "you must just take one of these. It's nothing new; they're what my mother used to give me at your age. And for one hour you must go out and get some fresh air, and then you can come back."

"Must I, Granny?"

"Yes; you must keep up your strength. Kiss me."

Nedda kissed a cheek that seemed extraordinarily smooth and soft, received a kiss in the middle of her own, and, having stayed a second by the bed, looking down with all her might, went out.

Frances Freeland, in the window, wasted no thoughts, but began to run over in her mind the exact operations necessary to defeat this illness of darling Derek's. Her fingers continually locked and interlocked themselves with fresh determinations; her eyes, fixed on imaginary foods, methods of washing, and ways of keeping him quiet, had an almost fanatical intensity. Like a good general she marshalled her means of attack and fixed them in perfect order. Now and then she gazed into her bag, making quite sure that she had everything, and nothing that was new-fangled or liable to go wrong. For into action she never brought any of those patent novelties that delighted her soul in times of peace. For example, when she herself had pneumonia and no doctor, for two months, it was well known that she had lain on her back, free from every kind of remedy, employing only courage, nature, and beef tea, or some such simple sustenance.

Having now made her mental dispositions, she got up without sound and slipped off a petticoat that she suspected of having rustled a little when she came in; folding and popping it where it could not be suspected any more, she removed her shoes and put on very old velvet slippers. She walked in these toward the bed, listening to find out whether she could hear herself, without success. Then, standing where she could see when his eyes opened, she began to take stock. That pillow wasn't very comfortable! A little table was wanted on both sides, instead of on one. There was no odorator, and she did not see one of those arrangements! All these things would have to be remedied.

Absorbed in this reconnoitring, she failed to observe that darling Derek was looking at her through eyelashes that were always so nice and black. He said suddenly, in that faint and cheerful voice:

"All right, Granny; I'm going to get up to-morrow."

Frances Freeland, whose principle it was that people should always be encouraged to believe themselves better than they were, answered. "Yes, darling, of course; you'll be up in no time. It'll be delightful to see you in a chair to-morrow. But you mustn't talk."

Derek sighed, closed his eyes, and went off into a faint.

It was in moments such as these that Frances Freeland was herself. Her face flushed a little and grew terribly determined. Conscious that she was absolutely alone in the house, she ran to her bag, took out her sal volatile, applied it vigorously to his nose, and poured a little between his lips. She did other things to him, and not until she had brought him round, and the best of it was already made, did she even say to herself: 'It's no use fussing; I must make the best of it.'

Then, having discovered that he felt quite comfortable—as he said—she sat down in a chair to fan him and tremble vigorously. She would not have allowed that movement of her limbs if it had in any way interfered with the fanning. But since, on the contrary, it seemed to be of assistance, she certainly felt it a relief; for, whatever age her spirit might be, her body was seventy-three.

And while she fanned she thought of Derek as a little, black-haired, blazing-gray-eyed slip of a sallow boy, all little thin legs and arms moving funnily like a foal's. He had been such a dear, gentlemanlike little chap. It was dreadful he should be forgetting himself so, and getting into such trouble. And her thoughts passed back beyond him to her own four little sons, among whom she had been so careful not to have a favorite, but to love them all equally. And she thought of how their holland suits wore out, especially in the elastic, and got green behind, almost before they were put on; and of how she used to cut their hairs, spending at least three-quarters of an hour on each, because she had never been quick at it, while they sat so good—except Stanley, and darling Tod, who WOULD move just as she had got into the comb particularly nice bits of his hair, always so crisp and difficult! And of how she had cut off Felix's long golden curls when he was four, and would have cried over it, if crying hadn't always been silly! And of how beautifully they had all had their measles together, so that she had been up with them day and night for about a fortnight. And of how it was a terrible risk with Derek and darling Nedda, not at all a wise match, she was afraid. And yet, if they really were attached, of course one must put the best face on it! And how lovely it would be to see another little baby some day; and what a charming little mother Nedda would make—if only the dear child would do her hair just a little differently! And she perceived that Derek was asleep—and one of her own legs, from the knee down. She would certainly have bad pins and needles if she did not get up; but, since she would not wake him for the world, she must do something else to cure it. And she hit upon this plan. She had only to say, 'Nonsense, you haven't anything of the sort!' and it was sure to go away. She said this to her leg, but, being a realist, she only made it feel like a pin-cushion. She knew, however, that she had only to persevere, because it would never do to give in. She persevered, and her leg felt as if red-hot needles were being stuck in it. Then, for the life of her, she could not help saying a little psalm. The sensation went away and left her leg quite dead. She would have no strength in it at all when she got up. But that would be easily cured, when she could get to her bag, with three globules of nux vomica—and darling Derek must not be waked up for anything! She waited thus till Nedda came back, and then said, "Sssh!"

He woke at once, so that providentially she was able to get up, and, having stood with her weight on one leg for five minutes, so as to be quite sure she did not fall, she crossed back to the window, took her nux vomica, and sat down with her tablets to note down the little affairs she would require, while Nedda took her place beside the bed, to fan him. Having made her list, she went to Nedda and whispered that she was going down to see about one or two little things, and while she whispered she arranged the dear child's hair. If only she would keep it just like that, it would be so much more becoming! And she went down-stairs.

Accustomed to the resources of Stanley's establishment, or at least to those of John's and Felix's, and of the hotels she stayed at, she felt for a moment just a little nonplussed at discovering at her disposal nothing but three dear little children playing with a dog, and one bicycle. For a few seconds she looked at the latter hard. If only it had been a tricycle! Then, feeling certain that she could not make it into one, she knew that she must make the best of it, especially as, in any case, she could not have used it, for it would never do to leave darling Nedda alone in the house. She decided therefore to look in every room to see if she could find the things she wanted. The dog, who had been attracted by her, left the children and came too, and the children, attracted by the dog, followed; so they all five went into a room on the ground floor. It was partitioned into two by a screen; in one portion was a rough camp bedstead, and in the other two dear little child's beds, that must once have been Derek's and Sheila's, and one still smaller, made out of a large packing-case. The eldest of the little children said:

"That's where Billy sleeps, Susie sleeps here, and I sleeps there; and our father slept in here before he went to prison." Frances Freeland experienced a shock. To prison! The idea of letting these little things know such a thing as that! The best face had so clearly not been put on it that she decided to put it herself.

"Oh, not to prison, dear! Only into a house in the town for a little while."

It seemed to her quite dreadful that they should know the truth—it was simply necessary to put it out of their heads. That dear little girl looked so old already, such a little mother! And, as they stood about her, she gazed piercingly at their heads. They were quite clean.

The second dear little thing said:

"We like bein' here; we hope Father won't be comin' back from prison for a long time, so as we can go on stayin' here. Mr. Freeland gives us apples."

The failure of her attempt to put a nicer idea into their heads disconcerted Frances Freeland for a moment only. She said:

"Who told you he was in prison?"

Biddy answered slowly: "Nobody didn't tell us; we picked it up."

"Oh, but you should never pick things up! That's not at all nice. You don't know what harm they may do you."

Billy replied: "We picked up a dead cat yesterday. It didn't scratch a bit, it didn't."

And Biddy added: "Please, what is prison like?"

Pity seized on Frances Freeland for these little derelicts, whose heads and pinafores and faces were so clean. She pursed her lips very tight and said:

"Hold out your hands, all of you."

Three small hands were held out, and three small pairs of gray-blue eyes looked up at her. From the recesses of her pocket she drew forth her purse, took from it three shillings, and placed one in the very centre of each palm. The three small hands closed; two small grave bodies dipped in little courtesies; the third remained stock-still, but a grin spread gradually on its face from ear to ear.

"What do you say?" said Frances Freeland.

"Thank you."

"Thank you—what?"

"Thank you, ma'am."

"That's right. Now run away and play a nice game in the orchard."

The three turned immediately and went. A sound of whispering rose busily outside. Frances Freeland, glancing through the window, saw them unlatching the wicket gate. Sudden alarm seized her. She put out her head and called. Biddy came back.

"You mustn't spend them all at once."

Biddy shook her head.

"No. Once we had a shillin', and we were sick. We're goin' to spend three pennies out of one shillin' every day, till they're gone."

"And aren't you going to put any by for a rainy day?"

"No."

Frances Freeland did not know what to answer. Dear little things!

The dear little things vanished.

In Tod's and Kirsteen's room she found a little table and a pillow, and something that might do, and having devised a contrivance by which this went into that and that into this and nothing whatever showed, she conveyed the whole very quietly up near dear Derek's room, and told darling Nedda to go down-stairs and look for something that she knew she would not find, for she could not think at the moment of any better excuse. When the child had gone, she popped this here, and popped that there. And there she was! And she felt better. It was no use whatever to make a fuss about that aspect of nursing which was not quite nice. One just put the best face upon it, quietly did what was necessary, and pretended that it was not there. Kirsteen had not seen to things quite as she should have. But then dear Kirsteen was so clever.

Her attitude, indeed, to that blue bird, who had alighted now twenty-one years ago in the Freeland nest, had always, after the first few shocks, been duly stoical. For, however her fastidiousness might jib at neglect of the forms of things, she was the last woman not to appreciate really sterling qualities. Though it was a pity dear Kirsteen did expose her neck and arms so that they had got quite brown, a pity that she never went to church and had brought up the dear children not to go, and to have ideas that were not quite right about 'the Land,' still she was emphatically a lady, and devoted to dear Tod, and very good. And her features were so regular, and she had such a good color, and was so slim and straight in the back, that she was always a pleasure to look at. And if she was not quite so practical as she might have been, that was not everything; and she would never get stout, as there was every danger of Clara doing. So that from the first she had always put a good face on her. Derek's voice interrupted her thoughts:

"I'm awfully thirsty, Granny."

"Yes, darling. Don't move your head; and just let me pop in some of this delicious lemonade with a spoon."

Nedda, returning, found her supporting his head with one hand, while with the other she kept popping in the spoon, her soul smiling at him lovingly through her lips and eyes.

CHAPTER XXXII

Felix went back to London the afternoon of Frances Freeland's installation, taking Sheila with him. She had been 'bound over to keep the peace'—a task which she would obviously be the better able to accomplish at a distance. And, though to take charge of her would be rather like holding a burning match till there was no match left, he felt bound to volunteer.

He left Nedda with many misgivings; but had not the heart to wrench her away.

The recovery of a young man who means to get up to-morrow is not so rapid when his head, rather than his body, is the seat of trouble. Derek's temperament was against him. He got up several times in spirit, to find that his body had remained in bed. And this did not accelerate his progress. It had been impossible to dispossess Frances Freeland from command of the sick-room; and, since she was admittedly from experience and power of paying no attention to her own wants, the fittest person for the position, there she remained, taking turn and turn about with Nedda, and growing a little whiter, a little thinner, more resolute in face, and more loving in her eyes, from day to day. That tragedy of the old—the being laid aside from life before the spirit is ready to resign, the feeling that no one wants you, that all those you have borne and brought up have long passed out on to roads where you cannot follow, that even the thought-life of the world streams by so fast that you lie up in a backwater, feebly, blindly groping for the full of the water, and always pushed gently, hopelessly back; that sense that you are still young and warm, and yet so furbelowed with old thoughts and fashions that none can see how young and warm you are, none see how you long to rub hearts with the active, how you yearn for something real to do that can help life on, and how no one will give it you! All this—this tragedy—was for the time defeated. She was, in triumph, doing something real for those she loved and longed to do things for. She had Sheila's room.

For a week at least Derek asked no questions, made no allusion to the mutiny, not even to the cause of his own disablement. It had been impossible to tell whether the concussion had driven coherent recollection from his mind, or whether he was refraining from an instinct of self-preservation, barring such thoughts as too exciting. Nedda dreaded every day lest he should begin. She knew that the questions would fall on her, since no answer could possibly be expected from Granny except: "It's all right, darling, everything's going on perfectly—only you mustn't talk!"

It began the last day of June, the very first day that he got up.

"They didn't save the hay, did they?"

Was he fit to hear the truth? Would he forgive her if she did not tell it? If she lied about this, could she go on lying to his other questions? When he discovered, later, would not the effect undo the good of lies now? She decided to lie; but, when she opened her lips, simply could not, with his eyes on her; and said faintly: "Yes, they did."

His face contracted. She slipped down at once and knelt beside his chair. He said between his teeth:

"Go on; tell me. Did it all collapse?"

She could only stroke his hands and bow her head.

"I see. What's happened to them?"

Without looking up, she murmured:

"Some have been dismissed; the others are working again all right."

"All right!"

She looked up then so pitifully that he did not ask her anything more. But the news put him back a week. And she was in despair. The day he got up again he began afresh:

"When are the assizes?"

"The 7th of August."

"Has anybody been to see Bob Tryst?"

"Yes; Aunt Kirsteen has been twice."

Having been thus answered, he was quiet for a long time. She had slipped again out of her chair to kneel beside him; it seemed the only place from which she could find courage for her answers. He put his hand, that had lost its brown, on her hair. At that she plucked up spirit to ask:

"Would you like me to go and see him?"

He nodded.

"Then, I will—to-morrow."

"Don't ever tell me what isn't true, Nedda! People do; that's why I didn't ask before."

She answered fervently:

"I won't! Oh, I won't!"

She dreaded this visit to the prison. Even to think of those places gave her nightmare. Sheila's description of her night in a cell had made her shiver with horror. But there was a spirit in Nedda that went through with things; and she started early the next day, refusing Kirsteen's proffered company.

The look of that battlemented building, whose walls were pierced with emblems of the Christian faith, turned her heartsick, and she stood for several minutes outside the dark-green door before she could summon courage to ring the bell.

A stout man in blue, with a fringe of gray hair under his peaked cap, and some keys dangling from a belt, opened, and said:

"Yes, miss?"

Being called 'miss' gave her a little spirit, and she produced the card she had been warming in her hand.

"I have come to see a man called Robert Tryst, waiting for trial at the assizes."

The stout man looked at the card back and front, as is the way of those in doubt, closed the door behind her, and said:

"Just a minute, miss."

The shutting of the door behind her sent a little shiver down Nedda's spine; but the temperature of her soul was rising, and she looked round. Beyond the heavy arch, beneath which she stood, was a courtyard where she could see two men, also in blue, with peaked caps. Then, to her left, she became conscious of a shaven-headed noiseless being in drab-gray clothes, on hands and knees, scrubbing the end of a corridor. Her tremor at the stealthy ugliness of this crouching figure yielded at once to a spasm of pity. The man gave her a look, furtive, yet so charged with intense penetrating curiosity that it seemed to let her suddenly into innumerable secrets. She felt as if the whole life of people shut away in silence and solitude were disclosed to her in the swift, unutterably alive look of this noiseless kneeling creature, riving out of her something to feed his soul and body on. That look seemed to lick its lips. It made her angry, made her miserable, with a feeling of pity she could hardly bear. Tears, too startled to flow, darkened her eyes. Poor man! How he must hate her, who was free, and all fresh from the open world and the sun, and people to love and talk to! The 'poor man' scrubbed on steadily, his ears standing out from his shaven head; then, dragging his knee-mat skew-ways, he took the chance to look at her again. Perhaps because his dress and cap and stubble of hair and even the color of his face were so drab-gray, those little dark eyes seemed to her the most terribly living things she had ever seen. She felt that they had taken her in from top to toe, clothed and unclothed, taken in the resentment she had felt and the pity she was feeling; they seemed at once to appeal, to attack, and to possess her ravenously, as though all the starved instincts in a whole prisoned world had rushed up and for a second stood outside their bars. Then came the clank of keys, the eyes left her as swiftly as they had seized her, and he became again just that stealthy, noiseless creature scrubbing a stone floor. And, shivering, Nedda thought:

'I can't bear myself here—me with everything in the world I want—and these with nothing!'

But the stout janitor was standing by her again, together with another man in blue, who said:

"Now, miss; this way, please!"

And down that corridor they went. Though she did not turn, she knew well that those eyes were following, still riving something from her; and she heaved a sigh of real relief when she was round a corner. Through barred windows that had no glass she could see another court, where men in the same drab-gray clothes printed with arrows were walking one behind the other, making a sort of moving human hieroglyphic in the centre of the concrete floor. Two warders with swords stood just outside its edge. Some of those walking had their heads up, their chests expanded, some slouched along with heads almost resting on their chests; but most had their eyes fixed on the back of the neck of the man in front; and there was no sound save the tramp of feet.

Nedda put her hand to her throat. The warder beside her said in a chatty voice:

"That's where the 'ards takes their exercise, miss. You want to see a man called Tryst, waitin' trial, I think. We've had a woman here to see him, and a lady in blue, once or twice."

"My aunt."

"Ah! just so. Laborer, I think—case of arson. Funny thing; never yet found a farm-laborer that took to prison well."

Nedda shivered. The words sounded ominous. Then a little flame lit itself within her.

"Does anybody ever 'take to' prison?"

The warder uttered a sound between a grunt and chuckle.

"There's some has a better time here than they have out, any day. No doubt about it—they're well fed here."

Her aunt's words came suddenly into Nedda's mind: 'Liberty's a glorious feast!' But she did not speak them.

"Yes," the warder proceeded, "some o' them we get look as if they didn't have a square meal outside from one year's end to the other. If you'll just wait a minute, miss, I'll fetch the man down to you."

In a bare room with distempered walls, and bars to a window out of which she could see nothing but a high brick wall, Nedda waited. So rapid is the adjustment of the human mind, so quick the blunting of human sensation, that she had already not quite the passion of pitiful feeling which had stormed her standing under that archway. A kind of numbness gripped her nerves. There were wooden forms in this room, and a blackboard, on which two rows of figures had been set one beneath the other, but not yet added up.

The silence at first was almost deathly. Then it was broken by a sound as of a heavy door banged, and the shuffling tramp of marching men—louder, louder, softer—a word of command—still softer, and it died away. Dead silence again! Nedda pressed her hands to her breast. Twice she added up those figures on the blackboard; each time the number was the same. Ah, there was a fly—two flies! How nice they looked, moving, moving, chasing each other in the air. Did flies get into the cells? Perhaps not even a fly came there—nothing more living than walls and wood! Nothing living except what was inside oneself! How dreadful! Not even a clock ticking, not even a bird's song! Silent, unliving, worse than in this room! Something pressed against her leg. She started violently and looked down. A little cat! Oh, what a blessed thing! A little sandy, ugly cat! It must have crept in through the door. She was not locked in, then, anyway! Thus far had nerves carried her already! Scrattling the little cat's furry pate, she pulled herself together. She would not tremble and be nervous. It was disloyal to Derek and to her purpose, which was to bring comfort to poor Tryst. Then the door was pushed open, and the warder said:

"A quarter of an hour, miss. I'll be just outside."

She saw a big man with unshaven cheeks come in, and stretched out her hand.

"I am Mr. Derek's cousin, going to be married to him. He's been ill, but he's getting well again now. We knew you'd like to hear." And she thought: 'Oh! What a tragic face! I can't bear to look at his eyes!'

He took her hand, said, "Thank you, miss," and stood as still as ever.

"Please come and sit down, and we can talk."

Tryst moved to a form and took his seat thereon, with his hands between his knees, as if playing with an imaginary cap. He was dressed in an ordinary suit of laborer's best clothes, and his stiff, dust-colored hair was not cut particularly short. The cheeks of his square-cut face had fallen in, the eyes had sunk back, and the prominence thus given to his cheek and jawbones and thick mouth gave his face a savage look—only his dog-like, terribly yearning eyes made Nedda feel so sorry that she simply could not feel afraid.

"The children are such dears, Mr. Tryst. Billy seems to grow every day. They're no trouble at all, and quite happy. Biddy's wonderful with them."

"She's a good maid." The thick lips shaped the words as though they had almost lost power of speech.

"Do they let you see the newspapers we send? Have you got everything you want?"

For a minute he did not seem to be going to answer; then, moving his head from side to side, he said:

"Nothin' I want, but just get out of here."

Nedda murmured helplessly:

"It's only a month now to the assizes. Does Mr. Pogram come to see you?"

"Yes, he comes. He can't do nothin'!"

"Oh, don't despair! Even if they don't acquit you, it'll soon be over. Don't despair!" And she stole her hand out and timidly touched his arm. She felt her heart turning over and over, he looked so sad.

He said in that stumbling, thick voice:

"Thank you kindly. I must get out. I won't stand long of it—not much longer. I'm not used to it—always been accustomed to the air, an' bein' about, that's where 'tis. But don't you tell him, miss. You say I'm goin' along all right. Don't you tell him what I said. 'Tis no use him frettin' over me. 'Twon' do me no good."

And Nedda murmured:

"No, no; I won't tell him."

Then suddenly came the words she had dreaded:

"D'you think they'll let me go, miss?"

"Oh, yes, I think so—I hope so!" But she could not meet his eyes, and hearing him grit his boot on the floor knew he had not believed her.

He said slowly:

"I never meant to do it when I went out that mornin'. It came on me sudden, lookin' at the straw."

Nedda gave a little gasp. Could that man outside hear?

Tryst went on: "If they don't let me go, I won' stand it. 'Tis too much for a man. I can't sleep, I can't eat, nor nothin'. I won' stand it. It don' take long to die, if you put your mind to it."

Feeling quite sick with pity, Nedda got up and stood beside him; and, moved by an uncontrollable impulse, she lifted one of his great hands and clasped it in both her own. "Oh, try and be brave and look forward! You're going to be ever so happy some day."

He gave her a strange long stare.

"Yes, I'll be happy some day. Don' you never fret about me."

And Nedda saw that the warder was standing in the doorway.

"Sorry, miss, time's up."

Without a word Tryst rose and went out.

Nedda was alone again with the little sandy cat. Standing under the high-barred window she wiped her cheeks, that were all wet. Why, why must people suffer so? Suffer so slowly, so horribly? What were men made of that they could go on day after day, year after year, watching others suffer?

When the warder came back to take her out, she did not trust herself to speak, or even to look at him. She walked with hands tight clenched, and eyes fixed on the ground. Outside the prison door she drew a long, long breath. And suddenly her eyes caught the inscription on the corner of a lane leading down alongside the prison wall—"Love's Walk"!

CHAPTER XXXIII

Peremptorily ordered by the doctor to the sea, but with instructions to avoid for the present all excitement, sunlight, and color, Derek and his grandmother repaired to a spot well known to be gray, and Nedda went home to Hampstead. This was the last week in July. A fortnight spent in the perfect vacuity of an English watering-place restored the boy wonderfully. No one could be better trusted than Frances Freeland to preserve him from looking on the dark side of anything, more specially when that thing was already not quite nice. Their conversation was therefore free from allusion to the laborers, the strike, or Bob Tryst. And Derek thought the more. The approaching trial was hardly ever out of his mind. Bathing, he would think of it; sitting on the gray jetty looking over the gray sea, he would think of it. Up the gray cobbled streets and away on the headlands, he would think of it. And, so as not to have to think of it, he would try to walk himself to a standstill. Unfortunately the head will continue working when the legs are at rest. And when he sat opposite to her at meal-times, Frances Freeland would gaze piercingly at his forehead and muse: 'The dear boy looks much better, but he's getting a little line between his brows—it IS such a pity!' It worried her, too, that the face he was putting on their little holiday together was not quite as full as she could have wished—though the last thing in the world she could tolerate were really fat cheeks, those signs of all that her stoicism abhorred, those truly unforgivable marks of the loss of 'form.' He struck her as dreadfully silent, too, and she would rack her brains for subjects that would interest him, often saying to herself: 'If only I were clever!' It was natural he should think of dear Nedda, but surely it was not that which gave him the little line. He must be brooding about those other things. He ought not to be melancholy like this and let anything prevent the sea from doing him good. The habit—hard-learned by the old, and especially the old of her particular sex—of not wishing for the moon, or at all events of not letting others know that you are wishing for it, had long enabled Frances Freeland to talk cheerfully on the most indifferent subjects whether or no her heart were aching. One's heart often did ache, of course, but it simply didn't do to let it interfere, making things uncomfortable for others. And once she said to him: "You know, darling, I think it would be so nice for you to take a little interest in politics. They're very absorbing when you once get into them. I find my paper most enthralling. And it really has very good principles."

"If politics did anything for those who most need things done, Granny—but I can't see that they do."

She thought a little, then, making firm her lips, said:

"I don't think that's quite just, darling, there are a great many politicians who are very much looked up to—all the bishops, for instance, and others whom nobody could suspect of self-seeking."

"I didn't mean that politicians were self-seeking, Granny; I meant that they're comfortable people, and the things that interest them are those that interest comfortable people. What have they done for the laborers, for instance?"

"Oh, but, darling! they're going to do a great deal. In my paper they're continually saying that."

"Do you believe it?"

"I'm sure they wouldn't say so if they weren't. There's quite a new plan, and it sounds most sensible. And so I don't think, darling, that if I were you I should make myself unhappy about all that kind of thing. They must know best. They're all so much older than you. And you're getting quite a little line between your eyes."

Derek smiled.

"All right, Granny; I shall have a big one soon."

Frances Freeland smiled, too, but shook her head.

"Yes; and that's why I really think you ought to take interest in politics."

"I'd rather take interest in you, Granny. You're very jolly to look at."

Frances Freeland raised her brows.

"I? My dear, I'm a perfect fright nowadays."

Thus pushing away what her stoicism and perpetual aspiration to an impossibly good face would not suffer her to admit, she added:

"Where would you like to drive this afternoon?"

For they took drives in a small victoria, Frances Freeland holding her sunshade to protect him from the sun whenever it made the mistake of being out.

On August the fourth he insisted that he was well and must go back home. And, though to bring her attendance on him to an end was a grief, she humbly admitted that he must be wanting younger company, and, after one wistful attempt, made no further bones. The following day they travelled.

On getting home he found that the police had been to see little Biddy Tryst, who was to be called as a witness. Tod would take her over on the morning of the trial. Derek did not wait for this, but on the day before the assizes repacked his bag and went off to the Royal Charles Hostel at Worcester. He slept not at all that night, and next morning was early at the court, for Tryst's case would be the first. Anxiously he sat watching all the queer and formal happenings that mark the initiation of the higher justice—the assemblage of the gentlemen in wigs; the sifting, shifting, settling of clerks, and ushers, solicitors, and the public; the busy indifference, the cheerful professionalism of it all. He saw little Mr. Pogram come in, more square and rubbery than ever, and engage in conclave with one of the bewigged. The smiles, shrugs, even the sharp expressions on that barrister's face; the way he stood, twisting round, one hand wrapped in his gown, one foot on the bench behind; it was all as if he had done it hundreds of times before and cared not the snap of one of his thin, yellow fingers. Then there was a sudden hush; the judge came in, bowed, and took his seat. And that, too, seemed so professional. Haunted by the thought of him to whom this was almost life and death, the boy was incapable of seeing how natural it was that they should not all feel as he did.

The case was called and Tryst brought in. Derek had once more to undergo the torture of those tragic eyes fixed on him. Round that heavy figure, that mournful, half-brutal, and half-yearning face, the pleadings, the questions, the answers buzzed, bringing out facts with damning clearness, yet leaving the real story of that early morning as hidden as if the court and all were but gibbering figures of air. The real story of Tryst, heavy and distraught, rising and turning out from habit into the early haze on the fields, where his daily work had lain, of Tryst brooding, with the slow, the wrathful incoherence that centuries of silence in those lonely fields had passed into the blood of his forebears and himself. Brooding, in the dangerous disproportion that enforced continence brings to certain natures, loading the brain with violence till the storm bursts and there leap out the lurid, dark insanities of crime. Brooding, while in the air flies chased each other, insects crawled together in the grass, and the first principle of nature worked everywhere its sane fulfilment. They might talk and take evidence as they would, be shrewd and sharp with all the petty sharpness of the Law; but the secret springs would still lie undisclosed, too natural and true to bear the light of day. The probings and eloquence of justice would never paint the picture of that moment of maniacal relief, when, with jaw hanging loose, eyes bulging in exultation of revenge, he had struck those matches with his hairy hands and let them flare in the straw, till the little red flames ran and licked, rustled and licked, and there was nothing to do but watch them lick and burn. Nor of that sudden wildness of dumb fear that rushed into the heart of the crouching creature, changing the madness of his face to palsy. Nor of the recoil from the burning stack; those moments empty with terror. Nor of how terror, through habit of inarticulate, emotionless existence, gave place again to brute stolidity. And so, heavily back across the dewy fields, under the larks' songs, the cooings of pigeons, the hum of wings, and all the unconscious rhythm of ageless Nature. No! The probings of Justice could never reach the whole truth. And even Justice quailed at its own probings when the mother-child was passed up from Tod's side into the witness-box and the big laborer was seen to look at her and she at him. She seemed to have grown taller; her pensive little face and beautifully fluffed-out corn-brown hair had an eerie beauty, perched up there in the arid witness-box, as of some small figure from the brush of Botticelli.

"Your name, my dear?"

"Biddy Tryst."

"How old?"

"Ten next month, please."

"Do you remember going to live at Mr. Freeland's cottage?"

"Yes, sir."

"And do you remember the first night?"

"Yes, sir."

"Where did you sleep, Biddy?"

"Please, sir, we slept in a big room with a screen. Billy and Susie and me; and father behind the screen."

"And where was the room?"

"Down-stairs, sir."

"Now, Biddy, what time did you wake up the first morning?"

"When Father got up."

"Was that early or late?"

"Very early."

"Would you know the time?"

"No, sir."

"But it was very early; how did you know that?"

"It was a long time before we had any breakfast."

"And what time did you have breakfast?"

"Half past six by the kitchen clock."

"Was it light when you woke up?"

"Yes, sir."

"When Father got up, did he dress or did he go to bed again?"

"He hadn't never undressed, sir."

"Then did he stay with you or did he go out?"

"Out, sir."

"And how long was it before he came back?"

"When I was puttin' on Billy's boots."

"What had you done in between?"

"Helped Susie and dressed Billy."

"And how long does that take you generally?"

"Half an hour, sir."

"I see. What did Father look like when he came in, Biddy?"

The mother-child paused. For the first time it seemed to dawn on her that there was something dangerous in these questions. She twisted her small hands before her and gazed at her father.

The judge said gently:

"Well, my child?"

"Like he does now, sir."

"Thank you, Biddy."

That was all; the mother-child was suffered to step down and take her place again by Tod. And in the silence rose the short and rubbery report of little Mr. Pogram blowing his nose. No evidence given that morning was so conclusive, actual, terrible as that unconscious: "Like he does now, sir." That was why even Justice quailed a little at its own probings.

From this moment the boy knew that Tryst's fate was sealed. What did all those words matter, those professional patterings one way and the other; the professional jeers: 'My friend has told you this' and 'My friend will tell you that.' The professional steering of the impartial judge, seated there above them all; the cold, calculated rhapsodies about the heinousness of arson; the cold and calculated attack on the characters of the stone-breaker witness and the tramp witness; the cold and calculated patter of the appeal not to condemn a father on the evidence of his little child; the cold and calculated outburst on the right of every man to be assumed innocent except on overwhelming evidence such as did not here exist. The cold and calculated balancing of pro and con; and those minutes of cold calculation veiled from the eyes of the court. Even the verdict: 'Guilty'; even the judgment: 'Three years' penal servitude.' All nothing, all superfluity to the boy supporting the tragic gaze of Tryst's eyes and making up his mind to a desperate resort.

"Three years' penal servitude!" The big laborer paid no more attention to those words than to any others spoken during that hour's settlement of his fate. True, he received them standing, as is the custom, fronting the image of Justice, from whose lips they came. But by no single gesture did he let any one see the dumb depths of his soul. If life had taught him nothing else, it had taught him never to express himself. Mute as any bullock led into the slaughtering-house, with something of a bullock's dulled and helpless fear in his eyes, he passed down and away between his jailers. And at once the professional noises rose, and the professional rhapsodists, hunching their gowns, swept that little lot of papers into their pink tape, and, turning to their neighbors, smiled, and talked, and jerked their eyebrows.

CHAPTER XXXIV

The nest on the Spaniard's Road had not been able to contain Sheila long. There are certain natures, such as that of Felix, to whom the claims and exercise of authority are abhorrent, who refuse to exercise it themselves and rage when they see it exercised over others, but who somehow never come into actual conflict with it. There are other natures, such as Sheila's, who do not mind in the least exercising authority themselves, but who oppose it vigorously when they feel it coming near themselves or some others. Of such is the kingdom of militancy. Her experience with the police had sunk deep into her soul. They had not, as a fact, treated her at all badly, which did not prevent her feeling as if they had outraged in her the dignity of woman. She arrived, therefore, in Hampstead seeing red even where red was not. And since, undoubtedly, much real red was to be seen, there was little other color in the world or in her cheeks those days. Long disagreements with Alan, to whom she was still a magnet but whose Stanley-like nature stood firm against the blandishments of her revolting tongue, drove her more and more toward a decision the seeds of which had, perhaps, been planted during her former stay among the breezy airs of Hampstead.

Felix, coming one day into his wife's study—for the house knew not the word drawing-room—found Flora, with eyebrows lifted up and smiling lips, listening to Sheila proclaiming the doctrine that it was impossible not to live 'on one's own.' Nothing else—Felix learned—was compatible with dignity, or even with peace of mind. She had, therefore, taken a back room high up in a back street, in which she was going to live perfectly well on ten shillings a week; and, having thirty-two pounds saved up, she would be all right for a year, after which she would be able to earn her living. The principle she purposed to keep before her eyes was that of committing herself to nothing which would seriously interfere with her work in life. Somehow, it was impossible to look at this girl, with her glowing cheeks and her glowing eyes, and her hair frizzy from ardor, and to distrust her utterances. Yes! She would arrive, if not where she wanted, at all events somewhere; which, after all, was the great thing. And in fact she did arrive the very next day in the back room high up in the back street, and neither Tod's cottage nor the house on the Spaniard's Road saw more than flying gleams of her, thenceforth.

Another by-product, this, of that little starting episode, the notice given to Tryst! Strange how in life one little incident, one little piece of living stress, can attract and gather round it the feelings, thoughts, actions of people whose lives run far and wide away therefrom. But episodes are thus potent only when charged with a significance that comes from the clash of the deepest instincts.

During the six weeks which had elapsed between his return home from Joyfields and the assizes, Felix had much leisure to reflect that if Lady Malloring had not caused Tryst to be warned that he could not marry his deceased wife's sister and continue to stay on the estate—the lives of Felix himself, his daughter, mother, brother, brother's wife, their son and daughter, and in less degree of his other brothers, would have been free of a preoccupation little short of ludicrous in proportion to the face value of the cause. But he had leisure, too, to reflect that in reality the issue involved in that tiny episode concerned human existence to its depths—for, what was it but the simple, all-important question of human freedom? The simple, all-important issue of how far men and women should try to rule the lives of others instead of trying only to rule their own, and how far those others should allow their lives to be so ruled? This it was which gave that episode its power of attracting and affecting the thoughts, feelings, actions of so many people otherwise remote. And though Felix was paternal enough to say to himself nearly all the time, 'I can't let Nedda get further into this mess!' he was philosopher enough to tell himself, in the unfatherly balance of his hours, that the mess was caused by the fight best of all worth fighting—of democracy against autocracy, of a man's right to do as he likes with his life if he harms not others; of 'the Land' against the fetterers of 'the Land.' And he was artist enough to see how from that little starting episode the whole business had sprung—given, of course, the entrance of the wilful force called love. But a father, especially when he has been thoroughly alarmed, gives the artist and philosopher in him short shrift.

Nedda came home soon after Sheila went, and to the eyes of Felix she came back too old and thoughtful altogether. How different a girl from the Nedda who had so wanted 'to know everything' that first night of May! What was she brooding over, what planning, in that dark, round, pretty head? At what resolve were those clear eyes so swiftly raised to look? What was going on within, when her breast heaved so, without seeming cause, and the color rushed up in her cheeks at a word, as though she had been so far away that the effort of recall was alone enough to set all her veins throbbing. And yet Felix could devise no means of attack on her infatuation. For a man cannot cultivate the habit of never interfering and then suddenly throw it over; least of all when the person to be interfered with is his pet and only daughter.

Flora, not of course in the swim of those happenings at Joyfields, could not be got to take the matter very seriously. In fact—beyond what concerned Felix himself and poetry—the matter that she did take seriously had yet to be discovered. Hers was one of those semi-detached natures particularly found in Hampstead. When exhorted to help tackle the question, she could only suggest that Felix should take them all abroad when he had finished 'The Last of the Laborers.' A tour, for instance, in Norway and Sweden, where none of them had ever been, and perhaps down through Finland into Russia.

Feeling like one who squirts on a burning haystack with a garden syringe, Felix propounded this scheme to his little daughter. She received it with a start, a silence, a sort of quivering all over, as of an animal who scents danger. She wanted to know when, and being told—'not before the middle of August', relapsed into her preoccupation as if nothing had been said. Felix noted on the hall table one afternoon a letter in her handwriting, addressed to a Worcester newspaper, and remarked thereafter that she began to receive this journal daily, obviously with a view to reports of the coming assizes. Once he tried to break through into her confidence. It was August Bank Holiday, and they had gone out on to the heath together to see the people wonderfully assembled. Coming back across the burnt-up grass, strewn with paper bags, banana peel, and the cores of apples, he hooked his hand into her arm.

"What is to be done with a child that goes about all day thinking and thinking and not telling anybody what she is thinking?"

She smiled round at him and answered:

"I know, Dad. She IS a pig, isn't she?"

This comparison with an animal of proverbial stubbornness was not encouraging. Then his hand was squeezed to her side and he heard her murmur:

"I wonder if all daughters are such beasts!"

He understood well that she had meant: 'There is only one thing I want—one thing I mean to have—one thing in the world for me now!'

And he said soberly:

"We can't expect anything else."

"Oh, Daddy!" she answered, but nothing more.

Only four days later she came to his study with a letter, and a face so flushed and troubled that he dropped his pen and got up in alarm.

"Read this, Dad! It's impossible! It's not true! It's terrible! Oh! What am I to do?"

The letter ran thus, in a straight, boyish handwriting:

"ROYAL CHARLES HOSTEL,

"WORCESTER, Aug. 7th.

"MY NEDDA,

"I have just seen Bob tried. They have given him three years' penal. It was awful to sit there and watch him. He can never stand it. It was awful to watch him looking at ME. It's no good. I'm going to give myself up. I must do it. I've got everything ready; they'll have to believe me and squash his sentence. You see, but for me it would never have been done. It's a matter of honour. I can't let him suffer any more. This isn't impulse. I've been meaning to do it for some time, if they found him guilty. So in a way, it's an immense relief. I'd like to have seen you first, but it would only distress you, and I might not have been able to go through with it after. Nedda, darling, if you still love me when I get out, we'll go to New Zealand, away from this country where they bully poor creatures like Bob. Be brave! I'll write to-morrow, if they let me.

"Your

"Derek."

The first sensation in Felix on reading this effusion was poignant recollection of the little lawyer's look after Derek had made the scene at Tryst's committal and of his words: 'Nothing in it, is there?' His second thought: 'Is this the cutting of the knot that I've been looking for?' His third, which swept all else away: 'My poor little darling! What business has that boy to hurt her again like this!'

He heard her say:

"Tryst told me himself he did it, Dad! He told me when I went to see him in the prison. Honour doesn't demand what isn't true! Oh, Dad, help me!"

Felix was slow in getting free from the cross currents of reflection. "He wrote this last night," he said dismally. "He may have done it already. We must go and see John."

Nedda clasped her hands. "Ah! Yes!"

And Felix had not the heart to add what he was thinking: 'Not that I see what good he can do!' But, though sober reason told him this, it was astonishingly comforting to be going to some one who could be relied on to see the facts of the situation without any of that 'flimflam' with which imagination is accustomed to surround them. "And we'll send Derek a wire for what it's worth."

They went at once to the post-office, Felix composing this message on the way: 'Utterly mistaken chivalry you have no right await our arrival Felix Freeland.' He handed it to her to read, and passed it under the brass railing to the clerk, not without the feeling of shame due from one who uses the word chivalry in a post-office.

On the way to the Tube station he held her arm tightly, but whether to impart courage or receive it he could not have said, so strung-up in spirit did he feel her. With few words exchanged they reached Whitehall. Marking their card 'Urgent,' they were received within ten minutes.

John was standing in a high, white room, smelling a little of papers and tobacco, and garnished solely by five green chairs, a table, and a bureau with an immense number of pigeonholes, whereat he had obviously been seated. Quick to observe what concerned his little daughter, Felix noted how her greeting trembled up at her uncle and how a sort of warmth thawed for the moment the regularity of his brother's face. When they had taken two of the five green chairs and John was back at his bureau, Felix handed over the letter. John read it and looked at Nedda. Then taking a pipe out of his pocket, which he had evidently filled before they came in, he lighted it and re-read the letter. Then, looking very straight at Nedda, he said:

"Nothing in it? Honour bright, my dear!"

"No, Uncle John, nothing. Only that he fancies his talk about injustice put it into Tryst's head."

John nodded; the girl's face was evidence enough for him.

"Any proof?"

"Tryst himself told me in the prison that he did it. He said it came on him suddenly, when he saw the straw."

A pause followed before John said:

"Good! You and I and your father will go down and see the police."

Nedda lifted her hands and said breathlessly:

"But, Uncle! Dad! Have I the right? He says—honour. Won't it be betraying him?"

Felix could not answer, but with relief he heard John say:

"It's not honorable to cheat the law."

"No; but he trusted me or he wouldn't have written."

John answered slowly:

"I think your duty's plain, my dear. The question for the police will be whether or not to take notice of this false confession. For us to keep the knowledge that it's false from them, under the circumstances, is clearly not right. Besides being, to my mind, foolish."

For Felix to watch this mortal conflict going on in the soul of his daughter—that soul which used to seem, perhaps even now seemed, part of himself; to know that she so desperately wanted help for her decision, and to be unable to give it, unable even to trust himself to be honest—this was hard for Felix. There she sat, staring before her; and only her tight-clasped hands, the little movements of her lips and throat, showed the struggle going on in her.

"I couldn't, without seeing him; I MUST see him first, Uncle!"

John got up and went over to the window; he, too, had been affected by her face.

"You realize," he said, "that you risk everything by that. If he's given himself up, and they've believed him, he's not the sort to let it fall through. You cut off your chance if he won't let you tell. Better for your father and me to see him first, anyway." And Felix heard a mutter that sounded like: 'Confound him!'

Nedda rose. "Can we go at once, then, Uncle?"

With a solemnity that touched Felix, John put a hand on each side of her face, raised it, and kissed her on the forehead.

"All right!" he said. "Let's be off!"

A silent trio sought Paddington in a taxi-cab, digesting this desperate climax of an affair that sprang from origins so small.

In Felix, contemplating his daughter's face, there was profound compassion, but also that family dismay, that perturbation of self-esteem, which public scandal forces on kinsmen, even the most philosophic. He felt exasperation against Derek, against Kirsteen, almost even against Tod, for having acquiesced passively in the revolutionary bringing-up which had brought on such a disaster. War against injustice; sympathy with suffering; chivalry! Yes! But not quite to the point whence they recoiled on his daughter, his family, himself! The situation was impossible! He was fast resolving that, whether or no they saved Derek from this quixotry, the boy should not have Nedda. And already his eyes found difficulty in meeting hers.

They secured a compartment to themselves and, having settled down in corners, began mechanically unfolding evening journals. For after all, whatever happens, one must read the papers! Without that, life would indeed be insupportable! Felix had bought Mr. Cuthcott's, but, though he turned and turned the sheets, they seemed to have no sense till these words caught his eyes: "Convict's tragic death! Yesterday afternoon at Worcester, while being conveyed from the assize court back to prison, a man named Tryst, sentenced to three years' penal servitude for arson, suddenly attacked the warders in charge of him and escaped. He ran down the street, hotly pursued, and, darting out into the traffic, threw himself under a motor-car going at some speed. The car struck him on the head, and the unfortunate man was killed on the spot. No reason whatever can be assigned for this desperate act. He is known, however, to have suffered from epilepsy, and it is thought an attack may have been coming on him at the time."

When Felix had read these words he remained absolutely still, holding that buff-colored paper before his face, trying to decide what he must do now. What was the significance—exactly the significance of this? Now that Tryst was dead, Derek's quixotic action had no meaning. But had he already 'confessed'? It seemed from this account that the suicide was directly after the trial; even before the boy's letter to Nedda had been written. He must surely have heard of it since and given up his mad idea! He leaned over, touched John on the knee, and handed him the paper. John read the paragraph, handed it back; and the two brothers stared fixedly at each other. Then Felix made the faintest movement of his head toward his daughter, and John nodded. Crossing to Nedda, Felix hooked his arm in hers and said:

"Just look at this, my child."

Nedda read, started to her feet, sank back, and cried out:

"Poor, poor man! Oh, Dad! Poor man!"

Felix felt ashamed. Though Tryst's death meant so much relief to her, she felt first this rush of compassion; he himself, to whom it meant so much less relief, had felt only that relief.

"He said he couldn't stand it; he told me that. But I never thought—Oh! Poor man!" And, burying her face against his arm, she gave way.

Petrified, and conscious that John at the far end of the carriage was breathing rather hard, Felix could only stroke her arm till at last she whispered:

"There's nobody now for Derek to save. Oh, if you'd seen that poor man in prison, Dad!"

And the only words of comfort Felix could find were:

"My child, there are thousands and thousands of poor prisoners and captives!"

In a truce to agitation they spent the rest of that three hours' journey, while the train rattled and rumbled through the quiet, happy-looking land.

CHAPTER XXXV

It was tea-time when they reached Worcester, and at once went up to the Royal Charles Hostel. A pretty young woman in the office there informed them that the young gentleman had paid his bill and gone out about ten o'clock; but had left his luggage. She had not seen him come in. His room was up that little staircase at the end of the passage. There was another entrance that he might have come in at. The 'Boots' would take them.

Past the hall stuffed with furniture and decorated with the stags' heads and battle-prints common to English county-town hotels, they followed the 'Boots' up five red-carpeted steps, down a dingy green corridor, to a door at the very end. There was no answer to their knock. The dark little room, with striped walls, and more battle-prints, looked out on a side street and smelled dusty. On a shiny leather sofa an old valise, strapped-up ready for departure, was reposing with Felix's telegram, unopened, deposited thereon. Writing on his card, "Have come down with Nedda. F. F.," and laying it on the telegram, in case Derek should come in by the side entrance, Felix and Nedda rejoined John in the hall.

To wait in anxiety is perhaps the hardest thing in life; tea, tobacco, and hot baths perhaps the only anodynes. These, except the baths, they took. Without knowing what had happened, neither John nor Felix liked to make inquiry at the police station, nor did they care to try and glean knowledge from the hotel people by questions that might lead to gossip. They could but kick their heels till it became reasonably certain that Derek was not coming back. The enforced waiting increased Felix's exasperation. Everything Derek did seemed designed to cause Nedda pain. To watch her sitting there, trying resolutely to mask her anxiety, became intolerable. At last he got up and said to John:

"I think we'd better go round there," and, John nodding, he added: "Wait here, my child. One of us'll come back at once and tell you anything we hear."

She gave them a grateful look and the two brothers went out. They had not gone twenty yards when they met Derek striding along, pale, wild, unhappy-looking. When Felix touched him on the arm, he started and stared blankly at his uncle.

"We've seen about Tryst," Felix said: "You've not done anything?"

Derek shook his head.

"Good! John, tell Nedda that, and stay with her a bit. I want to talk to Derek. We'll go in the other way." He put his hand under the boy's arm and turned him down into the side street. When they reached the gloomy little bedroom Felix pointed to the telegram.

"From me. I suppose the news of his death stopped you?"

"Yes." Derek opened the telegram, dropped it, and sat down beside his valise on the shiny sofa. He looked positively haggard.

Taking his stand against the chest of drawers, Felix said quietly:

"I'm going to have it out with you, Derek. Do you understand what all this means to Nedda? Do you realize how utterly unhappy you're making her? I don't suppose you're happy yourself—"

The boy's whole figure writhed.

"Happy! When you've killed some one you don't think much of happiness—your own or any one's!"

Startled in his turn, Felix said sharply:

"Don't talk like that. It's monomania."

Derek laughed. "Bob Tryst's dead—through me! I can't get out of that."

Gazing at the boy's tortured face, Felix grasped the gruesome fact that this idea amounted to obsession.

"Derek," he said, "you've dwelt on this till you see it out of all proportion. If we took to ourselves the remote consequences of all our words we should none of us survive a week. You're overdone. You'll see it differently to-morrow."

Derek got up to pace the room.

"I swear I would have saved him. I tried to do it when they committed him at Transham." He looked wildly at Felix. "Didn't I? You were there; you heard!"

"Yes, yes; I heard."

"They wouldn't let me then. I thought they mightn't find him guilty here—so I let it go on. And now he's dead. You don't know how I feel!"

His throat was working, and Felix said with real compassion:

"My dear boy! Your sense of honour is too extravagant altogether. A grown man like poor Tryst knew perfectly what he was doing."

"No. He was like a dog—he did what he thought was expected of him. I never meant him to burn those ricks."

"Exactly! No one can blame you for a few wild words. He might have been the boy and you the man by the way you take it! Come!"

Derek sat down again on the shiny sofa and buried his head in his hands.

"I can't get away from him. He's been with me all day. I see him all the time."

That the boy was really haunted was only too apparent. How to attack this mania? If one could make him feel something else! And Felix said:

"Look here, Derek! Before you've any right to Nedda you've got to find ballast. That's a matter of honour, if you like."

Derek flung up his head as if to escape a blow. Seeing that he had riveted him, Felix pressed on, with some sternness:

"A man can't serve two passions. You must give up this championing the weak and lighting flames you can't control. See what it leads to! You've got to grow and become a man. Until then I don't trust my daughter to you."

The boy's lips quivered; a flush darkened his face, ebbed, and left him paler than ever.

Felix felt as if he had hit that face. Still, anything was better than to leave him under this gruesome obsession! Then, to his consternation, Derek stood up and said:

"If I go and see his body at the prison, perhaps he'll leave me alone a little!"

Catching at that, as he would have caught at anything, Felix said:

"Good! Yes! Go and see the poor fellow; we'll come, too."

And he went out to find Nedda.

By the time they reached the street Derek had already started, and they could see him going along in front. Felix racked his brains to decide whether he ought to prepare her for the state the boy was in. Twice he screwed himself up to take the plunge, but her face—puzzled, as though wondering at her lover's neglect of her—stopped him. Better say nothing!

Just as they reached the prison she put her hand on his arm:

"Look, Dad!"

And Felix read on the corner of the prison lane those words: 'Love's Walk'!

Derek was waiting at the door. After some difficulty they were admitted and taken down the corridor where the prisoner on his knees had stared up at Nedda, past the courtyard where those others had been pacing out their living hieroglyphic, up steps to the hospital. Here, in a white-washed room on a narrow bed, the body of the big laborer lay, wrapped in a sheet.

"We bury him Friday, poor chap! Fine big man, too!" And at the warder's words a shudder passed through Felix. The frozen tranquillity of that body!

As the carved beauty of great buildings, so is the graven beauty of death, the unimaginable wonder of the abandoned thing lying so quiet, marvelling at its resemblance to what once lived! How strange this thing, still stamped by all that it had felt, wanted, loved, and hated, by all its dumb, hard, commonplace existence! This thing with the calm, pathetic look of one who asks of his own fled spirit: Why have you abandoned me?

Death! What more wonderful than a dead body—that still perfect work of life, for which life has no longer use! What more mysterious than this sight of what still is, yet is not!

Below the linen swathing the injured temples, those eyes were closed through which such yearning had looked forth. From that face, where the hair had grown faster than if it had been alive, death's majesty had planed away the aspect of brutality, removed the yearning, covering all with wistful acquiescence. Was his departed soul coherent? Where was it? Did it hover in this room, visible still to the boy? Did it stand there beside what was left of Tryst the laborer, that humblest of all creatures who dared to make revolt—serf, descendant of serfs, who, since the beginning, had hewn wood, drawn water, and done the will of others? Or was it winged, and calling in space to the souls of the oppressed?

This body would go back to the earth that it had tended, the wild grass would grow over it, the seasons spend wind and rain forever above it. But that which had held this together—the inarticulate, lowly spirit, hardly asking itself why things should be, faithful as a dog to those who were kind to it, obeying the dumb instinct of a violence that in his betters would be called 'high spirit,' where—Felix wondered—where was it?

And what were they thinking—Nedda and that haunted boy—so motionless? Nothing showed on their faces, nothing but a sort of living concentration, as if they were trying desperately to pierce through and see whatever it was that held this thing before them in such awful stillness. Their first glimpse of death; their first perception of that terrible remoteness of the dead! No wonder they seemed to be conjured out of the power of thought and feeling!

Nedda was first to turn away. Walking back by her side, Felix was surprised by her composure. The reality of death had not been to her half so harrowing as the news of it. She said softly:

"I'm glad to have seen him like that; now I shall think of him—at peace; not as he was that other time."

Derek rejoined them, and they went in silence back to the hotel. But at the door she said:

"Come with me to the cathedral, Derek; I can't go in yet!"

To Felix's dismay the boy nodded, and they turned to go. Should he stop them? Should he go with them? What should a father do? And, with a heavy sigh, he did nothing but retire into the hotel.

CHAPTER XXXVI

It was calm, with a dark-blue sky, and a golden moon, and the lighted street full of people out for airing. The great cathedral, cutting the heavens with its massive towers, was shut. No means of getting in; and while they stood there looking up the thought came into Nedda's mind: Where would they bury poor Tryst who had killed himself? Would they refuse to bury that unhappy one in a churchyard? Surely, the more unhappy and desperate he was, the kinder they ought to be to him!

They turned away down into a little lane where an old, white, timbered cottage presided ghostly at the corner. Some church magnate had his garden back there; and it was quiet, along the waving line of a high wall, behind which grew sycamores spreading close-bunched branches, whose shadows, in the light of the corner lamps, lay thick along the ground this glamourous August night. A chafer buzzed by, a small black cat played with its tail on some steps in a recess. Nobody passed.

The girl's heart was beating fast. Derek's face was so strange and strained. And he had not yet said one word to her. All sorts of fears and fancies beset her till she was trembling all over.

"What is it?" she said at last. "You haven't—you haven't stopped loving me, Derek?"

"No one could stop loving you."

"What is it, then? Are you thinking of poor Tryst?"

With a catch in his throat and a sort of choked laugh he answered:

"Yes."

"But it's all over. He's at peace."

"Peace!" Then, in a queer, dead voice, he added: "I'm sorry, Nedda. It's beastly for you. But I can't help it."

What couldn't he help? Why did he keep her suffering like this—not telling her? What was this something that seemed so terribly between them? She walked on silently at his side, conscious of the rustling of the sycamores, of the moonlit angle of the church magnate's house, of the silence in the lane, and the gliding of their own shadows along the wall. What was this in his face, his thoughts, that she could not reach! And she cried out:

"Tell me! Oh, tell me, Derek! I can go through anything with you!"

"I can't get rid of him, that's all. I thought he'd go when I'd seen him there. But it's no good!"

Terror got hold of her then. She peered at his face—very white and haggard. There seemed no blood in it. They were going down-hill now, along the blank wall of a factory; there was the river in front, with the moonlight on it and boats drawn up along the bank. From a chimney a scroll of black smoke was flung out across the sky, and a lighted bridge glowed above the water. They turned away from that, passing below the dark pile of the cathedral. Here couples still lingered on benches along the river-bank, happy in the warm night, under the August moon! And on and on they walked in that strange, miserable silence, past all those benches and couples, out on the river-path by the fields, where the scent of hay-stacks, and the freshness from the early stubbles and the grasses webbed with dew, overpowered the faint reek of the river mud. And still on and on in the moonlight that haunted through the willows. At their footsteps the water-rats scuttled down into the water with tiny splashes; a dog barked somewhere a long way off; a train whistled; a frog croaked. From the stubbles and second crops of sun-baked clover puffs of warm air kept stealing up into the chillier air beneath the willows. Such moonlit nights never seem to sleep. And there was a kind of triumph in the night's smile, as though it knew that it ruled the river and the fields, ruled with its gleams the silent trees that had given up all rustling. Suddenly Derek said:

"He's walking with us! Look! Over there!"

And for a second there did seem to Nedda a dim, gray shape moving square and dogged, parallel with them at the stubble edges. Gasping out:

"Oh, no; don't frighten me! I can't bear it tonight!" She hid her face against his shoulder like a child. He put his arm round her and she pressed her face deep into his coat. This ghost of Bob Tryst holding him away from her! This enemy! This uncanny presence! She pressed closer, closer, and put her face up to his. It was wonderfully lonely, silent, whispering, with the moongleams slipping through the willow boughs into the shadow where they stood. And from his arms warmth stole through her! Closer and closer she pressed, not quite knowing what she did, not quite knowing anything but that she wanted him never to let her go; wanted his lips on hers, so that she might feel his spirit pass, away from what was haunting it, into hers, never to escape. But his lips did not come to hers. They stayed drawn back, trembling, hungry-looking, just above her lips. And she whispered:

"Kiss me!"

She felt him shudder in her arms, saw his eyes darken, his lips quiver and quiver, as if he wanted them to, but they would not. What was it? Oh, what was it? Wasn't he going to kiss her—not to kiss her? And while in that unnatural pause they stood, their heads bent back among the moongleams and those willow shadows, there passed through Nedda such strange trouble as she had never known. Not kiss her! Not kiss her! Why didn't he? When in her blood and in the night all round, in the feel of his arms, the sight of his hungry lips, was something unknown, wonderful, terrifying, sweet! And she wailed out:

"I want you—I don't care—I want you!" She felt him sway, reel, and clutch her as if he were going to fall, and all other feeling vanished in the instinct of the nurse she had already been to him. He was ill again! Yes, he was ill! And she said:

"Derek—don't! It's all right. Let's walk on quietly!"

She got his arm tightly in hers and drew him along toward home. By the jerking of that arm, the taut look on his face, she could feel that he did not know from step to step whether he could stay upright. But she herself was steady and calm enough, bent on keeping emotion away, and somehow getting him back along the river-path, abandoned now to the moon and the bright, still spaces of the night and the slow-moving, whitened water. Why had she not felt from the first that he was overwrought and only fit for bed?

Thus, very slowly, they made their way up by the factory again into the lane by the church magnate's garden, under the branches of the sycamores, past the same white-faced old house at the corner, to the high street where some few people were still abroad.

At the front door of the hotel stood Felix, looking at his watch, disconsolate as an old hen. To her great relief he went in quickly when he saw them coming. She could not bear the thought of talk and explanation. The one thing was to get Derek to bed. All the time he had gone along with that taut face; and now, when he sat down on the shiny sofa in the little bedroom, he shivered so violently that his teeth chattered. She rang for a hot bottle and brandy and hot water. When he had drunk he certainly shivered less, professed himself all right, and would not let her stay. She dared not ask, but it did seem as if the physical collapse had driven away, for the time at all events, that ghostly visitor, and, touching his forehead with her lips—very motherly—so that he looked up and smiled at her—she said in a matter-of-fact voice:

"I'll come back after a bit and tuck you up," and went out.

Felix was waiting in the hall, at a little table on which stood a bowl of bread and milk. He took the cover off it for her without a word. And while she supped he kept glancing at her, trying to make up his mind to words. But her face was sealed. And all he said was:

"Your uncle's gone to Becket for the night. I've got you a room next mine, and a tooth-brush, and some sort of comb. I hope you'll be able to manage, my child."

Nedda left him at the door of his room and went into her own. After waiting there ten minutes she stole out again. It was all quiet, and she went resolutely back down the stairs. She did not care who saw her or what they thought. Probably they took her for Derek's sister; but even if they didn't she would not have cared. It was past eleven, the light nearly out, and the hall in the condition of such places that await a morning's renovation. His corridor, too, was quite dark. She opened the door without sound and listened, till his voice said softly:

"All right, little angel; I'm not asleep."

And by a glimmer of moonlight, through curtains designed to keep out nothing, she stole up to the bed. She could just see his face, and eyes looking up at her with a sort of adoration. She put her hand on his forehead and whispered: "Are you comfy?"

He murmured back: "Yes, quite comfy."

Kneeling down, she laid her face beside his on the pillow. She could not help doing that; it made everything seem holy, cuddley, warm. His lips touched her nose. Her eyes, for just that instant, looked up into his, that were very dark and soft; then she got up.

"Would you like me to stay till you're asleep?"

"Yes; forever. But I shouldn't exactly sleep. Would you?"

In the darkness Nedda vehemently shook her head. Sleep! No! She would not sleep!

"Good night, then!"

"Good night, little dark angel!"

"Good night!" With that last whisper she slipped back to the door and noiselessly away.

CHAPTER XXXVII

It was long before she closed her eyes, spending the hours in fancy where still less she would have slept. But when she did drop off she dreamed that he and she were alone upon a star, where all the trees were white, the water, grass, birds, everything, white, and they were walking arm in arm, among white flowers. And just as she had stooped to pick one—it was no flower, but—Tryst's white-banded face! She woke with a little cry.

She was dressed by eight and went at once to Derek's room. There was no answer to her knock, and in a flutter of fear she opened the door. He had gone—packed, and gone. She ran back to the hall. There was a note for her in the office, and she took it out of sight to read. It said:

"He came back this morning. I'm going home by the first train. He seems to want me to do something.

"DEREK."

Came back! That thing—that gray thing that she, too, had seemed to see for a moment in the fields beside the river! And he was suffering again as he had suffered yesterday! It was awful. She waited miserably till her father came down. To find that he, too, knew of this trouble was some relief. He made no objection when she begged that they should follow on to Joyfields. Directly after breakfast they set out. Once on her way to Derek again, she did not feel so frightened. But in the train she sat very still, gazing at her lap, and only once glanced up from under those long lashes.

"Can you understand it, Dad?"

Felix, not much happier than she, answered:

"The man had something queer about him. Besides Derek's been ill, don't forget that. But it's too bad for you, Nedda. I don't like it; I don't like it."

"I can't be parted from him, Dad. That's impossible."

Felix was silenced by the vigor of those words.

"His mother can help, perhaps," he said.

Ah! If his mother would help—send him away from the laborers, and all this!

Up from the station they took the field paths, which cut off quite a mile. The grass and woods were shining brightly, peacefully in the sun; it seemed incredible that there should be heartburnings about a land so smiling, that wrongs and miseries should haunt those who lived and worked in these bright fields. Surely in this earthly paradise the dwellers were enviable, well-nourished souls, sleek and happy as the pied cattle that lifted their inquisitive muzzles! Nedda tried to stroke the nose of one—grayish, blunt, moist. But the creature backed away from her hand, snuffling, and its cynical, soft eyes with chestnut lashes seemed warning the girl that she belonged to the breed that might be trusted to annoy.

In the last fields before the Joyfields crossroads they came up with a little, square, tow-headed man, without coat or cap, who had just driven some cattle in and was returning with his dog, at a 'dot-here dot-there' walk, as though still driving them. He gave them a look rather like that of the bullock Nedda had tried to stroke. She knew he must be one of the Malloring men, and longed to ask him questions; but he, too, looked shy and distrustful, as if he suspected that they wanted something out of him. She summoned up courage, however, to say: "Did you see about poor Bob Tryst?"

"I 'eard tell. 'E didn' like prison. They say prison takes the 'eart out of you. 'E didn' think o' that." And the smile that twisted the little man's lips seemed to Nedda strange and cruel, as if he actually found pleasure in the fate of his fellow. All she could find to answer was:

"Is that a good dog?"

The little man looked down at the dog trotting alongside with drooped tail, and shook his head:

"'E's no good wi' beasts—won't touch 'em!" Then, looking up sidelong, he added surprisingly:

"Mast' Freeland 'e got a crack on the head, though!" Again there was that satisfied resentment in his voice and the little smile twisting his lips. Nedda felt more lost than ever.

They parted at the crossroads and saw him looking back at them as they went up the steps to the wicket gate. Amongst a patch of early sunflowers, Tod, in shirt and trousers, was surrounded by his dog and the three small Trysts, all apparently engaged in studying the biggest of the sunflowers, where a peacock-butterfly and a bee were feeding, one on a gold petal, the other on the black heart. Nedda went quickly up to them and asked:

"Has Derek come, Uncle Tod?"

Tod raised his eyes. He did not seem in the least surprised to see her, as if his sky were in the habit of dropping his relatives at ten in the morning.

"Gone out again," he said.

Nedda made a sign toward the children.

"Have you heard, Uncle Tod?"

Tod nodded and his blue eyes, staring above the children's heads, darkened.

"Is Granny still here?"

Again Tod nodded.

Leaving Felix in the garden, Nedda stole upstairs and tapped on Frances Freeland's door.

She, whose stoicism permitted her the one luxury of never coming down to breakfast, had just made it for herself over a little spirit-lamp. She greeted Nedda with lifted eyebrows.

"Oh, my darling! Where HAVE you come from? You must have my nice cocoa! Isn't this the most perfect lamp you ever saw? Did you ever see such a flame? Watch!"

She touched the spirit-lamp and what there was of flame died out.

"Now, isn't that provoking? It's really a splendid thing, quite a new kind. I mean to get you one. Now, drink your cocoa; it's beautifully hot."

"I've had breakfast, Granny."

Frances Freeland gazed at her doubtfully, then, as a last resource, began to sip the cocoa, of which, in truth, she was badly in want.

"Granny, will you help me?"

"Of course, darling. What is it?"

"I do so want Derek to forget all about this terrible business."

Frances Freeland, who had unscrewed the top of a little canister, answered:

"Yes, dear, I quite agree. I'm sure it's best for him. Open your mouth and let me pop in one of these delicious little plasmon biscuits. They're perfect after travelling. Only," she added wistfully, "I'm afraid he won't pay any attention to me."

"No, but you could speak to Aunt Kirsteen; it's for her to stop him."

One of her most pathetic smiles came over Frances Freeland's face.

"Yes, I could speak to her. But, you see, I don't count for anything. One doesn't when one gets old."

"Oh, Granny, you do! You count for a lot; every one admires you so. You always seem to have something that—that other people haven't got. And you're not a bit old in spirit."

Frances Freeland was fingering her rings; she slipped one off.

"Well," she said, "it's no good thinking about that, is it? I've wanted to give you this for ages, darling; it IS so uncomfortable on my finger. Now, just let me see if I can pop it on!"

Nedda recoiled.

"Oh, Granny!" she said. "You ARE—!" and vanished.

There was still no one in the kitchen, and she sat down to wait for her aunt to finish her up-stairs duties.

Kirsteen came down at last, in her inevitable blue dress, betraying her surprise at this sudden appearance of her niece only by a little quivering of her brows. And, trembling with nervousness, Nedda took her plunge, pouring out the whole story—of Derek's letter; their journey down; her father's talk with him; the visit to Tryst's body; their walk by the river; and of how haunted and miserable he was. Showing the little note he had left that morning, she clasped her hands and said:

"Oh, Aunt Kirsteen, make him happy again! Stop that awful haunting and keep him from all this!"

Kirsteen had listened, with one foot on the hearth in her favorite attitude. When the girl had finished she said quietly:

"I'm not a witch, Nedda!"

"But if it wasn't for you he would never have started. And now that poor Tryst's dead he would leave it alone. I'm sure only you can make him lose that haunted feeling."

Kirsteen shook her head.

"Listen, Nedda!" she said slowly, as though weighing each word. "I should like you to understand. There's a superstition in this country that people are free. Ever since I was a girl your age I've known that they are not; no one is free here who can't pay for freedom. It's one thing to see, another to feel this with your whole being. When, like me, you have an open wound, which something is always inflaming, you can't wonder, can you, that fever escapes into the air. Derek may have caught the infection of my fever—that's all! But I shall never lose that fever, Nedda—never!"

"But, Aunt Kirsteen, this haunting is dreadful. I can't bear to see it."

"My dear, Derek is very highly strung, and he's been ill. It's in my family to see things. That'll go away."

Nedda said passionately:

"I don't believe he'll ever lose it while he goes on here, tearing his heart out. And they're trying to get me away from him. I know they are!"

Kirsteen turned; her eyes seemed to blaze.

"They? Ah! Yes! You'll have to fight if you want to marry a rebel, Nedda!"

Nedda put her hands to her forehead, bewildered. "You see, Nedda, rebellion never ceases. It's not only against this or that injustice, it's against all force and wealth that takes advantage of its force and wealth. That rebellion goes on forever. Think well before you join in."

Nedda turned away. Of what use to tell her to think when 'I won't—I can't be parted from him!' kept every other thought paralyzed. And she pressed her forehead against the cross-bar of the window, trying to find better words to make her appeal again. Out there above the orchard the sky was blue, and everything light and gay, as the very butterflies that wavered past. A motor-car seemed to have stopped in the road close by; its whirring and whizzing was clearly audible, mingled with the cooings of pigeons and a robin's song. And suddenly she heard her aunt say:

"You have your chance, Nedda! Here they are!"

Nedda turned. There in the doorway were her Uncles John and Stanley coming in, followed by her father and Uncle Tod.

What did this mean? What had they come for? And, disturbed to the heart, she gazed from one to the other. They had that curious look of people not quite knowing what their reception will be like, yet with something resolute, almost portentous, in their mien. She saw John go up to her aunt and hold out his hand.

"I dare say Felix and Nedda have told you about yesterday," he said. "Stanley and I thought it best to come over." Kirsteen answered:

"Tod, will you tell Mother who's here?"

Then none of them seemed to know quite what to say, or where to look, till Frances Freeland, her face all pleased and anxious, came in. When she had kissed them they all sat down. And Nedda, at the window, squeezed her hands tight together in her lap.

"We've come about Derek," John said.

"Yes," broke in Stanley. "For goodness' sake, Kirsteen, don't let's have any more of this! Just think what would have happened yesterday if that poor fellow hadn't providentially gone off the hooks!"

"Providentially!"

"Well, it was. You see to what lengths Derek was prepared to go. Hang it all! We shouldn't have been exactly proud of a felon in the family."

Frances Freeland, who had been lacing and unlacing her fingers, suddenly fixed her eyes on Kirsteen.

"I don't understand very well, darling, but I am sure that whatever dear John says will be wise and right. You must remember that he is the eldest and has a great deal of experience."

Kirsteen bent her head. If there was irony in the gesture, it was not perceived by Frances Freeland.

"It can't be right for dear Derek, or any gentleman, to go against the law of the land or be mixed up with wrong-doing in any way. I haven't said anything, but I HAVE felt it very much. Because—it's all been not quite nice, has it?"

Nedda saw her father wince. Then Stanley broke in again:

"Now that the whole thing's done with, do, for Heaven's sake, let's have a little peace!"

At that moment her aunt's face seemed wonderful to Nedda; so quiet, yet so burningly alive.

"Peace! There is no peace in this world. There is death, but no peace!" And, moving nearer to Tod, she rested her hand on his shoulder, looking, as it seemed to Nedda, at something far away, till John said:

"That's hardly the point, is it? We should be awfully glad to know that there'll be no more trouble. All this has been very worrying. And now the cause seems to be—removed."

There was always a touch of finality in John's voice. Nedda saw that all had turned to Kirsteen for her answer.

"If those up and down the land who profess belief in liberty will cease to filch from the helpless the very crust of it, the cause will be removed."

"Which is to say—never!"

At those words from Felix, Frances Freeland, gazing first at him and then at Kirsteen, said in a pained voice:

"I don't think you ought to talk like that, Kirsteen, dear. Nobody who's at all nice means to be unkind. We're all forgetful sometimes. I know I often forget to be sympathetic. It vexes me dreadfully!"

"Mother, don't defend tyranny!"

"I'm sure it's often from the best motives, dear."

"So is rebellion."

"Well, I don't understand about that, darling. But I do think, with dear John, it's a great pity. It will be a dreadful drawback to Derek if he has to look back on something that he regrets when he's older. It's always best to smile and try to look on the bright side of things and not be grumbly-grumbly!"

After that little speech of Frances Freeland's there was a silence that Nedda thought would last forever, till her aunt, pressing close to Tod's shoulder, spoke.

"You want me to stop Derek. I tell you all what I've just told Nedda. I don't attempt to control Derek; I never have. For myself, when I see a thing I hate I can't help fighting against it. I shall never be able to help that. I understand how you must dislike all this; I know it must be painful to you, Mother. But while there is tyranny in this land, to laborers, women, animals, anything weak and helpless, so long will there be rebellion against it, and things will happen that will disturb you."

Again Nedda saw her father wince. But Frances Freeland, bending forward, fixed her eyes piercingly on Kirsteen's neck, as if she were noticing something there more important than that about tyranny!

Then John said very gravely:

"You seem to think that we approve of such things being done to the helpless!"

"I know that you disapprove."

"With the masterly inactivity," Felix said suddenly, in a voice more bitter than Nedda had ever heard from him, "of authority, money, culture, and philosophy. With the disapproval that lifts no finger—winking at tyrannies lest worse befall us. Yes, WE—brethren—we—and so we shall go on doing. Quite right, Kirsteen!"

"No. The world is changing, Felix, changing!"

But Nedda had started up. There at the door was Derek.

CHAPTER XXXVIII

Derek, who had slept the sleep of the dead, having had none for two nights, woke thinking of Nedda hovering above him in the dark; of her face laid down beside him on the pillow. And then, suddenly, up started that thing, and stood there, haunting him! Why did it come? What did it want of him? After writing the little note to Nedda, he hurried to the station and found a train about to start. To see and talk with the laborers; to do something, anything to prove that this tragic companion had no real existence! He went first to the Gaunts' cottage. The door, there, was opened by the rogue-girl, comely and robust as ever, in a linen frock, with her sleeves rolled up, and smiling broadly at his astonishment.

"Don't be afraid, Mr. Derek; I'm only here for the week-end, just to tiddy up a bit. 'Tis all right in London. I wouldn't come back here, I wouldn't—not if you was to give me—" and she pouted her red lips.

"Where's your father, Wilmet?"

"Over in Willey's Copse cuttin' stakes. I hear you've been ill, Mr. Derek. You do look pale. Were you very bad?" And her eyes opened as though the very thought of illness was difficult for her to grasp. "I saw your young lady up in London. She's very pretty. Wish you happiness, Mr. Derek. Grandfather, here's Mr. Derek!"

The face of old Gaunt, carved, cynical, yellow, appeared above her shoulder. There he stood, silent, giving Derek no greeting. And with a sudden miserable feeling the boy said:

"I'll go and find him. Good-by, Wilmet!"

"Good-by, Mr. Derek. 'Tis quiet enough here now; there's changes."

Her rogue face twinkled again, and, turning her chin, she rubbed it on her plump shoulder, as might a heifer, while from behind her Grandfather Gaunt's face looked out with a faint, sardonic grin.

Derek, hurrying on to Willey's Copse, caught sight, along a far hedge, of the big dark laborer, Tulley, who had been his chief lieutenant in the fighting; but, whether the man heard his hail or no, he continued along the hedgeside without response and vanished over a stile. The field dipped sharply to a stream, and at the crossing Derek came suddenly on the little 'dot-here dot-there' cowherd, who, at Derek's greeting, gave him an abrupt "Good day!" and went on with his occupation of mending a hurdle. Again that miserable feeling beset the boy, and he hastened on. A sound of chopping guided him. Near the edge of the coppice Tom Gaunt was lopping at some bushes. At sight of Derek he stopped and stood waiting, his loquacious face expressionless, his little, hard eye cocked.

"Good morning, Tom. It's ages since I saw you."

"Ah, 'tis a proper long time! You 'ad a knock."

Derek winced; it was said as if he had been disabled in an affair in which Gaunt had neither part nor parcel. Then, with a great effort, the boy brought out his question:

"You've heard about poor Bob?"

"Yaas; 'tis the end of HIM."

Some meaning behind those words, the unsmiling twist of that hard-bitten face, the absence of the 'sir' that even Tom Gaunt generally gave him, all seemed part of an attack. And, feeling as if his heart were being squeezed, Derek looked straight into his face.

"What's the matter, Tom?"

"Matter! I don' know as there's anything the matter, ezactly!"

"What have I done? Tell me!"

Tom Gaunt smiled; his little, gray eyes met Derek's full.

"'Tisn't for a gentleman to be held responsible."

"Come!" Derek cried passionately. "What is it? D'you think I deserted you, or what? Speak out, man!"

Abating nothing of his stare and drawl, Gaunt answered:

"Deserted? Oh, dear no! Us can't afford to do no more dyin' for you—that's all!"

"For me! Dying! My God! D'you think I wouldn't have—? Oh! Confound you!"

"Aye! Confounded us you 'ave! Hope you're satisfied!"

Pale as death and quivering all over, Derek answered:

"So you think I've just been frying fish of my own?"

Tom Gaunt, emitted a little laugh.

"I think you've fried no fish at all. That's what I think. And no one else does, neither, if you want to know—except poor Bob. You've fried his fish, sure enough!"

Stung to the heart, the boy stood motionless. A pigeon was cooing; the sappy scent from the lopped bushes filled all the sun-warmed air.

"I see!" he said. "Thanks, Tom; I'm glad to know."

Without moving a muscle, Tom Gaunt answered:

"Don't mention it!" and resumed his lopping.

Derek turned and walked out of the little wood. But when he had put a field between him and the sound of Gaunt's bill-hook, he lay down and buried his face in the grass, chewing at its green blades, scarce dry of dew, and with its juicy sweetness tasting the full of bitterness. And the gray shade stalked out again, and stood there in the warmth of the August day, with its scent and murmur of full summer, while the pigeons cooed and dandelion fluff drifted by....

When, two hours later, he entered the kitchen at home, of the company assembled Frances Freeland alone retained equanimity enough to put up her face to be kissed.

"I'm so thankful you've come back in time to see your uncles, darling. Your Uncle John thinks, and we all agree, that to encourage those poor laborers to do things which are not nice is—is—you know what I mean, darling!"

Derek gave a bitter little laugh.

"Criminal, Granny! Yes, and puppyish! I've learned all that."

The sound of his voice was utterly unlike his own, and Kirsteen, starting forward, put her arm round him.

"It's all right, Mother. They've chucked me."

At that moment, when all, save his mother, wanted so to express their satisfaction, Frances Freeland alone succeeded.

"I'm so glad, darling!"

Then John rose and, holding out his hand to his nephew, said:

"That's the end of the trouble, then, Derek?"

"Yes. And I beg your pardon, Uncle John; and all—Uncle Stanley, Uncle Felix; you, Dad; Granny."

They had all risen now. The boy's face gave them—even John, even Stanley—a choke in the throat. Frances Freeland suddenly took their arms and went to the door; her other two sons followed. And quietly they all went out.

Derek, who had stayed perfectly still, staring past Nedda into a corner of the room, said:

"Ask him what he wants, Mother."

Nedda smothered down a cry. But Kirsteen, tightening her clasp of him and looking steadily into that corner, answered:

"Nothing, my boy. He's quite friendly. He only wants to be with you for a little."

"But I can't do anything for him."

"He knows that."

"I wish he wouldn't, Mother. I can't be more sorry than I have been."

Kirsteen's face quivered.

"My dear, it will go quite soon. Love Nedda! See! She wants you!"

Derek answered in the same quiet voice:

"Yes, Nedda is the comfort. Mother, I want to go away—away out of England—right away."

Nedda rushed and flung her arms round him.

"I, too, Derek; I, too!"

That evening Felix came out to the old 'fly,' waiting to take him from Joyfields to Becket. What a sky! All over its pale blue a far-up wind had drifted long, rosy clouds, and through one of them the half-moon peered, of a cheese-green hue; and, framed and barred by the elm-trees, like some roseate, stained-glass window, the sunset blazed. In a corner of the orchard a little bonfire had been lighted, and round it he could see the three small Trysts dropping armfuls of leaves and pointing at the flames leaping out of the smoulder. There, too, was Tod's big figure, motionless, and his dog sitting on its haunches, with head poked forward, staring at those red tongues of flame. Kirsteen had come with him to the wicket gate. He held her hand long in his own and pressed it hard. And while that blue figure, turned to the sunset, was still visible, he screwed himself back to look.

They had been in painful conclave, as it seemed to Felix, all day, coming to the decision that those two young things should have their wish, marry, and go out to New Zealand. The ranch of Cousin Alick Morton (son of that brother of Frances Freeland, who, absorbed in horses, had wandered to Australia and died in falling from them) had extended a welcome to Derek. Those two would have a voyage of happiness—see together the red sunsets in the Mediterranean, Pompeii, and the dark ants of men swarming in endless band up and down with their coal-sacks at Port Said; smell the cinnamon gardens of Colombo; sit up on deck at night and watch the stars.... Who could grudge it them? Out there youth and energy would run unchecked. For here youth had been beaten!

On and on the old 'fly' rumbled between the shadowy fields. 'The world is changing, Felix—changing!' Was that defeat of youth, then, nothing? Under the crust of authority and wealth, culture and philosophy—was the world really changing; was liberty truly astir, under that sky in the west all blood; and man rising at long last from his knees before the God of force? The silent, empty fields darkened, the air gathered dewy thickness, and the old 'fly' rumbled and rolled as slow as fate. Cottage lamps were already lighted for the evening meal. No laborer abroad at this hour! And Felix thought of Tryst, the tragic fellow—the moving, lonely figure; emanation of these solitary fields, shade of the departing land! One might well see him as that boy saw him, silent, dogged, in a gray light such as this now clinging above the hedgerows and the grass!

The old 'fly' turned into the Becket drive. It had grown dark now, save for the half-moon; the last chafer was booming by, and a bat flitting, a little, blind, eager bat, through the quiet trees. He got out to walk the last few hundred yards. A lovely night, silent below her stars—cool and dark, spread above field after field, wood on wood, for hundreds of miles on every side. Night covering his native land. The same silence had reigned out there, the same perfume stolen up, the same star-shine fallen, for millions of years in the past, and would for millions of years to come. Close to where the half-moon floated, a slow, narrow, white cloud was passing—curiously shaped. At one end of it Felix could see distinctly the form of a gleaming skull, with dark sky showing through its eyeholes, cheeks, and mouth. A queer phenomenon; fascinating, rather ghastly! It grew sharper in outline, more distinct. One of those sudden shudders, that seize men from the crown of the head to the very heels, passed down his back. He shut his eyes. And, instead, there came up before him Kirsteen's blue-clothed figure turned to the sunset glow. Ah! Better to see that than this skull above the land! Better to believe her words: 'The world is changing, Felix—changing!'

John Galsworthy, eldest son of John Galsworthy (1817-1904), a solicitor and company director of Old Jewry, London, and Blanche Bailey (1835-1915), daughter of Charles Bartleet, a needlemaker in Redditch. His father's ancestors originated in Wembury, near Plymouth in England, and Galsworthy, for whom family origins were of significant importance, maintained a close connection with Devon. His more immediate family were considerably wealthy and well established in the shipping industry, and owned a fine estate in Kingston-upon-Thames called Parkfield, where Galsworthy was born on the 14th August 1867. At the age of nine he began education at Saugeen, a Bournemouth preparatory school, before starting at Harrow school in 1881 where he remained until 1886, distinguishing himself as an athlete.

His education at Harrow being successful enough to gain him entrance to Oxford, he began at New College to read law and gained a second-class degree with honours in 1889. Following Lincoln's Inn he was called to the bar in 1890. Despite this recognition he realised that he was not keen to actually begin practising law and so he resolved instead to look after the family's shipping business while specialising himself in Marine Law. This decision saw him take to the seas to destinations such as Vancouver, Island and South AFrica, though it was at the age of twenty-five on one particular journey to Australia, motivated by an (unfulfilled) intention to meet Robert Louis Stevenson on Samoa that he would being to realise fully his literary interests: though he was not considering becoming a writer at this time, his enjoyment of literature was enough to encourage an attempt at meeting a great writer and eventually enabled one of the most significant encounters of his life. He made the journey with his friend Edward Sanderson and, though he missed Stevenson, he met Joseph Conrad, a fellow future author famed for his novels which were often nautically themed. At the time Conrad was the first mate of the sailing-ship Torrens moored in the harbour of Adelaide, Australia; still very much focused on his ship-borne career, he was yet to begin his writing in earnest.

Indeed, though neither knew at the time, both Conrad and Galsworthy were at similar junctures in their lives, their time spent as sea acting as a transitional period during which each found their literary calling. It is perhaps owning to this unknown common ground that they became close friends. During his time on the Torrens Galsworthy recorded several details, offering a frank and valuable characterisation of Conrad while also illuminating his own experiences as a student of Marine Law.

"I supposed to be studying navigation for the Admiralty Bar, would every day work out the position of the ship with the captain. On one side of the saloon table we would sit and check our observations with those of Conrad, who from the other side of the table would look at us a little quizzically."

On his return to England and the cessation of his nautical voyaging, Galsworthy began an affair with the wife of his first cousin, Major Arthur John Galsworthy. Ada Nemesis Pearson Cooper (1864-1956), the daughter of Emanuel Copper, an obstetrician from Norwich, remained married to the Major for ten years and the affair remained secret for its duration. In order to conceal the affair they took considerable pains to avoid suspicion. One such tactic was to stay in a secluded farmhouse called Wingstone in the village on Manaton on Dartmoor, in Devon. In Galsworthy's decision to choose Devon as the location for their clandestine rendezvous we see evidence of Galsworthy's affection for the place of his father's origin. It was only when, in 1905, she divorced the Major that their affair became known following their marriage on 23rd September of that year.

Galsworthy now took to writing sometime after having met Conrad and his career began in earnest when, in 1897, his first work, From the Four Winds, a volume of short stories, was published under the pseudonym John Sinjohn. He succeeded this in 1898 with Jocelyn, his first novel, and then his second in

1900, Villa Rubein. In 1901 he published a second volume of short stories, A Man of Devon, which was the last of his work to be published under pseudonym. The first of his work to be published under his own name was The Island Pharisees in 1904, a novel of social observation, seasoned with flashes of satire and propaganda. His decision to write under his own name is arguably owing to the recent death of his father, either as a mark of respect to his name or because now he was able to publish freely without incurring the possibility of paternal disappointment at his choice of career. It also marked a shift in his professionalism; he had hitherto published with small, independent publishers, but The Island Pharisees was published by Heinemann, a far more established House and one with whom he remained for the duration of his writing career.

He arguably cemented his position and maturity as a writer when, in 1906, he saw the publication of both his first major play, The Silver Box, and the novel The Man of Property. Each was published to considerable critical acclaim, and to achieve both in such a short space of time was impressive. the Silver Box concerns the imbalance in the justice system with regards to criminals of differing class by contrasting the treatment of a poor thief and a rich thief, both of whom stole silver cigarette cases but for very different reasons. The complexity of individual experience when not dealt with in public is highlighted and questioned in a bravely critical manner; despite the clear issues it raises with class and privilege, the final night was attended by the Price and Princess of Wales. The Man of Property was the first novel in the famous The Forsyte Saga, a trilogy of novels with an 'interlude' between each one, written between 1906 and 1921. Dealing with the questions of status, class and materialism, The Man of Property introduces us to the Forsyte family, particularly Soames Forsyte, who is acutely aware of his status as 'new money' and equally keen to assert himself as a wealthy man. Jealous of his wife and desperate to own things in order to confirm his wealth to those observing him, he engineers a plan to keep his wife from her friends which backfires spectacularly when, instead of cutting her off, all Soames achieves is enabling her to have an affair. This drives Soames to terrible actions with terrible consequences, which Galsworthy depicts with confidence.

Very typically Edwardian, the novel focuses on conflict between property and art, and to a certain degree much of its emotional power is drawn from Galsworthy's own life, particularly his affair with Ada. Their rendezvous in the countryside of Devon mirror the manner in which Forsyte seeks to relocate his wife and; though theirs was a much healthier relationship, there are clear similarities. By examining the fragile nature of the class system and those moving within it Galsworthy offered an important perspective on the relationships between material wealth, personal happiness and obsession, and the manner in which these change over time. His contemporaries widely regarded the publication of this novel as marking the end of Victorianism. His friend Conrad praised it as "indubitably a piece of art" and, though the notoriously risqué D.H. Lawrence lamented the novel's timidity in the face of sexuality and sensuality, he considered it potentially "a very great novel, a very great satire".

Though he continued to write both plays and novels, it was his work as a playwright for which he was most celebrated by his contemporaries. Indeed, his next novel, The Country House, seems uncharacteristically unfocused, its satirical view of those belonging to the country set comparatively unremarkable and weakly characterised, while at times the tone of satire becomes one of ironic detachment. In 1909 he published Fraternity, an exploration of of the various connections between urban society and the social classes therein, though its representation of lower-class Londoners is utterly unconvincing and ill-informed. Remaining with the subject of the landed gentry and the society surrounding it, in 1915 he published The Freelands, which does not stray far from conservative discussions of capitalism, the rural economy and their interrelationship.

His drama, however, featured a convincingly muted realism, directed at a relatively small, educated and politically-aware audience. His social agenda is prevalent here too, and is represented in a simple and static manner producing arresting instances of high drama. This talent for creating moments of captivating theatre is complimented by an instinctual sense of balance enabling his narratives to vacillate between their emotional high- and low-points, ultimately reaching conclusive equilibrium. This is particularly evident in one of his most popular plays, Strife, published in 1909 and examining the antagonists in a strike at a Cornish tin mine. In this, and in 1910's Justice, he approaches his subject with sympathy, irony and balance, which establishes a position of narrative authority while garnering the audiences trust that he is representing his characters and their motives justly. Justice condemns the use of solitary confinement in prisons, a reformist agenda which caught the liberality of his contemporary audiences along with the home secretary, Winston Churchill. Despite he was careful to disassociate himself with politics and professed himself apolitical, he and his work were nevertheless aligned with the views of the Liberal establishment. He spent much of the duration of the First World War working in a field hospital in France as an orderly having been passed over for military service.

Despite the popularity and brilliance of his work, it was only in 1920 that he had his first true commercial success with The Skin Game, a melodrama dealing with ethics, property and class. The play was adapted by Alfred Hitchcock in 1931. Galsworthy, meanwhile, had turned down a knighthood in 1918, considering his work not sufficient to be made a knight of the realm. He did, however, accept the Belgian Palmes d'Or in the following year. In 1920 he published the second novel in the Forsyte Saga, In Chancery, in which he resumes many of the themes of the first novel, focusing on the marital disharmony between Soames Forsyte and his wife. Katherine Mansfield considered it "a fascinating, brilliant book" in her review in The Atheneum. Then, in 1921, he was elected as the PEN International Literary Club's first president. The concluding novel to The Forsyte Saga, To Let was published in 1921 with a kind of peace being found between Forsyte and his now-ex wife, though he is left contemplating his losses and his greed. More ironic treatment of class confusions followed in Loyalties, bringing with it more popular success which lasted until 1926 and Escape, the last of his popular plays. Though he enjoyed popular success it was inconsistent and relatively small. His Collected Plays was published in 1929.

Over the course of time the appreciation of his work has gradually shifted from his plays to his novels, and particularly the detail and intricacy of his chronicle of English social difference, tension and pretension in The Forsyte Saga. Its success encouraged Galsworthy to revisit Soames Forsyte in a second trilogy, A Modern Comedy, which follows Soames's obsessive love of his daughter Fleur. In its three volumes, The White Monkey (1924), The Silver Spoon (1936) and Swan Song (1928) he examines the English commercial upper-middle class and its ideologies, its instinct to possess as its only way of distinguishing itself manifested in the poisonous materialism of Soames. Interestingly, this emergent social class which he so vehemently criticises is the very class from which he emerged. He witnessed first-hand its insularity, its chauvinism, its restrictive and oppressive morality, its stubborn imperialism and its materialism, and it is this experience which enables him to write so comfortably about it. Swan Song is widely considered among the best of Galsworthy's writing for the depth of its exploration of society and its heightened emotional subtlety. In 1929 he was appointed to the Order of Merit, despite having turned down a knighthood earlier. He spent his last years writing a third trilogy, End of the Chapter, beginning in 1931 with Maid in Waiting, Flowering Wilderness in 1932 and concluding with Over The River in 1933. These are significantly less coherent works and are indicative of his deteriorating health. Indeed, in 1932 he was awarded the Nobel Prize, though he was too ill to attend the ceremony.

Throughout the course of his career he received honorary degrees from the universities of St Andrews (1922), Manchester (1927), Dublin (1929), Cambridge (1930), Sheffield (1930), Oxford (1931), and Princeton (1931). In 1926 New College, Oxford, elected him as an honourary fellow. In photographs he is portrayed as handsome, fastidiously dressed and dignified. He was unusually compassionate and this saw him involved in several charitable and humane causes throughout the course of his life, including penal reforms, attacks on theatrical censorship and campaigning for animal rights. Though he spent the majority of the final seven years of his life at his home in Bury, West Sussex, it was at his home in Hampstead, London, that he died of a brain tumour on 31st January, 1933, six weeks after having been too ill to attend the ceremony in honour of his receiving the Nobel Prize. According to demands made in his will he was cremated and his ashes scattered over the South Downs from an aeroplane. Also in his will was his wish to leave cottages to several of his astonished tenants. He is memorialised in Highgate 'New' Cemetery and in the cloisters of New College, Oxford, where he was an honourary fellow.

John Galsworthy – A Concise Bibliography

From the Four Winds, 1897 (as John Sinjohn)
Jocelyn, 1898 (as John Sinjohn)
Villa Rubein, 1900 (as John Sinjohn)
A Man of Devon, 1901 (as John Sinjohn)
The Island Pharisees, 1904
The Silver Box, 1906 (his first play)
The Man of Property, 1906 – First book of The Forsyte Saga (1922)
The Country House, 1907
A Commentary, 1908
Fraternity, 1909
A Justification for the Censorship of Plays, 1909
Strife, 1909
Fraternity, 1909
Joy, 1909
Justice, 1910
A Motley, 1910
The Spirit of Punishment, 1910
Horses in Mines, 1910
The Patrician, 1911
The Little Dream, 1911
The Pigeon, 1912
The Eldest Son, 1912
Quality, 1912
Moods, Songs, and Doggerels, 1912
For Love of Beasts, 1912
The Inn of Tranquillity, 1912
The Dark Flower, 1913
The Fugitive, 1913
The Mob, 1914
The Freelands, 1915
The Little Man, 1915
A Bit o' Love, 1915

A Sheaf, 1916

The Apple Tree, 1916

The Foundations, 1917

Beyond, 1917

Five Tales, 1918

Indian Summer of a Forsyte, 1918 – First interlude of The Forsyte Saga

Saint's Progress, 1919

Addresses in America, 1912

In Chancery, 1920 – Second book of The Forsyte Saga

Awakening, 1920 – Second interlude of The Forsyte Saga

The Skin Game, 1920

To Let, 1921 – Third book of The Forsyte Saga

A Family Man, 1922

The Little Man, 1922

Loyalties, 1922

Windows, 1922

Captures, 1923

Abracadabra, 1924

The Forest, 1924

Old English, 1924

The White Monkey, 1924 – First book of A Modern Comedy

The Show, 1925

Escape, 1926

The Silver Spoon, 1926 – Second book of A Modern Comedy

Verses New and Old, 1926

Castles in Spain, 1927

A Silent Wooing, 1927 – First Interlude of A Modern Comedy

Passers By, 1927 – Second Interlude of A Modern Comedy

Swan Song, 1928 – Third book of A Modern Comedy

The Manaton Edition, 1923–26 (collection, 30 vols.)

Exiled, 1929

The Roof, 1929

On Forsyte 'Change, 1930

Two Essays on Conrad, 1930

Soames and the Flag, 1930

The Creation of Character in Literature, 1931 (The Romanes Lecture for 1931).

Maid in Waiting, 1931 – First book of End of the Chapter (1934)

Forty Poems, 1932

Flowering Wilderness, 1932 – Second book of End of the Chapter

Autobiographical Letters of Galsworthy: A Correspondence with Frank Harris, 1933

One More River (originally Over the River), 1933 – Third book of End of the Chapter

The Grove Edition, 1927–34 (collection, 27 Vols.)

Collected Poems, 1934

Punch and Go, 1935

The Life and Letters, 1935

The Winter Garden, 1935

Forsytes, Pendyces and Others, 1935

Selected Short Stories, 1935

Glimpses and Reflections, 1937